MOMENTARY STASIS

P R ADAMS

PROMETHEAN TALES

MOMENTARY STASIS

Cover Art by Adam Burn.

Logo Text Design © Tom Edwards.
TomEdwardsDesign.com

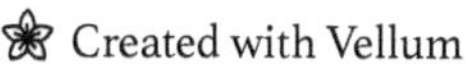 Created with Vellum

ALSO BY P R ADAMS

For updates on new releases and news on other series, visit my website and sign up
for my mailing list at:

http://www.p-r-adams.com

Books in the On The Brink Universe

The Stefan Mendoza Trilogy

Into Twilight

Gone Dark

End State (2018)

The Rimes Trilogy

Momentary Stasis

Transition of Order

Awakening to Judgment

The ERF Series

Turning Point

Valley of Death

Jungle Dark

Chariot Bright

Dawn Fire (2018)

<u>The Burning Sands Trilogy</u>

Beneath Burning Sands

Across Burning Sands

Beyond Burning Sands

~

<u>Books in The Chain Series</u>

The Chain: Shattered

The Journey Home

Rock of Salvation

From the Depths

Ever Shining

DEDICATION

For Tina, who made this possible.

1

20 February 2164. Singapore. Pei Fu Complex, Hougang Industrial Sector.

Sergeant Jack Rimes jerked awake as his Battlefield Awareness System chimed. The BAS's display showed a string of green text, bright against the evening dark: *Mission authorized by United Nations Special Security Council.*

Even before the Special Security Council's approval, Rimes had been running on adrenaline. He needed something more now. He popped a stimulant and winced at the bitter aftertaste.

Nearly twenty hours to give the go. So much for the element of surprise.

Rimes looked through the window he'd been leaning against, taking in the shadowy shell of the abandoned house he and the rest of the team had been hiding inside since their arrival. The BAS overlaid what he could see with imagery and data harvested from every security system it could discreetly access. A rusty, wrought-iron gate hung limply from a crumbling brick wall that enclosed a cratered courtyard. Beyond the gate, a cracked asphalt road ran southeast, framing apartment complexes before connecting to Lim Teck Boo Road.

Rimes was tense, a compressed spring waiting to be released. The rest of the team, all in black nano-particle bodysuits, weren't much better. In particular, the Indian Marine Commando, Tendulkar, was driving them nuts, pulling a boot-knife out and jamming it back into its sheath for hours on end.

Rimes had shared his concerns in private with Major Uber, the German in command of the mission, and his second, Captain Nakata. The three had worked together before. Petty Officer Tendulkar and Senior Sergeant Pachnine, a Russian who towered over even Rimes, had been inserted into the team at the last minute.

"Now we see if this was just politics or if these two are legitimate," Uber whispered to Rimes over a private BAS channel.

Rimes returned his gaze to the window and softly snorted. "Taking out four LoDu agents? Not the sort of mission I'd like to use as a learning opportunity. I'm already missing the old team."

The road was still deserted. A line of amber lamps lit a towering wall that sealed off a maze of sagging, scarred apartment buildings to the southwest. To the northeast, the wall transformed into a security tunnel and disappeared under a sickly forest. Inside the complex, a dozen uniformed guards patrolled on foot and in electric cars, their locations marked by the BAS. A light rain had fallen, leaving behind a mist that covered everything, clinging to the walls and twisted vegetation. Rainbow halos formed around the lamps, washing the street in ghost light.

Uber subvocalized the mission's final details over his BAS, then whispered, "Let's go."

Rimes glanced over the data: imagery and incontrovertible evidence connecting the agents to the Indonesian Finance Minister's assassination; criminal records; and most importantly, authorization for elimination.

They slipped out the building's front door in a loose line with Uber leading. From the courtyard, they ran low onto Lim Teck Boo Road, while the mist hid their boots and enhanced their camouflage systems.

The wall of the Pei Fu Complex rose four meters with pressure sensors and a meter of concertina wire lining the top. Rimes's BAS showed the closest security guard twenty-eight meters out and moving away.

Rimes looked the other team members over. One mistake, any sudden shift in the situation, and Pachnine or Tendulkar could derail the mission without fear of reprisals. It was the sort of political reality that Rimes hated having to deal with.

Uber turned to look at the team.

Captain Nakata raised his hand; Uber nodded. Rimes raised his hand, then Pachnine, then Tendulkar. After Uber nodded, each settled into place, eyes focused on his BAS display.

Nakata slowly extended a hand until he touched the wall. Then he leapt nearly three meters up, his now-tacky gloves gripping the surface, but stopped short of the top. He then extended his left hand to unleash a data burst that overwhelmed all sensor systems within range.

Rimes climbed after Nakata. As Rimes reached the top, Nakata leapt, easily clearing the concertina wire, twisting and catching the wall's opposite side with his gloves. Rimes waited as Nakata released his grip and dropped to a crouch on the opposite side, then followed. The others cleared the wall quickly and settled in its shadow.

Pachnine raised his hand, and Uber nodded. Pachnine sprinted east, choosing speed over cover. Inside the complex, time became the enemy.

They approached Building 5, breathing heavily. Before the Third Great Depression of '62, Building 5 had been a specialty manufacturing facility, a boutique operation for discriminating customers. Now it housed their targets, four unmoving red squares glowing brightly on their optics, data signatures captured nearly two days prior.

Tendulkar whispered, "Halt."

They dropped to their knees simultaneously. Rimes scrutinized his image over the BAS's display. Pachnine was blinking rapidly, his hand over his boot. Something must have changed—they'd been spotted, an alarm had gone off, a guard had modified his patrol ...

It only took a second before Rimes saw it on his BAS. Their targets were moving, separating.

The mission had been compromised.

2

20 February 2164. Singapore. Pei Fu Complex, Hougang Industrial Sector.

THEY SQUATTED, caught in the misty open space between their ingress point and target. Heads swiveled as the team sought a consensus. Tendulkar shook his head. Pachnine immediately nodded, as did Nakata.

Rimes hesitated for a moment before shaking his head. This far into such a critical mission, he would normally be in favor of proceeding, but normally he would be with his own team, people he could trust with his life. He didn't know if he could trust Tendulkar or Pachnine yet. There was too much at stake to continue forward with so much unknown.

Everyone turned to Uber. He considered for a moment before nodding.

There was no further discussion, no protest.

Pachnine went into a crouching run, absolutely silent, even for his bear-like size. The others trailed him in a staggered line, carbines out. Pachnine reached the western cement wall surrounding Building 5 and pressed himself tight to the left of the gate. Rimes and Uber took position to his left, with Nakata and Tendulkar opposite. The Pei Fu security teams had showed no deviation from regular patrol patterns, but the four icons inside Building 5 were now dispersed across four floors.

Uber signaled to Tendulkar to open the gate, then waved Pachnine inside. Rimes and Nakata followed, and Uber pulled up the rear.

They crossed the fifteen meters to the front entry of Building 5, at times struggling to keep their footing on the fractured cement. Nakata quickly destroyed the door's lock with a rapid carbine buttstroke, and they entered the building.

The interior was drywall, dust-covered posters proclaiming the company's greatness, and a door—dented and scraped from years of use—that opened onto a stairwell. A ten-meter corridor led to another door, and beyond that was the manufacturing floor. The nearest of their targets was in a room on the manufacturing floor, four meters to the left of the door.

Uber assigned Pachnine to the fourth floor, Rimes to the third. Nakata he signaled to go to the manufacturing floor. Then Uber headed into the stairwell, stopping only long enough to spray silicone on the door's hinges. Pachnine and Rimes followed.

Uber stopped at the second-floor door, once again spraying the hinges. He searched the corridor, then stepped through.

Rimes proceeded to the third floor with Pachnine close behind. At the third-floor door, Rimes stopped and sprayed the hinges, quietly popped the door open, then checked the hallway beyond. According to the BAS, his target was hiding in a room three meters away.

He nodded Pachnine on, watching him until he'd disappeared up the stairs. Rimes stopped just inside the corridor and waited.

The Special Security Council's intelligence agency had identified the LoDu lead agent as Wen Jintao, a Chinese native with political connections. Wen's muscle included Dung Trang, a fugitive Vietnamese gunman, and Akkarat Suttikul, a Thai known as much for his knife-work and kickboxing as his connections to what remained of the Tongs. The mystery man of the four was Kwon Myung-bak, a Korean with an impossibly small background file.

All four agents had combat experience. Whatever advantage Rimes had from his gear would be diminished by the building's tight quarters. He switched out his carbine for his pistol, his eyes never leaving the BAS display, then brought up another overlay that set down a three-dimensional wireframe of the building interior.

Rimes watched his teammates' icons on the display, then focused on the agents' icons.

Why separate? Why not create a single ambush point? There are a lot of great places to attack from. Were our systems compromised?

No, I'm being paranoid.

Uber and Nakata waited, motionless, for Pachnine to get into position. Pachnine approached the fourth-floor door. His target was just across the hall. Pachnine hesitated, probably bracing for a quick shot when he opened the door.

Pistol arm straightened to his waist, safety off, left arm extended for the door handle, Rimes moved down the corridor toward his target.

The BAS showed a cubicle to the immediate right of the door. The cubicle made any shot through the wall risky with his pistol, probably ineffective. He toyed with switching back to his carbine.

Pachnine reached his door. They were all in position.

Rimes signaled he was ready. Uber's signal showed ready, then Nakata's. Finally, Pachnine's.

Two seconds. One. Uber gave the go.

Rimes twisted the doorknob and pushed the office door in. He caught a flash of movement—a large, frighteningly fast shadow—and then the door slammed back at him, bending his arm aside and knocking him off-balance.

He dropped.

Three muffled gunshots sounded as three holes appeared in the door at chest level. He rolled away and returned fire, sending three rounds into the door in a diagonal, starting at an imaginary thigh and ending at an imaginary torso. He rolled again, this time coming to a stop to the door's right, flat on the ground, pistol ready. He breathed shallowly, not making the slightest sound, and listened.

Gunfire sounded again, first from upstairs, then from the room before him. Holes appeared above him, cutting a left-right diagonal one-and-a-half meters above the floor. Rimes counted to three and sat up, again guessing where his target might be, based off the BAS. Rimes fired three shots, pivoted on his butt, and kicked off from the floor. He came to a stop halfway to the door's left side.

He waited a moment before reaching for a magazine, another moment before reloading. Gunfire echoed throughout the building.

Rimes stood, twisted the handle, and threw a shoulder against the door's center.

The shadow came again, this time slower. Rimes saw the flash of a metal blade and knew he'd drawn the Thai. Rimes got off a shot before the shadow was on him, knives flashing terrifyingly fast. Rimes managed to block three of the slashes with quick forearm strikes, and then let his left shoulder take a fourth. The nano-particle weave absorbed the worst of the blow.

Rimes drove an elbow into the Thai's face, provoking a satisfying grunt. The Thai staggered for a moment, and Rimes stepped back, getting off another shot.

The Thai collapsed in a wheezing heap. Rimes kicked the Thai onto his stomach and fired three rounds into the base of his skull, then knelt to confirm the kill. Gunfire still echoed throughout the building.

Rimes took the Thai's communication earpiece and extracted a blood sample from the corpse for confirmation before exiting the office and collecting his discarded magazine.

As Rimes headed for the stairwell, he reloaded. Uber's and Nakata's icons were moving slowly. He could hear gunfire from below, less frequent now: confrontations reaching their conclusions. Pachnine had stopped moving. The fourth floor was silent.

As Rimes entered the stairwell, he brought up the vitals overlay long enough to see Pachnine's signals. *Dead.*

Rimes squatted and edged toward the stairs leading up. He sighted up the stairwell with his pistol, then ascended—slow, quiet.

The agent's red square moved toward the stairwell door as Rimes reached the midway landing. He squatted, sighted on the door, and braced for a shot. The square stopped and moved away from the door.

Rimes blinked.

Now the square was accelerating away from the door.

As though he had my signature, too.

Rimes moved up the steps, struggling to maintain his calm. The gunfire below was more infrequent now, a single shot followed by seconds of silence.

Rimes stopped at the fourth-floor door. Holes had penetrated the door and the cement wall beyond. The LoDu agents were using specialized ammunition capable of penetrating cement walls—not to mention the team's armor. The BAS showed Pachnine just beyond the door. He'd probably been shot immediately after entering.

Rimes watched the icons on his display. His target was at the other end of the floor now, hiding in an office there.

Rimes tried to push the stairwell door open, but Pachnine's corpse was in the way, and Rimes had to throw his body into the effort. The corpse gave ground grudgingly. Pistol aimed down the corridor, Rimes squeezed through the opening.

He set his back to the wall and advanced in a low crawl. The gunfire below had stopped. He switched back to the vitals overlay.

Rimes mouthed a curse.

Uber's vitals were dropping, his target moving into the stairwell two floors below. Nakata's vitals were steady, but he'd been wounded. At least his target was down.

Rimes switched back to the wireframe overlay.

Five meters from the office door, the target was coming toward Rimes's position. He went to his belly. A second later, rounds tore through the wall centimeters above him. He returned fire, emptying his magazine before rolling across the floor to the opposite wall. He reloaded and crawled forward two meters before holstering the pistol and readying his carbine.

Belly-crawling, he advanced another meter before focusing on the BAS again. Below him, Uber's target had now reached the first floor, heading toward the exit.

"Target exiting building west," Rimes whispered.

The Council took too long. If anyone had the element of surprise, it wasn't us.

Rimes's target was edging away from the door separating them. Rimes brought his carbine up and fired three short, controlled bursts. The target accelerated for the building's edge. Rimes heard a window shatter.

He leapt out of the building. Four stories up, and he leapt.

Rimes ran through the office door, then cut through a sea of furniture.

At the window, he risked a glance down. His target limped toward a four-meter-high security wall, then leaped to the top.

Rimes fired three short bursts, and the target fell.

"Two targets down," Rimes said as he ran back to the stairwell door. "Pachnine's dead."

"Target down," Nakata said. "Uber is badly wounded."

"No sign of the fourth target," Tendulkar said after several seconds. "I saw him moving toward the door, but nothing after. His icon, it just vanished."

A quick check confirmed that it had.

Rimes closed his eyes and played out where the fourth target could go without Tendulkar seeing him. There weren't many options. "No visual?"

"No," Tendulkar said.

Rimes heaved Pachnine over his shoulder and scanned the area for any magazines, but Pachnine had died without getting a shot off. Rimes groaned under the corpse's weight. The mission was becoming messier with each second, accelerating toward a nightmarish disaster.

His BAS alerted him that Pei Fu security teams were now approaching and would arrive in less than a minute.

"Check the target just inside the north wall," Rimes said. "Suttikul confirmed."

"Trang confirmed," Nakata said.

That leaves Wen and Kwon, the brains and the mystery man.

Rimes descended the stairs, ready at any moment for the missing LoDu agent to open fire on him. As Rimes approached the second floor, Nakata burst through the second-floor door with Uber over his shoulder. They hustled down the stairs to the first floor with Rimes in the lead, carbine at the ready. He opened the door to the corridor, half-expecting the missing target to attack.

The corridor was empty.

"Wen confirmed inside the north wall," Tendulkar said.

We lost Kwon. With security rapidly closing in, they couldn't risk searching for him.

Rimes ran through the first floor toward the door. Nakata kept up, but he was clearly struggling with Uber.

"North wall," Rimes said. He kicked open the exit and burst through.

Something—luck, instinct, training—caused him to pull up and twist as he cleared the door. Even as quick as he was, the attack connected. Pachnine's body took the worst of the blow, but the force knocked Rimes backwards. He lost his balance and tumbled to the ground, shrugging Pachnine off as he fell.

Rimes recovered and rolled to put some distance between him and his attacker. He came up in a crouch and again barely managed to deflect the flurry of kicks and punches that came at him, some striking his raised arms, some catching his shins. Wherever they landed, they tested the armor's limits and left the limb slightly numb.

Finally, the attacker lost his footing on the broken ground and a kick went wide. Rimes landed a punch. It was clumsy and feeble, but it was in the groin. The attacker stumbled backwards, and Rimes rose to his feet.

He was looking at Kwon, the missing target. *He's bigger than his data would imply.*

"Rimes?" Nakata called.

Rimes backpedaled and shifted to a defensive posture. His limbs felt sluggish and responded only stubbornly. "I've got Kwon. West courtyard."

Kwon closed, and again the blows came, stunning in power. They were blurs that drove Rimes backwards, testing his balance and resolve.

A shot rang out, and the round ricocheted off the west wall. Kwon turned, saw Nakata, and bolted, running for the west wall. He leapt and cleared it with ease.

Nakata ran toward Rimes.

Rimes waved Nakata back. "Go!"

They gathered up Pachnine and Uber and ran for the north wall. The numbness was fading, replaced by tingling, then aching. Rimes fell behind.

Tendulkar lay atop the wall in a gap of cut concertina wire, flat on his belly, arm extended to help them up. Getting the giant Pachnine over the wall proved a challenge, but they were quick enough that Rimes, the last one over, dropped to the other side of the wall just as Pei Fu security opened Building 5's western gate.

They were in the forest east of the complex by the time the security team raised the general alarm.

An hour later, they were aboard a Japanese helicopter carrier, the living and the dead, Australia-bound.

3

———

20 February 2164. JSS *Okazaki*.

RIMES SAT ALONE outside the infirmary watching the seconds pass on his earpiece's projected display. The waiting area was a tight space, with a cheerful facade—white paint, plastic plants, bright lighting, and two thick-cushioned chairs. He could just as easily have been squeezed into the belly of the ship for all it mattered.

The heat and humidity were worse than on any ship he could recall. Sleep was an undertow, dragging him out to the deep. The adrenaline rush had passed, and the stimulants were wearing off. His shoulder ached where Suttikul had slashed him, and his forearms and shins were tender and bruised from Kwon's strikes.

The team was gone.

Pachnine was dead.

Fortunately, Tendulkar had stabilized Uber before they'd reached the waiting inflatable boats. Uber had seemed fine when the helicopter had lifted them from the ocean, but an hour had already crawled by, and each time Rimes asked, he was told that he couldn't visit.

Nakata and Tendulkar had disappeared shortly after boarding the *Okazaki*. Nakata had received several stitches before being released to bed rest, and Tendulkar had headed off to give his briefing to the Special Security Council.

Uber should've been the one to give the executive brief to the Special Security Council. What if I missed something? What if Nakata or Tendulkar contradict me in their reports?

At twenty-five, Rimes was the team's youngest member. He was a highly decorated American Army Special Forces operative—a Commando—and the Council had made no secret of its regard for his perspective in the past. Still, he was the team's most junior member.

Rimes sighed. *It's just the fatigue. I didn't miss anything. They aren't going to contradict me.*

Rimes's leave was slated to begin in two days. Thanks to bio-restoratives and healing accelerants, he'd be largely healed by then. Only sleep could deal with the fatigue that was dragging on him.

He thought of home—Oklahoma: Fort Sill, Lawton, Grandfield. It was a long-overdue trip. Seeing Molly, visiting friends he hadn't seen for too long. And family. He fought off another sigh.

Bad with the good.

"Sergeant Rimes?"

Rimes looked up, alarmed that he hadn't heard approaching footsteps, much less the door opening, but he recognized the pudgy nurse who'd met him upon arrival, a man with thick glasses and greasy hair. Perspiration glistened on his brow and dampened his surgical grays along the ribs and chest.

"Your friend, Major Uber, he will be fine," the nurse said with a reassuring smile.

Rimes stood. His tall, wiry frame contrasted with the nurse's shorter, wider one. "Thanks. Can I see him?"

"The doctor says two hours."

"Great. I'd like to freshen up and catch a nap."

"I will call Ensign Watanabe. She will see to your quarters." The nurse's oily hair glistened brightly. He bowed and left through the infirmary door.

Now that he knew that Uber would be all right, Rimes could feel a crash coming. He'd faced them often enough to know the signs. He paced, clenching and unclenching his hands, biting his tongue, breathing deeply. He shook his head violently, did several deep knee bends. It was enough for the moment, but the moments kept creeping by.

Finally, the waiting room door opened, and a seaman entered. He looked like a wire frame with a crisp blue uniform hanging off it.

"Sergeant Rimes? Ensign Watanabe sent me. You need quarters?" The young man's accent would have been a challenge even if Rimes weren't in the middle of a crash.

Rimes grunted acknowledgement, and the young man darted back through the door. Rimes gathered his kit and followed the man down several corridors. Rimes was too tired to keep track of where he was and just trusted that the young man wouldn't lead him astray.

Finally, they stopped outside an open hatch.

"The head," the seaman said, then pointed at another hatch down the corridor. "Your berth. No one here now. You can rest." He disappeared around a corner.

The bathroom was a modest affair—open shower bay, a few toilet stalls. The quarters were slightly better, even with four bunks squeezed into a relatively tight space. Everything looked clean. Rimes stowed his kit beneath the foot of a bunk, fished out his field hygiene kit, returned to the head, relieved himself, and showered.

Rimes took a moment to brush his teeth, then checked himself in the mirror as he repacked his kit. Bruises discolored light cinnamon skin, and a shallow scrape—already healing—stood out on his left cheek, more noticeable because of his prominent cheekbones.

Somewhat refreshed, he made his way to the bunks, shirt slung over his left arm, boots and socks gripped tightly in his left hand. He tossed his shirt onto the top bunk opposite the hatch, set his boots and socks at the foot of the lower bunk, and slipped under the covers, immediately drifting into sleep.

Too soon, someone shook him awake.

A female ensign in tight Navy whites squinted at him intensely from a half-crouch at his shoulder. She was cute despite the serious, borderline-angry look on her long face.

It took Rimes a moment to realize he was staring at her. He looked away.

The ensign straightened up and adjusted her uniform. "Sergeant Rimes, you have a call in the comm room."

Rimes searched for his earpiece and panicked.

Lost it. I can't connect to the Grid, can't—

He found it and glanced at the time display. Just over an hour of sleep. He was shaking. He needed coffee.

"Thanks, ma'am. The comm—"

"I will take you there."

"I appreciate it, ma'am."

"Ensign Watanabe," she corrected.

Rimes spun around on his butt until he was sitting, closed his eyes, and let the dizziness pass. He pulled on his socks and boots, stood, and tested his balance. He looked toward the hatch, grabbing his shirt. "After you, ma'am."

Watanabe adjusted her uniform again and headed out the hatch, walking stiffly.

By the time Rimes got his bearings, he was outside the communications room with Ensign Watanabe walking swiftly away.

Crewmen watched him curiously from their workstations. Rimes stepped inside, for the first time truly feeling like the outsider he was. One of the crewmen pointed to a small office off the main room, not even bothering to ask who he was. Rimes muttered a "thank you" and crossed between the staring crewmen to the office, closing the door behind him.

Nobody was there.

The office was empty except for a desk that held a portable, secure communications terminal; it was flashing, indicating a held connection.

Rimes synced his earpiece with the device and sat on the desk.

His earpiece buzzed and chirped—the telltales of encryption negotiation—and then he was connected.

"This is Lieutenant Commander Derrick Cross of the USS *Sutton*. Who is this, please?"

"Sergeant Jack Rimes here, sir."

"Sergeant, we have a 121 *en route* to you, ETA fifty-seven minutes."

Rimes blinked. "I don't understand, sir. I'm supposed to fly to Darwin this afternoon. I have a flight back to the US tomorrow."

"Your leave's canceled," Cross said. "I'm sorry to have to report that, but we've had an incident hit the radar. Your Commando team is already *en route* to the *Sutton*. Captain Moltke said he needed everyone for this one."

Rimes bowed his head and rubbed his forehead. "Understood, sir."

It was his third leave canceled in the last two years.

He'd managed a short weekend with Molly in Italy three months ago, but since then he'd had to rely on electronic communications, only a few of them semi-private vids.

It was tough on a marriage, but he'd become used to that sort of sacrifice since enlisting. Molly, on the other hand, was becoming less patient with each passing month, but at least she was realistic enough to know there weren't a lot of other job opportunities for someone who didn't have a graduate degree and whose work experience amounted to killing people.

"We'll see you on the *Sutton*, Sergeant."

The connection terminated.

Rimes unsynced his earpiece. Whatever was up, it was big.

He couldn't recall any information about the *Sutton*, but he'd been on a dozen ships in his relatively short career, all of them helicopter carriers. If the *Sutton* had its own CH-121, it had, at minimum, a modest flight deck.

Rimes stepped into the communications room and asked a young man to call Ensign Watanabe. She arrived so quickly, Rimes wondered if she'd been waiting outside the door the whole time.

Once they were away from the communications center, she stopped and looked at him with her arms folded across her chest. "Where do you need to go, Sergeant Rimes?"

Rimes tried to smile charmingly. "I could really use some coffee, ma'am."

She tapped her fingers on her arm impatiently.

He sighed. "And I'd like to swing by the infirmary if it's possible to visit Major Uber before leaving?"

Wantanabe's brow furrowed. "There's no hurry. We won't be close enough to fly you to Darwin for some time."

"I won't be heading to Australia, unfortunately, ma'am. Look, I was serious about the coffee, and I'd very much like to see the major if he's awake."

Watanabe spun and walked quickly down the corridor. Rimes waited a moment, admiring the swing of her slender hips. He'd been away from Molly for far too long, and he was starting to feel it, even in his fatigued state. With a shake of his head, he fell in behind Watanabe.

The officer's mess was surprisingly small, but compared to what he'd seen on other ships, he was impressed. In one quick glance, he'd noticed a great deal of attention to detail—personalized bamboo trays, ranks engraved into tabletops, a cart for serving *saké*, and a sushi bar.

Even the coffee bar was impressive, its gleaming stainless steel brewing machine surrounded by matching sugar and creamer dispensers. The shelf below held rows of silver-framed, intricately cut crystal cups. A teal-colored Japanese tea set and matching tray with a painted beach scene rested on a shelf immediately beneath the cups.

Rimes helped himself to one of the crystal cups and stared at the coffee machine for a moment.

Watanabe pointed to a button on the machine's base.

He pushed the button. A seam in the side of the machine opened to lower a spout. Rimes quickly caught the steaming coffee in his crystal cup before it spilled.

"This is quite a setup."

Watanabe lifted her chin and almost smiled. Her voice softened. "You know Major Uber well?"

"He and Captain Nakata and I have worked together a few times—Minsk, Montevideo, Tunis." Rimes stirred sugar into the cup with a tiny silver spoon, enjoying the coffee's aroma. His saliva glands woke from their slumber. He sipped from the cup and was pleasantly surprised at the burst of flavors. *Real coffee. They live a different life.* "I just want to let him know I'll be in touch."

"Your work," Watanabe said, pausing uncertainly, shifting from question to statement. "It is dangerous."

"It can be, just like yours," Rimes said, smiling around a sip. "The better you are at it, the safer it is."

Watanabe returned the smile, hesitantly. "You were in Singapore?"

"Yes, ma'am." There was no value in denying what was common knowledge.

"It was about the Indonesian Finance Minister assassination?"

Rimes stared into his coffee cup.

Watanabe quietly cleared her throat. "LoDu has filed a protest with the United Nations. They deny any involvement with the assassination. They claim stories of their displeasure with Indonesian policy are greatly exaggerated."

Rimes looked at her. "Do you believe that, ma'am?"

"I am not sure."

"Well, it's typical metacorporate behavior—denial, obfuscation, misdirection, and if none of that works, offer up one of the smaller corporate entities to take the blame and scapegoat some low-level executive. At least it wasn't ADMP or EEC. Or SunCorps. I don't want to even think about how SunCorps would handle something like this. Probably tell the Council to take a walk. I can't believe what the metacorporations have done to us."

"I want to work for a metacorporation one day. Wang, HuCorp, maybe even LoDu."

"Oh, sorry, ma'am!"

"No. I am not blind to their behavior. They can do ..." She lowered her head. "Terrible things. And there are rumors about their ambitions in the colony worlds. It seems the larger they get, the worse they might behave?"

Rimes took another sip of the coffee, mulling the sophisticated blend of flavors. There were contrasts and complements, strong and subtle differences.

Complicated. Like us.

Finally, he said, "We're all capable of terrible things."

Watanabe blinked slowly. "The coffee, you like it?"

"It's wonderful." Rimes drained his cup and set it down on a nearby table, relieved. The awkward moment was over. He felt an immediate boost, but he knew it was really psychological. "Thank you, ma'am."

Watanabe bowed her head slightly, then adjusted her uniform and picked up the cup and spoon, setting them in a nearby plastic tub, then quickly led the way out of the room and through the ship.

They arrived at the infirmary a couple minutes later. Watanabe spoke to the nurse, then left Rimes alone outside Uber's room, peering through the door at the only occupied bed.

"Jack?" Uber, looking every bit the corpse warmed over, beckoned Rimes into the room. "Come in."

Rimes crossed to the bedside, his eyes playing across the equipment and displays before settling on Uber's pale, strained face. The room smelled of rubbing alcohol and latex.

"How're you feeling, sir?"

"Like hell," Uber said with a strained smile, then bit his upper lip for a moment. "The nurses tell me I will make it, whether I like it or not. I cannot complain."

They both laughed quietly, even though it wasn't funny.

Rimes looked at the equipment displays again. He was no expert, but Uber's vitals seemed weak. His eyes were watery and tired. Uber's wound was close to the heart; he was lucky to be alive.

They all were.

Uber wheezed, sounding even weaker than before. "You stop by to say hello or goodbye?"

"Goodbye, sir," Rimes said. Not heading home to Molly hurt. "Orders just came through. I'm being redeployed."

"It can be demanding, this life."

Rimes grunted.

Uber extended his right hand. "I wish you good luck, Jack."

His hand trembled.

Rimes gripped the hand gently and shook.

Uber gripped back hard, then pulled Rimes close.

"We were compromised," Uber whispered. "Not me. Not you or the Russian."

Rimes nodded once. "We know Nakata."

Uber raised an eyebrow. "Whichever one it was, LoDu got to him. There is money to be had, a lot of it."

Rimes glanced at the doorway. "The Special Security Council assigned Tendulkar."

Uber released Rimes' hand. "They assigned us all. Watch yourself, Jack. It is a complex world, and you are too trusting for your own good."

Rimes shrugged. He'd heard the accusation before, but without trust, he couldn't perform his job.

No soldier could.

"Get better, sir."

Uber winked, then winced. "I think it is time to sleep now. Pleasant dreams await me, no doubt. Thank you, Jack."

Rimes started to leave the room.

Uber called after him, his voice a whisper. "What we discussed? Think about it, please."

4

20 February 2164. JSS *Okazaki.*

RIMES STEPPED out of the room. Ensign Watanabe straightened and adjusted her uniform. Everything about her said she was ready to be done with this. Rimes wondered if she saw him merely as an inconvenience, or if the quiet moment at the coffee bar had been closer to her true nature.

They stopped by his quarters to gather his kit, then took several flights of stairs up before reaching the flight deck. Rimes scanned the horizon as he stepped into the open air, watching for any sign of the CH-121. He checked his earpiece's data feed: the helicopter was due in twenty-four minutes.

"Sergeant Rimes, I must return to duty now," Watanabe said, bowing slightly. "You wait only on your transport?"

Rimes saluted. "Yes, ma'am. You have been a most helpful and gracious host."

Watanabe returned the salute before smiling and waving awkwardly, then disappeared inside the ship. Rimes watched after her for several heartbeats, wondering at the way bridges could so easily be built. It seemed even easier to destroy them.

He returned his gaze to the sky. The ship moved beneath him, tons of steel driving through deep, blue waves. Each movement vibrated through his feet. He counted the waves until he saw the CH-121 in the distance.

A crew chief ran his team out to the forward landing pad, readying for the helicopter's landing. Rimes watched them as they waved the bird down. The engine's whine died, and the rotors began their slow spin down.

Rimes walked forward, saluting the pilot as he exited the aircraft. Rimes tossed his kit into the passenger bay and looked the bird over. "She's a beauty, Lieutenant."

The pilot returned the salute. "She is. Not even three years old." He gave the fuselage a loving rub.

"Is the *Sutton* new, sir? I've never heard of her."

"New enough," the pilot said. He pulled off his aviator glasses, then began chewing on one of the legs and twirling the glasses as he watched the crew connect the fuel hose.

Rimes looked the cockpit over for a few minutes. "What package does she have installed, sir? Looks like long-range transport?"

The pilot nodded distractedly at the extra fuel tanks slung beneath the belly. "That's enough fuel to get us wherever we need to go." He turned to look at Rimes. "We're not here for sub hunts or search and rescue, Sergeant. I think you know that."

"I've been on a few helicopter carriers."

"Not like the *Sutton*," the pilot said with a wink. He saluted the crew chief, who signaled the bird was ready to go. "She's a special ship. You'll see."

Rimes climbed in and buckled up. The engine started, rising from a whine to a thunderous whipping of the air. It was a comforting, familiar sound.

Rimes looked around the empty bay. No crew chief, one pilot—it wasn't a normal flight. The mission was becoming more troubling each passing second.

He tried to get some sense of where he was going and why. The first thing he considered was the location. The Pacific was simply too large a region, filled with too many potential targets, even when considering the whole team had been scrambled.

It's big, whatever it is, but that just takes some of the minor powers out of the picture. Maybe they've located Kwon already? Maybe LoDu flexed a bit too much muscle for its own good?

He connected to the helicopter's communications system and began downloading available regional intelligence and news feeds. That didn't help, either. Names, situations, and places merged into gibberish.

He yawned and stretched, trying to fight off his need for sleep. A moment later, his head fell forward and he realized it was hopeless. He nodded off.

He woke to the pilot's voice in his earpiece. The *Sutton* was visible far below, speeding west. It was afternoon, the ocean a brilliant sparkle in the sunlight. To the north, Rimes could make out the bend of a distant shore. He linked into the *Sutton*'s systems with his earpiece and confirmed he was looking at the Indian–Bangladeshi coastline.

A knot formed in his stomach as he considered the implications.

When the UN Special Security Council had recruited him for their previous mission, he'd spoken with the Indian representative, Deepa Bhatia.

Representative Bhatia's sorrowful description of her Indian homeland came back to him clearly. She had described it as a land dragged down by the weight of its own former greatness and the insistence on worshiping that same greatness. For more than a century, its government had been caught up in a cycle of corruption and ineptness, collapsing before transitioning to some semblance of order, always driven by wealthy and corporate influences.

The Special Security Council seemed intent on reshaping things. They wanted to protect and to correct the global landscape. Eventually, they hoped to extend that to the colonies. It was inevitable they would bump against the rival influences, the same wealthy and corporate powers that had led India to its collapse.

Rimes sighed. *Why would we want to get involved in India's affairs? We can't even handle our own.*

Rimes returned his attention to the flight deck. The *Sutton* was a helicopter carrier, larger than others he'd seen. It must have been a relatively new class, because he wasn't familiar with the design. He spotted a few unique weapons systems. The configuration was clearly even more expensive than the helicopter carriers he'd been aboard before.

A crew chief guided them in. Several meters back, Rimes saw four men. As the CH-121 settled to the deck, the men advanced, and Rimes recognized his fellow Commandos—Martinez, Pasqual, Wolford, and Chung.

Edward "Marty" Martinez was nearly as tall as Rimes but with hints of gray in his dark hair; Rick Pasqual was thick through the chest, copper-skinned, and handsome; Lewis Wolford was broad-shouldered and bald, intimidating even when he gave his friendliest smile; Patrick Chung was a ball of energy, even while standing still.

Another figure joined them on the deck, a woman.

She wore a jungle boonie hat secured by its straps; it fluttered in the rotor wash. A simple, loose-fitting uniform made it impossible to gauge her by her physique. Large sunglasses hid the rest of her identity.

Nevertheless, something about her seemed familiar—and troubling.

Rimes stepped out of the helicopter and made his way over to his friends, greeting each as appropriate: a handshake for Martinez, a slap on the shoulder for Pasqual, a fist bump for Chung, a bear hug for Wolford. He'd trained with them, been on missions with them, said goodbye to the fallen with them. They were friends, brothers.

Martinez, with his gruff voice and uncertain gait brought on by more wounds than even he could recall, was like a father to the rest of them.

"You got someone waitin' for you, Jack," Martinez said, jerking his head back toward the woman as he shook Rimes's hand. "How the hell did you let this one get away?"

Rimes looked over Martinez's shoulder at the woman, frowning. "A lot of fish got through the net before I closed it, Marty. You know how it is."

"Not like this one." Martinez released Rimes and turned to the woman, nodding at her.

The woman approached, her curves becoming more apparent with each step, despite the baggy uniform. Curly, golden-brown hair peeked from beneath the boonie cap. She held out a pale copper hand in the fading afternoon sun.

"Sergeant Rimes," she said, with a smile that brought back memories he had no interest in revisiting.

"Dana."

"Special Agent Kleigshoen, if it makes you more comfortable," she said. "I'm with the Intelligence Bureau now."

"IB?" Rimes shook her hand.

It was softer than he remembered. The last time he'd held it, it had been calloused and strong. Her hair had been shorter back then, the curls tighter. She'd put on weight that had softened her face and filled out her form.

It suited her—extremely well.

"They're ready to brief us." Martinez gave Rimes a warning glance. "The captain's on edge about this one."

"Shit," Wolford said, his face breaking out in a broad grin. "He's spittin' fire."

Chung tsked. "They pulled him off leave while he was rolling down the runway at Heathrow. He'd already gone through two of those little airplane whiskey bottles. He was one angry son of a bitch."

Rimes chuckled. "He loves his whiskey. I don't know how he can afford it."

"Man's got to have his priorities," Martinez said.

Wolford sneaked a peek at Kleigshoen, then looked at Rimes. "You got priorities of your own, right?"

Rimes winced. Wolford always said that he would have bailed from Army life years before if not for the crippling debt of marriage and divorce. Rimes didn't want this—he thought of Molly, of being away from her. "Makes you wonder why we do this, doesn't it?"

Martinez snorted. "That's not how I taught you to think, Sergeant. Duty and honor."

"Hoo-ah," the men shouted in unison.

Kleigshoen pointed toward the stairs. "I think we can proceed now, Gentlemen? You're going to want to hear this."

Martinez waved Kleigshoen ahead. Chung and Pasqual fell in behind her, each watching her swaying hips. Wolford looked back at Rimes and mouthed a whistle. Rimes held up his wedding band and shook his head. Wolford gave him a dismissive wave and moved past.

"You don't need woman trouble," Martinez whispered in Rimes's ear.

"It's all in the past," Rimes said.

"Uh huh. She's *still* trouble," Martinez whispered in Rimes's ear. "I hope you know that."

Rimes sighed.

5

---

20 February 2164. USS *Sutton*.

RIMES SETTLED in between Martinez and Wolford as Kleigshoen made her way to the head of the conference room table. Nearly twenty people were seated around the table or in rows along the back wall. The air was warm and smelled of boot leather and freshly scrubbed flesh.

Rimes recognized most of those gathered. He nodded and smiled at those he knew best. He hesitated when he saw Barlowe and Stern.

Stern was one of the better Commandos, a sturdy, strong-jawed, respected soldier. But he was still rehabilitating from a serious knee injury that at one point Rimes had heard had been a serious threat to Stern's career. He was coming along, but his mobility was limited. His inclusion didn't make a lot of sense.

Barlowe's involvement was even less understandable. He was a good kid, and he was brilliant with computers, but he was a project. Slight of build, baby-faced, and uncomfortable in his own skin, he never seemed at ease. Everyone knew he'd completed the qualifying course with the lowest score possible and was a Commando only after intervention from Colonel Weatherford, the Special Forces Group commander at Fort Sill.

Martinez had been mentoring Barlowe for more than eight months. There was no better mentor to have, yet Barlowe hadn't progressed much.

We've all had to cover for Barlowe just to keep him in the unit. Some of us more than others.

Martinez looked at Rimes. Rimes could see the annoyance in Martinez's eyes until he slowly closed them. Martinez shook his head once; no words needed to be spoken.

This is Weatherford's team. No one else would have made these choices. If he's involved, this has to be serious.

Pasqual leaned in from his seat behind Rimes, drawing him out of his thoughts. Pasqual traced an hourglass in the air over Kleigshoen's figure with his stubby index fingers.

"Any regrets now, baby?" Pasqual asked. "Little girl's all grown up since her Ranger days."

Rimes scratched the back of his head with an extended middle finger in reply. Pasqual chuckled and slapped Rimes on the back.

At the head of the table, Kleigshoen bent to speak quietly to Captain Moltke, who nodded and stood. The lieutenant commander to Moltke's right also stood, and Kleigshoen stepped back from the table. Moltke exchanged a mysterious smile with Kleigshoen, then turned his attention to the seated Commandos.

The lieutenant commander cleared his throat, silencing the room.

"Gentlemen, thank you. For those I haven't met yet, I'm Lieutenant Commander Cross. As the *Sutton*'s Deputy Ops Chief, it has been my unfortunate duty to inform many of you of canceled leave. I don't expect that's earned me any friends."

A chuckle ran through the room; Moltke grimaced uncomfortably.

In that moment, Rimes couldn't help but notice the stark contrast between the two officers. Moltke had been an operator for three years and was extremely fit. He had close-cropped, brown hair, tanned, bronze skin, and a strong jawline. Cross was pale and had little chin to speak of, just a stretch of pock-marked skin where his face and neck met. He was soft, the first hints of a paunch visible under his khaki shirt.

Cross continued: "I want to welcome you to the *Sutton*. I believe you'll find her to your liking. She's a good ship with a good crew. If you need anything, I want you to come straight to me. Now, I think I've wasted enough of your time, so I want to turn you over to Captain Moltke. Captain?"

Moltke moved away from the table, coming to a stop in the shadows near Stern. Moltke cleared his throat. "Thanks, Commander. All right, let's get to it. You've got eyes, so you've already seen we've pulled out all the stops on this one. It's big. The IB has a physical presence here with Agent Kleigshoen. We'll be running three teams—Red, Green, and Blue. Marty, you've got Red; Kirk, you've got Blue. Rimes, Green."

Martinez gave Rimes a quick elbow to the ribs.

It would be Rimes's first formal team lead, something he'd dreamed of since becoming a Commando. He normally operated on Martinez's team or ran solo. He'd have to tell Molly. Running a team was part of the path to promotion, to better money, and to a better life.

"I've already worked out rosters. I'll upload them after Agent Kleigshoen's briefing. We'll take questions at the briefing's conclusion. Agent Kleigshoen?"

Kleigshoen stepped forward. She activated the conference room's briefing system, which automatically dimmed the lighting. A simple graphic appeared, noting the *Sutton*'s position relative to accepted political boundaries.

"Thank you, Captain, Commander. As you're no doubt aware, we're in the Bay of Bengal, 200 klicks off the Indian coast. Three days ago, we intercepted some troubling communications between T-Corp management from off-world and their main facility in Mumbai about a secret research facility near here."

The graphic transitioned to a hi-res satellite image of a forested area bisected by a wide north-running river and criss-crossed by several smaller ones.

Two callouts highlighted areas of interest. The first was a surprisingly large compound with several buildings. The compound, labeled "T-Corp 72," was integrated into the forest's natural contours; it could have slipped past the imaging analysis software on an older satellite, before advanced confluent inference systems had been installed. The second was a clump of small forms labeled "T-Corp Ops."

"T-Corp 72—" Kleigshoen circled the compound with a wave of her finger, and a yellow circle highlighted the compound. "—was a T-Corp research facility illegally built in the Sundarbans. It was abandoned nearly thirty-six years ago, after a joint Europe-Africa military raid unleashed a virus that Eurica agencies estimate killed more than fifty thousand in India, Egypt, Turkey, and Italy.

"Officially, T-Corp shut the facility down because of international treaties protecting the region from any form of economic exploitation outside tourism. Unofficially, there's very strong evidence T-Corp was conducting illegal genetics research."

"Weapons?" Martinez asked, ignoring Moltke's briefing protocols.

"We believe it was early genie research. The virus was likely an unfortunate incident after accidental release of some of the research materials." Kleigshoen circled the "T-Corp Ops" forms with her finger. "Apparently, something has renewed T-Corp's interest in the facility. As you can see, as of 0200 this morning, a team of T-Corp operatives approached the facility in clear violation of the agreements signed following the outbreak."

The graphics transitioned again, this time showing gruesome images of outbreak casualties before changing to a close-up of T-Corp 72 itself. There were six buildings, each identified by callouts.

"Thanks to the Eurica agencies sharing intelligence from that previous raid with us, we have two areas of interest. The first is the research building, here." Kleigshoen circled the compound's largest building. "The second is the operations center, here." She circled the next largest building, south of the first. "We believe whatever T-Corp is going after would be in one of those two buildings."

Moltke spoke from the shadows again as Kleigshoen stepped aside. The Sundarbans map returned to the screen. Moltke's earpiece projected an interface in the darkness. His fingers manipulated an application, tracing a trail across the interface, and two helicopter icons appeared at the map's southern edge.

"We will receive the standard proactive treatments—general immune system boosters and restoratives. However, this is considered an NBC environment, so we will also be provided anti-viral injectors."

"Since it's not likely that T-Corp team sneaked a nuke in, are you saying that the biological agent's still a problem, sir?" Martinez asked.

Moltke sighed. "Biological is our main concern, yes. Please hold your questions to the end of the briefing, Sergeant."

Martinez looked at Rimes and rolled his eyes. Rimes tried not to smile.

"Commander Cross has provided us two 121s. We will proceed north along the Goashaba River." Moltke traced their path in the air and a line appeared on the map, following along the winding river. "We'll exit the 121s here, on the northern shore, and proceed on foot. I'll direct the operation from the insert point."

Moltke traced a northern path along a slender river until it reached the curve of a slightly larger one that angled west, then north. He followed the larger tributary with his finger. "You'll keep this tributary on your left flank, then proceed on the western bank of this second tributary until you reach the target. This route is approximately ten klicks. We'll have one hundred fifty minutes to cover it."

Kirk shook his head. "In NBC gear, sir?" His drawl stretched the question out. He quickly glanced at Stern, then back at Moltke.

"Hydrate, people. For ... political reasons, our insertion can't happen until 0130. Arriving at the compound after 0400 puts the mission at extreme risk. We will have sixty minutes to clear the compound. The 121s will touch down here, in this old parking lot, at 0500. If the LZ is not clear by 0500, the next opportunity for the 121s to land ... will be 0130 the next morning."

At Moltke's hesitation, Martinez and Kirk exchanged a glance.

Rimes already knew what they were thinking: there would be no second opportunity.

Moltke always hesitated when lying; it was his tell when they played poker.

The operation was happening without explicit consent, and T-Corp would pressure the Indian government the second they detected the intrusion. As Bhatia had warned, the Indian government was still among the most corrupt and ineffectual in the world.

It would buckle at the first hint of pressure from T-Corp, the country's single greatest employer.

While Rimes had grown used to the hollow promises and outright lies the military casually told its troops, he'd never approve of it—even though he understood the necessity.

"That's it, people," Moltke said, shutting down the briefing system. "I'm uploading maps and relevant overlays to your systems now. I'll be running Horus from my position. Take the standard jungle kit: CAWS-5 assault and shotgun mix, six magazines, one frag each, two liters of water, and energy bars. Keep it under twenty kilos, or you won't make it."

Rimes relaxed slightly. Horus—an unmanned reconnaissance vehicle— often made the impossible possible. It carried extremely high-resolution optics and sensor packages and fed real-time data through each soldier's system. The systems interacted with feedback from each user, constantly updating intelligence and imagery. Paired with their full-blown BASs, the data could turn the tide in an engagement. It wasn't as advanced as the systems he used when on Special Security Council operations, but it was better than anything anyone else used.

"Any questions?" Moltke looked around the room, no one said a thing. "All right. Report to the dispensary for your injections and injectors. Rest up and hydrate."

Moltke nodded to Cross.

Cross stood. "Dismissed, gentlemen." He exited the conference room, followed by Agent Kleigshoen.

Rimes watched the rest of the team filter out, blushing when Pasqual and Wolford congratulated him, but stayed behind with Martinez and Kirk.

"Congratulations, Rimes." Kirk squeezed a pinch of dip into his mouth. He was a few years older than Rimes, but had also trained under Martinez and was considered the natural choice to replace him when he finally moved on. Kirk was a good soldier and a more than capable team lead.

Moltke circled the desk and approached them, his face a mask. His breath carried the slightest hint of whiskey.

"Let's hear it," he said.

"Ten klicks through jungle in NBC gear in two-and-a-half hours," Martinez said. "It seems like a bit much to ask, sir."

Stern's going to have a hard time of it. Barlowe, too.

Martinez looked at Kirk. They seemed to reach an agreement without speaking. "Especially with the likelihood we'll be on our own for some time if we run into trouble."

Moltke hesitated a moment, then said, "I don't like it any better than you do. This one's big, though."

"They're all big, Captain," Kirk drawled. "They don't send us in for the little shit."

"This is bigger than most. As big as it gets. That facility was built for genetic engineering research before T-Corp had the capacity to get an orbital station up.

"You heard Agent Kleigshoen: they were designing genies there. It's the last physical presence on-planet of potential materials of incalculable value." He hesitated again, his eyes jumping from Rimes to the other two. "You know I don't have all the details. I'm sharing what I can with you."

Rimes's forehead furrowed. "This is about money, sir?"

Moltke paused, then rubbed his jaw. "Everything's about money, Sergeant. When you get down to it, nothing else matters. Currency drives enterprise; enterprise drives politics. In this case, the currency is genetic materials—possibly the secret to the first significantly advanced wave of our genetically engineered friends. It doesn't get much more valuable than that."

Kirk squinted at Moltke. "If it was worth so much, why didn't we just take it before?"

"The agreements they signed thirty-six years ago were a mess. T-Corp agreed to shut down the facility and pay a fine. They also helped deal with the outbreak. They probably saved tens of thousands of people and millions of dollars by sharing critical data, too. In exchange, India extracted guarantees from every international body imaginable that the facility would be treated as Indian sovereign territory so long as T-Corp honored their end of the deal."

"India would go to war over something like this?" Rimes asked, trying not to sound too skeptical. "What sort of research could be so valuable, thirty years on?"

Moltke chewed his lip for a moment. "Just about two years before that facility went up, exploration vessels discovered an alien ship around the Epsilon Eridani system. That's pretty much common knowledge. What isn't common knowledge is just how close we came to war over that discovery.

"T-Corp and LoDu got their hands on alien DNA, and they weren't about to share it. Not with the international science community, not with universities, not with their host nations, not with anyone. And they applied enough economic pressure—threats to send every last asset and job off-planet—to just enough of those host nations to put us all at each other's throats. They ended up sharing the DNA with ADMP to get them onboard. With those three metacorps making threats ..."

"So T-Corp's violation of the agreements gives us an opportunity to seize this alien DNA?" Rimes already knew the answer, but he had to hear it from Moltke.

Moltke nodded. "For all we know, they may intend to unleash a weaponized viral agent against someone. So even though the Indian government won't act, we can and we will. We have key support in this."

Kirk hissed a curse. "But not enough to back us if things go wrong."

Moltke said, "You three need to get some rest."

Martinez muttered his acknowledgement, a signal to Kirk and Rimes to do the same. They headed for the door.

"Jack," Moltke said.

Rimes stopped. The three men looked at each other. Then Kirk shrugged, and he and Martinez left without him.

"Look, Jack," Moltke said. "I think you're ready for this mission. You have high potential and top marks. You've proven yourself in the field over and again. You're a by-name operator for the Special Security Council. Even so, I'm assigning the most experienced operators to your team. I expect we'll be relying on your team pretty heavily."

"Understood, sir."

"Success opens doors. You have a lot of doors ahead of you. You'll have to start making decisions soon. I know you've got some pretty big plans."

Moltke considered Rimes for a moment. He gave a satisfied grunt, then left. A hint of whiskey lingered in his wake.

Rimes's head buzzed. He desperately needed to talk with Molly. *You have a lot of doors ahead of you.*

6

———

20 February 2164. USS *Sutton*.

THERE WAS nothing to do but wait as the *Sutton*'s communications system synchronized with the civilian network, so that's what Rimes did. From what the tech had said, the ship's connection was fine; the difficulty was in dealing with an overloaded civilian Grid circuit.

"Sergeant Rimes?" The crewman's thinly-mustached face reappeared in the vid display.

"Good news, Chief?"

"You should be good to go," the tech said. "Give it a few seconds."

"I owe you," Rimes said.

The tech scratched his mustache. "Not a thing, Sergeant." He signed off.

On Rimes's display, a digital clock counted down: three, two, one ... the earpiece made a few clicks, and then another display opened.

Molly's face came into view. "Jack?"

Rimes smiled. He could see sunlight streaming through the apartment's kitchen window in the background. Molly had her hair up in a bun; several frizzy, coppery strands sprouted out defiantly.

She looked tired. She wore a tattered cleaning shirt that hung loose on her lean frame, and the glow in her green eyes that made it impossible for him to look away was missing.

His throat tightened. "Hey," he said, unable to get out anything further.

She squinted, trying to make out the background behind him. "Are you at the airport? I thought you wouldn't be home for a few days."

"No, not at the airport. I wanted to call as—"

Molly closed her eyes for a second, then stared at him. "They canceled your leave again?"

Rimes broke eye contact. Tears were threatening, and he wasn't about to break down in front of her and anyone who might see him from the common area.

"You know how it is," he finally managed.

She bowed her head to hide wiping a tear away. "I should've known. Karen said Chris was pulled off a plane in London." She looked at him, her lips pressed together. "So when are you coming home?"

Rimes winced at Molly's casual reference to Moltke and his wife by their first names. They all shopped at the same stores, went to the same events. Molly had never accepted the military's officer and enlisted separation. It chafed at her even more than it did Rimes.

"No more than a few weeks. I'll let you know the moment I know. It won't be long, and we'll be rotating back soon." Six months forward-deployed, six months back at Fort Sill. That's how it worked—in theory.

Molly knew better.

Her image broke up for a moment.

Rimes squinted. "You there?"

The image returned.

"Molly?"

"I'm here." Molly said. She wasn't even trying to hold back the tears now. "I was gonna make it a surprise, Jack. I had planned ..." She wiped her face.

Rimes sat back in his seat. His heart accelerated. Every time he talked to Molly, every time he saw her ... he was always braced for the inevitable breakup message.

Most Commandos' marriages ended in divorce. The statistics ran through his head. He'd always hoped he might be one of the lucky ones, that Molly's strength and love would see them through the hard times. Despite the constant separations, his marriage had been like a dream.

"Molly, wait—" his voice failed him.

"I'm—we're—pregnant, Jack."

Rimes flinched at the last moment, almost missing Molly's actual words in his fear of what she might say.

Finally, he muttered, "Pregnant? How far along?"

Molly looked at him as she would a simpleton. "Well, the last time we spent any time together was in Italy, Jack. You figure it out."

Rimes relaxed. A baby was life changing. It would be a serious financial drain. It would delay her degree.

It was still better to look forward to than a messy divorce.

"How ... ? When did you realize?"

Molly wiped away more tears. They were down to a trickle now. "I missed my period, then started feeling sick—terrible heartburn, y'know? I finally went in a few weeks ago."

Rimes decided it wasn't the time to question protection. He hadn't used any; he'd just assumed she still was. "We'll visit Cleo and Alejandra when I get back. We'll tell them together. And your mother—"

Molly sniffled. "She already knows." She smiled. "She says it'll be good for me."

"You'll need to push back your PhD."

Molly shook her head; now, anger made her eyes sparkle. "Rejected again, anyway. Thirteen positions, only two went to Americans. Six Chinese students, three Indian, one Russian, one Vietnamese. Charging foreign student rates means a higher profit. I'll never get in, not without changing my nationality. And after I finally get the degree, it's not like they're knocking down doors hiring social scientists. It's so damned broken, Jack."

"Don't worry about it." Rimes could see she was on the verge of crying again. "Look, you're going to be a little too busy to worry about it for a while, right? You have your Master's. That's going to open doors, eventually."

Molly nodded. Tears welled in her eyes again. She looked at him, fighting them back. "Life's what you make of it, right?"

Her image broke into static for a moment, returned, then broke into static again.

Finally, the connection stabilized.

"Jack?"

"Bandwidth," Rimes said. "I'll send you notice when I have a firm return date. Love you, Baby."

Molly blew him a kiss. With the light from the kitchen washing over her, she was angelic. "Come home to me," she whispered. "Come home to us." She tried to disconnect before breaking into tears again but failed.

Rimes sucked in a lungful of air and exhaled. He was mostly alone in the room; four sailors—a young woman and three men of varying age—were caught up in their own communications sessions. Rimes quickly exited the common area, stepping through the hatch into the corridor before anyone could make eye contact.

In his haste, he nearly bumped into someone standing immediately outside the hatch. He turned.

"Jack! Was that Molly?" Kleigshoen, wearing a form-fitting black T-shirt and battle dress pants, stepped back, then leaned against the corridor wall to his left. Her hair was slightly damp and smelled of sandalwood shampoo.

She smiled, but it was more like that of a hungry predator than an old teammate.

Rimes took a quick breath. "Yeah."

"Don't worry." Kleigshoen poked him mischievously. "I wasn't spying on you, I just heard you as I was hanging up on my father. I haven't talked to him in a month—you remember how he gets. You have it easy with Cleo and Alejandra."

Rimes took another step away from her and felt himself relax. "Sure."

"How are things, Jack? I didn't really get a chance to talk to you before. It's just been so crazy, you know?"

"Dana ..." He sighed quietly. "Things have been good, thanks. I've moved on."

"Married," Kleigshoen replied, looking at his ring. "I'm happy for you. I should be, right? She's pretty."

Molly was pretty. He knew that. Everyone knew that. But she was a candle to Kleigshoen's sun.

"Thanks," Rimes said. "You?"

Rimes wanted to leave, to catch a quick nap, but his window of opportunity was shrinking.

Kleigshoen held up her hand, wiggling her fingers. "Nope. I told you, career first. I meant it." She smiled again, cutting through his defenses. "I hope you're not still mad at me? To be fair, you were the only person to ever make me reconsider ... everything."

Rimes shook his head. "I've got a really good thing going."

Kleigshoen raised an eyebrow. "That is *so* wonderful. I don't know how you could do it. How long have you been married?"

Rimes struggled for a moment, summoning memories from an infinite abyss. He was tired and she was in his head, destroying anything that remotely resembled reason and control.

"Two years next month."

"You've been in Spec Ops the whole time. You two really must have something special."

"Molly has the patience of a mountain."

"I'd say. So what's your plan?" Kleigshoen tilted her head, exposing her long, soft, smooth neck.

"I need to catch a nap—"

Kleigshoen chuckled. He'd forgotten her deep, throaty laugh and how it affected him.

"I meant, what's your plan for the future," she said. "I've seen the recording from Singapore. Lots of the big guys have, and we all liked what we saw. Everything's changing."

Rimes nodded, surprised and embarrassed. He wondered how much of the mission she'd seen. *Probably all of it.*

"Well, if the Army can hold things together another twenty or so years, I guess I'll shoot for retirement. It's not like war is going out of style."

"The old wars will," Kleigshoen said. "It's only a matter of time before the last bits of national identity vanish. You've got to see that, Jack. The military isn't going to be there in twenty years, not like it is today. And the Commandos aren't going to make it even that far."

Rimes felt his pulse rising. "There's always going to be demand for someone like me."

"Someone like what? Someone brave? Someone loyal?"

"I get things done."

Kleigshoen shook her head. "You're getting defensive. Don't. I'm not attacking you. I'm trying to say you've got to plan. People like you ... Jack, you're a wonderful person. You're—"

A sailor entered the corridor.

Kleigshoen waited until he'd passed into the common room. "You're extremely capable, but ... going into the field, the kind of things you do now, it won't last forever."

"I'm applying for Officer Candidate School. I need to take a few more classes and wrap up my Master's thesis, that's all. Then I'll run operations, not just execute them."

Kleigshoen looked him in the eyes with an unsettling intensity. "Why don't you come to work for the Bureau? No matter what happens—the United States carries on, this American Hemisphere entity they keep talking about comes about, the United Nations takes over—the Bureau is going to be there in one form or another. There's too much going on here on Earth and out there in the colonies for the Bureau to ever become obsolete. With all the power the metacorporations have accumulated and with their willingness to use it, we're probably more important now than ever before."

Rimes had heard the pitch before. He shook his head. "I love field work. It's what I'm good at. As long as there are people, there's going to be a need for a military to protect them."

"The Bureau has field operators. I have connections. I've done well; you would be exceptional.

"It's not going to be the same, not forever. You got lucky. Think about it. You had a forty-percent fatality rate in Singapore. The three you killed were Jimmies, and I mean *extreme* genetic modification. The Thai—Suttikul— we've never seen anything like it. They were on radical stimulants, tailored drug cocktails like nothing else out there. It's going to be weeks reverse-engineering what they had in their bloodstream."

Rimes was grinding his teeth. "We did okay."

"*You* did okay, Jack. How'd the Russian do? And your German buddy was touch and go. His heart stopped twice before they stabilized him. He'll be behind a desk for the rest of his career unless they fund growing him a new heart. I've seen the AAR. You know how this goes."

"We all knew the risks."

"And I'm telling you, it's not going to be easy like this for much longer." Kleigshoen stretched, arching her back. "The risks for someone like you are going off the charts. Ten years from now, no normal humans will be going into the field. Not like today."

Rimes closed his eyes and wished her away. "I'm not completely against being a Jimmy, if I have to. I'll take more aggressive stims, whatever it takes.

"But even if the government decided to grow their own genies—and I don't believe they would, not considering what happened with them—I'll be retired before they're field-ready."

Kleigshoen gave him a knowing wink. "Twenty years at the outside, Jack. Trust me. Join us. You'll work the field, but without the risk."

It hit Rimes then. She had to be talking about remotes. Proxies. He'd heard about it before, but it had been purely theoretical at the time.

The first models had been crude robots, good for simple, high-risk work, like ordnance disposal. But the future lay in biomorphic robots— machines that could pass as humans, hosts capable of fully immersive awareness transfer.

The idea of remotely piloting a robot revolted him.

"Remotes? Not interested. That's Moltke's thing, not mine."

Kleigshoen rolled her eyes. "Jack, it's coming. You can get onboard or you can get run over by it. You keep going against these genies, you *will* die. They're not human."

Rimes knew what genetically engineered and modified humans were capable of, but he also knew what *he* was capable of.

The metacorporations had created their own small armies of genies and Jimmies years before. Increasingly, it was falling to people like him to deal with the fallout.

"I need to get some sleep," he muttered.

"Good night, Jack." She extended her hand. "Think about what I said."

Against his better judgment, Rimes took her hand in his own. Her touch, like her laugh and her smile, brought back memories. She was soft, warm, vibrant.

Rimes broke off the contact and headed for the berth he'd been assigned. His eyes were heavy, his pace sluggish, and his thoughts a twisted mess.

He had just enough time to catch a short nap, to think of his new life, to dream of his time with Kleigshoen.

He could still smell her perfume—musky, sweet.

7

———

21 February 2164. Sundarbans, India, 25 kilometers from the Bangladesh border.

LIGHTNING FLASHED across the dark sky for several seconds, momentarily revealing their camouflaged forms before Rimes closed his eyes to prevent pupil contraction. He squatted in the stunted underbrush, waiting for the light show to finish. Thunder crashed, built to a crescendo, settled into quiet rumbles, then faded to silence.

Finally, his optics came back to life.

Rimes opened his eyes, and the once-expansive mangrove forest returned to sight as a tapestry of greens and blacks. Four decades before, he would have been concerned about tigers, crocodiles, even snakes. But now the forest, in slow recovery from decades of abuse, offered little more than angry kingfishers for a threat.

The animals that concerned him walked on two feet.

A low-lying haze remained, obscuring everything, rendering trees and grass otherworldly, dream-like. The storm was passing, but the damage was done; critical minutes had been lost.

Camouflage battle dress, grease paint, and a greasy residue from the rain covered Rimes head-to-toe. Ankle-deep in muddy water, closing on a potentially dangerous situation, and leading a team into action for the first time—he was simultaneously energized and nauseated.

It was the life he loved, for however long he could live it.

Rimes scanned the stunted trees around him, confirmed his team was in position, then whispered. "Green in position."

Chung, Wolford, and Pasqual were all with him. Bhat and Orr, two other Commandos he'd worked with before, filled out the rest of the team.

Every operational element was going by the book. Rimes had no intention of screwing anything up, not with so much of his career riding on this performance.

Three years before, he'd qualified for Commando training, and it had fit him like a glove. Now he had unofficial word his application for Officer Candidate School would be accepted, from Moltke, no less.

The future's mine to control.

Crystal-clear whispers confirmed Red and Blue were in position.

Captain Moltke ordered them into bounding overwatch movement. Kleigshoen's briefing had identified twenty-five T-Corp operators, a significant challenge for the unit should they lose the element of surprise. Like most metacorporations, T-Corp recruited heavily from seasoned military units for its security forces—mostly from India, but Afghanistan, Iraq, and Pakistan were also targeted. Every one of their security teams had at least one veteran in its ranks. This close to potential enemy positions, a staggered advance made sense.

At the order, Red moved first.

Rimes sighted through the CAWS-5's scope. There was a millisecond blur as his helmet's optics—a lightweight, integrated flip-down shield—synchronized with the weapon's scope.

Scanning the forest to his right, he located the Red team. They were doing well, making optimal use of cover, minimizing their silhouettes. Rimes scanned the forest ahead of the advancing team, watching for signs of movement or anything that broke the normal terrain silhouette.

"Red in position." Martinez's voice had a calm Rimes could only hope he'd have one day.

Moltke spoke again. "Green, move forward."

Rimes began a slow, crouched jog, making use of what cover he could. To his left, Chung and Wolford followed. A moment later, Pasqual, Bhat, and Orr separated from the undergrowth to his right.

Moving across the soggy ground was slow going. In addition to the all-too-frequent patches of slick mud, there were hidden roots and water-filled holes just waiting to break a man's leg.

His mission team drew parallel to Red, then continued past, securing a position fifteen meters forward.

Moltke ordered the Blue team to advance.

They repeated the process three times before Martinez spotted the compound perimeter. They were all on edge, waiting for an attack from the positions Intel had identified.

But there was nothing.

"Any movement, Gold?" Martinez whispered after a moment.

In his mid-30s, Martinez was the most experienced among them, yet the lack of engagement after Horus's earlier report of movement seemed to have rattled him. His team consisted of recent high-potential graduates and Barlowe, all on their first major mission. They were combat-proven, but not necessarily ready for operations of this nature.

Coming out of Commando school, Rimes had been labeled as similarly high-potential and had exclusively trained under Martinez during his first year.

Even then, Martinez had been under pressure to take a position at Commando school. Martinez had deferred the "promotion," opting for another stint in the field.

Rimes's thoughts turned to Barlowe, who was consistently lagging behind the rest of Red. *Get it together, Ladell. We don't want to lose anybody.*

Rimes moved his team toward Red's position, securing the left flank. Kirk moved Blue up to secure the right. Like Barlowe, Stern was pulling up his team's rear.

"C'mon, Stern, pick it up," Kirk said. "We're almost there."

Communications went silent for a moment.

"Green, breach perimeter two meters from the western edge. Ops should be in the two-story building about thirty meters east-northeast, in a secure room at the northwestern end of the first floor."

Rimes moved his team forward, taking position near the perimeter fence. They went prone in the knee-high grass, watching through the fence for movement. The compound looked clear. Rimes signaled Chung forward from the leftmost position and covered him as he squatted at the fence.

Chung slung his weapon over his shoulder and quickly unraveled a strand of centimeter-thick therm cord. He pressed the cord onto the fence to create a meter-wide semicircle, then shoved a thumb-sized device into the cord.

Once in position, he pulled a small detonator from his pocket and glanced at Rimes.

Rimes scanned the perimeter, then nodded.

Chung pressed the detonator, and the therm cord flared momentarily, burning through the fence. Rimes moved forward, punched down the sagging links, and ducked through the opening.

The team followed, each entry separated by five seconds. Less than a minute after Rimes signaled the breach, their backs were pressed against the operations building's south wall.

Dark green creepers covered the exterior of all the buildings except one. The research building, made of naked sandstone and rose-colored glass, was a middle finger raised to the skies.

Aside from the research building, the compound was modest and functional, nothing like the commercial parks that had sprung up during India's years of explosive growth—the growth that had eventually decimated so much of the country.

Rimes edged along the wall, stopping at a door, then signaled for Pasqual to open it.

While Pasqual worked on the lock, the rest of the team scanned the darkness. Nothing moved. Even the sounds amplified by their helmets were insignificant—gentle rain, a soft wind, Pasqual's work on the door, the occasional bug or reptile hardy enough to have survived ecological ruin.

Finally, Pasqual slid his tools into his jacket pocket and resumed his position, weapon ready. With Bhat at his side, Rimes edged toward the door, then held up three fingers.

Bhat centered his CAWS-5 on the door.

Rimes squatted and counted down, then opened the door and ducked out of Bhat's arc of fire.

The door was clear. Lights reflected dimly off once-polished walls.

Rimes brought his weapon up and scanned for movement. "Gold, this is Green. Entry is clear. Power is on." He was sure his pulse was drowning out his words.

"Repeat, Green."

Rimes looked inside the entry again. He hadn't imagined it. "The power is on."

"Proceed, Green."

Rimes waved Bhat and Chung into the room. They took positions covering the entries, and Rimes sent the rest of the team in.

Inside, Rimes's BAS overlaid the building map in a pale green wireframe.

According to Intel, the room had been a processing center for the main research group. About thirty cubicles still held terminals and communications units—bulky, dust-covered anachronisms that must have been outdated even when the facility was active.

The room's northern doorway opened into an east-west corridor, with access to the second floor through a stairwell. Three north-south corridors led off the east-west corridor, one to the far left, one almost straight ahead, and one to the far right.

Their target was the left corridor.

"Bhat, secure that stairwell door. Chung, cover him. Orr, watch that right corridor, Pasqual, the central corridor. Wolford, left corridor. Go."

Rimes waited until everyone was in position, then advanced toward the end of the far-left corridor. He stopped shy of the corridor and waited. Wolford signaled all-clear. A moment later, Orr and Pasqual did the same.

Rimes signaled Chung forward. Once Chung was in place, Rimes glanced down the left corridor. He signaled for Wolford to hold position, then moved forward. Chung followed.

The overlay showed six doors along the corridor's length: four to his right, two to his left. The overlay of the northernmost left-hand door flashed.

Based off the room size and location, it would be a fairly typical T-Corp operations center. However, unlike most metacorporations, which located operations centers in basements or windowless interior rooms, T-Corp preferred operations rooms to have two outside walls. There was no way to know why; T-Corp was one of the few metacorporations the military hadn't cracked.

Rimes kept his back to the wall and moved quietly down the corridor. Drywall and lightweight aluminum couldn't stop a high-powered round, but it still provided some sense of security.

At the room, Rimes reached for the doorknob but stopped at the last second, when he realized the door wasn't completely closed.

"Gold, door to target is ajar," he whispered.

"Proceed with caution, Green."

Rimes signaled the rest of the team forward. They arrived a few seconds later. Wolford took up position watching the team.

Pasqual and Chung brought their carbines up. Once again, Bhat positioned himself in front of the door, shotgun ready.

Bhat looked around quickly. "Anyone know any good knock-knock jokes?"

Rimes counted down from three with raised fingers.

On one, he shoved the door in.

The door hit resistance, and he stumbled.

Without losing a beat, Bhat squat-walked into the room, swinging the weapon barrel in a semicircle, but there was no movement. The others followed.

They froze, heads sweeping to take everything in.

It took them all a moment to absorb what they were seeing—a dozen bodies spread around the room, their backs arched, their faces contorted, and their fingers curled in agony.

"NBC," Rimes called over the communication channel, trying to keep his voice from betraying his near panic.

He unfurled the thin plastic shielding from the top of his helmet, wrapping it around the optics shield and quickly pressing the shielding material to his coat to seal off his face and throat. He retrieved his gloves from a pants pocket, pulling them on as he watched his team seal up.

The plastic shielding's micro-filter would block ninety percent of known weaponized materials, allowing them to breathe in relative safety for twenty-four hours.

They each had atropine injectors for nerve agents, antibiotic and anti-viral cocktail injectors for bacterial and viral agents, and a broad-based aerosol formula for most other chemical agents. Vaccinations and immunity boosters provided defense against common, preventable threats.

But, depending on what they'd been exposed to, all those defenses still meant they only had a slim chance of survival.

8

____

21 February 2164. Sundarbans, India.

RIMES LOOKED around the operations room. The T-Corp operatives had died terrible deaths.

As if there could be a good death. I'm going to see this in my dreams.

"Green, confirm NBC," Moltke demanded, some concern understandably leaking through.

Pasqual was already testing surfaces and corpses with wipes taken from a hip pocket.

"NBC confirmed," Rimes said. "We have ... eleven ... thirteen ... fourteen dead. No wounds. Indications of rapid reaction to vector."

Pasqual set aside the last of a dozen wipes, shaking his head at Rimes.

"Negative on testing," Rimes said.

Moltke was silent for a minute. "Hold position. Radio check. Any symptoms?"

"Red One, all clear."

"Red Two, all clear."

Rimes responded when the other teams were done. No symptoms

among eighteen men, no reaction on any of the wipes, no sign of residue or particulate matter—but he was looking at fourteen corpses of seemingly healthy men. Whatever had killed them was fast-acting and left no detectable signature.

"Hold position for five minutes. Green, estimate the time the agent took to act."

Rimes considered the corpses. Some were still holding weapons. One had collapsed over a portable computer array; another, the one Rimes had shoved aside upon entry, had been headed for the door.

"Seconds." Rimes shook his head. "Or hours, possibly."

It was possible—although unlikely—that prolonged exposure had caused the reaction. But if it had been prolonged exposure, differences in immune systems and exposure levels should have led to different reaction times. *No, they died in seconds and almost certainly within seconds of each other.*

"Correction. It must have been within seconds."

"Green, secure the roof. Red, hold until my signal, then move to Ops. See if you can retrieve data from any of the equipment there. Blue, take up Red's position on my signal. Maintain NBC posture."

Rimes led his team to the stairwell door, pausing until Bhat disarmed the alarm he'd set on it. They took the stairs in a staggered line.

Whatever killed them, it has to be something new, something we can't detect. Maybe it's outside the known arsenals. It's not the virus that hit the Eurica teams. Those had extremely high temperatures, connective tissue disintegration, hemorrhaging. That took hours, days.

That wasn't a weapon. This was.

On the roof, Rimes deployed his team to the corners, with Orr covering the door. Then, from the north wall, he scanned the research building windows for any threats.

After a moment, he reported the team in position.

Perspiration rolled down his face. He did his best to blink it away.

Moltke ordered the Red team in to secure the operations building and Blue to remove the corpses before redeploying to the building to the northwest.

After several minutes, Rimes watched Kirk and the Blue team spread out across the other rooftop, less than fifty meters away.

There was still no sign of any other activity in the compound.

"Barlowe's downloading data from the T-Corp computer," Martinez reported.

"Barlowe, can you give me an estimate?" Moltke asked.

Barlowe clucked into his earpiece. "It's taken some damage, Captain. It'll be a while."

"Is it intact?"

Barlowe clucked again. "I think there's a chance I can recover it."

A few heartbeats passed, then Moltke responded. "Red, leave Barlowe on the computer work. Take the rest of your team to the research building. We've got eleven operators unaccounted for."

Rimes opened a private channel to Moltke. "Gold, did you say leave Barlowe in there alone?"

"Roger, Green," Moltke said with a hint of irritation. "Keep your focus."

Barlowe's not ready for this.

Rimes tracked the Red team's movement through his scope, running his sights ahead of them in an arc. He stopped suddenly twenty meters shy of the research building, where a small structure stood in a clearing that had long ago been a parking lot.

He'd seen something.

"Movement, twenty meters southeast of research building," Rimes said calmly. "One Tango." He caught another flash of movement in his limited peripheral vision. "Two. Two Tangos."

"Red, take cover," Moltke ordered. "Green, identify Tangos."

"Lost visual," Rimes said. He looked to his right. Chung, positioned at the northeastern corner, looked up from his scope, signaled there were three targets, but he'd lost sight of them.

"Update. Three Tangos. Lost visual at the structure in the southeast of the parking lot. They were moving fast."

"Blue?"

"Negative, no visual."

"Red, increase spacing and interval. Bringing Horus in for a closer look."

Rimes listened for Horus's telltale hum. Moltke was understandably reluctant to risk their eye in the sky, but the situation justified it.

Rimes scanned the structure in the clearing again. The rain had completely stopped, and he was slowly cooking inside the sealed suit.

Another flash of movement.

Rimes fired. "Red, eastern flank, *down!*"

The target sprinted first north, then east, then disappeared completely behind a stunted tree. Almost as if he'd sensed what was coming.

Horus's hum became audible as it bathed the field in ultraviolet light that their optics picked up. Moltke hissed a curse under his breath as the high-resolution imaging system identified potential threats.

"Red, fall back to Ops," Moltke said hurriedly. "Blue, fall back to Ops, double time. Green, cover them. Focus attention on north and northeast. Six Tangos, closing."

Chung opened fire, a controlled burst of three rounds. Wolford joined him a moment later. Rimes saw a blur of movement headed for a trailing Red team member—Martinez.

There was no time to shout a warning.

Rimes sighted and squeezed off a three-round burst, striking center mass.

The target staggered, slowed. It had a knife in one hand, its other hand struggled to un-holster a pistol. It was within a meter and still closing.

Martinez turned, put another burst at point-blank range into the target. It fell.

"Tango down," Martinez said.

He'd been a heartbeat away from a body bag and seemed completely unfazed.

Six rounds to take down one target. What the hell?

They used specialized rounds that would take a normal man down with one hit, two at the outside. Then again, a normal man couldn't move as quickly as what he'd just seen.

Genies. We could really use the latest BAS upgrades.

Moltke fed Horus's imaging into everyone's optics. Two targets were advancing on Rimes's building from the east, while Chung and Wolford were maintaining a steady cover fire. Two more were moving toward Blue's building to the northwest.

With one down, that left another unaccounted for.

Rimes moved to the west wall, scanning Horus's targeting feeds. Pasqual and Bhat were doing the same. They found one of the targets as it sprinted toward the north door of Blue's building and opened fire, driving the target back to cover.

"Blue, target advancing at high speed on your building from the northwest," Rimes said.

He let off a burst in front of the target as it cleared cover. A second burst and the target staggered. A third and it dropped.

"Tango down." Rimes continued scanning as he reloaded. "Gold, this is Green. I can't find the sixth Tango."

"One second, Green."

Horus gained altitude and increased UV output. Digital signals replayed the last minute on Rimes's optical display. Two signals stopped where the targets had been dropped.

Rimes surveyed the display, identifying the two targets Chung and Wolford had engaged, and the one Pasqual and Bhat had pinned down. Finally, he spotted the sixth. He cursed.

"Blue, Tango in your building."

As if in response to his call, Rimes heard gunfire. He spotted along the other building's eastern wall, looking through windows for any possible targets. He couldn't see anything. The gunfire stopped.

"Blue, status," Moltke said calmly. "Blue, report."

There was no response. Rimes brought up a window with the Blue team's vitals. One was dropping fast, the others were flat-lined.

"Their vitals—" Rimes said.

"I can see their vitals, Green," Moltke said, his voice emotionless. "We've lost Blue."

A crack of gunfire followed by a wet gurgle caught Rimes's attention. He turned. Wolford collapsed backward from the southeastern corner of the wall, clutching his throat.

Lewis!

Rimes ran across the roof and took Wolford's position.

The target was hidden behind a low cinderblock wall, part of a drainage system.

Rimes pulled a grenade from his belt, waited a beat, pulled the pin, and threw it to the right of the wall.

Before the grenade detonated, the target moved to the left—into Rimes's sights.

Three bursts and the target went down.

"Tango down," Rimes said.

Gunfire erupted to his left.

"Tango down," Chung said.

Rimes signaled for Chung to move to the western wall, then checked Wolford. There was a pulse, but it was weak. Wolford's eyes looked at something far away for a few seconds before closing. Blood spurted from his ruined throat, pooling on the rooftop.

Rimes closed his eyes for a moment. "Wolford's down." Rimes took Wolford's grenade and hoped he wouldn't have to leave the body.

He hoped there wouldn't be more.

Silence settled over the communication channel for a moment.

Rimes scanned the parking lot, looking for flashes of more-than-human speed.

The silence was broken by an almost sheepish announcement: "Red in Ops. Room is secure."

Rimes moved back to the west wall. Pasqual and Bhat still had their target pinned down, but were no closer to eliminating it. Rimes signaled Chung; a moment later, a grenade landed on either side of the target, forcing it out of cover. Pasqual and Bhat dropped it.

"Tango down," Pasqual said.

Bhat looked at Rimes. "Please tell me that's the last one?"

Rimes held up a finger and pointed to the building where the Blue team had been slaughtered. The Tango was still in the building, possibly escaping out of sight to the west. It was equally possible that it had circled and was now inside the building somewhere below them.

"Gold, this is Green. Permission to engage final target."

Rimes signaled Pasqual and Bhat for a grenade and directed them to observe the northwestern building while Orr moved to cover Wolford's position. Once confident Orr was going to be okay working next to

Wolford's corpse, Rimes slung his carbine over his back and took Bhat's assault shotgun.

"Granted, Green," Moltke said, finally.

Rimes tapped Chung, and the two descended to the first floor. Rimes reviewed Horus's image overlay, relieved to see the sixth target hadn't yet exited Blue's building.

They were halfway to Blue's building when shots rang out. Glass shattered, and the sound of Horus's motor changed: the target had hit the UAV. A moment later, the motor gave out completely, and Horus crashed to the ground.

"Horus is down," Moltke said, with more emotion than when he'd lost the entire Blue team.

Rimes reached the building first, pressing tight against its wall. He had the assault shotgun at the ready, hoping the greater area it covered would compensate for having to fight indoors. Pasqual and Bhat suddenly opened fire, their bullets shattering windows and ricocheting off the wall a few meters from Rimes.

The firing intensified. Bullets thudded and bounced nearby. Rimes turned, saw the target round the corner, heading for him. Rimes got a shot off, clipping the target. Chung fired and missed.

The target was on Rimes then, a flurry of blows—fist and knife, punching and slashing.

Rimes gave ground, letting the fists land, trying to redirect or block the knife with the shotgun. Blood trickled from wounds on his forearms and the backs of his hands.

Rimes managed a lucky swing with the shotgun's stock, stunning the target. He followed it up with a kick to the abdomen, getting a knife in his thigh for his troubles.

But the kick put room between him and the target.

Pasqual and Bhat opened fire again.

The target shuddered, then dropped.

Rimes brought the shotgun butt down hard into the target's throat, then followed up with a brutal stomp on the target's face.

"Tango down," Bhat reported.

9

24 February 2164. USS *Sutton*.

THE WORLD WAS DIVIDED into two spaces: quarantine, and everything beyond.

A plexiglass wall—thick, impassable, suffocating—defined the limit of his freedom. The smudge-free wall teased him, allowing him to imagine he wasn't a prisoner for whole seconds at a time. Beyond it, three nurses in fully sealed hazmat suits focused on another round of blood work.

The *Sutton* didn't just have extra weapons systems and a larger deck. Snuggled tight at the stern, immediately below decks, was a small compartment accessible by a single set of stairs. The compartment, including a small lab and a slightly larger suite of rooms, was rated for Biosafety Level 4 work.

Rimes paced his prison. The room he was in was three meters deep and two meters across. It was white, sterile—simultaneously empty and cluttered. With a bunk, card table, and two chairs, it offered little open space, but the absence of any personal effects made it feel hollow.

Rimes and Martinez were hot-bunked with Moltke, who was asleep. An adjoining room, accessible through the shared head, held the rest of the team. Rimes and the others faced days of quarantine, assuming they weren't already dying from whatever agent the genies had used. It would be weeks before the techs would know what had killed the T-Corp agents.

We lost seven men. And for what?

Rimes ran through the inventory: two storage devices, a dozen specimen containers, a spent chemical-weapon canister, several tailor-made weapons retrieved from the genie corpses, and petabytes of data.

Along with the remaining T-Corp agents in the other buildings—dead like the rest—they'd found another portable computer array, busily downloading and analyzing data.

T-Corp had suddenly decided they had to violate a decades-old agreement. The genies—so fast, so deadly—should have fled the moment the Commandos arrived. And whatever had been in the recovered weapons canister somehow fell outside the broad spectrum the Commandos' kit could detect.

Everything was random data points and inconsistencies, absent of any connecting elements or explanations. Try as he might, Rimes could make no sense of it.

Genies were genetically engineered, lab-grown servants designed to perform specific tasks. These had been Asian, almost certainly LoDu products. Rimes had never heard of genies directly engaging military units before. Outside of attacks on other metacorporate assets, there was simply no record of direct engagement with military forces. And the few who escaped their owners were generally wary of hiring on for anything other than corporate espionage. Of course, the bodies had no identification on them, no way of telling who had hired them and for what purpose.

The CH-121s had been Valkyries, carrying home the fallen.

Lewis, buddy. Body bags, loot. Why? What was in the computer arrays? What was worth the risk? All this death—maybe my own—and I'm going to be a father. If I survive.

As he watched the nurses cautiously catalog the blood samples, Rimes's thoughts turned to Kleigshoen's offer. To look at her—the soft hair, the manicured nails, the perfume—it was obvious an Intelligence Bureau agent was treated well.

He'd worked with a few over the years. They'd seemed capable—if cocky and prone to callous disregard for their military counterparts. Most had been burdened with a dangerous sense of entitlement.

Rimes wondered if he could ever become like that. A flash of his baby's imagined face, of Molly's warm caress, and he realized he very well might. Family was an obligation he didn't take lightly.

Martinez returned to the room with a quiet sigh, pulling a cotton ball out of his right elbow crease. "Damned vampires," he whispered as he settled at the table. He pulled a deck of cards from his thigh pocket and pointed at the table.

Rimes settled into the chair across from Martinez, and the two began a series of half-hearted games. They had access to thousands of entertainment options, but the cards' tactile sensations and mind-numbing repetition held the greatest appeal. They passed hours without speaking, quietly shuffling, dealing, and playing.

Rimes yawned and checked the time. They'd been aboard the ship a little over fifty-two hours.

Finally, Moltke sat up in the bunk. Martinez stood, offering up his chair. Moltke waved him away and stumbled toward the head with a loud yawn.

Moltke paused at the entry and looked back. "You two up for some poker?"

Martinez shook his head. "I can't afford it, sir." He settled into the bunk and flipped the pillow before stretching out. "What about the old gang?"

Moltke glared at Martinez for a moment, then looked to Rimes. "What about you? I don't feel like giving my money away to Babyface. You up for a little adventure?"

Rimes chuckled and shuffled the cards. "Is Ladell really that good, sir?"

"He knows cards like he knows computers. And don't be fooled by that innocent face. He's impossible to read."

Rimes's earpiece chirped, and he placed it in his ear. Kleigshoen was requesting a channel.

Rimes accepted.

"Jack?"

Kleigshoen was close. Rimes turned to look into the lab. Two people stood at the wall in hazmat suits.

He walked forward, peering into the faceplates. "Dana?"

A smile spread across the face in the slightly smaller suit. "Good news," Kleigshoen said. "We made an educated guess on the weapon used to kill the T-Corp team, and just confirmed it. X-17 nerve gas. No contagion. You'd have been killed within seconds had you been exposed to meaningful quantities."

"No one is showing any signs of exposure, Sergeant Rimes," said the other person, a doctor who'd been one of the first to interview the returning Commandos. "We should have you all out of here by tomorrow morning. One more round of tests and you're home free."

Rimes rubbed his face. He was relieved, but something about the situation left him feeling hollow, too. "How'd they get hold of X-17?"

Kleigshoen looked from the doctor to Rimes. "There was an incident. We don't know who, but someone managed to steal a shipment. That's actually why I came to see you. Jack, this is an important case. I'd like to interview you about any details you may have missed during the debrief."

Her words, although friendly enough, stung.

Even though it ultimately didn't matter, he'd somehow worked himself into believing she'd come to share the good news because she still cared for him.

It was stupid; he was a happily married man with a child on the way, and his relationship with Kleigshoen had been relatively short and, for Kleigshoen, nothing but a solution for a physical need.

Rimes finally nodded.

"Great. Would now be okay?" Kleigshoen looked at him hopefully, and he nodded again.

She thanked the doctor, who exited the lab.

Rimes looked at the slumbering Martinez, then at Moltke, who wasn't even pretending to ignore the one-way conversation.

"It was X-17, sir," Rimes explained. "No contamination. A few more tests, and we should be out of here by morning."

"X-17? No shit?" Moltke looked surprised for a moment, then turned his attention to the cards. He snorted. "I wasn't even fucking exposed. Maybe I can salvage my vacation after all."

We could've been completely wiped out, and that's all he feels? Ice in his veins.

"Roger that, sir," Rimes said with a smile.

Moltke shook his head. "I guess we know who stole the X-17 now."

Rimes turned back to Kleigshoen.

He took in a deep breath and tried to focus on the helicopter flight into the Sundarbans ... then the trek through the forest ... the arrival at the compound ...

Kleigshoen played back the debriefing for him, to help jog his memory.

"Okay, Jack," Kleigshoen said. "I'm looking for anything that might have escaped your attention, anything that might have seemed trivial or obvious during the debriefing. Everything matters at this point: How did your weapons function? How did you feel before entering the compound compared to afterwards? How did your team perform? Did you see *anything* that was in retrospect out of the ordinary?"

Rimes closed his eyes in concentration. It wasn't uncommon on critical missions to go through more than one debriefing. After a moment, he looked at Kleigshoen. "Sure. Shoot."

"Great. Let's start with the team, then. Did anyone act odd?"

"Odd?" Rimes rubbed his forehead for a moment, then shook his head. "Not that I can think of. I mean ... like what?"

"Maybe they exhibited signs of exposure," Kleigshoen offered. "Maybe they were a little sluggish. Maybe they were sloppy or had discipline problems?"

Rimes thought back through the operation. Other than Barlowe and Stern, everyone had been at the top of their game. "No," he said, hesitating, then again with more confidence. "No. We did about as well as could be expected."

"All right." Kleigshoen seemed content with the answer. She replayed a segment from the debriefing where Rimes described initial contact with the genies. "You saw movement."

"Right. I saw one break from cover."

"How many did you ultimately see?"

"See? Well, Horus picked up six forms. Their suits were pretty advanced. We could barely pick them up with our own optics. Our systems aren't as advanced as what the Special Security Council has, and it showed.

It wasn't just the suits, though. They moved so fast … I've heard of genies being fast. I've seen video. This was … it was amazing."

"I told you," Kleigshoen said. "There are thousands of them out there. Tens of thousands. And that's only what the metacorporations have publicly registered. Legally, they're property, so we can't be completely sure the metacorporations have revealed everything. It was only a matter of time before something like this happened."

"Like I said, the suits were high-end stuff, as good as anything I've ever seen or used," Rimes said. "I put a three-round burst into the first one, center mass. At that range, it should've put him down. I saw the corpse. The rounds got through, but the wounds were almost … superficial. Even so, they would've put a normal man down, probably permanently. What the hell can they do to make that possible?"

Kleigshoen thought for a moment. "Toughened skin? Denser bones? Did you see anything odd when you looked at the corpses? What did they look like?"

They'd laid the genies out next to one of the buildings, pulled off their headgear, and exposed their wounds for the video record. "Young, maybe mid-twenties. My age, maybe a little older. Asian, mostly—the eye shape—"

"Epicanthic fold?"

Rimes nodded. "Right. And straight, dark hair. Male. About my height, but leaner. You couldn't tell they had less mass by the force of their attacks. There was … the eyes were different. The shape was slightly off. And the color was different. There was something strange about the iris."

"Can you be more specific?"

Rimes closed his eyes. "The video should have caught it. But maybe not, in that lighting. Something about the placement and the size. There was … an animal-like appearance about them. Does that make any sense?"

"You mean they glowed when the light hit them?"

Rimes half-shook his head. "Not quite, but something like that."

"We've got their DNA. Our scientists are going to be tearing this data apart for months. Go on."

"That's about it, really. The kit was the sort of thing you'd find only with an elite unit. Modular weapons, unique materials. Specialized. Their physical capabilities—strength, speed, resiliency—were off the charts. Whatever tailoring they did, it started with Asian DNA. I'm confident they were LoDu."

"What are the odds they made off with some of the data?"

Rimes thought for a moment. "I don't think so. The computer arrays were still downloading and decrypting the data when we found them. They could have done a parallel download and left with incomplete data, but Barlowe said this sort of stuff is usually stored so that you have to have all the files to decompress and decrypt fully. Barlowe did all he could with the systems. They took some damage, and there's some sort of complex encryption algorithm involved. Really, you should talk to him about the computers. He's pretty amazing. Plus ... we didn't see any genies leaving as we approached the facility. No. I don't see how they could've gotten the data out."

"You didn't see any once you were in the facility, either," Kleigshoen reminded him. "Not until it was almost too late."

Rimes nodded. Even Horus had missed the genies until Moltke had sent it in closer. "Okay, sure. It's possible, although I still question the value of what they could have gotten away with. We can't know. If they can make some that are as smart as those were tough, though ..."

Kleigshoen watched him for a moment. "You killed three of them, Jack."

"No, a team of eighteen Commandos killed six of them, and we suffered a nearly forty-percent fatality rate in the process."

Just like Singapore.

Rimes shook his head as Wolford's last seconds played out in his mind. "It could've been much worse. They could've succeeded with their ambush. One or two fewer mistakes, a break that had gone their way, and they would've gotten us all. I don't think they were very experienced. Not against military."

She pressed a gloved hand against the wall. "I'm sorry about your friends. Jack ... Don't forget my offer. It's too dangerous out there."

Rimes nodded.

He wondered what Molly would think—he'd have to share at least a little of what he'd been through with her.

He wasn't looking forward to it.

10

---

25 February 2164. Oklahoma City, Oklahoma.

RIMES WOKE WITH A START. His neck ached, and his head throbbed where he'd just smacked into the bus window. The old man beside him cursed as he tried to find a comfortable spot. The old man's wife, looking weaker than when they'd boarded in Los Angeles, tried to scoot back from the crowded aisle. Filthy young men swayed unsteadily in the aisle, shouting curses to no one in particular.

With a glance out the grease-smudged window, Rimes realized they were finally approaching the outskirts of Oklahoma City.

The highway had fallen into even greater disrepair—spiderweb cracks, craters, washed-away shoulders—since his last trip home, no doubt victim to more violent storms.

And Oklahoma City's broken skyline served as painful testimony to the lack of will and wherewithal for any kind of intervention.

He blinked the sleep away and yawned, immediately regretting taking in the bus's foul air through his scented surgical mask. Even living in the field and going days without a shower couldn't match the rank odor permeating everything around him: unwashed bodies, clothes long overdue for disposal, grease- and dirt-covered travel bags, and patches of exposed cushion that absorbed each passenger's scent, mingling it with its predecessor's until it produced a nauseating stench. The end result unsettled him more than the sounds of combat ever could.

He recalled traveling in his youth with Cleo, his father. They'd traveled occasionally by car, but mostly by bus on private seats, with blankets purchased to protect their clothing. Rimes had heard that travel even as recently as thirty years ago hadn't been so bad. More people had flown, and private or shared vehicle ownership had been common.

But the city had been deep into its death throes, even in his earliest memories. Fires raged for days at a time with no one to fight them, roads cracked and buckled with no one to repair them, and gangs terrorized anyone foolish enough to enter their territories.

Rimes had seen it all—the crime, the violence, the utter despair born of economic hopelessness and helplessness—without even realizing what it was, riding on his father's lap in a battered HuCorp mini-sedan.

His father had been an American football star and had been relatively well-off—but that life had been fleeting. His political career, almost as short as his football career, had been built on the idea that the shattered American landscape and institutions could be restored. Two stints in Congress had helped recoup some of his squandered wealth, but corruption trials had siphoned even more off than had been regained, leaving them a very modest life and, eventually, leading to a broken home.

Another pothole, more swaying and cursing. The old man reached across his wife and pushed away a young man who'd lost his grip on the ceiling rails.

The young man was of southern Indian descent, dressed in tattered paper pants and a shirt haphazardly patched together from at least three others. An ugly scar angled across his forehead and nose. Something about the man troubled Rimes, and he kept "Scarface" in his peripheral vision the rest of the way to the bus station.

The bus came to a stop at the rear of the station, the autodriver shutting down with a staticky announcement of their arrival. Folks exited in a ragged, sluggish line, their pace set as much by malnutrition as stiffness and fatigue. Scarface disappeared in the bustle, but Rimes felt certain he'd gone into the terminal.

Rimes exited last. He gave a final scan around to be sure he wasn't being watched. After putting the bus between him and the other passengers, he set his earpiece into his ear.

"Molly Rimes," he muttered.

A moment later, Molly's voice came over the line. "Hello?"

"Molly, it's me. We just reached Oklahoma City."

Rimes looked across the street to an empty lot that had once held a row of houses. Children played football, shouting and running over the packed dirt. Rimes closed his eyes for a moment to remember his father's stories of American football, before it had collapsed in the same economic maelstrom that had obliterated so much else of the country.

Americans used to call the sport the kids were playing "soccer," not "football." Now, none of them knew any better. The US was just another poverty-stricken land that embraced the simpler and cheaper sport.

"I'll be about forty minutes," Molly said, excitement in her voice. "Oh, Jack ..."

Rimes smiled, imagining his son leaping and kicking amongst the grimy kids running through the packed-dirt lot. "I'll see you when you get here, Baby."

With one fluid motion, he signed off and put his earpiece away.

After another glance to ensure he wasn't being watched, he stepped from behind the bus, adjusting his travel pack on his shoulder. He walked casually toward the terminal, stepping through the entry and locating the bathroom.

The old man who'd sat beside Rimes on the bus bumped into him as he entered the bathroom. They exchanged a nod, and the old man walked to the women's bathroom entry, where he leaned against the wall.

Fumbling in one of the travel bag's pockets, Rimes entered the bathroom. He fished out his payment card, a new pair of shoes, and a change of clothes. He moved to the farthest sink and stripped, tossing his paper clothes and shoes into the corner recycler. He purchased a minute of cold running water and two shots of soap. He quickly washed himself, then purchased a half-minute under the dryer before dressing. Finally, he pulled a clean travel bag from the old, stained one and transferred his belongings to it.

Content that he no longer reeked of the road, he tossed the old bag into the recycler and left the bathroom to wait for Molly.

"Hey, Mister."

Rimes turned, saw Scarface, saw the knife. Scarface's stench hit even before he swung the knife.

Rimes stepped into the swing, intercepting Scarface's forearm with an elbow. Before Scarface could adjust, Rimes drove his fist into Scarface's throat, eliciting a wet, choking sound and a look of complete surprise. A woman's scream echoed through the terminal as Rimes instinctively locked Scarface's greasy forearm and upper arm, dislocating his elbow with a quick lock. The knife clattered to the ground as Scarface silently struggled for air and stared down at his ruined arm in horror.

People stepped away from the ticket booth to watch as Rimes kicked the knife away and patted Scarface. Rimes found a slim, filthy wallet with a payment card and a national ID identifying the man as Ram Gundtra. Rimes wiped the ID card clean on his pants leg and stuffed it into a pocket. He walked to the ticket booth. People parted as he approached, eventually revealing the station's sole human employee.

"Could you call Emergency Services?" Rimes asked as calmly as he could.

The bug-eyed attendant looked over at Gundtra's gasping form. "Is he … ?"

"He'll be fine if they can get here quick enough. He was trying to rob me."

The attendant activated his earpiece and nodded. "Emergency Services."

Rimes walked away while the attendant hashed out the details with the care center. He watched Gundtra's terrified face for a few seconds, then exited the terminal. The police would receive the surveillance video and assign it to some overworked detective to determine whether to contact Rimes for questioning. He doubted they'd deem it worthwhile; Gundtra would seem like a simple thief.

Rimes wouldn't do a thing to dissuade them of it, even though he suspected someone had hired Gundtra to kill him.

Several minutes passed before Molly pulled up in one of the apartment complex's cars, an ancient HuCorp two-seater.

She stepped out and hugged him.

They kissed. She smelled like she'd been working in the kitchen—onions, cumin, oregano, garlic, and chili powder.

Rimes slipped into the passenger seat and set his travel bag on the floor. Molly turned the car around, her face glowing. The car's automatic driver was broken, and she seemed to be having a hard time focusing on the road.

"I took a little something for the nausea," Molly said. "Dinner should be ready when we get back. I went ahead and splurged on a little chicken and a bottle of wine. I thought it would be okay?"

Rimes leaned back in the chair. It was stiff and meant for someone much smaller, but it was bliss compared to the bus. "It should be fine." He was annoyed about the wine, but he let it go. He wanted to talk to her about Gundtra, about the Sundarbans, about Singapore, but he couldn't. *Not yet.*

"Michael called last night," Molly said.

His younger brother only called when he needed money. His job at the penitentiary paid enough for their small family to survive on, but Michael's daughter had cri du chat syndrome and required therapy he had to cover out of pocket. Rimes did what he could. Sometimes, however, things went a little awry, and Michael needed to push for a little more.

Michael's drinking problems only complicated things.

Like father, like son.

"He said they can't afford the gene therapy, so she's going to need surgery," Molly continued.

After a moment, Rimes asked, "How much does he need?"

"Five thousand."

Rimes closed his eyes.

Five thousand would wipe them out. They'd been saving to pay for their graduate school and stay out of debt. It would push them back another year, easily.

"I guess I could volunteer for an early rotation." Rimes wasn't keen on being away from home, but combat pay made it easier to save.

Molly suddenly focused on the road. "There's part-time work at the Statton Mall."

Rimes chewed his cheek. The Statton Mall was a chain of retail outlets owned by ADMP, one of the more predatory metacorporations. Everything in retail was contract, and the pay was purely market-based. Molly would be bidding against people with no education or skills: people who could afford to drive the bids low.

"It would give me something, Jack."

"They'll release you the second you can't keep up."

Molly smiled weakly. "I know. But J.C. says she can get me on."

Rimes looked out the passenger window.

Martinez and his wife are always coming through for us. They've saved our marriage how many times? And what have we done to pay them back?

Outside the window, they passed collapsing husks of houses and apartments. There were no lights, no signs of electricity as the sun set. It would approach freezing in a few hours, and whole families would huddle in the dark structures beneath foul, tattered blankets to stay warm.

He thought of Michael's family shivering in the cold. "I guess we don't have much choice."

They were silent the rest of the trip. Molly pulled into the apartment complex and parked the car. They held each other's hands as they strolled back to their apartment. The temperature was already dropping from pleasantly cool to chilly.

At the base of the apartment stairs, Rimes pulled Molly close and gently patted her slender belly.

"Is it ... ?"

"What?" Molly asked, smiling mischievously. "Safe? Painful? A boy or girl?"

Rimes laughed. "All three, I guess."

"They'll run a test in a few weeks to predict the gender. Unless you want to pick? It's still early enough. We'd have to pay for it, but it's only a few hundred dollars."

Rimes shook his head. "I'm good with whatever happens."

Molly's smile spread. "Me too. Other than nausea, there's no real pain right now. From everything I've read and heard, there's going to be discomfort as it grows. It'll sit right on my bladder, so I'll have to pee a lot."

Rimes processed the idea for a few seconds. "Okay."

"And, yes, it's perfectly safe. I asked Dr. Sheehan first thing." Molly squeezed his hand and led him up the stairs and into the apartment.

Rimes stepped into the bathroom. He relieved himself and showered, washing away the last of the filth and despair, then headed for the bedroom to dress in clean clothes, pulling on a real cotton T-shirt and jeans, some of the only extravagances he allowed himself.

Molly was setting out their plates as he stepped into the kitchen. Rimes popped the cork off the wine bottle she'd left on the table and poured them each a glass. He tried not to think of the cost of the wine and the chicken or of the risk the wine posed.

We're past that now. She's got it under control.

Molly turned on the entertainment center display and purchased a news broadcast. They watched while they ate, struggling with the reader's French accent.

Rimes commented in general on the situations in Singapore and India without acknowledging his involvement in either. The news ended as they finished their meals. He cleaned the kitchen while she took her turn in the bathroom. A few minutes later, she poked her head into the kitchen and giggled nervously.

"You better hurry if you want to have some fun. I'll be fat before you know it."

He tossed the towel onto the kitchen table.

Molly stood in the hallway outside the kitchen.

He thought of Kleigshoen—a little weight would do Molly well. She took his hand and they retreated to their bedroom, past the tiny guest bedroom.

And he thought of the life that would soon call it home.

11

26 February 2164. Elgin, Oklahoma.

THE EARPIECE'S high-pitched squeal shattered Rimes's dream. He twisted in bed, spotted the earpiece on the nightstand, and snatched it up before the second ring completed. Molly rolled onto her side and wiped the sleep from her eyes. The display showed 0452.

His gut twisted. An early call on a Sunday morning was never a good thing.

"Sergeant Rimes?" The voice belonged to Colonel Weatherford.

Rimes's gut twisted more. He and Molly had made plans, and he'd hoped to at least visit his parents before he had to report back in.

"Yes, sir."

"I need you in the Seminole briefing room by 0600," Weatherford said.

Rimes covered his eyes with his right hand. "Understood, Colonel."

The channel closed, and Rimes massaged his face.

Molly rolled out of bed and hurried to the bathroom. He could hear the first of her quiet sobs.

He looked around the bedroom. Molly's little touches were everywhere

—his were absent. Aside from a few of his uniforms, their small closet held only her handful of dresses and outfits and a few blankets she'd inherited from her family. Her few pieces of jewelry were kept in a scuffed teakwood box on the dresser; a few tubes of lotion and a bottle of perfume gifted from a now-passed friend sat next to it.

The only things he kept there—that weren't disposable—were two worn pairs of jeans and a few simple pullover shirts. Everything else belonged to the military.

With a heavy sigh, he opened the dresser and pulled out underwear and shorts. He slipped them on and quietly padded to the kitchen. The entertainment display glowed dimly in the darkness. It quietly hummed to life with a gesture, and Rimes reserved one of the complex's vehicles under Molly's name for the morning.

He checked the refrigerator and was delighted to see Molly had also splurged on some eggs. He fished one out along with the soy milk carton, tofu, and a mealworm-vegetable paste. Within minutes, he had the paste and tofu slices sizzling in a shallow pool of oil next to a scrambled egg. The intoxicating aroma of coffee filled the kitchen.

Molly, wearing his T-shirt, settled at the table, her eyes puffy and red. She fidgeted with the towel he'd left on the table the night before, refusing to meet his eyes. He poured her a cup of coffee, distractedly comparing the simple, chipped cup to the intricate crystal and silver set aboard the *Okazaki*. He set the powdered sweetener and a spoon down in front of Molly, doing his best not to dwell on the second-hand container and spoon.

They ate in silence.

As Rimes finished off his coffee, Molly finally looked at him. Her face was drawn, tired.

If I have to go somewhere, she'll have to do all the preparation and planning alone. Like she's had to do so often before. She deserves better.

"Any idea how long? Where?"

Rimes cleared the table. "It may be nothing," he said, then almost laughed at himself. "I mean, it may be something short. Most of the team is still forward-deployed, so this must be ... different."

At least it will be a free flight home if they send me abroad.

Molly followed him to the bathroom where they quickly showered together, sharing coffee- and tear-flavored kisses. While Molly ran down to grab the car, Rimes shaved and brushed his teeth. He pulled a uniform out of the closet and quickly dressed before rushing down the stairs.

The entire drive, Molly fought to hold back her tears; Rimes tried not to dwell on the sheer ecstasy of holding her in his arms the night before—and the imminent ache of her absence.

THE SEMINOLE BRIEFING room was simply furnished: a long, old, oak table, several well-worn chairs, and a semi-static digital display on each wall. It was one of the smaller rooms in Fort Sill's Building 1215, but it was just down the hall from Weatherford's office.

Rimes was alone. The lights were on in Weatherford's office, but the building was otherwise empty and dark. Rimes took a seat to the left of the head of the table and waited.

Weatherford, shaved and in uniform, stepped through the doorway. He was tall and silver-haired, raspy-voiced. "Jack. Thanks for making it here so quick."

Rimes stood and accepted Weatherford's proffered hand. "No problem, sir."

"Of course it's a problem," Weatherford said. "I wouldn't drag your ass in at this hour if it wasn't." He motioned for Rimes to sit again. "We have a call in fifteen minutes. You were a by-name request."

"Special Security Council?"

"Intelligence Bureau," Weatherford said. "It's exceedingly rare. They have their own operators, a lot of them straight from us or Delta. You remember Fairchild? He went to IB just after you arrived here."

Rimes nodded. He thought back to the *Sutton*, the quarantine, and to Kleigshoen's offer.

She'd taken the next step without consulting him; he was surprised to feel not anger, but excitement.

"Tough thing, losing Kirk and his men." Weatherford shook his head. "I've watched the videos three times now, and I still don't get it. What happened? Did we step on an ant's nest? Genies attacking US military? It's unheard of."

"Yes, sir. The whole thing seemed ... off. They used X-17. That's pretty crazy right there, sir."

After a moment, Weatherford patted Rimes's shoulder. "We've put a lot of stress on you the last six months."

"It comes with the job, sir."

"Some folks handle it better than others. I think you're ready for the next step. Your request for OCS would fly through quick enough if you submitted it today. Something like this with the IB ... It's a feather in your cap. You've shown you can work with folks across the board. That's exactly what the officer corps wants."

Rimes felt as if he were floating in a dream. He always wanted to be an officer. He'd seen how Moltke and Weatherford lived. The difference in pay alone was staggering, but the doors opened by a commission meant a completely different life, both while he was on active duty and once he retired. "I would be honored to serve as an officer, Colonel."

"What do you have left to wrap up your graduate work?"

"Three classes, and I need to present my thesis." Rimes decided not to mention his financial situation.

Weatherford nodded. "You can wrap that up on your next rotation. What's your thesis?"

"'The Creation of the American Hemisphere Economic Zone Led to the Collapse of the Guatemalan Labor Party.' My mother's from Guatemala, and her mother's still there. She was active in the party until its collapse. They both provided a great deal of insight."

Weatherford glanced at the clock on the wall. As if by signal, the room's communication display notified them of an incoming call. They waited as a series of encryption handshakes squealed and chirped from the speakers.

Weatherford looked at Rimes—as if for approval—before speaking. "This is Colonel Tim Weatherford, Commander 6th SFG, Fort Sill. To whom am I speaking?"

An image hovered over the scarred briefing room table, a balding man in shirt and tie sitting at a desk. He sported a bulbous nose with a fine network of inflamed capillaries.

"Colonel Weatherford! My name's Jim Marshall, wonderful to speak to you again. We met at the Global Threat Assessment Conference in Dallas a few years back."

Weatherford squinted at the man. "How can I help you, Agent Marshall?"

Marshall smiled broadly. "Executive Assistant Director now, actually."

"Congratulations."

"I assume that's Sergeant Rimes with you, Colonel?"

"As requested," Weatherford responded coldly. "It's 0616, Executive Assistant Director Marshall. On a Sunday morning. That's not normally a time for IB to make personal calls."

Marshall's grin widened. "All right." He folded his hands together. "We have a minor situation that requires special experience and expertise. Based on his recent operations, and on the recommendation of Agent Dana Kleigshoen, we believe Sergeant Rimes matches our needs. We would like your approval for him to work with IB for a short period of time."

Weatherford's brow wrinkled. "How long is a 'short period of time'? Sergeant Rimes is currently on deployment."

"Not that it matters, but I thought he was on leave at the moment? He was recently assigned to the Special Security Council for more than a week. Wouldn't want to play favorites, would we?" Marshall smiled again. "Colonel."

"What special experience and expertise do you think Sergeant Rimes could bring to this situation?" Weatherford asked.

Marshall's grin disappeared. "Okay, Colonel, here's how it is. We know Sergeant Rimes was part of the team sent to Singapore to dispatch the four LoDu agents responsible for the assassination of Indonesian Finance Minister Sembiring. You can correct me if I'm wrong, of course."

"I was under the impression IB had their own assassins," Weatherford said.

Marshall's brow creased, and he suddenly leaned toward the camera, his smile stretched into a snarl. But, just as suddenly, he leaned back, adjusted his tie, and chuckled.

"You know how these things are, Colonel. Thanks to Sergeant Rimes's input, we've made a breakthrough. A few breakthroughs, actually. What I can confirm right now is that the genies killed at T-Corp 72 were also LoDu operatives ... using HuCorp gear."

Marshall tapped his forefingers together. "This points to a continued strengthening of relationship between the two metacorporations, matching what we've seen with ADMP and Cytek. We're very concerned about some of these metacorporate alliances. Sergeant Rimes was the only person on the ground involved in both the LoDu operations." Marshall clasped his hands and leaned forward. "It could be the difference between success and failure, Colonel."

Weatherford looked into the distance for a moment; he had once said that it was his way of stepping out of the present to see the big picture.

After a few seconds, Weatherford looked back. "I'll need to talk with Sergeant Rimes for a moment."

Marshall opened his hands. "Of course." He smiled and jabbed at something, and his image froze.

"The man who escaped in Singapore ..." Weatherford said.

"Kwon Myung-bak."

"Your report indicated he had a minimal file. You also said you were sure you'd been compromised, but apparently everyone in the world knew about this operation, so it's hard to know by whom. You think this Kwon Myung-bak was getting his feed from the Korean government? That maybe he's a Korean plant?"

It didn't sound likely. The Koreans weren't part of the Security Council or the even more selective Special Security Council—how would they have known? But Rimes hedged his bets, trying to see where Weatherford was leading.

"It's possible, sir. Security was clearly compromised. But there were several potential sources."

But Weatherford was looking away again. "Kleigshoen ... the name rings a bell. Where would I have heard of her before?"

"She was in the Commando qualification course when I went through, sir. Came in with a marksman badge, made it further than any woman before her. Her father was an ambassador in the Arturo administration."

Weatherford's eyes zeroed in on Rimes. "You know her."

"She was in my class, sir. She was in my Ranger unit before that."

"Is she trustworthy?"

"Well, she's a spook now, sir. I guess she's as trustworthy as any of them can be."

Weatherford looked away again. "Ambassador Kleigshoen. I remember him. She's from money."

Rimes nodded. "Her grandfather was sitting on a lot of the right stocks when the metacorporations formed. She's not about the money, sir; it's career for her."

Weatherford re-opened the communication channel. The frozen image faded; Marshall was looking off-camera, arguing with someone.

Weatherford cleared his throat. "When do you need Sergeant Rimes?"

Marshall looked back at Rimes and Weatherford, his smooth smile returning instantly. "Can you get him on a plane by noon?"

Rimes looked at Weatherford. "I can be ready by noon, sir."

Marshall clasped his hands together so quickly he clapped. "Then we'll see you tonight. Thank you, Colonel."

Marshall disappeared.

Weatherford stood, shaking his head, and Rimes immediately shot to attention.

Weatherford frowned. "I don't know what they're up to, but I don't trust them. I'd advise you do the same."

"Will do, sir," Rimes said.

"How's Molly?"

Rimes smiled. "She's a good woman, sir. She'll be okay."

"She's pregnant ..." Weatherford's voice was neutral, his gaze off in the distance again. It could have been a question or a statement.

"Yes, sir."

"You hurry, you can spend a little more time with her before you fly out." He extended a hand and Rimes shook it once more. "You explain to her how important this mission is, what it can mean for your career if it turns out right."

Rimes nodded. "Count on it, sir."

~

THIRTY MINUTES LATER, at the first, vague hints of approaching dawn, Rimes and Molly were *en route* to the apartment. Molly yawned. Her features were drawn, and he guessed the nausea had returned.

Rimes watched the fields full of struggling dogwood saplings. Red sunlight reflected off the ice-covered branches.

"It's a big opportunity," he said, finally. "The colonel thinks it's the last piece I need to build my OCS application."

Molly said nothing.

"It's inter-organization, exactly the sort of credentials you need for promotions. I'd be going into the officer corps with a leg up."

Molly kept her eyes on the road. "How long?"

Rimes blinked. He couldn't lie, although he sensed it was what she needed. "I don't know. It doesn't sound like it'll be too long."

"You're supposed to be on leave, Jack. Our anniversary is coming."

"If it's a short enough operation ..." He didn't sound convincing, even to himself.

"We've got a baby on the way." Molly shot a glance at him that contained a frightening mix of pain, love, and fury.

"I know," Rimes whispered.

12

———

27 February 2164. Washington, D.C.

FOG ROSE off the James River, cloaking the capital in a dreamy shroud. Looking to the north, where the river cut through a scrawny stretch of oak, he could make out a metal framework rising from the fog, a commercial development project to house metacorporate representatives as they dictated to the fragile remnants of government.

As promised, Marshall had been waiting, smelling of alcohol and cologne, when Rimes had arrived. Yet despite the fact that the combination spelled money and politics, Marshall still seemed likable. After a quick meeting and setting up Rimes's temporary IB account, Marshall sent Rimes to acquire—on IB's tab—"appropriate wear."

Rimes glanced down at his jacket, a charcoal-gray, pinstriped cotton-wool-paper blend. He smiled for a moment at the matching pants, crisp white cotton shirt, and poly-blend tie that rounded out his outfit. The office he'd been given was as big as his and Molly's bedroom.

But the suit felt unfamiliar, and the office lacked any hint that it was his, really.

"Jack?" Kleigshoen poked her head into the room. "May we come in?"

Rimes waved her in and stepped around the bare desk. Marshall was arranging for a terminal access point, but for the moment Rimes was using his earpiece to access IB databases—tracking Scarface's case both in order to learn the system's interface and out of curiosity about his assailant.

As Kleigshoen stepped in, Rimes caught his breath.

She wore a black jacket and skirt that accented her form rather than clumsily hiding it as the uniform had. Her hair, while still held up in a bun, seemed to glow in the soft light. Makeup brought perfection to an already remarkable face.

She looked nervously behind her, and a man followed her in.

"I probably should've warned you," she said with an awkward smile. "This is Brent Metcalfe. He'll be running this operation. He taught me everything there is to know about field work. I think you two are going to really get along."

Tall and thin, Metcalfe wore a charcoal-gray mohair suit. Rimes pegged him as having North African descent, probably a second- or third-generation citizen following the immigration waves caused by the Arabic Rebellions.

"Jack." Metcalfe extended a hand and nodded at the window. "Beautiful view, isn't it? When you work in the vault, you don't get to see much. Dana has told me quite a bit about you. It all sounds very impressive."

"I'll try not to disappoint, sir."

Metcalfe frowned. "*Sir*? What the hell does that mean? Are you trying to imply I'm old?"

Kleigshoen put a hand on his shoulder. "That's the way he's used to addressing superiors, Brent. It's just part of military life." She looked at Rimes for support. "You didn't mean anything by that, right, Jack?"

Rimes blinked, confused. "Of course not. I'm sorry. Did I say something wrong?"

Metcalfe glared at Rimes for a moment, then gently took Kleigshoen's hand from his shoulder. "Don't worry about it."

Rimes stepped backwards and waved at two chairs opposite his desk. They'd seen better days, but he'd already grown attached to them. Somehow, in his mind, they represented him in this new world of glittering skyscrapers and well-dressed civilians. "Please, make yourselves comfortable."

Metcalfe closed the door behind them as Kleigshoen settled into the more battered of the two seats. Rimes stepped back to his desk and sat on it, adjusting his pants self-consciously as he looked at the two of them. He felt cheap and out of place.

"I'm betting you're wondering what this is all about." Metcalfe looked at Kleigshoen with an inscrutable smile. "Does he have any idea?"

Kleigshoen shook her head. "Jim wouldn't have gone into detail about something like this."

Metcalfe's eyes lingered over Kleigshoen.

"All Director Marshall would disclose is that it's related to Sundarbans," Rimes finally said, watching the satisfaction spread across Metcalfe's face.

"Partly." Metcalfe stood, unbuttoned his jacket, and pulled it open so he could hook his thumbs on his hips as he paced. "We've got some real problems we need to iron out, Jack, some dots to connect. We've got holes in our data, and that's not a good thing. Follow?"

Rimes nodded.

"For instance, what was LoDu doing in that T-Corp facility? It was a genetics research lab that worked on alien DNA, building genies, right? Not just perfect humans, special ones. But LoDu had access to the same DNA. They got it from the same operation, because they worked together on it."

Rimes offered, "Maybe T-Corp made some advancements LoDu wanted access to."

Metcalfe waved the suggestion away, but Rimes kept going.

"It's been thirty-something years. Maybe T-Corp had something, and LoDu wanted a shortcut. Maybe the virus T-Corp developed for the DNA work was more effective."

Metcalfe was already shaking his head before Rimes finished. "LoDu would have used the same virus. Hell, it became public domain after the outbreak. That facility was only cooking up genie stew, drugs, gene therapies—stuff LoDu could easily reverse engineer. Why take that kind of risk for decades-old materials? And why would T-Corp re-enter a closed facility, at the same exact time LoDu did? Can't be coincidence."

Rimes could see Kleigshoen clearly respected Metcalfe, just seeing the way she watched him pace the room's limited space.

"I'm sorry." Rimes felt uncomfortable challenging Metcalfe, especially given Kleigshoen's obvious infatuation.

"Yes?"

"That doesn't address the basic problem."

Metcalfe smirked. "The basic problem. Maybe you could elucidate for us, what with us only being intelligence analysts?"

Rimes fought back the urge to sigh. "Doesn't this all assume T-Corp has something LoDu would want to steal? When was the last time T-Corp was an innovator? All of their corporations copy and refine and squeeze costs down like no one else can. They're a conservative organization; they don't lead the charge."

Metcalfe looked at Kleigshoen. "Dana?"

She smiled up at him, but it wasn't the same kind of look he'd given her earlier. She crossed her legs and centered herself; she'd obviously rehearsed what she was about to say.

"The LoDu hit team you targeted in Singapore may hold the key; however, we believe your connection with Ritesh Tendulkar will be of more help. His uncle is a T-Corp senior director for colonial exploitation, and his cousin is a senior bio-engineering scientist at their Mumbai facility."

Rimes looked from Kleigshoen to Metcalfe, surprised. "That's it? That's what you need me for? You want me to contact Tendulkar out of the blue and ask him to get his relatives to roll over on their employer? Maybe we can toss back a beer and talk about overthrowing their government? I hardly even know the guy. We carried out one op together."

Metcalfe smirked. "We're not idiots, Jack."

"As I said, the team you hit in Singapore is key," Kleigshoen said. "Kwon Myung-bak survived the attack. We have every reason to believe he's a genie. We also believe he's connected to one of the genies you killed at T-Corp 72."

"Connected?"

"Same batch," Metcalfe said. "Same genetic build. Brothers, in a sense."

Kleigshoen transferred an image to Rimes's earpiece. He examined it. It was two faces side by side—the last genie killed in the Sundarbans, bruised and misshapen from the fight, and Kwon's. Rimes blinked, shocked.

That's not Kwon. That's the genie, some sort of file photo. They could almost be twins.

Rimes considered the implications. "So what's the angle? How do we pitch this to Tendulkar? Kwon has a grudge and he's going to come after the team that tried to kill him?"

"In a nutshell," Kleigshoen said. "You felt the mission was compromised. You knew the German and the Japanese soldiers, you didn't know the Indian or the Russian. The Russian is dead. Who does that leave as your prime suspect?"

They've seen my report to Bhatia.

Rimes wasn't surprised. Representative Bhatia made no secret of the relationship between the Special Security Council and IB. But he was surprised that Kleigshoen and Metcalfe had inferred so much from what he'd put in the report. He hadn't included even the subtlest of accusations of compromised security; the Special Security Council wouldn't have accepted it.

"You contact Tendulkar with an innocent offer," Kleigshoen said. She looked at Metcalfe. "Friends of yours in the intelligence world—that would be us—have contacted you to solicit your assistance with Kwon. This is the easy part, it being true. We believe Kwon is involved in a broader effort by LoDu to acquire T-Corp technology. Also true. You believe LoDu had an inside man that nearly got you all killed. This is the tricky part. You'll say you believe the traitor was Nakata."

Rimes raised his eyebrows. "Nakata?"

"He has some ... questionable friends at LoDu," Kleigshoen said. "It's actually entirely possible that Nakata *is* your man."

"For now," Metcalfe said, "we're only concerned about the perception. You believe Nakata was the weak link. He bungled things in Tunis. He has a gambling problem. You need Tendulkar to ask a favor. We've given you the information about Tendulkar's cousin, and you just need any hint of what LoDu could be after. And Kwon has killed Uber, so you think he's coming after the rest of the team."

Rimes blinked, stunned. "Uber's dead?"

"No," Kleigshoen said. She had a disturbing gleam in her eye that hinted at how much she enjoyed deception. "But he's off the Grid. We're working with the Germans and Aussies. They've got him stashed away in Darwin."

It was a stretch. On the one hand, the lie was simple and at least influenced by fact. On the other, he would be asking Tendulkar to get his cousin to compromise his position at T-Corp.

"Well?" Metcalfe stopped pacing in front of Rimes's desk and smiled down at him. "It's not airtight, but nothing ever is in this business."

Rimes shook his head, stopping himself from saying what he really wanted to say. "I don't think he's going to fall for it."

"You might be surprised," Metcalfe said. "We've convinced the military about a lot more outrageous things, right, Dana?" He winked at her.

Kleigshoen's face flushed slightly. "It could work, Jack. But even if it doesn't, it may give us some insight into T-Corp. They're a tough nut to crack."

Rimes thought about it for several seconds. He couldn't help but feel there was more to it than he was being told, something that was the foundation for Metcalfe and Kleigshoen's confidence.

"What's it going to be, Jack?" Metcalfe tapped the fingers of one hand on the desk.

The IB had already flown him out and put him up in a hotel; they weren't likely to take no for an answer.

"I'm in."

Metcalfe smiled broadly, then started pacing again, emphasizing his words with gestures. "Excellent! We leave tomorrow. You'll need some travel clothes, so we'll leave you to that; we've got some meetings and preparations and such. Why don't we get together for dinner later on? Six okay?"

Metcalfe strode out the door with barely a look back at Kleigshoen, who jumped out of her chair to follow him.

Numbness slowly crept through Rimes's gut as the door swung closed, leaving him alone in the office. The sense of things moving invisibly all around him left him feeling anxious and edgy.

He closed his eyes and thought of holding Molly the night before, but the memories were quickly stolen, Kleigshoen usurping Molly's place.

13

———

29 February 2164. Mumbai, India.

RIMES JOGGED in place for a moment to check his heart rate. His earpiece showed it well within optimal range. A motorized bike passed. Its engine sputtered and its headlamp blinked intermittently.

Rimes blinked, and it was gone in the clinging, acrid smog.

Mirage?

It was 5:06 A.M., but the city was already waking from its slumber. He'd been jogging north in the shadow of the JJ Flyover, sticking close to building fronts to try to avoid the city's chaotic traffic system.

He was past Nesbit Road now, approaching the fringe of the slums. Hotel security warned him to avoid them, but it wasn't the citizenry that concerned Rimes, and he needed another five minutes out before heading back.

He coughed to clear his lungs, but the smog refused to release its grip. His throat burned; the stench had become a stinging, metallic taste. Then the wind shifted, and the reek of the slums hit him.

Rimes pushed on; his earpiece laid down a route through the maze of slick, muddy paths. Morning sounds echoed in the tight space—babies crying, dry coughs, water splashing. People appeared momentarily, then disappeared again in the mist.

Five minutes later, Rimes circled a hut and retraced his route. A skinny, filthy boy staggered beneath the weight of a sloshing water pail. The water was the same dirty brown as the smog.

He waved at the boy and kept running, but his heart was heavy. Security had said the slums worsened the farther in you went. The outer area was depressing enough.

Somewhere to the west, the city's well-to-do slept in comfortable, expansive homes.

Once back in his room, a coughing fit hit. Rimes doubled over and finally spat up a muddy clump of phlegm. His stomach rolled at the sight of it.

No more jogging outside.

He dressed quickly: underwear, pants, shirt, and tie. Everything about the suit was alien—the texture, the cut, the look. It left him doubting the man looking back from the mirror.

Even on the thirty-third floor of the Golden Brahmin Hotel, Rimes could hear the cacophony of motorized bikes, taxis, and buses, but he couldn't see them. Mumbai was invisible below the brown smog carpet. All he could make out was T-Corp Primary Research Facility's glowing copper towers.

His earpiece chimed. It was nearly six. He had two minutes to meet Kleigshoen and Metcalfe in the lobby.

Rimes gathered his coat, checked his tie—deep burgundy with gold diagonal stripes—in the mirror, and exited his room. He was still adjusting to the Muxlan shoes. Stylish or not, they were uncomfortable.

A young woman waited down the hall for the elevator. She glanced at him casually as he approached. At the elevator's chime, she turned away.

Rimes hustled to catch the elevator rather than testing whether she would hold it for him. They exchanged awkward smiles and rode to the twentieth floor. Three more passengers joined them without exchanging a word. Two more stops, two more passengers, and not a word was spoken before the elevator opened onto the lobby.

Rimes watched the others exit the car. None of them seemed threatening. Still, the attack at the bus station was fresh in Rimes's mind.

As he entered the lobby, he saw Metcalfe feigning interest in a newscast on the main display. Rimes noted it was the same French newsreader he and Molly took a liking to some months back. However, there was only a Hindi voiceover to listen to—leaving Rimes to wonder if Metcalfe was bluffing about being able to understand the language.

"Morning, Jack," Metcalfe said. "More trouble in Jakarta. Looks like Minister Sembiring's family isn't happy with the names being floated to replace him. They've got the minority party riled up. At least twenty killed in riots an hour ago."

Rimes watched the video of crowds on a dawn march. The march transitioned into people burning vehicles and hurling rocks. Security forces turned them back with sonic crowd control weaponry, tear gas, and gunfire.

"Looks messy."

"You never see that sort of thing here," Metcalfe said, half-smiling. "Trained their citizens properly from the start, wouldn't you say? Dharma. Can't really go wrong building your society around a religious chassis that preaches acceptance of fate, can you? No better way to control the masses."

"We all have our filters and controls." Rimes frowned, but did his best to fight it. He watched the news reader, imagining her soothing French accent instead of Metcalfe's voice.

Metcalfe turned around, took in the rest of the lobby with a quick glance, then leaned in. "You know, Jack, I'm not blind. I know what's going on. You want to show you're the big dog, you might want to think about where you're at and what's at stake."

Rimes's brow wrinkled. Metcalfe's breath washed over him. Any hint of alcohol or other drugs was smothered by toothpaste and mouthwash. Rimes momentarily debated how to respond. "I have no idea what you're talking about, Brent."

Metcalfe glanced past Rimes and smiled, suddenly warm. "Well, there she is. Punctual as ever. You've gone with the lemon ensemble. Safe."

Rimes turned.

Kleigshoen wore a yellow pant suit with a modest neckline and a loose, modest fit that at least tried to hide her figure. It was the sort of outfit only she could pull off. She'd also gone light on makeup. "It's not my favorite outfit, but it's going to have to do." She looked at Rimes and raised her eyebrows. "What's the word?"

Before Rimes could answer, Metcalfe said, "Jack here arranged a meeting with Tendulkar at Café Noorani at eight this morning. That leaves us enough time to swing by T-Corp's administrative office north of the docks."

"What do we want with the T-Corp office?" Rimes asked, his eyes slowly drifting away from more images of violence in Jakarta to look at Metcalfe.

"Background investigation," Metcalfe said with a patronizing smile. "You think it's all running around shooting people, Jack? Nothing comes easy, and it's not like in the vids."

"I didn't mean that," Rimes said coolly.

"Of course you didn't." Metcalfe stood, straightening out the creases of his tailored pants. "I have a few questions and a contact who might be able to help. We'll need to get moving. Fifteen kilometers can take forever here."

14

———————

29 February 2164. Mumbai, India.

RIMES RODE in the front seat, his eyes scanning the streets: pedestrians, huddled beggars, the staggering array of patched and makeshift vehicles. The hotel SUV's driver banged into more than a few bumpers, coming away with crumpled scraps of fiberglass or rusted metal for his trouble, but deposited them on the steps of their building after only twenty minutes.

The T-Corp Administrative Facility Southwest Region Two building was a four-story affair with stone walls and thin strips of copper-tinted glass that gave the impression that the building was a miniature T-Corp Primary Research Facility tower.

Rimes shook his head, perplexed that a simple administrative building could so significantly outshine the austere structures of Fort Sill.

As he climbed out of the SUV, he inadvertently took a deep breath. The air left a foul, gritty feel in his mouth. He coughed as he climbed the stained steps to the entry. "How do they breathe this?"

"They don't have a choice, really." Kleigshoen shielded her eyes with a cupped hand. "You could wear a mask, but that would probably offend people."

"Great."

Metcalfe approached the front desk receptionist, a young woman with an oversized head and a left shoulder that appeared warped, even through her sari's layers. The desk was isolated, apart, something co-workers could avoid completely. Her deformities marked her as one of the millions damaged by T-Corp chemical spills, a national embarrassment.

Rimes watched Metcalfe talk with the young woman; never once did he appear distracted by her appearance. Rimes couldn't help but admire the man's ability to deal with people. *Other people.*

"What were you two talking about in the lobby?" Kleigshoen asked.

"Honestly, I'm not really sure," Rimes admitted. "He seems to be concerned about the Indonesia situation, but I'm not getting the connection."

"That's nothing to worry about. ADMP will step in and settle things down; they have billions invested in sweatshops there and in Malaysia. Your Muxlans were probably bathed in Indonesian sweat and blood before they ever saw America." Kleigshoen said. "I lived there for a year, you know. It's a terrible place."

"The world's full of terrible places," Rimes said.

Kleigshoen's eyes hadn't left Metcalfe for a second. "Why don't you like him?"

"Metcalfe?"

"My father likes him. He says Brent has the makings of a diplomat. I think he ought to consider it. He's a good judge of character, and he knows how to work well with people." Kleigshoen waved at Metcalfe as he followed the receptionist out of the lobby. "He's also very, very good at this job. He could get you on with IB."

She turned to look Rimes right in the eye. "He likes you."

Rimes blinked. "What makes you say that?"

Kleigshoen wrinkled her nose. "We talk a lot; he makes a point of teaching me every nuance of the job. Like how to assess people. Including you. He's a great mentor. I mean, spectacular, really. Did you know I'll be up for promotion in six months?"

Rimes tried to hide his confusion, but he could feel his brow wrinkle. "I'm not really sure how IB promotions or ranks work. Is that a good pace?"

Kleigshoen put her hand on his chest. "It's quick all right, my second promotion since I joined. I get all the usual resentment and whispers—I'm sleeping with Marshall, I'm sleeping with Brent, my father's calling in favors. No one can just accept I'm damned good at my job. I'm doing the sort of work I've dreamed of since I was young. You know what I mean?" She pulled her hand back awkwardly, realizing the intimacy of it.

Rimes blushed from her touch. "You were a good Ranger. You'd have made a good Commando. I believe you've earned it."

"With Brent showing you the ropes, you could move up the ranks in no time. He'll take Marshall's place in a few years. Everyone knows it. You really need to get past whatever it is that's messing things up between you two."

"I ..." Rimes sighed quietly. "Sure. I'll work on it."

Several minutes later, Metcalfe reappeared in the lobby, all smiles. He stopped by the receptionist's desk and spoke with her again for a few moments. Rimes thought he saw Metcalfe push something into the woman's hands, but it was so quick that he couldn't be sure. The woman's eyes trailed Metcalfe until he joined them at the doorway.

"We can just make Café Noorani if we hurry," Metcalfe said as he hurried them out the door.

For Rimes, the drive to the café was even more nerve-wracking than the one to the administration building had been. Even the driver seemed stressed. Twice Rimes heard the driver muttering what was almost certainly a curse.

Most Commando operations happened in the pre-dawn hours, when even the busiest streets tended to be relatively empty. But now the traffic was near-impenetrable. A quick escape would be problematic.

They arrived at the café with a few minutes to spare. Metcalfe lingered a moment at the driver's door and gave him a hefty bundle of bills, producing a smile and several appreciative nods.

Rimes shook his head at the exchange. No one used cash anymore except for illicit transactions.

Like most buildings in Mumbai, Café Noorani had seen better days. Cracks and divots were all that held the baked clay façade together. What little remained of the paint hinted at an original cream and mustard color scheme.

The three of them headed inside.

Heat washed over them, and spices, herbs, hot grease, coffee, and other scents battled the staggering reek of body odor. The place was filled to capacity. Toothless old men in traditional *dhotis* and *sherwanis* were crammed next to younger men in casual Western attire.

"Well, isn't that something?" Metcalfe muttered through the quiet roar around them. Like Kleigshoen and Rimes, he was craning his neck to spot Tendulkar.

Kleigshoen pointed toward a booth near the back. "There."

Tendulkar sat in the booth with three uniformed men—Marines—each nursing a steaming cup. One of the men nodded at the Americans. The other Marines took a final, rushed sip and exited the booth, pulling berets from their belts.

Rimes led the others to the rear, nodding to the Marines as they passed. Tendulkar waved one of the staff over, and the man gathered the cups quickly onto a tray. Rimes and Kleigshoen squeezed into the booth opposite Tendulkar, and Metcalfe sat beside him, trapping him in.

Rimes nodded at Tendulkar. "Were they from your unit?"

Tendulkar nodded slowly. He blinked. "Good friends, yes. You should order breakfast."

Metcalfe smiled. "How is their *puttu* here?"

"Good, good" Tendulkar said, head bobbing happily. He looked at Kleigshoen and Rimes patiently.

"Something light for me," Kleigshoen said.

"Honestly, I'm starving," Rimes said. "What would you recommend?"

"You like rice? You could get *idli*, a steamed ... um, rice cake with fermented lentils. A *vada*, like a spicy donut. Or you could get a vegetable stew with rice—a *sambar*. It is filling."

"*Sambar* sounds interesting," Rimes said.

"I'll try the *vada*," Kleigshoen said. "And did I smell Turkish coffee when I came in?"

"Yes, yes," Tendulkar said. "They have all kinds of coffees and teas."

Rimes glanced around again at the locals crammed into every seat. The three of them seemed to be the only foreigners. Tendulkar ordered their meal in Hindi, assisted by Metcalfe, who engaged the waiter for a moment on some small detail.

So he is fluent.

Rimes thought back to Tendulkar's behavior during the Singapore mission. Tendulkar's tendencies when stressed had included rapid blinking and puckering his lips. He'd also pulled his knife in preparation for an imaginary lunge—something he couldn't do in the café.

As Tendulkar looked at them, in particular at Metcalfe, the blinking and puckering set in.

At first, Rimes attributed Tendulkar's behavior to discomfort with people he hadn't met, but as they made their well-rehearsed pitch, Tendulkar's behavior intensified. And when their food arrived, Tendulkar ate very little.

Metcalfe finished describing the details of Uber's death between sips of coffee. "So, Ritesh, what do you think? Is Nakata our man?"

For a moment, the blinking and puckering stopped. Tendulkar looked at Rimes as if he wanted to say something, then thought better of it.

He blinked several times. "It sounds like he is."

Rimes wondered what Tendulkar had seen on his face. He knew his own stress tendencies—chewing his lip, going silent. *Can you see through the lie?*

"Jack really nailed it earlier," Kleigshoen kept the coffee cup close to her face so she could breathe in the aroma. She was perfectly at ease with the deception. "The mystery here is what LoDu could want with the facility."

Tendulkar winced almost imperceptibly at the mention of the facility. Rimes imagined the assault must have felt like a slap to Tendulkar's national pride. The T-Corp agents killed by the LoDu team might just as easily have been Tendulkar's team instead. Tendulkar's nervousness made sense, but Rimes wasn't convinced of the real reason for it.

Rimes cleared his throat. "Nakata leaked information to LoDu. They knew we were coming. That got Pachnine killed and damned near got Uber killed, too. Then Kwon tracked Uber to Australia to finish the job. Why? LoDu agents attacking US military is unprecedented."

"Maybe they thought you were T-Corp," Tendulkar offered.

"It's possible," Rimes said. "But I doubt it."

Tendulkar nodded weakly. "I'll visit my cousin. He will know what was in 72. He will understand. It's very unfortunate. I'd hoped to go to work for T-Corp soon. The pay ..."

"No reason they can't hire you on." Metcalfe patted Tendulkar's shoulder. "Jack here is considering a career change for the very same reason, aren't you, Jack?"

Rimes winced. "Sure. Having a baby changes everything. You can't close doors."

Tendulkar picked at his *sambar*, leaving Rimes with the distinct impression doors were already closing. Tendulkar set his spoon down and sighed, as if that might grant him strength. "I will call you tomorrow, arrange a meeting. Someplace remote—quieter, safer."

Rimes tried to conceive of a place in Mumbai that could be considered quiet or remote. He couldn't. The city was thick with people.

Over Tendulkar's polite protestations, Metcalfe paid for the breakfast. As they left, Tendulkar lingered in front of the café, waving and smiling for a moment as the hotel SUV pulled away.

Then, frowning, he disappeared into the crowd.

15

---

1 March 2164. Mumbai, India.

RIMES FUMBLED IN THE DARK, struggling to wrap his hand around the soothing cerulean flash of his earpiece. It was an important call. He had the earpiece in place by the third ring.

"Jack?"

"Ritesh, what's up?" Rimes blinked and rubbed his eyes. He willed himself awake and looked around the room.

The earpiece display showed 0400.

"Can you meet me in an hour?" Tendulkar whispered.

Rimes activated the earpiece's recorder. "Sure. Where at?"

"Where are you staying?"

Rimes suddenly longed for Molly. He missed her smile, her touch, her taste and smell. He hated this job and what it demanded of him.

Rimes hesitated a moment, embarrassed at staying at such a swanky hotel instead of barracks. "The Golden Brahmin."

"I know it. It is very nice. Maybe I can take my fiancée there once we marry and I take a job with T-Corp."

"She'd like it," Rimes said. "My wife would love it, but we couldn't afford it."

They laughed awkwardly.

"There is an old place north of there," Tendulkar said. "Sewri Mudflats. Take the P D'Mello Road. You can beat the traffic if you hurry. It is quiet, like I promised. We can talk."

"All right. 0500. We'll be there." Rimes looked around at the mess he'd made of the bed. The blankets and pillows were everywhere. He stood and began straightening everything up.

"Good, good. Thank you."

"Ritesh, I want to tell you how much I appreciate this. I know you're taking a risk, but Kwon is a very dangerous problem."

Tendulkar paused for a moment. "Sure, sure. He is a very dangerous man. Genies are bad trouble. No problem."

Rimes set the last pillow back on the bed. "Okay. See you in a bit."

Rimes killed the connection and dropped back onto the bed, favoring his left shoulder. It felt tender and weak, and his head ached too much from staying out late with Kleigshoen and Metcalfe to remember why.

Rimes played back the recorded message and had the earpiece search for directions; then he called Metcalfe.

"What is it, Jack?" Metcalfe's voice was heavy with sleep.

"Tendulkar called," Rimes said as he stumbled to the room's modest desk and turned on the lamp. "He wants us to meet him in an hour."

"Where?"

"Sewri Mudflats." He suddenly realized how unpleasant the name sounded. "It's about a half-hour drive."

Metcalfe noisily fiddled with his earpiece. "That's certainly remote enough. Okay. I'll arrange for a vehicle. You call Dana yet?"

"I just got off the call with Tendulkar. I'll call her now."

Metcalfe dropped the call without another word. Rimes called Kleigshoen. It took a few rings before she answered.

"Jack? It's not ..." Kleigshoen's voice drifted off into slow, seductive breathing.

"Dana, we have to leave in about thirty minutes." The connection stayed silent for several seconds. "Dana? Ritesh called. He wants to meet us. We need to—"

"We should've thought of this before last night, Jack." Kleigshoen sighed heavily. "You two let me drink way too much. I'm a disaster. I can't believe you're any better."

"Thirty minutes in the lobby," Rimes said, working his stiff shoulder.

He disconnected and tossed his old underwear into the bathroom recycler. Yawning, he ran through a series of stretches, trying to work the kinks out of his back.

Razor in hand, he started the shower. Suddenly, he didn't care about running up the Bureau's bill and cranked the shower to full heat. A minute later, he was gasping beneath the steaming spray, shaving as quickly as he could.

He toweled off, applied his antiperspirant, and pulled on his underwear. Bloodshot eyes stared back at him as he brushed his teeth. Cursing himself for indulging in one drink too many the night before, he gargled with the courtesy mouthwash. He eschewed his suit for a black T-shirt, dark slacks, and navy windbreaker. Ten minutes later, he was in the elevator, headed for the lobby.

METCALFE PROVED to be a competent but impatient driver. The hotel had loaned them a small T-Corp three-seater with an anemic engine that supposedly boosted its electric motor. There was barely enough room in the back for Rimes and Kleigshoen to squeeze in. They were pressed tight against each other, their bodies warm in the cool air.

The back of the front seat dug into Rimes's knees. Ten minutes into the drive, they ached as if they'd been worked over with a lead pipe. With each pothole strike, the car sputtered and gasped and threatened to die, drawing another string of curses from Metcalfe.

"He's got some sense of timing," Metcalfe muttered over the clattering and squeaking. "We're not going to get there in time to do any sort of recon."

"I'm having a hard time getting a connection to the Imagery system."

Kleigshoen massaged her temples. With each jolt, she looked ready to vomit. "The latest image I have is from three hours ago."

"Send me a copy," Metcalfe said as he glared at Rimes in the rear-view mirror. "Did he give any reason for having to meet so soon?"

"No," Rimes said. "We didn't really talk much."

Rimes looked out the half-window to his right. What leaked through the grime was a sleeping city: the occasional bus and more infrequent scooter or small car. There were no pedestrians in sight. The car's engine gasped; Rimes worried about their chances, should things unravel.

A thunderous crack sounded, and the car suddenly went airborne. Metcalfe screamed furiously as he fought to regain control. They landed hard, and Metcalfe fought to get the petulant little beast moving in a straight line again.

"I simply cannot believe people live in these conditions," Metcalfe shouted. "There's more hole than road—oh, hell."

Rimes saw the lights before he heard the brief siren wail. The police mini-SUV approaching them in the oncoming lane pulled a U-turn as it passed, then accelerated to catch up to them.

Rimes and Kleigshoen twisted in the seat to watch through the rear window as the police vehicle closed on them. In the confined space, Kleigshoen was pressed against him, filling his awareness with her scent, her heat and touch. He looked down at her for just a moment, long enough to catch her turning to look up at him. She pushed tighter against him.

Without moving his head, Rimes said. "I see two in uniform. They're definitely following us."

Metcalfe mumbled and pulled over to the left. He rolled the window down and twisted in his seat to watch the police. "We've got five minutes to get there, so this is going to be tight. Let me deal with them."

Rimes saw Metcalfe slip something out of his pocket: cash. Then the police vehicle's floodlight kicked on, nearly blinding them. Rimes blocked the light with his hand and watched the policemen exit their vehicle. Both had unsnapped their holsters; the second officer's right hand hovered over the weapon's grip.

"Something's not right," Rimes said. "They're ready to draw."

Metcalfe watched the driver in the side-view mirror. "Dana, what's our little friend doing back there?"

Kleigshoen strained a little to get a better view of the passenger. "Jack's right. He's got his hand on his gun."

"Okay then." Metcalfe slid the cash back into his jacket pocket. "Stay sharp, right?"

The driver, a small, pudgy man, finally arrived at the open window. His hand now rested directly on his pistol butt. He made a face, as though detecting alcohol in the air. He stared at Metcalfe.

"You been drinking?"

"Last night, officer," Metcalfe said with a smile. "We're well over it, I assure you."

Metcalfe switched to Hindi and said something that seemed to set the officer at ease. They spoke for a few moments, Metcalfe pointing back in the direction of the hotel. The officer nodded and headed back to his vehicle.

With practiced ease, Metcalfe popped open the glove compartment and pulled out a small booklet. "I want you ready to act," he said, never losing his smile. "Understand?"

Kleigshoen nodded.

Metcalfe popped open the door, waving the booklet and calling to the driver in Hindi. Rimes watched as the policemen focused on Metcalfe. The second officer seemed worried, looking back down the road. Rimes followed his head and saw an approaching black SUV.

It was accelerating.

"Get down," Rimes shouted. He shoved the driver's seat forward and hooked his arm around Kleigshoen's chest, pulling her down as automatic gunfire roared. Glass shattered and bullets tore through the car. The firing stopped as suddenly as it had started, replaced by an accelerating engine's whine.

Kleigshoen gasped. She pulled away from Rimes and put a hand to her back. Twisting, she looked through the shattered windows.

"They're down!" She scrambled to get out of the car and made her way to the battered police vehicle.

Rimes grimaced in sudden pain as he carefully navigated through the glass-covered door. Outside, he braced his butt against the ruined car—the vehicle wasn't going anywhere. A quick inspection revealed a dozen cuts across his hands, but it was his left leg that troubled him: he'd been hit in the thigh.

Kleigshoen squatted over Metcalfe, then helped him up. Metcalfe was covered in blood, but he seemed alert and functional, which was more than could be said for the policemen.

"You all right?" Metcalfe called to Rimes. He brushed Kleigshoen's hands away, then took her shoulders, turned her around, and looked at her back.

"Caught one in the thigh." Rimes put weight on the leg. It was numb but seemed functional. "Just cut up other than that. You?"

Metcalfe said, "I used our friend here for cover when I noticed his passenger watching the road. Get the passenger's gun. We need to be ready if they come back."

Rimes took a tentative step, then another. "Is she okay?"

"She was grazed along the back," Metcalfe said after a moment. "I'll get you two to someone we can trust."

Metcalfe hooked his wrists under the driver's arms and pulled him onto the side of the road. Metcalfe grunted as he lowered the policeman to the ground. "We'll take their vehicle."

As he approached the passenger-side door, Rimes saw the other policeman. He was still alive but slipping into shock. Rimes took the policeman's gun and searched him for extra magazines or loose bullets, gently swatting away the policeman's bloody hands when he resisted. When he was done, he pulled the policeman to the side of the road.

Wincing at the stiffness in his shoulder, Rimes pulled off his windbreaker and wrapped it around his hand to sweep the glass from the back seat, then let Kleigshoen in. Once he was sure she was in safely, he swept off the passenger seat, climbed in, and closed the door.

Metcalfe pulled his jacket off and swept the driver's seat clear. After checking the gun he'd taken from the dead policeman, he pulled onto the road, already chatting in Hindi with someone over his earpiece.

A minute later, they were off the main road, heading toward the slums.

"I guess we have our answer about Petty Officer Tendulkar," Metcalfe finally said. He gave Rimes a rueful smile.

"Or about T-Corp," Rimes replied. "Or both."

Metcalfe nodded. "I don't think Tendulkar would do something like this on his own. We'll find out soon enough. For now, though, we stay off the Grid. There's no reason to take any risks."

The SUV bumped and rattled as they approached the slum's outskirts and the road turned into little more than packed dirt. Metcalfe drove for several minutes, searching down the maze of winding paths before pulling into one. He stopped the SUV beneath a tattered overhang and killed the engine.

Jacket draped over his gun, Metcalfe exited the vehicle. He looked around quickly, then entered the maze. Kleigshoen and Rimes followed.

"We've got a few minutes to kill before our Good Samaritan will be ready for us," Metcalfe said. "She runs a tight schedule."

They wandered through the tightly packed slums for several minutes, Metcalfe frequently checking the map overlay on his earpiece.

Finally, they reached what constituted a nice house, for the slums. Light leaked from beneath the heavy drapes covering the door, revealing a scooter chained against the outer wall.

The drapes lifted as they approached, and an elderly man wearing a crisp shirt and baggy, tattered pants gave a quick glance around, then waved them in.

Metcalfe and the older man spoke quietly just inside the entry as a young woman in a nurse's uniform stepped from behind a curtain to the left of the entry. The place reeked of curry, onions past their prime, and unwashed bodies. The young woman whispered quickly to the old man, then pointed Kleigshoen and Rimes toward the hut's central room.

The place was half the size of his apartment and served as dining room and kitchen. The floor was hard-packed dirt.

The young woman set out a bowl of water and her medical kit while Metcalfe slipped the old man a wad of cash, silencing his protestations.

The nurse quickly examined Kleigshoen and Rimes, carefully cutting away as little clothing as she could in order to get to their wounds. Kleigshoen's shoulder and back had a long gash where a round had grazed her. It was shallow, but it was bleeding and would be vulnerable to infection without treatment.

The nurse washed the wound clean before swabbing it with alcohol and applying an ointment. She taped a gauze strip over it, then turned to the superficial hand wounds they'd received from the broken glass. The crude medicine and equipment she worked with was a painful reminder to Rimes of how fortunate he was.

After washing away the blood and applying antiseptic, she turned her attention to Rimes's leg wound. She carefully examined the wound, then explained to him in English that the bullet had passed through without doing serious damage. Rimes grimaced as she cleaned and sewed shut both ends of the wound while warning him that he risked infection if he didn't get a more thorough cleaning at a hospital.

It was growing light out by the time the nurse closed her kit and emptied the bloody water outside the house. She spoke with Metcalfe for a few moments, then pulled two cellophane-wrapped hospital shirts from beneath a stack of blankets. She handed the shirts to Metcalfe and stepped through the front entry.

Rimes looked the shirts over. They were distinctive in their plainness. Stolen clothing might catch someone's attention.

We wouldn't stand out any more than we already do, and it's not like we'd be the first to steal clothing. Anyway, who's to say we aren't recent patients?

A moment later, he heard someone unchain the scooter. The motor came to life, and Metcalfe entered the house alone.

Metcalfe looked the two of them over. "Are you waiting for something nicer?"

Rimes smiled. He helped Kleigshoen into her shirt, then pulled his own on. The shirts were stiff and smelled stale, but they were clean.

Metcalfe watched the entry for a moment, finally turning to look at Kleigshoen and Rimes. "We're staying here for now. If they're looking for us, they won't find us. I'd suggest you get some sleep. We'll go looking for our friend Tendulkar tonight, so we'll need to be sharp. He's almost certain to be on his guard. Everyone's going to be on their guard."

16

2 March 2164. Mumbai, India.

THEY WERE PARKED off a secondary road leading into an upscale housing area. A towering privacy wall blocked out the street lights, cloaking them in shadow. Metcalfe sat in the vehicle's front seat, eyes focused on the Grid security video. Rimes watched the feed over his earpiece.

"Think he has any idea?" Kleigshoen asked.

Rimes defocused from the video feed to watch Metcalfe's face in the weak glow of hacked-together surveillance equipment.

IB's apparently unlimited funding amazed Rimes. Metcalfe had purchased a stolen SUV, equipment, guns, and a change of clothes without batting an eye. Objectively, it was the same operational concept—"Get it done"—that the Commandos lived by, but on a completely different scale. It *felt* different.

Metcalfe stared into space for a moment. "No." He lowered his head and returned to the security video.

The police killings had stirred up surprisingly little activity. According to a newscast Rimes had heard earlier in the day, the official line was that radical dissidents had targeted the policemen. By all indications, the three of them weren't even fugitives from the law—at least officially. It had even been frighteningly easy to locate and close in on Tendulkar: he had no police protection, no extra security.

Rimes closed his eyes and relaxed, enjoying the dreamlike quality of the moment: a moment of calm in a turbulent mission that had sapped his energy and resolve.

Tendulkar's voice suddenly came over the communication channel. Tendulkar was speaking with his cousin, the senior T-Corp scientist. The two talked about trivial matters for a few moments before the cousin asked Tendulkar if he'd heard from his friends. Tendulkar quickly said he had not. They both sounded nervous. The cousin assured Tendulkar he'd done the right thing and disconnected.

"Okay," Metcalfe said, replaying a security video that showed the front of an impressive two-story, gated house. "This is where Tendulkar is hiding, his brother's place. His brother's a senior government engineer, and Poppa Tendulkar was a T-Corp administrator until last year, so they're not hurting for money.

"Tendulkar's brother shares this place with their parents, his own family, a cousin, and his cousin's wife. I make eight inside right now, plus Tendulkar, so nine.

"Right now you can see the woman I believe is Tendulkar's fiancée, who arrived ten minutes ago.

"I haven't had any luck getting a floor plan. Best I can determine, it's fairly similar to the floor plan I'm laying over the image now."

A pale-blue wireframe settled over the house to match the security camera's perspective. Metcalfe adjusted the obvious problem areas, aligning the door and windows and knocking off a small side patio.

A glowing finger appeared over the image on Rimes's display. "Dining room, living room, bedrooms. According to energy use patterns, they'll fire up their entertainment console and run it until about ten. That should put Ritesh and his sweetie out the door a few minutes later. Factor in a goodbye peck, and Ritesh is headed this way on his scooter by a quarter past."

They'd wrapped a cable around a nearby pole. When the time came, Rimes would run across the street and wrap the cable around a signpost on the opposite side. In the dark, Tendulkar wouldn't see it. It would knock him off scooter, and Rimes would be on him before he could get off the ground.

It would then be up to the IB's interrogation techniques to pry out the desired data.

"What's our extraction plan?" Kleigshoen asked.

"There's a private airstrip sixty kilometers north," Metcalfe said. "A pilot will be waiting for us. Then we get to Pune and hire a shuttle to wherever the heck we need to go next."

"Simple enough," Rimes said. "What are our possible destinations?"

Metcalfe thought for a moment. "Seoul. Darwin. Tokyo. Who knows at this point?"

Rimes shook his head.

"What?" Kleigshoen leaned forward, crossing her arms on top of the seat and resting her chin on her hands. "Too much travel?"

Rimes chuckled quietly. "Too much uncertainty. I'm used to knowing where to go, what to do, and what I have to do it with."

Metcalfe glared back at him. "Who do you think makes that possible? We have people all around the globe pulling down data, listening in on countless conversations, buying information, analyzing targets, and more, all so you can have the sort of certainty you're used to. People risk their lives every day on some of the most mundane and innocuous things, all in the name of intelligence gathering."

Rimes nodded. "I get that. It doesn't make the transition from operator to collector any less jarring, though."

Kleigshoen punched him gently on the shoulder. "What we're doing here is critical. Of course we're uncertain. For all we know, the bad guy could be one of us."

Metcalfe cleared his throat. "What Dana's trying to say is that we can't even identify what's at stake between these two metacorporations. There's simply no way for us to say we have actionable material to work with just based off what we've dug up to date—"

Rimes held up a hand. "Wait. Play back the audio for the call that just went out."

Metcalfe waved his fingers around his console. The audio played back.

It was Tendulkar's cousin from T-Corp and his brother, exchanging pleasantries. The cousin promised to see his brother at their father's house that weekend.

"No, before that. Just before that."

Metcalfe waved a finger through the air. The conversation reversed itself at high speed.

"Stop," Rimes said.

A few seconds of garbled audio played.

"There," Rimes said. "Can you decrypt that?"

Kleigshoen leaned back in the rear seat and piggybacked off Metcalfe's session. Rimes watched them at work, running through cracking modules, analyzing the packet with interpolators and assessors.

After several tense seconds, Metcalfe grunted. The audio piece played again, this time unencrypted.

"In position."

It was a voice Rimes hadn't heard before.

"What's that mean?" Rimes looked from Kleigshoen to Metcalfe. "And where did that come from? The local Grid?"

"I don't know yet." Metcalfe scanned through the video feeds.

Kleigshoen began tracing the source and destination. Precious seconds slipped by. Rimes lowered his window and craned his head out, trying to see around the wall.

"There," Metcalfe said.

A large, black SUV appeared on their screens. Metcalfe pulled the view back until they could see the SUV in relation to the Tendulkar house.

The SUV was one house over.

Metcalfe enhanced the image, highlighting two men in the front seat and what looked like a possible third man in the rear. The two in front wore dark jackets and held submachine guns.

"That message's destination was T-Corp Administrative Facility Southwest Region Two," Kleigshoen said.

"A T-Corp hit team," Rimes said.

Metcalfe started the engine and popped the SUV into gear as another garbled message flew across the network. "I see the vehicle; it's closing on the house." Metcalfe turned onto the secondary street and accelerated toward Tendulkar's house.

"They don't want any loose ends," Rimes said as he checked his weapon.

Kleigshoen readied her weapon as the decryption module cracked the message. "They've given them the go."

Rimes felt powerless as he watched the SUV stop outside the Tendulkar house. Four men exited the vehicle; two ran around the side of the house while the third shoved another man toward the front door. The fourth scanned the street, then walked to the house.

Gunfire and screams shattered the night.

Metcalfe braked quickly in order to turn down a side street and come up behind the Tendulkar house. He parked the SUV.

"Okay, no heroics, Jack. Grab Ritesh if he's alive and get the hell out."

Rimes nodded.

They all jumped out of the vehicle.

Rimes's leg was a mess, but it supported his weight enough that he could manage a jump-hop motion that got him to the back gate as Metcalfe opened it. The three of them advanced on the house quickly, guns down, watching. They dropped as they heard the SUV at the front of the house pulling away, then quickly closed the final stretch to the back door.

The back door opened onto the kitchen, where two young women lay in a pool of blood. An older woman was slumped against a blood-spattered wall nearby, her dead eyes still open. Beyond the kitchen, they found the others, some in the dining area, some in the living room. The walls and furniture were riddled with bullet holes. Tendulkar and his cousin had each taken a bullet to the head, erasing any potential for extraction—or interrogation.

Rimes stared at Tendulkar's dead eyes. "We got him killed. This deception ... he was in over his head."

Metcalfe patted down the bodies. "He got himself killed, Jack. Snap out of it. You can't feel guilt about something like this."

Rimes looked at Kleigshoen, saw the shock in her eyes. "He was a good soldier, Dana. He was just doing his job. What the hell did we drag him into? Why would T-Corp need to kill all of them?"

Kleigshoen looked away.

"It's done," Metcalfe said. He stood, inspecting the haul—earpieces and slim wallets. He stuffed them in his pants pockets with shaking hands. "He turned us in to T-Corp and they killed him. That's all that matters, isn't it?"

They retraced their path through the kitchen and out the back door. Rimes stole another glance at the women: innocent victims. A quick dash across the back yard, and they were in their vehicle, speeding away.

Six hours later, they were bound for Seoul.

17

3 March 2164. Seoul, Korea.

SEOUL WAS A GARISH, neon mess, a glowing scab over an unhealed wound buried beneath tons of cement and steel. Reunification had come for Korea, but only after weeks of war, the result of one psychotic act too many. The scars were generations old and would last generations more.

You wish to know more about Kwon. We all wish many things.

Rimes replayed the call that had brought him out from the hotel and listened to the directions to the unnamed café again; for a moment, he thought he'd lost his way, but then he spotted one of the landmarks. He was close, and he still had a minute.

Rimes felt as if he'd stepped into an alien, nightmarish parody of Earth.

How many had been buried alive? How many had been abandoned, screaming for help?

Rimes moved through the crowds, struggling not to react to people brushing into him. He was on a deadline. He began to emulate the thugs around him, pulling his gray jacket's hood over his head, shoving his hands into the pockets, then leaning into his walk. The cold was biting, numbing.

The hood couldn't protect his face, either from the cold or the suspicious glares. His height marked him as a foreigner—an enemy all Koreans could come together to despise.

Rimes tried not to get angry with the people. The reunified Koreans were the offspring of two inbred, antagonistic cousins. The new nation, still eaten by internal strife, had become little more than a shadow of either of its former halves.

Rimes stopped beneath a glowing sign—a bottle, a cup, and an infantile creature, all dancing. *This is it.*

Unfortunately, the cartoonish art was ubiquitous, and it hadn't been easy to find the right sign. He glanced through the window, saw a sign in English ("Coffee!"), then stepped inside. It was small and cramped, with several tables and chairs, and a counter. The customers were almost exclusively Korean, two of them hunched over, trying to hide deformities—one with a sheet of flesh where there should have been an eye, the other a shabbily constructed nose.

Rimes moved to a two-seat table at the back and settled into a chair opposite a similarly dressed man with Slavic features: his contact. The man smiled as though he were simply a foreigner finding comfort in the company of a fellow outsider. His teeth were surprisingly bright, his face cleanly shaved. Rimes made him for a corporate man.

"We buy from the same tailor," the man said with a slight Russian accent, pointing to his gray jacket.

"I recommend him to all my friends," Rimes said. "You picked this out?"

"Yes. It suits you well," the Russian said, extending his right hand. "Anton Tymoshenko. And you are Jackson Rimes. It's good to finally meet you in person. I've heard quite a bit about you."

Rimes shook with him. "Jack, if you don't mind."

"Of course." Tymoshenko chuckled. It was a pleasant sound after the discordant roar outside. "No offense intended."

"I can't take offense to being called by my name, Mr. Tymoshenko," Rimes said.

"Anton, please." He nodded at the counter. A dainty, young Korean woman stood behind it. She was staring off into the distance, smiling. "You should try some of their coffee."

"I will, thanks." Rimes stood. "What's good?"

"Nothing I've tried yet," Tymoshenko said with a wink. "Truly, life is full of adventure."

Rimes stepped to the counter and waited for the young woman to acknowledge him. She finally closed her eyes and sighed heavily. For a moment, Rimes thought she might have forgotten him; then her eyes opened again. She gave a slight eye roll, then looked at him with a completely blank stare.

Rimes spent several minutes trying to order a small coffee, struggling with the young woman's weak grasp of English and his even weaker grasp of Korean. Eventually he returned to the table with a paper cup that smelled like one of the open sewer ditches running through the city.

After further investigation, he discovered it smelled better than it tasted. He cringed and pushed the cup aside. "Eight dollars for that. Brutal."

"There are few places that could manage something so bad," Tymoshenko said. "They probably take pride in it. How many other places are so proud about their inability to speak English?"

Rimes bit his bottom lip to keep from laughing. A standing law prohibited the teaching of English, although many Koreans sought private tutoring anyway. "It's an odd choice."

"Koreans imagine humanity spawned here, but only the best stayed behind," Tymoshenko laughed. "But it makes it easy for us to discuss things out in the open, yes?"

Rimes looked around to see if anyone was listening. Aside from the occasional inquisitive glance, they had been deemed unworthy of attention. "I'm not so sure the best would stay behind. Not … here."

Tymoshenko winked. "Not everyone wants to leave home, you know?"

Rimes said, "I'm curious why you contacted me … and how you knew to reach me here."

Tymoshenko leaned forward, his elbows resting on the table. "You are a smart man. Why don't you tell me what you think."

"Well, I'd start by assuming you're a company man, metacorporate, probably EEC. And you want to know what I'm doing in Seoul after visiting Mumbai."

Tymoshenko laughed. "You like to dance around what you mean, yes? However, I like to get to the point," Tymoshenko said. "I am a businessman, an ambitious one with a bright future. I must seize it, take risks, take charge."

Rimes nodded.

"I've been following you for a little while now. That shouldn't be a surprise. What you do, it's not so secret as you think. You have your intelligence gatherers, like your Bureau friends, and we have ours. Sometimes, we're all closer than we realize. We have mutual friends. And enemies."

Rimes shifted in his seat.

Had Pachnine been an EEC spy? Did the Special Security Council know, and still assign him to the team? Tendulkar, Pachnine, Nakata ... who can I trust?

Tymoshenko sipped his coffee, grimacing. "It is no secret we are in an extremely competitive situation. Biotech is key. Two tables away, you see potential customers for gene therapy. We can create cures no one would have dreamed possible twenty years ago."

"I understand the potential," Rimes said.

"New worlds out there wait for exploitation, for humans who are stronger or who can breathe ammonia or who can withstand one-hundred-degree temperatures without protective gear. We can get part of the way there looking at Earth species, maybe. We do a great deal with that already. But what exists out there—" Tymoshenko indicated the heavens with a wave of his coffee cup. "That is what will crack open the gateway to the stars."

"What about remotes?"

Tymoshenko smiled. "Proxies? Maybe an answer. But they are not *our* answer. People spend tens of thousands of dollars to have tiger fur. Imagine what they will pay for the ability to fly ... or to swim through an alien ocean. To live out there. To have adventures of their own."

Rimes tried the coffee again; it was still undrinkable. "All right. There will always be a fringe that sort of thing appeals to, but most folks aren't going to give up their humanity permanently for a few thrills."

Tymoshenko winked again. "You are right, of course. Certain assumptions must be made, certain paths must be taken. We must be adaptable in this regard, or we cannot compete. Which gets me to my point. Your friends are playing a dangerous game with you. I would like to help you, but, as you know, I am a businessman."

Rimes leaned in closer. "What are you offering?"

"You should ask what I want," Tymoshenko said. "But of course you already know."

Rimes gritted his teeth. "If I knew, I wouldn't be in this little slice of heaven."

"Maybe. Maybe not." Tymoshenko finished his coffee and set the cup down. "I think I am going to be sick after drinking that. There's simply nothing we can do to inoculate humanity against such a thing." He stood, made a face and placed a hand on his gut. "You'll excuse me, I hope? I'm not so strong as I'd imagined."

Rimes stood, concerned. "Are you—"

Tymoshenko patted him on the shoulder. "I will be fine." He pressed his empty paper cup into Rimes's hand. "Here, take my cup. A smart man learns from little things, yes?"

Rimes watched Tymoshenko head out into the cold. It was starting to rain. Tymoshenko pulled his hood up and pushed his way into the crowd, a giant among the stunted masses.

Rimes studied the cup, then stuffed it into his pocket and exited the shop, pulling his hood up and walking in the opposite direction.

A sliver of data film was curled around the cup bottom.

EXCEPTING A FEW SUBTLE DIFFERENCES, the Emperor's Palace could have been the Golden Brahmin. Even the smog was the same.

Rimes set aside his earpiece and closed his eyes while his stomach lurched. He'd already destroyed the data film, but there was no way to destroy what he'd seen. He couldn't conceive of some of the numbers, couldn't imagine living with himself to attain those numbers.

Why am I making such a big deal about this? The genie's already out of the bottle, literally. Why pretend otherwise? It's not really breaking the law. EEC needs data on the genetic materials behind these genies, Anton wants to be the one to acquire it. Anton wins, EEC wins, I win.

But that's not me. No matter how Anton likes to play it, I'm not a mercenary. He's got such good access, he can get the blood samples we took from the Sundarbans and reverse engineer them himself.

But that won't do for Anton. The offer makes that clear. They want a pure sample to start from. There's no love lost between these metacorporations. Nearly thirty-thousand registered genies, probably twice as many hidden away in labs or off-world, and EEC's responsible for fewer than five thousand, none with this alien DNA. It irks them. And it limits their revenue stream.

"We make your tomorrow today." Doesn't that say it all?

A gentle knock broke through the stormy clouds of his thoughts. He glanced out the peephole; Kleigshoen and Metcalfe stood in the hallway, dressed in casual attire. Rimes opened the door, then sat on his bed.

"Feeling any better?" Kleigshoen settled into the room's entertainment console chair as Metcalfe turned the desk chair around and seated himself.

"Not really." Rimes rubbed his eyes. "They can't make coffee here to save their lives, apparently."

Metcalfe laughed. "I have a friend who swears by all things Korean. He's of Korean descent, though."

Rimes let the comment go. "Any luck?"

"Yes," Metcalfe said. "You might even call it the jackpot."

"We've got Kwon," Kleigshoen said.

Rimes stood. "What? Where?"

Metcalfe chuckled. "Whoa, slow down. We don't *have* Kwon, we have a solid lead on Kwon. A very solid lead. We also have confirmation on the identities of the team you took down in Sundarbans. They weren't LoDu."

Rimes gaped. "What? How do you know that?"

Metcalfe assumed an official air. "We are investigating the attack by LoDu operatives on an international military unit enforcing Special Security Council orders—"

"You lied?"

"Embellished," Metcalfe said. "We were dealing with LoDu, so we had to stay close to the truth. They ran it up the chain, used their contacts in the Chinese diplomatic corps. The Chinese have too much at stake to be lackeys this time around, and the Council knew full well what was going on, sanctioned or not."

"No." Rimes paced the room for a moment, shaking his head. "LoDu gave up the team. They're dead, they were compromised. There's nothing to be gained saying they were operating on LoDu's behalf."

Kleigshoen looked at Metcalfe. "Actually, we think they're telling the truth."

"To an extent," Metcalfe said. "It certainly looks like a rogue operation, and it wouldn't be the first. LoDu has had a handful of genies go their own way the last few years. It's nothing on the scale of ADMP or EEC, but they've had several incidents. Even T-Corp has had problems, and they engineered theirs to be more compliant."

Rogue genies?

Rimes settled back on the bed, tired again. "What about Kwon?"

"Another problem child, apparently," Kleigshoen said. "With a criminal history. Even the Korean police consider him problematic. They've assigned us an officer—Inspector Chae Kang-joh—to help move this along."

"I'm almost disappointed LoDu didn't send a security team to kill us," Rimes said.

"They'll still have plenty of opportunities," Metcalfe said. "Don't be so sure they won't."

18

4 March 2164. Seoul, Korea.

Seoul Metropolitan Police Bureau 102 was a narrow, ten-story building with a stained, yellow brick facade, built upon the blasted ruins of its predecessor. It was early, but lights were already glowing from several windows.

The interior was plain, with faux stone paneling, cracked pink-gray floor tiles that echoed even the quietest footfall, and a noisy, lurching elevator.

At the fifth floor, Rimes held the elevator door open for Kleigshoen and Metcalfe, and they made their way to where they had been told they would find Inspector Chae Kang-joh's cubicle.

The meticulously clean, organized cubicle was filled with digital frames that looped through pictures of what were probably Chae's wife and two daughters. Kleigshoen smiled wistfully as a photo of Chae and his daughters flashed for several seconds. Chae was nowhere to be seen.

Were we dumped off on some useless obsessive-compulsive?

Minutes dragged as they waited. At 7:50 sharp, the stairwell door opened, revealing a man who walked with a brisk, purposeful stride, adjusting his cuffs and brushing imaginary dust from his jacket.

Chae.

He stopped abruptly, and his nostrils flared when he saw Rimes, but his eyes ultimately settled on Metcalfe. "How may I help you?"

Metcalfe extended a hand. "Brent Metcalfe." His deep voice echoed in the empty office. "These are my partners, Dana Kleigshoen and Jack Rimes. We're from the Intelligence Bureau."

"Inspector Chae Kang-joh." Chae stared at Metcalfe's hand and adjusted his tie.

Metcalfe gave his most charming smile through clenched teeth. "We were told to seek you out, Inspector."

Chae shook his head. The man's lack of even the flimsiest of social subterfuges was shocking. "It would be easier if you spoke Korean."

"I'm afraid I don't," Metcalfe said.

Chae didn't answer, offering only a sour, disapproving look. He glanced at Kleigshoen and Rimes without making eye contact.

Metcalfe sighed. "I apologize for the trouble. I understand you're in charge of the Kwon Myung-bak case?"

Chae adjusted his tie and checked his cuffs again. "The Kwon Myung-bak case is mine. It has been classified as a cold case."

Metcalfe said, "The Bureau wants to speak to Mr. Kwon on a very sensitive matter. We would greatly appreciate your cooperation."

Chae's jaw muscles worked as he ground his teeth.

"I understand it can be frustrating, Inspector." Metcalfe winked and nodded at Kleigshoen. "We've been through some fairly frustrating challenges ourselves. In India. We received excellent cooperation there."

Rimes caught the hint of a smile touching Kleigshoen's lips.

Chae sighed loudly, then pushed past Metcalfe. Another sigh and Chae dropped into his chair, synchronizing his earpiece with the desktop console.

After several seconds of ignoring them, his face flushed. "It would appear I have been assigned to help you until you have been satisfied."

"I'm very sorry for the trouble, Inspector. We'll do our best to make this as quick and painless as possible." Metcalfe looked at Kleigshoen and smiled. "We just need some help locating Mr. Kwon, and we'll be on our way."

Chae nodded once and submitted a series of requests. After several seconds, he detached from his console and stood. "If you will follow, please."

Kleigshoen looked at Metcalfe curiously.

Metcalfe waved her back. "Inspector, where are we going?"

Chae looked at Metcalfe impatiently. "I would like to end my involvement in this quickly. Please?"

He led them to the first floor, where he stopped at the car pool, then brusquely directed Metcalfe to wait at the front of the building before disappearing into a stairwell.

Metcalfe led them outside. He looked at Kleigshoen and Rimes with a pained expression. "You two have been remarkable," Metcalfe said. "The rudeness ... If it's any consolation, I think we could have done worse."

Rimes shrugged. "They still haven't gotten used to foreigners. We see it all the time, in the Commandos."

The three of them walked to the corner. It was chilly out, and pedestrians were beginning to crowd the sidewalks. The stench of garlic hung heavy in the air; food carts were setting up all along the street.

Rimes, used to covert missions in the dead of night, hated it. "So much activity, so many people packed into such a small area. What do they do? How do they avoid going insane?"

"Who said they haven't?" Metcalfe asked, half-joking. "They spend more time connected to the Grid than any other culture in the world."

Rimes watched in disbelief as a man looking at something on his earpiece casually bumped into him, then did the same to Kleigshoen, acting as if neither were present. The man pushed his way into a group waiting at a crosswalk and started into the busy street just as the light changed.

Rimes shook his head at the disturbing sight. The man was in another world, oblivious to reality. "Any idea what the police want Kwon for?"

Metcalfe turned as Chae pulled up in a small HuCorp electric SUV and stopped in front of them. "Homicide, I guess."

They climbed into the SUV without a word. Chae drove south for several minutes, meticulously working his way through foot traffic and reckless drivers until finally turning west onto quieter streets.

Metcalfe twisted in his seat slightly. He caught Kleigshoen and Rimes's eyes, then looked at Chae. "So, Inspector, maybe you could share some details of the Kwon case you were working on?"

Chae stiffened and looked straight ahead.

Metcalfe's eyebrows shot up in surprise. He put on another winning smile. "To help the Intelligence Bureau?"

Chae said nothing, instead sighing quietly.

The buildings turned from crude, brutish skyscrapers and glass-fronted shops to darker, more menacing stone and steel towers. With their asymmetrical lines and crude materials, they looked both new and ruined. As the SUV stopped in front of one of the buildings, Rimes realized that most of the materials must have been salvaged from the ruins after the war.

Chae switched the motor off and watched the traffic for a moment, his thoughts far away.

"Last year, Kwon Myung-bak killed three ... young women. That's what we could prove. They were prostitutes and performers, of no special value. I worked the case and arrested him. He confessed to the killings; he was unconcerned about breaking the law. I do not believe he felt the law applied to him at all."

Chae closed his eyes. "An hour after I logged the case, I received a call from Senior Superintendent Cho informing me the evidence and confession were inadmissible. He had the case immediately classified as cold.

"I released Kwon Myung-bak."

Chae sighed quietly. He straightened in the seat and opened his eyes. He looked at the building, adjusting his tie and smoothing the front of his jacket distractedly. The SUV remained quiet for several seconds.

Metcalfe pointed to the building. "Is this where he killed them?"

Chae looked at his hands, now resting on his lap. "Kwon Myung-bak had an apartment to the northwest. I worked out of the headquarters building then, before I was transferred. His building was twelve-and-a-quarter kilometers from my office, far enough away to not hear the screams, but close enough to feel the ... horror."

"The girls lived here?" Metcalfe asked, his voice quiet.

Chae nodded. "One did. Park Hyun-ok. Sixteenth floor."

"Why are we here? Is this where he killed her?" Metcalfe asked.

Chae took a cleansing breath. "No. The killings were performed at Kwon's apartment. He had a ... private room there. Padded to contain the screams. A drain for the blood. Wall hooks for the tools he used." He shook his head. "Based on what I saw at the rest of his apartment, he is a very successful man, very valuable."

"Wealthy enough to buy his own freedom?"

"No," Chae said with a quiet, vicious chuckle. Then he brushed the front of his jacket again. "Apparently, LoDu intervened on his behalf. He said they would. He also said I would pay for my mistake. I have always hoped my transfer was the whole of the price.

"Two of the victims were thirteen." Chae pulled a slender wallet from his jacket, swiping a finger across the surface of a display panel within. An image of a smiling young girl materialized. "My older daughter turns thirteen in six months, you see."

Despite the poor treatment Chae had given them, Kleigshoen patted him on the shoulder.

Chae put his wallet away.

Metcalfe asked, "What's the significance of this building? Are we going to see Miss Park's apartment?"

"Lee Sang-woo lives here," Chae replied. He glanced at the side-view mirror, then opened his door. "You want Kwon Myung-bak, you need to speak to Lee Sang-woo."

The apartment building interior made the damaged exterior look cheerful by comparison. The halls were dark, with light fixtures nothing more than murky shadows. Paint chips and trash littered the floor. Rimes picked his steps carefully and tried to block out the stench—urine, feces, decomposition. It saturated everything around them.

Chae led them up six flights of stairs, then down two corridors. He stopped at an unmarked metallic door and knocked. The echoes banged back up the empty hallway.

In the darkness, time seemed to come to a stop. Finally, Rimes spotted a thin, black strip sliding out from beneath the door. A micro-camera curled upward.

Chae squatted in front of it. "Inspector Chae and three others. These people wish to speak with you about Kwon."

Why not tell him we're IB?

The camera retreated beneath the door. A few seconds later, they heard a heavy, metallic scrape and several locks rattling.

The door opened into absolute blackness.

Chae whispered something, and another voice replied. Chae swept a hand forward for Metcalfe to enter. Metcalfe led, and Chae entered last.

The door closed behind them, and an iron bar slammed home.

Bright lights hit them in the face, blinding them. Rimes closed his eyes and instinctively raised his hand to block out the light.

"We need to speak to you about Kwon Myung-bak," Metcalfe said.

The lights went out again.

The same voice spoke, and Chae answered. Rimes caught Kwon Myung-bak's name, but nothing else.

Rimes stood still, waiting.

The lights returned, this time more dimly.

Rimes closed his eyes again and controlled his breathing in an effort to fight the dilation. He opened his eyes and scanned the entryway for something to focus on, finally settling on a sickly young man at the far end of the room.

Unkempt dark hair, acne-racked face, a pair of goggles on his forehead, sunken cheeks, yellow teeth, and a raised HuCorp 8xH pistol eventually resolved themselves from the blur.

Even as sickly as the man looked, Rimes couldn't help recognizing Kwon Myung-bak from the file images.

19

———————

4 March 2164. Seoul, Korea.

"WHAT DO YOU WANT WITH 731?" the sickly figure demanded.

The pistol he held moved slowly between the three Americans. He stood in a hallway, his back to a corner, his right side to a wall, his left to a black plastic table that held a bright white backpack and several photo frames. Images of a young woman scrolled across each of the frames.

"Kwon Myung-bak?" Rimes gauged the likelihood he could close on the man without being shot. The odds weren't favorable. The man's face glistened with perspiration, and his breathing was rapid and shallow. He seemed strung out on something, yet still uncomfortably in control of his faculties.

Chae turned his back to Rimes and looked at Metcalfe. "This is Lee Sang-woo. He is sometimes referred to as 729."

"They're brothers," Metcalfe whispered.

Lee sneered. "Even my people can't choose their family."

729? 731? Genies have families?

Rimes struggled to control his surprise. "How many of you are there?"

"Two, now." Lee exposed his yellow teeth in a wicked grin. "730 is dead. Mourn the good son."

Chae twisted to look at Rimes momentarily, then turned toward Metcalfe again. "Dr. Hwang Sung-il, their 'father,' liked to work in threes."

Lee tilted his head sideways. "You shouldn't be so rude, Chae. You're so blind that you'll talk to a motherless Korean but refuse to acknowledge a black man."

Chae barked something in Korean that made Lee smile again, baring his yellow teeth.

"Anything Korean is acceptable, even a monstrosity like me? What about 731?" Lee looked at Rimes. "You still haven't told me what you want with 731."

"We believe he can answer some very important questions about a sensitive operation," Rimes answered.

"So Chae says," Lee replied. "But I want to know the truth. You. Your friends may be Bureau, but you don't have the look."

"Mr. Rimes," Metcalfe said, looking at Chae, "is attached to my mission from the military. We're not at liberty to discuss the particulars of our investigation."

Lee casually dropped his pistol on the table and stepped away from the corner. He ruffled Chae's hair as he went past. "Chae will say nothing if it would hurt the great and powerful nation of Korea. Isn't that right, Chae?"

Chae fixed his hair and brushed his jacket but didn't reply.

"Wake up, Little One," Lee said.

A console that consumed an entire wall lit up. Lee settled into a chair facing the screens. He swiveled around to face them.

"So, Mr. Metcalfe, let's start with you. You're the one running this mission, not Mr. Rimes. Why don't we give it a look?"

Behind him, the console helpfully lit up with several projected images.

One showed Metcalfe in Chae's SUV. Another showed Metcalfe standing next to Kleigshoen at the airport. A third showed Metcalfe and Rimes at the Pune airport, waiting outside the women's bathroom for Kleigshoen. A fourth showed all three of them standing at the private Mumbai airport, talking to the pilot. A fifth showed the three of them walking through the capital airport in Virginia. Travel itineraries filled the final display.

"D.C. to Mumbai, right when the dissident activity experienced a sudden, inexplicable spike. Mumbai to Pune via private jet and then Pune to Seoul." Lee pointed to a display showing the dead policemen. "Have you come here to stir up dissidents too? If so, you'll find Koreans are much less likely to accept your rabble-rousing."

Is he making fun of us? Rimes looked at Metcalfe, who was frowning. *Not making friends, that's for sure.*

"Dream worlds are so much more appealing than riots." Lee waved his hand to indicate the screens. "The Grid … an inexpensive means of controlling the populace, isn't it?"

Metcalfe's face darkened as he looked at the displays. Rimes waited for the storm to come, but Metcalfe kept it under control.

"That's not important. We're here to understand why LoDu would send a team of genies into India, why that team would consider it acceptable to attack a military operation inside a closed compound, and why they would use illegal weaponry to do so."

Lee looked at Rimes. "That was *your* operation in India."

"I was part of it, yes," Rimes acknowledged, ignoring Metcalfe's glare.

"Give me the names of the operatives." Lee spun his chair from side to side.

Metcalfe pulled his wallet from his suit pocket and carefully flipped open a hidden flap within. He patiently worked out a strip of data film, then handed it to Lee. Lee swiveled to his console and fed the film into a reader, extracted the data, and tossed the film on the floor. He looked the names over for a moment, his fingers steepled beneath his chin.

He swiveled around in his chair. "My services aren't cheap. I can get you more details on these operatives, but it will take some time. LoDu doesn't give me access. They do, however, frequently hire my services, which gives me a way in. One hundred thousand."

"Too much," Metcalfe said.

"One hundred thousand, or a better explanation and fifty thousand. You've given me no reason to believe 731 is in any way associated with this operation."

Rimes looked to Metcalfe for approval. Metcalfe nodded, and Rimes cleared his throat.

"I was involved in an operation against Kwon and some other operatives in Singapore."

"The Sembiring assassins," Lee said with a casual nod. "The Special Security Council's bold counter-strike."

Rimes blinked, then continued. "The operation was supposed to be classified, but Kwon's team knew we were coming for them. We believe he can tell us who gave us up. Right now, the only common link between the two operations is LoDu genies." He looked at Chae. "Your brothers."

Lee leaned forward, brow wrinkled in concentration and fingers steepled again. "Fifty thousand," he said after a long minute. "Come back tomorrow."

"WHAT'S HE ON?" Metcalfe asked as they climbed back into the SUV.

Chae shrugged. "He will not admit it, but he is shamed that LoDu discarded him. One side of his face says he hates them and doesn't need them, the other side spits bile and fury that they found him inadequate."

"What happened to him?" Kleigshoen asked.

Chae glanced at Kleigshoen out of the corner of his eye, then answered her. "He developed an illness. He could not perform fieldwork. He was always considered a disappointment, but he was exceptional with computer systems, so they were willing to overlook his shortcomings. He became an addict ... of many things. They would have eliminated him, but he was too valuable. He proved this by sending them some ... uncomfortable data he had on key executives."

"He blackmailed them?" Kleigshoen asked, surprised. "And they let him live?"

Chae nodded. "They give him enough work to keep him stocked with drugs. But there will come a day where he becomes too expensive to keep."

Rimes blinked at the realization. "He's how you were able to arrest Kwon."

Chae said nothing but started the motor and pulled into traffic. They were halfway back to the station when he spoke again.

"We knew of the disappearances. Seven girls between the ages of twelve and sixteen, all of them pleasure women. The one who disappeared from Lee's apartment building was special to him."

Rimes shivered slightly. "That display by Lee's door. That was the victim?"

Chae grunted. "Park Hyun-ok. Kwon took her out of spite. In the end, Lee was able to get evidence to connect Kwon to three murders. We caught him in the act of ... eating a girl."

"Eating?" Kleigshoen buried her face in her hands. "What is *wrong* with him?"

Chae stopped for a group of youngsters slowly walking across the street, laughing and arguing with each other.

"Genies are not like us. They do not have to select which path to walk in life. They do not have to worry if they will be good enough or if they will be able to feed their families. They are designed for one purpose. They are either good enough to serve that purpose and are allowed to grow to adulthood, or they are deemed a failure and are eliminated."

"I'd be worried about the survivors resenting the hell out of their siblings being killed," Metcalfe said. He looked out the window, suddenly distant.

"They believe they are more than human," Chae said. "They are free from the responsibilities we face, yet they are slaves to their creators. It is a complex relationship."

"You seem to know a lot about them," Kleigshoen said quietly. "From the case?"

"Yes. Lee provided ... valuable insight into the life of a genie. He made it possible to understand how someone like Kwon can exist. As I said, it is a complex relationship."

THEY WERE WALKING the kilometer back to the hotel. The wind had picked up and a light drizzle was falling.

"I've never cared for genies." Metcalfe rubbed his hands to warm them. "In fact, I'm beginning to really dislike them at this point. Then again, I think I'm beginning to understand them a bit more."

Kleigshoen's features were pinched. "Cannibalism? What could motivate a human to create something that *eats* humans?" She edged closer to Rimes until they were touching. "Doesn't it bother you, Jack?"

"Humans have done it too," Rimes said matter-of-factly; he widened the distance between the two of them, conscious of Kleigshoen's closeness. "We'll do damn near anything to survive. And if you follow that line of thinking, it's not really cannibalism. They're eating a lesser creature. Just like we do."

Kleigshoen glared at Rimes. "You're defending cannibalism?"

"They built the perfect killers, trained them to kill, and told them they were better than us, *more* than us. It's inevitable some of them would develop some sort of problem."

Metcalfe laughed and pulled Kleigshoen behind him, pressing his body against hers to "protect" her. "Be careful, Dana. He's been trained to be the perfect killer."

Kleigshoen shook herself free. "That's not even remotely funny, Brent. Jack wasn't created to kill, and he wasn't engineered to be more than human and then told he was better than us. He kills for his country. He knows the difference between right and wrong."

"Oh come on, Dana. I was just ..." Metcalfe shoved his hands into his pockets and shot Rimes a dirty look. "All right. I'm sorry."

So I'm not the only one Dana drives nuts with her conflicting signals. Maybe that's why he's always so surly?

Rimes thought back to Kleigshoen's comments about her promotion ... she hadn't explicitly denied sleeping with Marshall or Metcalfe. At least he didn't think she had.

He wondered why it even mattered to him.

20

5 March 2164. Seoul, Korea.

Dawn came early, and with it a hint of warmth, but only a hint. Rimes's earpiece's alarm tore him from a dream. He pulled on his jogging outfit in the dark and stepped into the hallway light, still struggling to shake himself awake.

He shook away lingering fragments of the dream: fire, a staircase, a terrible weakness and confusion.

I was older. Is it normal to dream of the future? It was so real.

The parking lot he'd been running through abruptly ended at a small, grassy span bracketed by two impressive trees. A flight of stone stairs descended down a hill to a miniature park that looked down onto the city. Rimes stopped at a cement bench and stretched, wishing for something to fill the void where the dream had been. He watched the city below—like him, awakening slowly—with only a few pedestrians puttering about.

Rimes wondered at their lot in life. Some wore tattered paper home-spun, others—a few company serfs—wore modest casual attire. Vehicles drove past them, ranging from half-sized cars to stylish faux luxury sedans driven by apparatchiks who must fancy themselves untouchable, chosen, secure.

Secure. How would that even feel?

Rimes chuckled quietly. There was nothing to do but marvel at the global nature of the play. The script was the same wherever he traveled; only the language changed. He wondered what name his Korean doppelganger would answer to.

"You find entertainment in the strangest things."

Rimes casually turned around to scan the nearby benches.

Tymoshenko sat at a bench in front of several ducks, feeding them what might have been pieces of a muffin. He wore *baji* pants and an unremarkable gray coat with the collar turned up. Except for his Slavic features and tall frame, he could have been just another Seoul resident.

"I feel stupid asking, but how'd you know I'd be here?"

Tymoshenko laughed. "You follow a predictable path."

Rimes winced. *I need to change it up more.* "You said I found entertainment in strange things?"

"For some, entertainment is expensive, yes?" Tymoshenko said, throwing the rest of the crumbs on the ground for the ducks to work out. He stood, wiped his hands on his pants, and strolled casually toward Rimes. "If we are entertained by our career, we ask, how much power and influence can I accumulate? For others, it is family: we value our mate, our children, our parents. Or physical pleasures. Drugs to grant us dreams we hadn't thought possible, skydiving, or climbing snowy peaks."

Tymoshenko stood next to Rimes, overlooking the street. He laughed and raised an eyebrow knowingly. "Maybe even just a good screw, right?"

Rimes looked around, suddenly uncomfortable. "Are we being watched?" He scanned dark storefronts and the few parked cars. His skin crawled at a thought he couldn't quite grasp.

"Of course we are," Tymoshenko said. "Every minute of every day. All of us. Who can say when we have a private moment? Even a quick night of fun in a hotel room is part of the public domain. I'm not even sure privacy is possible anymore. I doubt it's a very healthy thing for business, actually. We want to know the real person, not some machine they live in."

Rimes met Tymoshenko's eyes. "Watched by your people."

"Your people, my people. You draw lines in the air and define words with them. Someone is watching us now. Whoever it is, we can have a copy of it if we want it. Your friends can too. It is easy to gain access to data if you know what to look for. Otherwise, it is a nanobyte of chocolate hiding in zettabytes of shit."

Why is he telling me this? What does he want?

Rimes shivered. "I need to head back. We have to be someplace in an hour or so."

"You really think Kwon will help you? He thinks he is free. None of us are free. We are all puppets."

"What do you want, Anton?"

Tymoshenko winked. "What do any of us want? What do you want?"

Rimes looked at his shoes. They were Army-issued running shoes. If he wanted his own pair, he could buy better ones almost anywhere for fifty, maybe sixty dollars. There were people who had to live off that much money for a month. There were people who needed so much more than that to survive a day.

In many ways, he enjoyed his life. He hated being away from Molly, but he was providing for her and would be able to provide for his child. He was doing the right thing.

"I'm still thinking about it," he said.

Tymoshenko looked back at the ducks, who were fighting over the last few crumbs. "I'm leaving now. This place is too big a strain on me, and there's no use hanging around. I would have thought you would have asked me if I could eliminate Kwon by now."

"Elimin—" Rimes looked around again. "You could do that? You know where he is?"

"Of course. There are no secrets anymore. Not really. You can hide something or someone for a short while, but not forever."

Rimes rubbed his forehead. "We don't want him dead."

Tymoshenko laughed. "Yes, you do."

"No. He's a monster, but it's ... there's more to it than simply killing him."

"If you change your mind, you know how to reach me, yes? From the data film? The window is still open, but it won't be forever."

Rimes watched Tymoshenko walk to the stone stairs that led up the hill Rimes had just descended. The breeze sneaked inside his hooded jacket, forcing another shiver from him.

THE MORNING ONLY WORSENED. Metcalfe put Rimes through another inexplicable, almost psychotic series of veiled threats in the hotel lobby until Kleigshoen arrived. Kleigshoen was no better, bitterly complaining about every problem, real and imagined, from the moment they left the hotel to the moment Chae stepped out of the fifth floor stairwell at the police building.

It's like being trapped in a sadistic maze with no escape.

The drive from the police station to the apartment building was uncomfortable. Chae was even more introspective and grumpy than the day before. At every stop, he looped through cycles of adjusting his tie and silently staring ahead.

Finally they reached Lee's apartment building.

Traffic rolled past their parked SUV as Metcalfe and Chae discussed the deal's particulars. Metcalfe had apparently bumped against the upper limit of his seemingly infinite cash reserve. All the while, Kleigshoen steamed beside Rimes, occasionally glaring at him from behind reflective sunglasses.

Rimes sneaked a look at her, trying to see through the lenses. He saw only his own frustrated face—and behind it, a black SUV.

The vehicle was across the street, its rear to theirs. He risked a quick glance and caught a reflection in its side-view mirror of a dark-haired man wearing sunglasses and a dark, corporate-style suit.

"SUV," Rimes said. "Eight o'clock."

Kleigshoen's glare didn't change, but she slowly tilted her head to glance past Rimes and out the window. "Inspector Chae, any idea whose SUV that is? Looks like we're not the only ones interested in Lee."

Chae and Metcalfe broke off their argument and sneaked a look at the vehicle. "LoDu."

"LoDu?" Rimes didn't doubt Chae, but there was no obvious reason for LoDu's interest.

"They still consider him valuable," Chae said. "They keep an eye on him to be sure he is safe."

"Safe? Safe from what?" Metcalfe asked, leaning to get a better look at the vehicle.

"Himself." Chae checked the traffic, then stepped out of the SUV. "They are family." He slammed the door, nodded at the LoDu vehicle, and headed for the building entry.

Metcalfe shook his head, and they all followed Chae. Rimes glanced back at the SUV before entering the building.

"Family," Rimes muttered. He thought about Molly and the bottle of wine and felt a flash of guilt that worsened when he thought of his brothers still deployed while he was living in posh hotels.

The interior was every bit as dark and grimy as it had been the day before, but somehow, the darkness felt more compressed, more menacing, and the air more foul. They picked their way up the stairs, sliding on rotting things that ruptured beneath their feet in the shadows and released fetid sighs.

Chae knocked at Lee's door and stepped back. Rimes waited for what he assumed was Lee's ritual of scanning his visitors and readying his weaponry. He looked the doorframe over and remembered Lee's high-level security measures—the iron bar, the bolt locks, the heavy door. The doorframe and walls would need to be sturdy, too—to provide significant time for escape or defense should someone attempt to force entry. Lee would have worked out an escape plan before moving into the apartment.

Rimes looked down the corridor. The closest two doors had little plaques Lee's door lacked, that glinted in the dim light. "What apartment number is this?"

Chae smiled, barely perceptible in the darkness. "731."

The door opened suddenly, revealing a strung out, sweat-soaked Lee standing in dim light. Lee's eyes flitted left and right. He hissed, "Inside, quickly."

Lee slammed the door behind them, dropped the bar, and slammed home the largest of the bolts. He shook visibly.

"We have guests." He jerked his head toward the wall.

"We saw their vehicle," Metcalfe said.

"Vehicle?" Lee dropped into his chair and powered up his terminals with a wave. "The SUV? That's only LoDu. Our guests are T-Corp. They've blocked my access to the Grid. They came in this morning and settled into 729."

Rimes tried to connect to the Grid. "He's right. No signal."

"How many?" Rimes asked.

"Five."

Chae's hand ran up and down the length of his tie. Metcalfe paced, looking ready to kick the walls. Only Kleigshoen seemed relatively calm, behind her black glasses.

"What are they here for?" Metcalfe snarled.

Lee steepled his fingers together, smiling through them. "They would have acted by now if they were here for me. They're here for you. More specifically, they're probably here for the data you've purchased."

"They want Kwon." Rimes said. The idea made sense, assuming Metcalfe's theory was correct and the Singapore and Sundarbans operations were related.

Lee's hands shook slightly. "You're getting your money's worth with the data, that's for sure."

He's really on edge.

Metcalfe handed a cash card to Lee, who exchanged it for a palm-sized disk.

"I want to see the data before I leave," Metcalfe said.

Lee pointed at his terminal and moved aside for Metcalfe to seat himself. Metcalfe gave the filthy chair a look of revulsion, then settled in. After several seconds of acquainting himself with the system, he loaded the media and spread it across several of the screens. Chae, Kleigshoen, and Rimes stepped forward to watch him navigate randomly through the data stream.

Data of every sort—video, audio, simple documents, captured messages—played out for several minutes. Metcalfe moved through it all with amazing speed that left everyone but Lee blinking.

Even so, Rimes heard enough message snippets and recorded meetings to answer the question of who the genies were working for.

He watched Kleigshoen. Surprise played across her features behind her glasses.

Metcalfe ran through a few more files before removing the disk and stuffing it inside his wallet. He rubbed his face for a moment, then stood. "This presents a problem."

"They were operating independently?" Kleigshoen's voice was barely more than a whisper. "How? They knew about T-Corp's plans to re-enter the compound. They had equipment LoDu couldn't afford to lose. LoDu had to have known."

"I can't help you any further," Lee said, standing. "I've given you all you need." He looked at Rimes. "You just need to spend some time working with it. It will come to you, eventually."

Lee waved at the screen. "Go to sleep, Little One." The console displays blanked, and the system powered off.

Chae gave Lee a slight bow. They walked together to the door, where Lee whispered something to Chae. Lee then placed something in Chae's hand.

"It's time to go," Chae said nervously.

Lee gripped a deadbolt. "You will no doubt find what you are looking for, but I'm afraid you won't find anything to change what you've already surmised. LoDu is safe in this matter. They won't try to stop you from leaving with this data. They've had no risk in this all along. That isn't their way. They're opportunists, stealing technology and improving upon it. They follow protocols and tradition, even when tradition no longer means anything. But in the end, they're pragmatic. They realized the information would become public one way or another. So they simply position them-selves to take advantage of that. T-Corp ... is much more possessive."

Lee slid back the bolt. The rest of the bolts followed, and the bar rose. The door swung wide.

"Thank you," Metcalfe said.

"Go."

They ran.

The door closed behind them with a metallic bang.

A few steps beyond Lee's door, Chae dropped whatever Lee had given him with a thud. The door of 729 slammed against the apartment wall behind them, drowning out the sound of their running feet. They were on the stairs when Chae's flash-bang grenade detonated, its echoes filling the corridor. The T-Corp agents shouted in surprise.

"Run," Chae shouted, as if anyone needed encouragement.

They reached Chae's SUV and climbed in. In his haste, Rimes roughly shoved Kleigshoen into the back seat. He suddenly realized he was still holding her. Her hands held his hands in place. In a moment that seemed to stretch an eternity, she looked into his eyes and squeezed his hands against her.

Rimes pulled away.

Chae started the motor just as their pursuers burst through the front door, hands reaching inside their jackets. Chae accelerated away from the sidewalk, cutting in front of a battered mini-car. Rimes watched as the pursuers—clearly T-Corp men—sprinted after them, only to stop as the LoDu SUV pulled onto the sidewalk in front of them, cutting them off. Chae turned hard right onto the next street, and in the distance, the T-Corp agents slapped the hood of the LoDu SUV in apparent anger.

21

———————

6 March 2164. Seoul, Korea.

Rimes woke from a fitful sleep. He'd dreamed of Kleigshoen. She was in his head, manipulating him, controlling his thoughts, sleeping and waking. He felt powerless and weak.

He checked the time on his earpiece. It read 0237. He rubbed his eyes and sighed.

He'd been sure he wouldn't be able to sleep well. He considered trying to go back to sleep but knew better.

He sat up in bed, suddenly grappling with the terrible weight of loneliness.

Molly, I miss you.

Rinsing his face with cold water freed him from sleep's final clutches. And Kleigshoen's.

Without a second thought, he started the coffee machine and pulled on a pair of shorts. As he settled at the desk, it hit him how easily he was being lulled into Bureau life. The hotel room, using the coffee machine and its expensive imported coffee without the least concern over the expense, even his frustrating meetings with Tymoshenko. None of it was in Rimes's nature, yet he was finding that nature surprisingly fluid once challenged. He wondered if he could escape the attraction when the time came to say goodbye.

The coffee machine emitted a quiet beep, drawing him out of his thoughts and back to the Kwon problem. They had looked at the terabytes of data from Lee, but none of it had seemed of any real use in figuring out where Kwon was and what he was doing. Rimes inhaled the coffee's comforting aroma before tapping a container of sweetener into the paper courtesy cup and swirling the dark fluid.

Sipping, he settled back at the desk and opened a private workspace inside the earpiece and began recording. The earpiece's cameras captured his hand movements, translating them into navigation commands for the virtual interface it projected before his eyes. His fingers selected then expanded a box. He transferred Kwon's vital data—birthdate, birthplace, siblings, father, education—to the box. He followed the box with a circle filled with disconnected but supporting data: the murder case, the mission history, the connection to the genies at the T-Corp facility. He had a starting place.

Something about the genies at the T-Corp facility made Rimes pause. He wondered if LoDu might have manipulated or even fabricated the security records connecting the genies killed at T-Corp 72 and Kwon.

They could have, easily. But why? He's from the same batch as 730. The connection is there. It's real.

But LoDu had as much to lose if they appeared incompetent and irresponsible as they did if they were caught sanctioning the operation. They were in a no-win situation, so there was no value fabricating or altering the records. He discarded the line of thinking.

Rimes created another circle to hold locations—birthplace, training facility, residences, operations, last seen. He examined the locations overlaid atop a global representation of Earth. He rotated the globe and pushed in for details, focusing on Asia.

Aside from some time in orbital training, Kwon had spent most of his life throughout the continent. Twenty-six missions, some with nothing more than travel dates and expenses to document their existence. Three in

Korea, four in Japan, three in Malaysia, two in the Philippines, four in Vietnam, one in India, two in Pakistan, one in Bangladesh, one in Sri Lanka, five in China, and one in Singapore. No pattern jumped out.

Rimes opened another circle and populated it with the mission data—dates, costs, nature, and connections to the genies killed at the T-Corp facility. He opened a separate feed to tap into the Grid for crimes or stories of interest around the times provided. Finally, he ran a series of sorts and comparisons based on simple raw and derived data points.

An error message appeared—a glitch that elicited a quiet growl and another trip to the coffee machine.

Eyes squinting, Rimes re-examined the mission data. Somehow, one of the mission dates had caused an error. He breathed in the coffee's rich aroma, took another sip, then repeated the process. This time, he watched for the error.

He caught it while sorting on mission counts. He manually counted the provided mission data and compared it to the LoDu summary. Twenty-six missions had been logged by LoDu, but there were twenty-seven missions in the data.

He had his anomaly.

He stared at the data for several seconds before it finally hit him. A comparison of the mission dates to other critical dates was the key. He ran the comparison.

The results came back instantly: 6 June 2107. Kwon had been in a prison cell at that time thanks to Chae. The record indicated he'd been on one of his China missions. The inconsistency piqued Rimes's interest. He opened the questionable China mission file.

According to the LoDu file, Kwon had been sent to Pingfang District to eliminate an EEC operative. Rimes wasn't familiar with Pingfang; he downloaded all the available data on LoDu operations there. He wasn't surprised to find LoDu had nothing significant in the area, and certainly nothing an EEC spy would have an interest in. An icy chill ran down his spine.

A false mission, or a false arrest? The arrest seemed real enough. Chae's fear of Kwon certainly seemed authentic. Could LoDu even pull off such a scam? Of course they could, but why fake it?

The EEC operative seemed the next logical point to focus on. Rimes pulled up the mission photos. He selected the first one. It quickly resolved: Anton Tymoshenko, wearing the same gray jacket from their meeting at the horrible coffee shop a few days earlier.

That answers it: Fake mission.

Tymoshenko was just pulling his hood over his head. The look of nausea and disgust on his face was unmistakable. It was definitely taken from outside the coffee shop, but some of the image had been modified. Since he hadn't been eliminated by Kwon in Pingfang District, the fake mission had meaning of some sort.

We're always being watched, just like he said. It's Lee's work. He placed this data. The Pingfang mission was a fake. Why? What's he stand to gain from this? Extortion? Intimidation? A false trail? A hidden message? Something else?

Rimes tried to come up with other possible reasons. None stood up to even cursory challenge.

It can't be extortion. Lee knows all about me. I don't have anything he'd want.

If I could figure out it's fake data, anyone who gives it a serious look could, so it's not effective as a false trail.

Intimidation? Maybe. Why, though? It's not my case. This is the Bureau's problem. Lee knows that. Why not scare Metcalfe off?

There must be a hidden message, something he wants me to find. But he's using Tymoshenko. No one else knows about him. Yet. He means this just for me. What did he say, that we'd find what we were looking for if we looked hard enough? Something like that.

Why me? What's he hiding from IB?

Rimes searched for Pingfang District and LoDu, tying the results back to several potential criteria: Tymoshenko, murders, Korea, EEC, T-Corp, and genies. Nothing stood out.

He tried several permutations with no better luck. He broadened his criteria set, adding in LoDu and X-17. Again, he found nothing.

Frustrated, he set his earpiece down and stood. He stretched, then paced for several minutes. The idea of a jog was appealing, but he decided to give the data another try before abandoning it. He settled back at the desk and put the earpiece back on.

After another set of searches proved fruitless, he decided to return to the China mission itself.

In the photo, which should have shown the horrible coffee shop's glass wall and cartoonish sign, a blank stone wall stood.

Chewing on his lip, Rimes inspected the image. He rotated it inside the workspace. He flipped it, reversed it, created a depth-accurate version. He pulled the focus out and pushed it in on Tymoshenko. Nothing came to him. There simply wasn't that much of Tymoshenko to see. The pedestrian traffic blocked everything below his chest. Only the hooded jacket and Tymoshenko's face stood out.

The jacket!

Rimes crossed to the closet where his own hooded jacket hung. Frowning, he spun it around by its hanger, looking for anything of interest. He photographed it and uploaded the photo for comparison.

Tymoshenko had been wearing the same jacket, identical except for size. Rimes rotated his own jacket inside the workspace and cut away everything he couldn't see of Tymoshenko's jacket. He shaded his jacket to match Tymoshenko's. That done, he ran a comparison of the images.

His headset beeped. It had only taken a few seconds for it to find what his eye was missing. He magnified and enhanced the difference, rotating it around to see it in three dimensions. He couldn't see any difference.

He ran interpolation analysis against it, and the image resolved: on the jacket near the collar, the number 731 was printed. Kwon's number at LoDu.

Hastily, Rimes returned to his queries and added 731 to the criteria, but they returned nothing. Rimes's brow wrinkled in frustration. He felt confident with his find: Lee had planted the message for him. There was some sort of connection between 731, Tymoshenko, and Pingfang. He just wasn't seeing it.

Recalling the roadblocks he'd encountered in his thesis research, Rimes decided to purchase access to archived print media. He billed the access to his hotel room and re-ran his query.

Long seconds passed as backend transactions ran through the orbital banking system's intricate web. Finally, the query returned. Rimes looked at the results in disbelief.

What had returned were references to Pingfang District during World War II and a Japanese biological weapons research group: Unit 731.

After some thought, he decided to read through the first few articles the search had returned.

Disgust washed over him at some of the atrocities the Japanese had committed: amputation, induced gangrene, surgical mutilation. The atrocities seemed too extreme to be real. Unit 731 must be one of Lee's fabrications.

After thinking for a moment, he decided to add a name to the search criteria: Dr. Hwang Sung-il, Kwon and Lee's creator.

A recent article—from the Grid rather than the archives—moved into the top list of returns; the date matched that of Kwon's arrest in Seoul and the false China mission.

Korean spy Sim Duk-ryong honored as World War II hero by President Park Myung-hwan.

LoDu Senior Scientist and luminary Dr. Hwang Sung-il attended the ceremony that finally granted official recognition to one of the few Koreans killed by the infamous Japanese Unit 731, Sim Duk-ryong. Also in attendance were Chinese historian Zhou Ji and Russian novelist Jerzy Tymoshenko, descendants of the men Sim Duk-ryong had been working for in China at the time of his capture.

Rimes ran a few more searches, confirming that Anton Tymoshenko was related to the Jerzy Tymoshenko mentioned in the article.

He still couldn't see the connection. With a frustrated sigh, he exited the workspace.

It was approaching three-thirty. He'd wasted nearly an hour on the effort. The results were useless, meaningless. He assumed they were fake. The odds of both families having such a legacy in espionage and tragedy were outrageously slim.

Just like that, I'm seeing Kwon, Lee, and Hwang as a family. But Kwon and Lee are genies.

Rimes closed his earpiece and considered returning to bed. He could use the sleep, but he knew it wouldn't come for him. The wasted time and money had him wound up—but his failure to make sense of Lee's message irked him even more.

He realized he was rubbing his chin, chafing it. He straightened in the chair. Failure had never been easy for him to accept. Failing spectacularly had irritated him, so he set his mind back to work.

Although he knew better, Rimes had expected the offline archived print data to be reliable. He'd fancied it safe, the uncorrupted key to unlocking Lee's message. But Unit 731 had been too much of a coincidence; it had to be faked. Realizing the print data could be compromised disturbed him, but not as much as Lee not leaving any obvious clues.

Rimes considered that thought—that Lee would leave a trail with no clear end.

No. There's an end. I'm missing something. It's not Lee, it's me.

A flick of his finger and the earpiece was reopened and resting on his ear. The virtual interface materialized before his eyes, and he re-opened the workspaces. He stared at them, trying to determine the best course to take.

He decided to work from the premise the article on the Pingfang District ceremony was a fake, too. That would make it the best starting point. Lee must have left a trail of breadcrumbs rather than an obvious message.

Rimes skimmed the article, stopping to fully read when he reached the details on Unit 731.

His skepticism about the unit quickly faded. He'd heard claims about atrocities during older wars, but most were considered exaggerated. And the Japanese atrocities of World War II were something he'd never heard of before.

However, the article detailed so many, so thoroughly, that they seemed frighteningly authentic.

After a second read-through, Rimes looked at the notes box he'd created. Three things stood out. First, the words "family" and "honor" were repeated throughout. Second, the article cast the Russians as cruel, almost cardboard villains. Third, Dr. Hwang Sung-il's home was explicitly identified as "bordering the southeastern Seoul fringe." The data seemed trivial, out of place—yet the article had made it sound important.

Rimes checked the time again. He wouldn't have breakfast with Kleigshoen and Metcalfe until nine; he had five hours. They were probably still asleep.

A quick check confirmed the temporary Bureau connection they'd given him in D.C. was still intact. Rimes searched Bureau records on Dr.

Hwang Sung-il; they listed a possible location for him. Rimes pulled the address to his earpiece and checked it against a map.

Got him! But if I've figured this out, who else might have? If Dr. Hwang is important, would LoDu move him? Would they silence him?

Rimes started to open a call to Kleigshoen. He stopped, finger hovering over the virtual button. He closed the communication application.

No. I've been playing their game long enough. I want this one without their interference. If I blow it, it's on me. But if I'm right and Dr. Hwang is where Lee is pointing me, I don't want there to be any chance someone could interfere.

Rimes opened the communication application again. He thought for a moment, then called Chae. Three rings passed before there was an answer.

Chae answered crisply in Korean.

"Inspector Chae, this is Jack Rimes."

Sheets rustled faintly, and a female voice mumbled something in the background. Rimes imagined he heard footsteps.

After what felt like an eternity, Chae said, "It is not even four in the morning."

"I need to speak to Dr. Hwang Sung-il," Rimes said. He struggled to remain calm. "It's very important to the Kwon case."

"I have no idea where Dr. Hwang Sung-il lives. LoDu is very protective of the privacy of its senior staff."

"Lee gave us the address," Rimes said, unconcerned that he was crafting a selective truth. He realized his voice was growing louder with each word. He took a breath to calm himself. "I think Lee's saying that Dr. Hwang is the key to understanding this Kwon situation. I'll need you to get me through the security. The address is in the middle of a LoDu campus just outside Seoul, not even an hour from here."

Chae went silent again. "I will need an hour. I can pick you up at the hotel." He disconnected.

Rimes smiled. He had a lead.

22

---

6 March 2164. Seoul, Korea.

DURING THE DRIVE, Rimes flipped through the Bureau's data pack on the Gwangju Gardens LoDu campus. Construction had begun in December 2096. It had reclaimed a three-kilometer stretch of valley southeast of Seoul, including parts of the Gwangju city ruins. According to the Bureau, the campus was home to thousands of LoDu employees, including hundreds of privileged elders.

Like Dr. Hwang Sung-il.

Rimes looked up as Chae's SUV approached the compound's front gate. As was usual with Korean architecture, towering skyscrapers covered most of the campus. Even during the early morning hours, it was brilliantly lit, a hypnotic neon rainbow.

They had to wait for seventeen minutes at the campus gate.

The guards never took their eyes off Rimes the entire time. Then a message came through; after some muttered exchanges and another check of Chae's badge, the guards waved them through. Rimes watched the guards shrinking in the passenger side mirror; they watched the SUV until they were out of sight.

A few minutes later, Rimes found himself standing beside an elevator cage at the base of Orchid Building 6. In the pre-dawn light, the building threw off a brilliant pink glow. Rimes counted twenty stories. His research indicated Hwang resided alone at the top.

Chae pressed the intercom for Hwang's floor. A dry, quavering voice angrily replied in Korean. Chae bowed his head and replied contritely, embarrassed. The elevator cage opened, and Chae nodded for Rimes to enter.

The surrounding buildings became their horizon as the elevator climbed. Rimes marveled at the startling aesthetics of the daring architecture—abrupt angles, hanging terraces, glass walkways. Midnight blue, jade, and burnt orange glows predominated their quadrangle. Beyond, the colors were equally bold and vivid. He could recall nothing so audacious and beautiful in his experiences at home or abroad.

With quiet clangs and rattles, the elevator cage came to a stop, and the door opened onto a short stretch of earth that ended in a rustic stone wall. Rimes stepped onto a path of river stones that led to a wrought-iron gate; Chae followed. As they approached, the gate opened.

An elderly man dressed in a grimy, gray *hanbok* stepped into view, his face inscrutable under his bushy eyebrows.

Rimes reached the gate. "Dr. Hwang."

His skin was dry and scaly and his hands wiry. "Yes?"

"I'm Jack Rimes. I asked Inspector Chae here to help me to reach out to you. I apologize for the early hour, but I greatly appreciate you giving us a few moments of your time."

Hwang stepped back and waved them in, closing the gate behind them. He shuffled down the path toward his apartment. Vines stretched across the path; the closer they came to the front door, the thicker the vines. Rimes and Chae were forced to choose their steps carefully.

Most of the plants were long dead, leaving only the hardiest to battle the weeds. Rimes glanced at Chae. Chae looked as disturbed as Rimes felt.

The apartment's façade was better maintained, but even it seemed forgotten. Chipped stone, cracked wood, dented metal—it was a blemish on the campus's complexion.

Hwang opened the front door and escorted the two of them inside. The air inside the apartment was thick with rot and filth. The door opened onto a foyer. Crumpled food containers, tattered wrapping paper, and moldy food covered everything, but Hwang showed no sign he was aware anything was amiss.

"Some tea?" Hwang asked.

Rimes shook his head; he'd be afraid to drink it. "Doctor, I was hoping you might be able to help us with a serious problem."

Hwang ignored him, shuffled into the equally filthy kitchen, and gathered a teapot from the top of the stove. Charred bits of food and containers covered the black cooking-stone stovetop. With a gentle shove, he cleared space at the overflowing sink to fill the teapot, unleashing a domino effect that sent tottering piles of dishes, pots, and pans onto the counter and floor with a crash.

Hwang didn't react to the clatter.

After filling the teapot, Hwang set it on the stove and turned on one of the heating elements, then stared at it, unmoving.

After a few moments, Rimes said, "We're looking for Kwon Myung-bak."

Hwang turned, his eyes focused on nothing. "What has he done?"

"Well," Rimes said, looking to Chae for support. "We believe he's involved in something that extends beyond the LoDu metacorporation. He seems to be operating without their approval."

Hwang frowned.

"He assassinated a high-profile politician in Indonesia recently," Rimes said. "He also seems to be connected to an operation in India involving a T-Corp research facility. LoDu has made it clear these were unsanctioned operations."

Hwang searched through a pile of dirty dishes, clumps of molding rice, and discarded packaging until he secured a mug. He scraped black paste out of it, dumping it on the floor. He muttered, then opened an empty cupboard, searching it repeatedly.

"Dr. Hwang?"

Rimes looked at Chae, who shrugged.

After several seconds, the muttering resolved into words, first Korean, then English. Hwang turned to look at Rimes as he spoke. Hwang's brow wrinkled as he struggled to concentrate.

His voice sounded clearer, less shaky. "What makes you believe LoDu?"

"They've provided a good deal of evidence implicating Kwon," Rimes said.

Hwang looked into the cup, then returned to the sink and rinsed it. He sighed. "What evidence?"

"Videos, communication records. Images. Enough to hold up in court. Lee Sang-woo ... was our intermediary."

Hwang looked at Chae, who nodded.

"Brother turns on brother," Hwang said, eyes drifting to Rimes. "Do you have children?"

"One on the way."

The teapot began to whistle. Hwang poured water into the cup, then stared at the steam.

"I have dozens. They are stars in the sky while we are ... rocks. Dirt. You understand?"

Rimes shook his head. He assumed Hwang was referring to the genies' engineered superiority, but the old man's mind seemed fragile and unpredictable.

"My final children for LoDu were 729, 730, and 731," Hwang said. He stared into the distance as he breathed in the steam rising from the mug. "Lee, Kim, Kwon. They were my favorites, my best work. Kim and Kwon, at least. 729 was a disappointment."

"Kim was your favorite?" Rimes asked.

Hwang smiled gently and nodded once. "Kim Jang-yop, they named him. They always gave them names, sometimes made up, sometimes from someone in history. To make them special. They were brothers, and I was their father." Hwang sipped his water. "And now he is gone."

"I'm sorry for your loss," Rimes said. *They must have told him.*

"Nothing pleases a father so much as a son who succeeds him."

"I understand, sir."

Hwang stared into his mug. His brow wrinkled. "How did he die?"

Rimes hesitated. "In battle. He fought bravely."

Hwang took another sip. "We have fallen."

Rimes looked at Chae. "I don't understand," he whispered.

Chae watched Hwang for a moment, then said in a hushed tone, "The family's honor has been undone. Lee because of his weakness, Kwon because of this betrayal. Kim's reputation will be undone. Their failures will reflect on Dr. Hwang. They will destroy his legacy."

Rimes wasn't sure if it was anything he could use to get Dr. Hwang to tell him what he wanted to know. Besides, direct questions seemed more effective for the moment, despite Hwang's erratic behavior.

Is he senile? Crazy?

"Dr. Hwang, can you tell me about 731? About Pingfang?"

Hwang's eyelids fluttered. He looked around the kitchen as if seeing it for the first time, wincing at the filth. His eyes traveled across Rimes and Chae's faces blankly, then returned to Chae's face, squinting.

Rimes and Chae exchanged looks of surprise.

Pingfang? 731? Something had changed. A trigger word?

"I know you," Hwang said, his voice stronger, his hands suddenly steady. "I can help you. Quickly."

"Dr. Hwang?" Chae said uncertainly.

"For the moment, yes," Hwang said tersely. "Your questions. You must be quick. You seek information on Kwon?"

Rimes nodded. "Lee embedded false information into the data he provided, a fake operation Kwon ran in Pingfang District, China. He supposedly assassinated an EEC spy there, but the mission data pointed back to another article Lee somehow planted in a printed media digital archive. The article referenced Sim Duk-ryong."

At the name, Hwang flinched.

Rimes kept going. "I couldn't make any sense of it. I thought it might be some sort of code."

"Sim Duk-ryong was real." Hwang looked at Rimes, his gaze intense and sharp. "I worked for LoDu for forty years, and I was head of their genetics engineering effort for the last twelve. Always, the elderly must step aside for the young. I mentored a brilliant young man, Dr. Kang Tae-suk, for the last four years. He replaced me. He was forty years old. Forty," the old man snarled.

"In the past, the policy was that no one would ascend to a senior post such as I held until they were sixty-two. Age reveals wisdom and patience. Kang was brilliant, but he was not patient. The LoDu leadership were not patient, either. They approved his promotion."

Rimes shook his head. "I don't understand, sir. How does Sim Duk-ryong relate to Dr. Kang Tae-suk?"

"Dr. Kang was Sim Duk-ryong's father," Hwang said.

"Sim Duk-ryong was … in the article, he was a World War II hero. Dr. Kang couldn't have been his father."

"Dr. Kang created a genie with the same name. Sim Duk-ryong … was his favorite. He was, as far as LoDu was concerned, the future."

"What, a brilliant scientist?"

"Not a scientist," Hwang said. "Brilliant, but not a scientist. You mentioned Pingfang District. Are you familiar with its significance?"

Rimes shook his head. He was struggling to contain mounting frustration and fear. He suspected the lucid Dr. Hwang would only be around for a short while. "Pingfang" must have been a trigger word of limited use.

Hwang needed to get to the point *now*, or the search for Kwon would come to a dead end.

"When the Japanese invaded China in the 1930s, they established a terrible operation in Pingfang District. The operation involved vivisection —live surgery, you understand?—biological experimentation of an inhuman nature. The operation was run by Unit 731. Biological agents, chemical agents … mostly, the victims were Chinese. Even among our Asian family, the Japanese had a special contempt for the Chinese.

"There was one Korean who was finally proven to have died there."

Chae bowed his head. "Sim Duk-ryong."

Hwang nodded. "We needed something to be proud of, after that war.

"Kang's main rival was a Japanese researcher. Sim was Kang's poke in the eye, you see? 731 was mine. So many rivals out of Tokyo, always looking down on us. Even within LoDu, there is division."

Rimes chewed his lip. "I'm still not following, Dr. Hwang. What's Sim's connection to Kwon?"

"Just as Kang replaced me, Sim replaced Kwon. Our original designs were humans, but faster, stronger, hardier. Alien DNA was used to take us into our future, not to ... Kang saw that as lacking ambition. Sim was created using newer theories. He was the first to render us completely obsolete."

"Us?" Rimes "You and your comrades?"

Hwang shook his head. "Humans." He blinked slowly and stared into his mug. "You can walk the corridors of memory forever in dreams."

"Dr. Hwang, wait, concentrate." Rimes loudly snapped his fingers. "Doctor? Please. Sim renders us obsolete?"

"Sim makes us obsolete, yes. All of us." Hwang stared into the distance, slumping. "He has destroyed the family, replaced it with his own. Kwon does not see himself as an outsider anymore. He does not see me as his father anymore. Kim did. Kim was the good son. Not like 729."

"How has he made us obsolete?" Rimes grabbed Hwang's shoulders. "Dr. Hwang? How has Sim made humans obsolete?"

Hwang smiled feebly. "His mind. It is everywhere. It is in everything. He is *Sansin*. He abandoned LoDu. The metacorporations transcend nations, even Earth itself. Now they have been transcended by their own creation. And they fear Shiva."

"Shiva?" Rimes swore quietly as the last vestige of intelligence left Hwang's eyes. He released the old man, who shuffled around the kitchen, muttering.

Rimes looked at Chae. "*Sansin*? Shiva? Does that make any sense?"

"*Sansin* was a powerful mountain spirit," Chae said.

"A spirit? Like a genie?" Rimes asked.

Chae thought for a moment, then he nodded.

"What about Shiva? Is that the same?"

Chae shook his head. "That is a Hindu god, I think. *Sansin* was from ancient Korean beliefs."

Rimes sighed. He pulled up a reference to Shiva on his earpiece, skimming through it as he watched Hwang stumble, as though he didn't see the garbage under his feet.

"Creator and destroyer," Rimes said, shaking his head. "Does that make any sense to you? Any connection?"

Chae stared at the ground. "I don't see one, no."

Hwang sat at the cluttered dining room table, picked up a pot and a spoon, and began singing happily.

With a heavy sigh, Chae led Rimes out.

The sun was a red scab low in the eastern sky as they drove back to the city.

23

6 March 2164. Seoul, Korea.

RIMES SHOWERED. The filth of Hwang's apartment had disturbed him even more than the induced dementia. He staggered out of the shower and dried off; then he sneaked in a quick nap.

As he walked into the hotel restaurant, Rimes wondered how Lee felt, knowing his father lived in such a state.

Not happy about it, I bet. A prisoner to his own memories. LoDu sells cures for this sort of thing, but they inflict it on their own. How horrible.

Kleigshoen and Metcalfe were sitting in a corner booth when Rimes walked in, both smiling at him. He wasn't sure what to make of their promptness, much less their demeanor after yesterday's surliness. He returned their smiles.

Kleigshoen pointed across from her. She was breathtaking in a bright red top, sleeveless and low-cut, with her hair hanging down and curled onto her left shoulder. Metcalfe's eyes drifted over her, lingering a moment, before he scooted over to make room for Rimes.

"You're early." Rimes ordered a vegetable and rice plate with slices of steamed tofu, then added a boiled egg, figuring the Bureau wouldn't complain about *that* extravagance compared to the data bill he'd piled up.

Kleigshoen looked at Metcalfe, mouth and eyebrows twitching. Metcalfe nodded at her.

"We've had a break," Kleigshoen said. "A huge break."

Rimes looked from Kleigshoen to Metcalfe, then back again. "Aren't you going to tell me what it is?"

Show me yours and I'll show you mine.

"They've got Kwon," Kleigshoen said.

Rimes's heart raced. *If they've got Kwon, it changes everything. They aren't going to care about what Hwang told me.*

"They?" It didn't really matter who had Kwon, so long as someone had him. There were so many questions to be answered. Kwon was the key to most of them.

"The Australian police," Metcalfe said. "They've got him locked up in Darwin. High security, someone watching him every minute of the day. He's pretty banged up, so he's not going anywhere."

Kleigshoen said, "Doesn't look like he was as rogue as LoDu wanted us to believe. But they've got four agents in the Darwin morgue right now and another two in ICU."

Rimes rubbed his forehead. "He killed LoDu agents?"

"That's what we're hearing," Kleigshoen said.

"Sounds pretty rogue to me." Rimes rubbed his forehead. "So LoDu knew where he was all along?"

"Apparently," Metcalfe said. "Or they knew enough to find him when they really wanted to. This changes the complexion of the case completely. Lee's data is pointless now. Fifty-thousand dollars wasted. Jim's going to ride my ass for that."

A waitress appeared and set their plates in front of them. Metcalfe tore into a slice of tofu drizzled with a garlic sauce and washed it down with a sip of hot tea. He gloated as he chewed, looking from Rimes to Kleigshoen.

Rimes kept thinking of Dr. Hwang, making "tea" and winced.

Metcalfe laughed. "We've got him, Jack. Aren't you happy?" He sucked tofu from his teeth before scooping up a large mouthful of rice.

"How did they get him?"

"The police report isn't clear," Metcalfe said around another sip of tea. "No one's in any condition to talk, but it looks like the agents went to Kwon's hotel and expected him to cooperate. Security video shows them approaching his door clumped pretty tight. Unless they were rank amateurs or extremely stupid, they weren't ready for a fight. He killed two of them before the others had any idea what was going on."

Rimes picked at his food and considered the scenario Metcalfe described. It was possible LoDu was so internally compartmentalized that their agents hadn't been informed Kwon had gone rogue. Yet something seemed wrong about it.

Rimes finished the last of his vegetables. "I don't like it."

"You don't like it?" Kleigshoen looked to Metcalfe.

"What don't you like, Jack?" Metcalfe smiled condescendingly over the top of his steaming teacup. "We've only been doing this job for a of couple decades between us, so we're probably missing something your sharper, fresher eyes have caught? Maybe you could share your insight with us, walk us through this little maze we've stumbled into?"

Kleigshoen's brow furrowed. "Brent—"

Metcalfe waved Kleigshoen down. "It could be the key piece we've been missing all along. Maybe he's dreamed up a solution to this whole puzzle. Have you, Jack? You put it all together and figured it out?"

Rimes sighed. Metcalfe was trying to turn the situation personal again, and it didn't serve anyone.

"All I'm saying is that it doesn't add up. The agents show up in Australia, and he kills them? Do we have the agents' communications records? How long were those agents in Australia before they went to his hotel room? How long was he in the hotel room before they arrived? Why was he there?"

Metcalfe chuckled. "Maybe we should just ask LoDu to tell us what they're doing."

"Brent." Rimes sighed and shook his head slowly. "I don't need the hostility, all right? I'm just trying to understand. Because right now, nothing is fitting together. Not for me."

Metcalfe snorted. "Well, why don't you ask Kwon for his help? We're on the next flight to Darwin. That is, assuming you want to come along?"

Kleigshoen caught Rimes's eye. "We thought this would be good news to you."

"It is. Obviously. It's a huge break." Rimes peeled the boiled egg, hoping the mundane activity would help defuse the situation. "But I'm not very good with things that aren't what they appear to be. You know how it is, Dana. It works against all my training and what I do. See the battlefield, know the battlefield."

Metcalfe poured them each more tea. He sighed, set the pot down, and looked Rimes in the eye. The smugness was gone.

"You've picked this all up so quickly, Jack. And I mean that when I say it. Dana said from the start that you're a sharp one. Thing is, you're still new to the game."

Rimes took a bite out of the egg. He tried to find serenity in the moment, but he suspected that Metcalfe was just setting him up for another personal attack.

"There's a world of difference between the sort of wetwork you do and the work we do," Metcalfe said. "It's probably tough to stay engaged in all the reading and listening and research we have to do when you're used to action and reaction."

Rimes felt his face flush. "I think I'm doing okay."

Metcalfe winked. "Sure. And I'll be the first to admit there are a lot of things about this case that we haven't connected yet. It happens. This one's complex. You have to be patient in this line of work. Keep your eyes open, watch for the clues. It'll come to you, eventually."

Metcalfe looked at Kleigshoen, as if waiting for some sign. If she gave it, Rimes couldn't sense it.

Metcalfe took a sip of his tea. "Anyway, we had a call with Executive Assistant Director Marshall this morning. He's very pleased, especially now that we have Kwon."

Rimes cocked an eyebrow. "He understands we don't actually have Kwon, right?"

"The Aussies do," Metcalfe said impatiently. "They'll cooperate fully. They're great allies."

"They've come to rely on us a great deal to manage some of the radicals they deal with." Kleigshoen.

Radicals. Terrorism—low-scale or not—probably won't go away in our life-time. Hate dies hard.

"If we can get Kwon to talk, we're all in a very, very good place." Metcalfe leaned back and offered his most charming smile. "Go ahead and admit it, Jack: you're starting to like this sort of work, aren't you?"

Rimes finished off the last of his breakfast and emptied his teacup. "Maybe I can visit Major Uber while we're there?"

Metcalfe winked at Kleigshoen. "We should be able to arrange that. I knew you were onboard, Jack. Wheels up at 1245."

24

———

7 March 2164. Darwin, Australia.

RIMES YAWNED as he reached their rental car from the airport. The sun was blinding; it burned away whatever coolness remained from the night before. Everything had a filmy, dreamy quality to it. Singapore, Los Angeles, Washington, Mumbai, Seoul, and now Darwin—the jet lag was catching up to him.

In the distance, a HuCorp orbital shuttle rocket roared. He turned and watched it rise into the sky, trailing misty fire. It quickly disappeared in the haze above. Obsolete or not, the insatiable demands of orbital platforms kept the older shuttles hopping.

Some things never truly become obsolete. They just go out of style.

To the west, skyscrapers vanished in the hovering smog.

Kwon was there, somewhere. Rimes felt a faint tingle of excitement.

"And I thought Seoul was muggy." Kleigshoen tossed her handbag into the rental car's back seat. Her blouse and skirt clung damply to her. "Can we get to the hotel quickly, please? I need a shower."

Metcalfe chuckled. "Don't worry, we'll have time to clean up and grab a bite. I'm going to squeeze in a nap. We won't head over to Nightcliff until later this afternoon. That's where the police have our Mr. Kwon secured."

The car was an odd little HuCorp contraption Rimes had never seen before. He climbed into the passenger seat. Cabbies and limousines rolled by.

"You know your way around?" Rimes buckled in.

Metcalfe shook his head. "Sydney. Melbourne. I've never driven here. Ought to be an adventure, right?"

They exited the airport and drove west, into the newer streets of Darwin City. Most of the buildings were less than ten years old, rebuilt after yet another devastating disaster nearly wiped the area off the map.

Darwin had a history of bad luck. Cyclones, bombing raids, and more—just over four decades back, an Indonesian radical had detonated a dirty bomb, killing twenty thousand people, because he'd been furious the city had hosted a bisexual Colombian entertainer. However, most recently the city had been rebuilding from Cyclone Jonathan's gentle touch.

Metcalfe pulled into the parking lot of the Queen Victoria Hotel. It was a modest, ten-story tower that looked over the rebuilt Bicentennial Park and, beyond that, Port Darwin.

After relieving himself and kicking off his shoes, Rimes set his room's thermostat as low as it would go. He set his suitcase on the bed and laid out his last pair of fresh underwear.

They'll need to be replaced soon. Not what I'd normally buy, but it's not like I had much choice when we lost everything in Mumbai.

He stripped and walked to the closet, pulling the laundry bag from its hanger. It would be cheaper to buy new undergarments, but he had no idea what sort he could find in the area, and he wasn't keen on lugging a suitcase full of dirty clothes around with him. He stuffed the dirty undergarments, two shirts, and a pair of pants into the bag.

The Bureau's paying, so why not?

He marked the bag for a full wash and softener, then set the bag by the door.

The jet lag hit him again as he headed for the bathroom. He shook himself and took a few energizing breaths.

The shower stall was narrow and had a frosted glass door and stainless steel controls. He cranked the water temperature as high as it would go and leaned into the spray. It heated quickly, and he was forced to turn it down slightly before lathering up.

As he rinsed, he stretched, working his stiff muscles until he felt some of the travel-induced tension and soreness leave them. His wounds were largely healed, but nothing could erase the fatigue but sleep.

With his mind on the verge of shutting down, he turned the water off and stepped out, toweling down briskly before wrapping the towel around his waist. He stepped out of the bathroom, swearing he'd make time for a call to Molly before they went to Nightcliff.

His vow drifted into the ether as his tired eyes spotted Kleigshoen sitting on the edge of his bed, bathrobe draped over her left arm.

"Dana?"

She smiled. "I'm all out of soap. I can't believe how often that happens, can you? You don't mind?"

She tossed her bathrobe onto the bed and walked past him, kicking her shoes off next to the bathroom door. She peeled off her clothes and turned, lingering a moment, silhouetted. She disappeared around the corner. A moment later, the shower kicked on.

Rimes sat on the bed, blinking.

He loved Molly more than anything. He thought of his child growing inside her. He thought of his career, of the integrity he embraced as a soldier.

When the shower shut off, he tensed.

She stood in the bathroom doorway, toned arms bracing her supple form in the frame. She could have been drawn from his deepest fantasies.

She crossed to the bed, trailing steam, and pulled back the covers. He started to ask her to leave, but she reached for him and pulled him to her. She kissed him, and he knew he was deceiving himself. She pulled his towel away, and her heat melted the last of his resistance.

Sunset cast long shadows as they turned off Casuarina Drive onto a dirt trail. Just outside the driver-side window, waves rolled onto the beach, then dragged themselves back into the deeps. The current tore detritus from the shore, then abandoned it to float aimlessly on the surface.

The HuCorp rental car bounced and shook, creaking in protest as the dirt trail turned onto a long-abandoned gravel path. Rimes wasn't sure the little car would make it.

He stared out his window.

A security camera was partially hidden inside some scrub brush by the road. It was the first operational piece of equipment he'd seen for kilometers.

Rimes watched it through the rear window, risking a momentary glance at Kleigshoen. She looked at him triumphantly. Rimes looked away. Metcalfe remained focused on the narrow path ahead.

"I haven't seen anyone for a good five minutes," Rimes said.

"This section took the brunt of Cyclone Jonathan, and they never rebuilt it." Metcalfe's voice was cold. "It's a shame. It used to be so pretty." He glanced into the rear-view mirror.

Kleigshoen looked away.

Rimes said, "There were some people in those shacks as we came into Nightcliff."

"Immigrants. Squatters," Metcalfe replied. "People move into your territory. If you don't do something about it, they ruin everything. We did everything we could to help them, but ... there's not much use trying anymore. They made their choice, right, Jack?"

Metcalfe swerved around a corner, and a cratered parking lot came into view, empty except for an older, rust-red EEC sedan in the center.

Three buildings, one of them surprisingly intact, stood beyond the broken stretch of asphalt. The crumpled remains of an Olympic-sized pool lay in shadows across a ruined lawn.

Their HuCorp sputtered and came to a halt next to the sedan.

"Is this a secure facility?" Kleigshoen leaned forward. "Brent, are you sure about this?"

Metcalfe's jaw muscles clenched. He exited the car without uttering a word.

Rimes got out of the car. His memories were a mess now, a tangle of the last few hours, the last few days, the moment. He wanted so badly to be with Molly in their modest little apartment. He wanted so badly never to have been with Kleigshoen, never to have been pulled into the whirlpool of passion, physicality, and political games he thought he'd escaped years ago.

"Brent, is this—are we using aggressive interrogation techniques? Is that why we're out in the middle of nowhere, away from legal authorities?"

Metcalfe thrust his hands into his pants pockets. "Careful now, Jack. We're all sacrificing a small part of our souls here, aren't we? What's a little torture in the grand scheme of things?"

Kleigshoen closed her car door. "Brent—"

Metcalfe turned on her. "What, you think his hands are clean? He's no better than me. Take a knife to someone, put a bullet in them, poke an eye out—we do what we have to do. Don't we? Am I right, Jack? Whatever it takes for the mission?"

"That's enough," Kleigshoen said. Pain and anger played across her face.

Rimes rubbed the heel of a palm against his forehead. "Dana's right. This stinks. We need better security."

Metcalfe stormed across the parking lot, nearly going head over heels as a patch of asphalt collapsed beneath his feet.

Kleigshoen started to run after him, but Rimes hooked her around the waist.

"Dana, wait."

She glared at Rimes. "He's not thinking straight. He could kill Kwon, and we'd lose everything."

"That's not going to happen," Rimes said calmly. "I think he may be thinking straighter than any of us right now. I need you to talk to me."

Kleigshoen pushed his hand away. "Talk to you about what?"

"This thing you've got going on with him. Do you even care that he's in love with you?"

Kleigshoen recoiled. "Brent?"

"That's why he's been such a jerk."

"He's like a father to me, Jack. What you're saying is ... sick."

Rimes sighed and lowered his head until his chin rested on his chest. "Dana, he doesn't see you that way. He feels betrayed."

Kleigshoen looked away, scanning the shoreline, the twisted, stunted palm trees covering the lawn. "I ... it was never ... supposed to be like that."

Metcalfe had disappeared into the one standing building.

"When this is all over, you need to talk with him." Rimes kicked up a piece of asphalt with his shoe and flipped it over. Beetles crawled away. "What happened can't happen again. I'm married, Dana. Happily married, if Molly will forgive me. You and I had our chance a long time ago, and it didn't work out. We need to move on."

Kleigshoen stormed off toward the building.

Rimes almost laughed at the insanity of what he'd allowed himself to fall into, but the fear of losing the thing that mattered most to him in the world silenced that impulse.

What's a little torture in the scheme of things?

He scanned the shoreline and the road they'd taken in, then walked around the sedan and headed toward the building.

A plainclothes cop of apparent Indian descent met them at the door. "G'day." He waved them through to a large common room, then closed the door behind them and casually leaned against it.

The room was empty except for an ancient but functional sofa and matching chair. Water bottles rested on an end table between the two pieces of furniture. Their hollow shadows stretched across a heavily scored wooden floor. The room opened onto a kitchen area partitioned by a long island.

A Chinese man with a pockmarked face and a burly Indonesian woman with spiked, gray-streaked hair stood in the common room across from a large bay window. The woman limped slightly as she stepped forward to shake their hands. Rimes noticed she had a thicker sole on her right shoe than her left.

"Sergeant Unu," the woman said. She nodded toward the Chinese and Indian men as she spoke. "This is my partner, Constable Chang. Constable Desai brought you in. Your friend's down there with Inspector Djerrkura," Unu said, nodding down a dark hallway. "First room on the right."

Constable Chang coughed into his hand, and Sergeant Unu gave him a look.

"He's right, I should tell you. This guy—"

Gunfire drowned out her words.

25

7 March 2164. Darwin, Australia.

Automatic gunfire shattered the bay window; shards of glass sprayed across the floor. Rimes knocked Kleigshoen to the ground. Unu dropped into a squat, then Chang. They drew their weapons.

Desai spun. Another burst, and several rounds punched through the front door, taking him full in the chest. He staggered for a moment, then collapsed.

Rimes crawled forward to check on Desai. Unu and Chang crawled toward the far wall, Chang trying to avoid the glass shards covering the floor, but Unu staying low.

A loud crack sounded. Chang quietly gasped, fell, and stopped moving.

"Sniper," Rimes called.

Desai was in shock, twitching and bleeding. Rimes pulled Desai's pistol from its holster and searched for any spare magazines, then skidded it across the floor to Kleigshoen.

Then Rimes crawled to Chang, blood pooling beneath the back of his ruined head. Rimes pulled Chang close enough to grab his gun and spare magazines.

"I've heard four shooters," Unu called from the corner. She glanced out the shattered window then over at Rimes. "Chang?"

"Dead," Rimes said. "And Desai's not going to make it. Can you raise someone?"

Unu nervously dug her earpiece out of her shirt pocket and placed it on her ear. She tried a few messages then shook her head. "They must be jamming somehow."

Rimes crawled back to Kleigshoen, who was now at the hallway entry. Djerrkura and Metcalfe were on their stomachs behind her.

"Four shooters, probably more," Rimes said. "One sniper, three automatic weapons. The sniper and two others to the south, one to the north. We've got two folks down so far."

Djerrkura closed his eyes and shook his head, muttering something beneath his breath.

Metcalfe crawled backwards, out of sight. A few moments later, something crashed to the floor. Rimes trained his pistol on the shadows, relaxing when Metcalfe returned.

"I knocked our friend's chair over," Metcalfe said. "Don't want him taking a stray round."

"We need to find that sniper," Rimes said. "He'll pick us off or keep us pinned down until the others are on top of us. Either way, we're dead."

"I'm open to suggestions," Metcalfe said grimly.

Rimes nodded, then looked at Djerrkura. "This place have a bathroom?"

"Down the hall. Take the first right, then the third left."

Rimes crawled down the hall, stopping a moment to check on Kwon. Kwon lay on the ground with his eyes closed.

Bright-colored synthetic rope criss-crossed his chest and legs, and carbon fiber restraints bound his wrists and ankles to the chair. He opened his eyes and glowered at Rimes, baring teeth. It was crude, but probably effective.

Those eyes. The amber coloring, the shape. Is that part of the alien influence?

Another round of automatic fire echoed from the hallway, and Rimes continued down the hall and into the bathroom.

The bathroom had a small window on the south wall. He belly-crawled across the floor until he reached it, then looked back toward the bathroom's north wall.

A cracked and grimy mirror stretched over three sinks, reflecting the shadowy stalls, the sinks—and the window. It wasn't perfect, but it let Rimes see outside.

Darkness was approaching fast. At least the attack had come at twilight rather than later in the evening; it might mean the attackers lacked experience and sophisticated gear.

However, the terrain couldn't have been worse if he'd pulled it from a nightmare. Several twisted palm trees and clumps of weeds cropped up between the building and an embankment. He could make out the very top of the embankment, but not much beyond. The sniper could be anywhere.

Sudden movement caught his eye. Two men with assault rifles were sliding down the embankment, heading for the building's northeastern side.

Rimes shouted a warning down the hallway. "Two Tangos coming in from the northeast."

Metcalfe shouted back, "Got it."

As the gunmen disappeared from sight, Rimes watched for any further flicker of movement, any glint of the dying sunlight off a sniper scope or rifle barrel. He saw nothing.

He shifted position.

Still nothing.

But as he shifted again, he saw it: the sniper was repositioning, moving along the embankment top. Rimes couldn't believe his luck. He watched until the sniper settled into his new position behind a stunted tree, then returned down the hallway to Djerrkura and Metcalfe. They were pressed against opposite sides of the hallway, Djerrkura watching the main entry door, Metcalfe the hallway.

"The sniper's behind the stunted tree to the west. Those gunmen are going to come in through the eastern side. Is there a door or an easy access point along the eastern wall?"

"Yeah, sure, the service door," Djerrkura said. "Opens onto the kitchen."

"Metcalfe, you and Djerrkura need to set up an ambush there." Rimes handed Chang's pistol and magazines to Metcalfe. "When the first one comes in, the other gunman will probably try the door we came through. We'll deal with him."

Metcalfe wiped sweat from his upper lip as Djerrkura jogged away in a half-crouch down the hall. Metcalfe looked at Kleigshoen, then back at Rimes. "Jack—"

Rimes nodded. "She'll be okay. I promise."

Metcalfe smiled ruefully toward Kleigshoen, who was staring out the shattered window, then squat-jogged after Djerrkura.

Rimes belly-crawled to Kleigshoen. "You catch that?" he whispered.

"It's about to get fun," Kleigshoen said with a quavering voice. She nervously brushed curls off her forehead.

Rimes studied her for a moment. "You going to be okay?"

"Yeah." Kleigshoen gave a quick nod. "It's been a while since I've been pinned down like this, that's all. Any idea who these guys are?"

"They're not wearing any special gear," Rimes said. "South Asian? They could be locals."

"Mercs?"

"Probably." He twisted around. "Unu, any metacorp field teams operate in this area normally?"

"Yeah, yeah, sure," Unu said, her voice shaking. "T-Corp, sometimes HuCorp. Mostly mercenaries, though. Brotherhood and the like."

"Mercs it is," Rimes said. *Brotherhood of Arms. Not the threat they used to be, but bad enough.* "They'll probably come through any minute now. Cover the door and stay where the sniper can't see you."

"No worries," Unu said. "I'm not moving."

Rimes belly-crawled to the front door, hugging the north wall as tight as he could. By staying atop the embankment, the sniper had limited his view into the room. Unu was safe so long as she stayed in the corner, and Kleigshoen was hidden in the hallway.

As he crawled past the door, he saw that Desai had stopped breathing, although his blood continued to spread on the floor. Rimes stopped just beyond the door and sat up, his heels beneath his butt and his hand pressed against the wall for balance. He kept his eyes level with the knob. He would be the first thing the gunman would see when he came through the door.

Surprise was all he had going for him.

Suddenly, the knob twitched and started to turn. Rimes held a hand up and pointed at the door.

Gunfire erupted at the eastern end of the building. An instant later, the door opened, and the gunman stepped in, barrel lowered.

Rimes launched himself and grabbed the barrel, putting his whole weight into the maneuver. His momentum pushed the two of them out the door.

The gunman tried to jerk the gun free, squeezing off a burst in the process. The rounds thudded into the ground. The barrel heated up, and Rimes gritted his teeth in pain. He shoved the gunman back, straining to keep the barrel pointed away and down, pushing until the gunman lost his footing, then driving a shoulder into his face and neck until he released the gun and tried to push Rimes off. Rimes pinned the gun between them with his hip, then pummeled the other man's face, breaking first his nose, then his cheek.

Rimes pinned the assault rifle to the ground with a shin, then scrambled onto the man's chest and pinning him down, all the while punching and throwing elbows against ever-weakening attempts to fend off the attacks. Finally, the other man's arms went limp.

Rimes freed the assault rifle and squatted low over the unconscious form. Sporadic gunfire sounded from the east. Rimes hastily retrieved two magazines, a knife, and an earpiece, then he delivered a swift kick to the bloody head, and retreated to the front of the building.

He stopped at the front door, then slipped the primitive earpiece on, adjusting it as best he could and setting it to mute. He listened to the earpiece intently.

It was quiet.

"Jack?" Kleigshoen whispered from the front room.

"Dana, you two make your way through this door to the parking lot," Rimes called. "Stay low. Don't go for the cars. We need to eliminate the gunmen on the eastern side of the building. Wait for me to engage the sniper."

"O-okay."

Rimes sneaked along the north wall until he had a view of the embankment. He scanned for any sign of the sniper, then squat-walked along the west wall.

He stopped at the sight of the stunted tree, dropped flat, and brought the assault rifle up.

He scanned the area through the rifle's sights, waiting.

Suddenly, the sniper moved, tracking to Rimes's left. Rimes fired. The sniper rifle sounded simultaneously.

The sniper pitched backwards. Kleigshoen screamed.

Rimes jogged for the front door, his heart racing wildly. "Dana!" The roar of an engine drowned out his voice.

Car. Approaching from the east.

Rimes rounded the north wall in time to see Kleigshoen collapse in the doorway. His heart skipped a beat.

He ran to her side.

Tears welled in her eyes. Blood—and clots of other matter—dripped from her face and hair. Rimes wiped her face. She was fine.

Next to her, Unu's skull had been shattered.

"He shot her," Kleigshoen sobbed in a whisper. "She was right next to me and he shot her."

Rimes stood. Too many times to count, he'd survived a close call only to watch someone else die, and he'd never gotten past the survivor's guilt.

The engine was closer now. He could hear brakes squealing. Voices shouted over each other in the earpiece. Someone said something about movement.

The gunfire to the east had stopped. Rimes cautiously jogged east along the north wall, stopping at the edge.

He heard a weak choking sound nearby and attempted to sneak a peek, but a round thudded into the corner, spraying his face with splinters.

Two men were sliding Kwon into the back of a large HuCorp car.

Rimes looked again. A third man with a pistol squatted behind the front of the car. He fired at Rimes but missed.

The car's engine roared. Blood trickled into Rimes's eyes. He popped around the corner just long enough to fire a burst toward the gunman.

He heard a satisfying howl, but then the car accelerated away.

Rimes wiped away the blood, pulling a pinky-length splinter from his forehead. He waited a few heartbeats, then glanced around the corner again.

The car was gone.

The gunman was on the ground. He was breathing shallowly and reaching for his pistol.

Rimes jogged forward, picked up the wounded man's gun, and took away his earpiece, kicking the man's hands away. Rimes muted the earpiece, then kicked the gunman in the head, stilling him.

Rimes took in the carnage along the eastern wall. Two more gunmen were slumped on the ground, their blood-soaked shirts testament to Djerrkura and Metcalfe's ambush.

Rimes jogged back to the building.

Inside the doorway, Djerrkura lay on the ground. The back of his head was blown in, and a tranquilizer dart stuck in the wall beside him.

Rimes pulled the dart from the wall and examined the room, imagining what had happened.

Kwon must have sneaked up on Djerrkura during the gun battle, then was knocked out by the mercs. Whoever they were, they weren't Kwon's friends.

Two meters beyond, Metcalfe was slumped over a table, his head twisted at a horrific angle. He was still alive, barely. He wheezed as he struggled to breathe.

His gun was gone.

"Brent?"

Metcalfe's eyes opened, reflecting fear and a terrible awareness. Tears rolled down his face.

He tried to speak, but didn't have the breath.

Rimes touched Metcalfe's shoulder. "Dana's okay. She's going to be all right. We're going to find these bastards. We—"

Rimes stopped.

Metcalfe was dead.

26

———————

7 March 2164. Darwin, Australia.

RIMES CREPT BACK to the front room and knelt beside Kleigshoen. He positioned himself between her and Unu's corpse. Kleigshoen was still a mess.

"We have to go," Rimes said, softly at first, then again more firmly, as she didn't respond.

"Get Brent first." Kleigshoen's head shook in time with her breathing.

Rimes hesitated.

She knows he's dead. She just needs me to tell her for her to accept it.

"He's gone."

Kleigshoen cupped her hands over her eyes. Her body shook, but no sound escaped.

"Dana, we don't have time for this. I need you to call the police. You need to tell them what happened, and they need to locate the mercs' car. There was—"

Kleigshoen shook her head and released a loud sob. She reached for Rimes and pulled him to her, clutching him tight. She shook violently for several seconds before sucking in a big gulp of air and slipping into a loud cry.

There was nothing he could do to stop it, so Rimes let her get it out of her system. He wrestled with conflicting feelings: anger, confusion, sorrow.

Foremost, though, was the anger. Not only over Metcalfe's death but over Metcalfe and Kleigshoen's deception, their games and secrets, the way they doled out information and manipulated him.

From the start, something had been amiss in the Bureau's request for his assistance. Pursuing Kwon had been legitimate, or at least there had been legitimate reasons to pursue him. But they'd never come clean about the true motivation, either about the mission or about their need to involve Rimes.

He held Kleigshoen. Her crying diminished slowly.

A chill wind blew in from the sea. Darkness was approaching. He pulled away from Kleigshoen, but her hair had matted to his bloody forehead. He gently tugged the hair free.

"Dana?" he whispered. "Can you contact the police? There was a security camera back up the road, just out of sight when we came off that dirt trail. They can get an image of the car off that."

Kleigshoen nodded. Rimes handed her his handkerchief, and she wiped her face. After a moment, she walked down the hallway.

He watched her go. When she was out of sight, he returned to the unconscious gunman on the front lawn.

Rimes pulled the gunman's belt from his pants, rolled him onto his stomach, then started to bind his hands behind his back. The man began to struggle. Rimes planted a knee in the small of the man's back, pinning him down, then finished the crude knot.

Rimes pulled a knife and put the blade against the man's neck. He quit struggling.

Rimes paused, letting the man imagine what might be in store for him.

Sometimes, imagination is worse than the reality.

On the back of the man's neck, Rimes found the edge of a partially hidden tattoo. Rimes pulled the man's collar back. The tattoo was a stylized fist—clenched and armored. A combat knife and a pistol crossed behind the fist.

Brotherhood.

"We don't have long to talk," Rimes said. "So I'd suggest you think carefully about what you say. The police will be here soon. There are four of their own dead in the building back there. What's T-Corp want with Kwon? Tell me and you're free."

The man tried to glare at Rimes from the corner of his eye. "They never told us. They want him alive. There is a ship. We were supposed to get him onboard." His voice had a nasal quality to it.

"Name?"

"The *Argo.*"

"How many were on your team?"

The gunman hesitated. "Nine."

"Counting you?"

"Ten."

Rimes considered the numbers. "You only brought eight."

"Basu, he got sick with the malaria. Atish ran the operation from the motel."

Rimes set the man's earpiece on the ground, then untied him and rolled him into a sitting position, still holding the knife at his throat.

Rimes fit the other earpiece in his ear. "I need you to do one last thing. Tell Atish you escaped and want to get back to them when things cool down. You'll need some medical attention, but you'll live."

The gunman looked at the earpiece uncertainly. He hesitated for a moment, then gritted his teeth and put it in. "Atish." He blinked slowly, waiting for the connection. "Atish, hello?"

Rimes tightened his grip on the knife, watching the man's face for any hint of artifice. The silence dragged on for several seconds.

Through his earpiece, Rimes heard a voice ask, "Anwar? Where have you been?"

"Atish, I am hurt." Anwar rubbed at his ruined face. "The bastards, they got me."

"We can't get you. It's too much trouble now."

"I know, I know. I need medical help, but I will be okay," Anwar said. "My nose, it is broken. I think my cheek too."

"Okay, yeah," Atish said after a moment. "Tomorrow. On the ship. Now don't call me again."

"Tomorrow. Do not leave me."

Rimes smiled as the link closed. He held out his free hand, and Anwar returned the earpiece.

"Don't try to contact them again." Rimes pulled the knife away from Anwar's throat and pointed to the west. "Go that way. I wouldn't go near the ship if I were you."

Anwar rose with one eye on Rimes, backed out of reach, then jogged away.

Kleigshoen stood in the north doorway. Her eyes were puffy, and she was shivering but otherwise in control.

"You shouldn't have let him go."

He looked Kleigshoen in the eyes. She held his gaze without blinking or looking away.

Good. I need your head in this. I'll need your help getting Kwon back, then you can answer whatever questions he can't.

The anger was back. He was going to get answers, no matter what it took.

"Did they identify the car?"

Kleigshoen nodded. "They found it dumped off Stuart Highway. They're gone."

"All right. I guess they're not totally incompetent." Rimes handed her Anwar's earpiece. "Can you run a trace on that, get a log of the calls? I want the location of the most recent one first. That's where we're headed."

Kleigshoen took the earpiece, still trying to stare him down. "You're not giving this to the police?"

"No," Rimes said. "We're going to handle this ourselves."

27

7 March 2164. Darwin, Australia.

THE DARWIN SEASIDE Resort Lodge consisted of three dirty, peeling two-story buildings in an inverted "U." Despite its name, it was positioned closer to the McMinn Street ramp onto Stuart Highway than to any shoreline.

Rimes watched the parking lot through his earpiece's display.

"What a sad little dump," Kleigshoen said.

Compared to the rest of Darwin City, it looked old and neglected. The place reeked of hopelessness, desperation. They'd seen an example of its typical clientele earlier: a lonely businessman opening his door for a grungy prostitute. It would appeal to unsavory sorts who preferred to be left alone.

Like the Brotherhood mercenaries.

"You see anything new?" Rimes asked.

"Nothing."

Rimes drilled down on the image on his display until he saw a grainy

"122" on the door. He pulled the zoom out, stopping when "123" showed on the adjacent door.

"At least the camera's working. Perfect placement."

For the last half hour, they'd been parked beneath a broken lamp, twenty meters from the parking lot. The only activity had been one of the mercenaries leaving from, then returning to, Room 122 with dinner, using a blue van.

For the third time since their arrival, Rimes checked the assault rifle he'd taken from Anwar. It was an ARDE AWS-3, a knockoff of the Cytek Advanced Assault Weapons System, and not a particularly good one. It had a reputation for jamming after less than a hundred rounds. The three magazines he'd taken from Anwar held twenty 6.8-mm rounds; one was already half-empty.

I don't even have enough rounds to worry about it jamming.

Kleigshoen had settled into a quiet calm. "What's your plan?"

Rimes adjusted the holster to Desai's pistol before replying. "When the time comes, I'll retrieve Kwon from our Brotherhood friends."

"And when is that?"

"It shouldn't be long." He locked eyes with her. "While we wait, why don't you tell me what you and Brent were really up to? It sure as hell wasn't figuring out what was behind T-Corp 72."

Kleigshoen looked out the passenger-side window, into darkness.

After a long pause, she sighed. "That's not completely true. We were very interested in what happened at T-Corp 72, just not in the compound."

"All right. What were you interested in?"

"The X-17."

"You knew all along they had that?" Rimes shook his head. "Wait. You knew those genies were going to be there?"

"We suspected. Jack, it's complicated."

Rimes's eyes narrowed. "Give me a try."

"You don't want to—wait." She held up a hand. "Who's that?"

She sent Rimes an overlay on the camera image through her earpiece. Rimes squinted at the image, then grabbed the assault rifle.

A man with a swollen nose was edging toward the motel parking lot, looking over his shoulder. Anwar.

"It's the gunman you let go. I told you not to—"

After a few seconds, Rimes opened the car door.

Kleigshoen turned. "What are—"

"Get ready."

He walked across the street and into the parking lot. He held the assault rifle vertically off his left hip, shielding it from the view of anyone looking from the front of the motel and maintaining a normal stride as he crossed the parking lot.

Anwar knocked on the door, talked to someone inside, then disappeared inside Room 122.

Rimes stopped at the door to Room 121, leaned against the wall, and edged to the right of Room 122's window. He shifted the assault rifle into both hands.

Raised voices leaked through the window. Anwar's voice was recognizable, although it was Atish and someone else doing the shouting.

Rimes was almost sure that Kwon was in the adjoining room, 123, away from the argument, with maybe a couple of guards. Rimes had planned to start with Room 123 and eliminate any men guarding Kwon first, but the shouting gave Rimes second thoughts. He'd wanted a distraction, and the mercenaries were as distracted as they were going to get.

He listened a moment longer, trying to visualize as well as he could where Atish and the other shouter were. Before planting the camera in the parking lot, Kleigshoen had managed a few image grabs of other rooms, so Rimes had a good idea of the rooms' layouts: rectangles, deeper than they were wide, with a bathroom and small closet at the back, a table and two chairs beneath the window looking out onto the parking lot, two beds on one wall, a dresser and console on the opposite.

Atish and the other shouter were near the window; Anwar sounded like he was still near the door. The one who had malaria should be in the room with them, too, away from the prisoner, on one of the beds.

The door to Room 123 opened.

One of the mercenaries started to exit, holding a plastic food container in his right hand. He froze.

Rimes sent a burst into the mercenary's chest and stepped in front of

Room 122's window, spraying four short bursts at waist level, focusing on the occupants' probable locations.

Rimes edged toward Room 123's door, then squatted by the wounded mercenary, waiting.

Three rounds flew through 123's door, giving away the shooter's position. Rimes ducked around the doorway and fired, then ducked back.

Nothing.

Rimes reloaded, then crawled past the door toward Room 123's window.

Kwon should be on a bed on the left wall, unconscious, bound.

There was no movement from Room 122 yet.

Rimes stood and sent five bursts into Room 123. A satisfying gasp and slumping sound told Rimes he'd guessed right.

He replaced the magazine and kicked in the door. Kwon was facedown on the room's farthest bed. The second mercenary was on the floor near the console, bleeding heavily, still clutching his pistol but unable to lift it. Rimes kicked the pistol away.

He checked Kwon for any obvious wounds, then felt for a pulse.

Alive.

Rimes threw Kwon over his shoulder and edged toward the door, assault rifle at the ready.

As Rimes peeked out, the door to Room 122 burst open. Rimes squeezed off a short burst just as one of the mercenaries appeared. The mercenary returned fire.

Rimes stepped back into Room 123 and sent three bursts through the wall, angling down and toward the parking lot to avoid collateral damage. A hail of gunfire answered him. He flinched, but one of the rounds grazed his leg, another his back.

"Bring it around," Rimes shouted into his earpiece. He fired into the wall, aiming low until he emptied the magazine.

He released the assault rifle, pulled Desai's pistol, and stepped into the parking lot.

He sent several shots through Room 122's front wall as Kleigshoen swung the bouncing car into the pitted parking lot.

Rimes fired into Room 122 again, stopping only long enough to heave

Kwon into the car. Another three shots, and he dove into the car beside Kwon.

Kleigshoen coaxed as much as she could from the HuCorp, getting it up onto two tires when she turned onto the Stuart Highway. Rimes felt the world shifting beneath them.

Kleigshoen glanced back at Rimes. "Are you okay?"

Rimes smiled at her weakly. "Yeah."

"Bullshit. You're slipping into shock."

Rimes chuckled. It was a quiet sound that ended suddenly. "I was going to visit Major Uber anyway …"

"Darwin City Police Dispatch. Yes, constable, this is Special Agent Dana Kleigshoen of the Intelligence Bureau. Check my credentials through the embassy, if you don't trust them. There's been an attack on Intelligence Bureau personnel at the Darwin Seaside Resort Lodge."

Rimes listened to Kleigshoen's side of the exchange, admiring the sudden calm in her voice. He had to concentrate to keep up with it. He was feeling woozy after the engagement.

"Yes, McMinn Street," Kleigshoen said. "Several wounded. What? Look, these are the bastards who killed your own officers, so I don't think you should be yelling at me. Yes, thank you."

Kleigshoen terminated the call. "I thought they'd never—" She looked over her shoulder at him. "Jack, you've been hit. Can you understand that? I need to get you to a hospital."

Everything seemed to be moving slower.

Kleigshoen went silent for a second. "Royal Darwin Hospital. Yes, this is Special Agent Dana Kleigshoen of the Intelligence Bureau. I'm two minutes out. I need priority treatment for my teammate. He's been shot."

Kleigshoen's voice was smooth and husky, dreamy. *Teammate. I like the sound of that.*

Rimes wondered how he'd ever escaped Kleigshoen—or how he'd ever let her escape him; he wasn't sure which. His memories were a jumbled mess at the moment. He smiled contentedly. It didn't matter. He would never be alone. He had someone waiting for him back at home. For a moment, he tried to remember what home meant, then slipped into darkness.

28

---

8 March 2164. Darwin, Australia.

"Jack?"

Rimes's eyes fluttered open. He was thirsty and tired, and his left side ached. He was on a hospital bed, dressed in a pale blue gown; his left arm had an IV in it.

A young, skinny Aboriginal Australian woman in nursing grays looked over at him from one of the monitoring system displays as he blinked. "I'll be right back with the doctor."

Someone touched his hand; Kleigshoen sat to his right. Her shirt was blood-stained, and her hair was a mess, but she was beautiful in the harsh light.

He tried to speak and at first found his throat too dry. He swallowed and finally managed a very weak gasping sound that made Kleigshoen smile.

Rimes saw a water cup with a straw sticking out of the top. He reached for it and missed. Kleigshoen guided his hand and helped him clench it. The water was surprisingly cool and sweet.

"Not too much." Kleigshoen pulled the cup away. "They said you'd just vomit it back up again."

"How am I?" Rimes asked.

"They took a bullet out of you, but not before you'd lost a bit of blood."

"What about Kwon?"

Kleigshoen shook her head. "They dug a bullet out of his neck. They have him on life support for now ... we have some budget left, but keeping a genie alive isn't going to receive approval, even though using him as a shield probably saved your life."

Rimes frowned. Kwon had held answers. They needed—Rimes needed—to know what Kwon knew. Kwon would be carrying everything to the grave. It was too easy a death, too painful a final act of defiance against those he'd wronged.

"We need to leave soon," Kleigshoen said, patting his hand. "The police ... aren't happy. The nurse gave you restoratives and stimulants. You should be ready to travel tomorrow, two days at the latest."

Bio-restoratives and stem-cell extract stimulants weren't cheap. Kleigshoen must be playing with the expense account now that Metcalfe was dead.

Rimes yawned, even through the stimulants. He needed to rest.

"I'm going back to the hotel and get some sleep," Kleigshoen said, standing. "We'll deal with Kwon in the morning."

"The mercs?"

"Two in prison, one in ICU. The rest are in the morgue. The guy you worked over at the secure facility took two to the chest, but they think he'll make it."

Rimes chewed at his bottom lip. "I dreamed about Major Uber."

Kleigshoen smirked. "You think he'd like to know Kwon's dead?"

Rimes chuckled dryly. "Is he here? Maybe I could visit him? I wouldn't mind being the one to tell him."

Kleigshoen shook her head. "I checked already. He's probably back in Germany by now."

"Damn. I'll send him a message. I'm sure he'll be happy."

"You do that," Kleigshoen said. She turned to go, then stopped. "*After* you get some rest."

Rimes waved weakly at Kleigshoen as she left.

As he drifted off, he thought about Kwon.

Although technically dead, Rimes wondered how much of Kwon's mind remained ... and whether his condition was really as hopeless as it sounded. Genies were considered disposable. That was certain to color any diagnosis.

An idea was forming in Rimes's mind.

RIMES YAWNED and stretched his left arm above his head. He grimaced at the stiffness in his ribs, then sat up. He felt much better but still thirsty, despite the IV.

"That tea will help you talk," the nurse said.

It was the same woman; she nodded approvingly when Rimes picked up the tea cup on the table next to the bed. It was still hot.

She watched him out of the corner of her eye as she took the IV out of his arm and powered down the last of the monitors.

"You have a cybernetics lab, right?" Rimes's voice cracked, but he managed to get through the question without swallowing.

She glared at him, and he sipped the hot tea again.

I wish I could have slept until the healing was complete.

"We have a fitting and adjustment lab," the nurse admitted. She took the teacup away from him and tilted the cup insistently, stinging his tongue.

Rimes swallowed quickly, ignoring the burn. "So you'd have an MMI technician, then?"

She looked into the cup. "You need to see him?

Rimes quickly drank the rest of the tea. "Please? Before I go."

She took the cup. "We have two. Brian's on duty today. Brian Chin. I saw him in the cafeteria earlier. Get dressed." The nurse pointed to the small bathroom. "Your friend's finishing checkout. I will ask Brian about seeing you after you have clothes on." She pointed toward a small stand at the foot of the bed, then left before he could thank her.

Rimes climbed from the bed. On his way to the bathroom, he scooped

up his jeans and a complimentary blue paper shirt and matching underwear from the stand.

In the bathroom, he rotated his left arm several times until the stiffness
lessened. A quick shower, and he returned to the bed area, dressed and
ready to go.

Kleigshoen waited at the edge of the bed. Her hair was still damp, the
golden curls tight. She wore a light cotton outfit that looked like it would
handle the humidity without losing its style.

"What's this about an MMI tech?"

"On the *Sutton*, you mentioned the next wave of remotes. It reminded
me that the older generation of remotes use the same man-machine interface as the more advanced cybernetics.

"A couple of years ago, one of our guys was on an operation in Chile,
and an RPG took out his helicopter. He broke his neck in the fall but
survived—only his brain went without oxygen for too long, and the medics
couldn't wake him up.

"He had valuable intelligence, so they did what they could to keep the
blood flowing and got him to a hospital. An MMI tech and a remote
systems designer, working together, were able to establish contact with his
mind. Unfortunately, the computers could never make sense of what they
downloaded."

Kleigshoen rubbed her fingers through her curls, pulling on a loose
strand. "You want to use the MMI gear to download Kwon's thoughts?"

"I want to interface directly with Kwon's brain." Rimes smiled hopefully.
"You keep implying remotes are the next big thing. So there had to have
been advances in the software. What I want—what I need—is to search
what's left of his brain. Now."

"He was a serial rapist and murderer, Jack." Kleigshoen pulled her legs
up on the bed and wrapped her arms around them. "It doesn't sound possible, and if it *is* possible, it certainly doesn't sound safe."

THEY FOUND the Cybernetics Lab on the third floor, connecting the hospital's neurosurgery and physical therapy wings. Bright colors covered the

hallways on the first floor, but when the elevator opened onto the third-floor hallway, they faced a sea of muddy brown with jarring spatters of orange and yellow. The lab was a small office situated in the middle of a spray of orange.

Aside from two simple, plastic chairs by the doorway, the tiny lab was dominated by a modest, tool-cluttered workstation and an examination table.

Rimes settled into the plastic chair farthest from the door.

Kleigshoen snorted. "This isn't going to work."

He glanced at the chair beside him then at Kleigshoen. She rolled her eyes and noisily sat down.

"You have an appointment?"

A pudgy young man with spiked hair and Asian features stood in the doorway. He wore nursing grays cinched by a vinyl tool belt with hip pouches.

Rimes stood and extended his right hand. "You must be Brian."

"Chin, yeah." Chin looked at Rimes's hand, then shook it once and pulled his hand away.

"I'm Jack Rimes. This is my partner, Dana Kleigshoen."

Chin looked at Kleigshoen, then scratched his stomach through his grays. "You the American came in all shot up last night?"

Rimes nodded.

Chin cocked an eyebrow. "You look pretty spry for someone near dead."

"They've got me on some pretty good stuff. Do you have a minute?"

"Nothing 'til after lunch." Chin edged past Rimes and pulled a rolling chair out from under the workstation. "What d'you want?"

"A couple quick answers," Rimes said. "A man came into the ER with me. He'd taken a bullet to the neck. They said he'd suffered too much damage to be saved."

"The genie in ICU, yeah?" Chin asked.

"His name's Kwon. What I need to know—is it possible to rig me up to him, let me interface with his mind through some of your equipment here?"

Chin looked from Rimes to Kleigshoen. "Is this a joke?"

Rimes held out his hands to forestall Chin and accidentally hit the exam table. The impact thundered in the room's cramped space. "Hear me out—"

"Sounds like that corpse isn't the only one suffered brain damage, mate."

"I know there's equipment and software for this. And there are all sorts of advances going on in MMI research. If you don't have anything capable of this, maybe you could connect me with someone who does? What about neurology?"

"Look," Chin said. "What you're describing isn't anything we do here. I'm a tech. I run tests, I manage upgrades, fittings, and adjustments. Tweaking and the like, see? Yeah, maybe the neuro boys could help you, but I doubt it. That's witchcraft, right? No one does man-machine-man interface research here. Maybe at university. Maybe at research—" Chin stopped and leaned back so far that two of the wheels on his chair left the floor.

"What is it?" Rimes asked.

Chin dropped his chair wheels back down. "Yeah, okay. So maybe it's not what you want, maybe it is. There's a private research facility down the street a ways. Vanguard something or other. I don't know who funds them right now, but they've done some pretty crazy stuff there the last few years, and they've been hiring a lot. You see a lot of new faces over there now."

Rimes smiled uncertainly. "You're not blowing me off, are you?"

"Yeah, but not completely." Chin squinted at him and leaned back in his chair again. "They're your best chance, regardless. They patented some new skin-graft technique about three months ago, and about a year ago, they patented a liquid bone replacement. It's not MMI, but it's advanced medical work, right? And Cathy said you mentioned cybernetics. They do that, too."

Rimes glanced at Kleigshoen and caught an impatient glare. "I'll try them. I'm also going to contact some folks back in the US, okay? Dr. Michaels."

Chin scratched his stomach slowly, looking at the two of them curiously. "Stefan Michaels? All right, yeah. I've heard about him. Practically created the latest MMI protocol single-handed. Okay. And if you come up with something, I'll work with you."

"It's a deal."

A few minutes later, Rimes had Michaels onboard with the idea and in communication with Chin. It was exactly the resolution Rimes wanted, but it was oddly unsatisfactory.

Rimes smiled at Kleigshoen and thought of asking her what irritated her so much about the idea of him connecting to Kwon's brain.

The look on her face told him not to bother.

29

---

8 March 2164. Darwin, Australia.

THEY DIDN'T SAY anything until reaching the garage.

Kleigshoen had traded the blood-soaked HuCorp in for an even smaller car, somehow managing to find something even uglier, in bright yellow.

She was rigid. Muscles stood out in her neck and shoulders. Her arms were crossed and she kept her back turned to him.

Angry. Understandable, I guess. But is she mad about the risk? Something else?

"Do you want to talk—"

"No," Kleigshoen said. Her voice was cold.

Rimes scowled as he looked the vehicle over, wondering what sort of fevered dream had been behind its design. "Was this a budget choice? I mean, it's … hideous."

"Get in."

Kleigshoen slammed her door; it made a tinny sound.

The car whined and shook as it pulled out from the dim garage into traffic. Bright sunlight quickly triggered the window tinting. In no time, the underpowered air conditioner was struggling hopelessly to keep them from boiling alive.

Kleigshoen wiped perspiration from her brow and glared at the traffic.

"Where are we going?"

Kleigshoen gave him a withering glance.

Rimes felt his temper threatening. "Look, I'm open to suggestions here. If you can think of a better idea to get what we need, I'm listening."

Another withering glance. "You know there's no other way. Not right now."

"All right. So why all the hostility?"

The car pulled off the main drag and into a small restaurant parking lot. Kleigshoen sighed and closed her eyes. With the car powered down, the interior quickly became unbearable.

"It's not just the physical risks, Jack. I don't care for ... never mind."

She climbed out and slammed her door.

Rimes pulled his legs up to his chest, pivoted in the seat, and dragged himself up and out of the car. "You've got your mission, I've got mine. It goes without saying we have different priorities."

And I can't even begin to guess what the hell your priorities are.

Kleigshoen crossed the parking lot without another word. Her shirt clung to her back. Rimes's eyes traced the curve of her spine, lingering on the small of her back. He shook away the thoughts.

One time, one error. I'm not going to make it worse.

Rimes opened the restaurant door, and the air conditioning hit him. Compared to the car's unit, it was divine.

A waitress seated the two of them in a booth at the rear. They ordered salad, iced tea, and cold soup—tofu, whey, cucumber, and curry—from the menu.

When the salads and tea arrived, Rimes dug in. He was famished, partly the result of the restoratives. Waiting around wasn't going to make Kleigshoen less angry.

Kleigshoen watched him for a moment, then turned to her own plate. She picked at it for several seconds, separating the greens from the other vegetables.

"Don't like the salad?" Rimes asked.

"It's fine." Kleigshoen shoved a forkful of greens into her mouth and chewed with her mouth open. "See?"

"I do," Rimes said. He smiled despite himself.

Might as well push her.

"We've got some time to kill ... why don't you finish telling me about T-Corp 72?"

Kleigshoen froze. She hastily finished what she was chewing and washed it down with a swig of tea. "I already told you, we were interested in the X-17."

"You said it was complicated. They were in the compound. They had the gas. You didn't tell us about it. We could've died. How much simpler could it get?"

She quickly tucked another leaf into her mouth and followed it up with a slice of carrot.

"We had you suited up in NBC gear," Kleigshoen said, finally. "We'd already run several satellite scans of the area. We knew ..."

"You knew they'd already used the X-17 when the T-Corp team didn't show up on your scans. What was the real target?"

The waitress, an elderly Chinese woman with bowlegs, brought them their soup.

Kleigshoen watched the woman slowly shuffle away. "The treatment for that condition costs about twenty-five thousand dollars. My grandmother underwent the treatment. It changed everything for her."

Rimes's brow wrinkled. "I'm happy for her."

"Your niece, Gina, she has a condition, right?"

"Cri du chat syndrome," Rimes said, annoyed. "Why?"

"You're still a sergeant. What's that pay?"

Rimes frowned. "You know damned well what it pays, Dana."

"Around twenty thousand?" She was suddenly remote, analytical.

"Around." Rimes shifted.

"Combat pay, jump qualified bonus, housing, subsistence ... all told, that's half again," Kleigshoen said. She tasted a spoonful of the soup. "Let's put you at thirty thousand. Not bad. You probably clear twenty-two. You spend maybe seventy-five hundred a year on rent, utilities, food. You're both going to school off and on, so probably the same amount in school bills.

That leaves you about seven, maybe eight thousand in the clear to cover whatever expenses come up: clothing, uniforms. You splurge every now and then—dinner, a movie."

"Fine," Rimes said. "You've seen my financial records. We live simple. We have a few thousand dollars saved up. I don't get your point."

"You recovered one canister from that compound, Jack. We think the genies purchased as many as a hundred. As best as we can tell, they paid five hundred thousand dollars, probably more. Five thousand each."

Rimes stared at Kleigshoen, a spoon of soup frozen halfway to his mouth. He could feel his face flushing. He set the spoon back in the bowl.

"There were twenty-five hundred canisters in the stolen shipment. The street value is in the millions of dollars. As much as we want to recover what the genies stole, we want the rest of the shipment more."

Rimes felt his stomach knotting. "What are you getting at?"

"You've given eighty-two hundred dollars to your brother in the last four years. That's a lot of money, but everything still adds up. As far as we can tell, you're clean."

Rimes clenched his fists. "Clean?"

"What do you know about the X-17 shipment heist, Jack?"

"Not much," Rimes said through clenched teeth. "I was on a Special Security Council mission when it happened. Several people killed, a shipment stolen. No one really knew what it was at the time, just some sort of weapon. We heard most of the shipment was destroyed during the heist or recovered later."

"That was a cover-up. The thieves got away with the whole thing. Twenty-one people died, mostly security personnel, former soldiers. It was a phenomenally well-planned and executed operation, and it represented a staggering breach in our security apparatus. An unprecedented breach."

Rimes looked down at his bowl. His vision was blurring, his hands shaking. "Dana ..."

"Only a few people could have pulled off something on this scale, with this level of success. It's exactly the sort of thing Commandos train for."

Rimes shook his head.

No. It's just more of your mind games.

"Did you know Captain Moltke has a gambling problem? He's more than thirty thousand dollars in the hole over the last two years. Sergeant Martinez's wife ran up nearly twenty-four thousand dollars in debt shopping. He just paid it off. Did you know that?"

Rimes stared into his soup.

"Sergeant Wolford purchased a three-thousand-dollar diamond ring for his fiancée. Sergeant Kirk, six thousand on a racing motorcycle. Corporal Stern, three thousand lost on investments. Barlowe spent five thousand dealing with his mother's addiction to bliss."

"No." Rimes looked at Kleigshoen, tears forming in his eyes. "You've got it completely wrong."

Kleigshoen reached for Rimes's hands; he pulled away. "I'm sorry, Jack. I told you it was complicated."

Rimes stood, unsteadily at first, got his balance, and walked to the door. He paused a moment outside, leaning against the splintered, peeling wall, trying to find strength.

There wasn't any to be found.

He wiped away a tear and walked for the car, finally coming to a stop at the passenger door. Heat radiated off the exterior. Rimes pressed his hand against the door handle and grimaced. He pressed his forehead against the car roof, letting the heat burn away the doubts.

She's telling the truth. I've refused to see what I found unpleasant. If I'm going to be mad at anyone, it should be me.

Rimes pulled away from the car. His skin burned where it touched the chassis.

Why am I doing this? Why is she doing this?

He looked back at the restaurant door, half-expecting Kleigshoen to charge out and ...

And what? Yell at me for living in denial? Mock me for missing obvious signs? Console me because I've had my little fantasy destroyed?

Sweat trickled down his back, and he cursed beneath his breath. He suddenly realized that, regardless of intent, Kleigshoen had probably done him a favor. If he was successful pulling memories out of Kwon's brain, he would almost certainly run into something implicating the compromised Commandos.

I'm a marked man if I succeed.

Kleigshoen opened the restaurant door and stepped into the heat. She was neither angry nor consoling as she approached, and she said nothing. Instead, she paused before opening the driver's-side door.

"Are you going to be okay?"

She seems to be asking me that a lot lately. He thought for a moment, then said, "Yeah."

"You still want to go through with this?"

Rimes closed his eyes. *No. No more closing your eyes.* He looked at her and wondered what was truly going on in her mind, if this was the last game she would play with him or if there was something more yet to be revealed.

"Yeah," he said with a sigh. "I can't turn back now."

30

8 March 2164. Darwin, Australia.

"What do you see?" Chin asked. His voice sounded like it came out of the dark clouds overhead.

Rimes looked at his hands, his pants, his shoes. "I'm me. I mean, I see me, down to the jeans and shirt and sneakers."

"And around you?"

Rimes glanced to his left, then to his right. He stood on a natural-looking rock structure rising roughly thirty meters above a dark plain. The sky was dark, formless, and inky. Lightning pulsed dimly in the far distance.

"It's dark, mostly. I'm on an outcrop above some ... plains. There's lightning way off in the distance."

"Lightning?" Kleigshoen's voice echoed off the rocks.

"Yeah. I think. It's not what I expected."

Chin grunted. "What were you expecting?"

"I don't know. Something more surreal, dream-like, indistinct?"

"Okay," Chin said. "What about now? Any difference?"

Rimes couldn't see any change. He moved down the outcrop until he had a better view. Details—boulders, rocky hills, shallow canyons—suddenly revealed themselves in the area below. Lightning flashed again, this time slightly closer.

"I can see the ground below me better now. There's more detail. The lightning is closer, coming a little more frequently."

Chin's channel clicked like he was tapping a fingernail on his desk. "I don't understand the lightning. Dr. Michaels didn't say anything about that. Can you make your way to the ground? Can you move easily?"

Rimes bent over and touched the rock beneath him. It was solid, steady, and smooth to the touch.

Colonel Weatherford had connected them with Dr. Michaels, who had set them up with software and interfaces, but Michaels had left Chin running the connections. He'd assured them Chin's experience was just as good as anything he could provide, since there was no one with practical experience.

His words hadn't improved Kleigshoen's mood.

Below him was a sheer drop, then a path. The rock, while smooth, offered handholds. He'd navigated worse in training. He squatted, then carefully began the descent to the path.

"I'm descending. It's ..."

The world shifted, twisting and collapsing with dizzying speed.

"What?" Chin asked. The clicking over his channel came quicker, as if the drumming had sped up.

"I'm ... I was climbing down to a path, then everything changed. I'm on the ground now. I don't know what happened."

Chin whistled. "One moment, right? I want to check your connections again."

Rimes could hear the sounds of cable harnesses squeaking from kilometers away, echoing through the heavens.

"Everything checks out." Chin's voice rolled like thunder. "It's just that all we see on the displays is a steep-walled canyon. You're sure it looks like an electrical storm in the distance?"

"Yeah," Rimes said. "And it's getting more intense."

"So what just happened?" Chin asked.

"I don't know," Rimes admitted. "I was climbing down. I guess I wanted it to be over. And suddenly it was, and I was on the ground."

"And now, what do you see?"

Rimes looked around him again. The outcrop was behind him, as expected, but the plains were now surrounded by shallow canyon walls. Lightning flashed again, closer.

"I'm in a canyon," Rimes said. "Not very deep."

"Okay," Chin said. "We can see where you are on the display now. These are the areas where Kwon still has functionality. Dr. Michaels says the more detailed the features, the stronger the coherence. He thinks these are Kwon's most recent memories, but he's not sure. What do the canyon walls look like?"

"They're brown with a hint of red to them." Rimes squinted at the walls. "There's an amazing amount of detail, actually. I can see ... I think that's quartz? Something's reflecting the lightning. And there are striations in the stone."

"Good." Chin paused. "Can you sense anything out of the rock itself?"

"What?" Rimes turned around in a circle with his hands out. "Like heat or something?"

"I don't know; Dr. Michaels wasn't clear," Chin said, exasperated. It sounded as though he took off his earpiece for a moment; his voice went faint. "Thoughts? How is he supposed to feel thoughts? These notes make no sense."

The world shifted again, and Rimes was standing less than a meter away from one of the canyon walls. He flung his arms out instinctively, trying to balance himself. The disorienting motion stopped as quickly as it had started.

Rimes shook his body as if that would drive off the sensation. He looked at the wall and took a cleansing breath, then placed both hands on the stone and concentrated.

Nothing happened.

But it reminded him of running for the wall with Pachnine slung over his shoulder, in Singapore.

Suddenly, he could see himself struggling to lift the big Russian up to where Tendulkar could reach his limp arm. The view spun, and he was running through the Pei Fu Complex, bleeding from a wound in his side, tasting blood—not his own. Then he was flying over the compound wall and into the forest.

He wasn't Rimes anymore.

Rimes pulled away instinctively. "I-I think I just found a memory."

Rimes's hands shook as he placed them on the canyon wall again. He thought of the motel room in Darwin, of Kwon being tranquilized. Voices came to him in darkness. Familiar accents, smells of Indian takeout, the sound of gunfire.

Rimes screamed as something shattered his neck.

Rimes heard movement, and Kleigshoen called nervously from the distance. "Jack?"

He took his hands off the wall and put one on his neck. Nothing.

"What happened?" Chin asked.

"I felt the bullet that took out his spine." Rimes's voice shook. "I'm fine. I'm moving down the wall. Are the memories sequential? Do I need to move a greater distance to find an older memory than a newer one?"

"Dr. Michaels said no one knows," Chin said.

"I've turned around a bend," Rimes said. "I'm trying again."

Rimes placed his hands on a rock. This time, however, he concentrated on nothing in particular, a point in the darkness above him. Lightning flashed as sensations struck him.

A young woman lay on a ceramic table, a bone saw, blood jetting, screaming, other women, more screaming, raw flesh in his mouth, release.

Rimes pulled back and fell to his knees, then vomited.

The sky came alive with piercing alarms and warning beeps.

"Jack!" Kleigshoen shouted.

Rimes forced himself to calm down, and the machines went silent. Someone wiped his face. It was disorienting, feeling himself in two places and yet not fully in either.

"I ... I found ... he ..." Rimes shook himself and stood. "Inhuman bastard."

Rimes concentrated on the opposite side of the canyon, and was there in a flash of lightning. He placed his hands on the stone.

He was in a bar, looking at Nakata. A small, stainless-steel table separated them. Amber alcohol danced gently in a glass near Nakata's hand.

Nakata wore stylish civilian clothes. Music played. Japanese techno. Nakata watched androgynous forms dancing, grinding against each other beneath strobing lights.

Kwon slid a card across the table. Nakata watched two forms kiss each other and took the card without acknowledging Kwon.

Kwon slipped out of the bar, stopping only long enough to pull one of the dancers after him.

Rimes pulled away.

Nakata.

He moved along the wall again, vaguely aware of a wind blowing through the canyon now. A mist began to drift down.

He somehow knew where he was supposed to place his hands next.

He—Kwon moved through a distinctly American bar—flickering beer signs, a deer head mounted on a wall, a tattered pool table. Women in skin-tight clothing watched hungrily from booths. One finally caught his eye, a dainty, young Thai in a HuCorp T-shirt. Kwon settled at a booth with the woman, not looking at the other occupants. The seats smelled unpleasantly of sweat and cigarettes.

Moltke leaned out of the shadows across from Kwon to lift a glass of beer, then gently tapped the napkin the beer had been resting on.

Kwon lifted the napkin, pulled a data card from within, wiped his face with the napkin, and slid another card into it.

The booth's other occupant pulled the napkin into the shadows for a moment before shoving it back.

Moltke returned his beer to the napkin top.

Rimes pulled his hands away from the canyon wall.

"What's happening?" Chin asked anxiously. "There's a great deal of electrical activity showing. I don't know what that means. I'm getting some very strange readings. Can I disconnect you?"

Rimes's voice sounded distant in his ears. "One more thing, and I'm done here."

Rimes moved along the wall, hands lightly brushing the stone. He could sense memories now without having to concentrate. A sensation washed over him. He planted both hands on the wall and let the sensation expand.

Kwon sat cross-legged on the floor of an apartment. His eyes were closed; his breathing was slow and measured. Somehow, he was *also* in the Sundarbans, moving through the T-Corp 72 complex.

Rimes looked around the apartment, confused. Kwon's eyes were closed, but he was able to see. Rimes/Kwon was able to see Kwon completely, as if through his own awareness.

How?

Abruptly, he was back in the canyon. Thick raindrops and ice were pounding him. Booming thunder assaulted his ears. Rimes pushed back into the memory.

Kwon moved through the complex in the Sundarbans, making his way through each of the buildings, identifying the critical computer systems that would need to be brought back online. He marked each step that would need to be taken to overcome the T-Corp security, to gain access to the data. Kwon visualized, memorized, traced and retraced, generated overlays and milestones, coded the data extract and decryption algorithms, gauged the storage required, planned for opti—

Rimes screamed as lightning flashed in the canyon. Electricity shot up his arm. His body convulsed and twisted. Current hummed across the bench surface.

Rimes tried to pull out of the connection, to abandon Kwon.

He couldn't.

There was another presence in Kwon's mind, and it wouldn't release Rimes. Lightning struck again. Rimes spasmed. Spittle rolled down his cheek. He tried to scream but failed.

Another bolt of lightning, more pain.

He slipped into oblivion.

31

9 March 2164. Darwin, Australia.

Deafening wind hurled thick, wet snow against every inch of his naked body. He shivered uncontrollably, rubbing his arms. He dropped to the ground and curled into a fetal ball to conserve his heat.

Darkness hid everything, even the ground he lay upon.

It felt like uncut stone—cold, hard, and rough against his frozen skin.

I'm going to die if I don't find cover. Clothing, shelter, heat. Especially heat.

He forced himself to stand. He staggered forward several meters, stopped. The darkness was absolute.

Maybe I'm blind? Damage from the lightning?

He extended his arms as he walked.

He had been sitting on a bench and Kwon had been lying on the examination table nearby. Chin had been placing sensors first around Kwon's head, then Rimes's.

I'm still in his head. He's dead now, and I'm still in his mind.

Rimes staggered on. "Dana!" The winds swallowed his voice.

Maybe it's not Kwon that's dead. Maybe it's me. Is this what the brain experiences when it powers down?

He'd seen research—solid science—about the brain's perception of time and how it might change with death: looping, reversing, rerunning out of sequence, losing any sense of time at all.

He ignored the cold. He'd been in Kwon's head. He'd seen Kwon's memories: disturbing, horrifying. But expected.

He'd seen something else, though. Something unexpected.

The lightning. The storm.

The presence.

It all came back to him then. Something—someone—else had been there, in Kwon's mind. He'd felt it, but too late.

This is not my body failing. I'm not here. This isn't real.

A crazy thought occurred to him, that he could will himself awake. It seemed impossibly simple.

He tried to wish himself awake.

Nothing happened.

"It is never that simple, Colonel Rimes."

The voice echoed in the void. It was everywhere. It was in everything. It was inside him. He was nothing but the voice.

"Hello?" Again, the wind swallowed his voice.

There was no way the other voice could have been heard over the wind.

It's not real. It's part of the experience, the dementia.

"I am every bit as real as you are," the voice said.

Rimes vibrated with the voice's power. He shivered from its existence. "Who are you? Where are you?"

"I am you," the voice said.

No.

"This is the moment of silence, the blade of grass standing erect before the tempest tears it from the ground by its roots," the voice said. "This is the calm before the storm."

The presence.

Memories came to him. Kwon's memories. Rimes's memories. The Sundarbans. Running through the jungle, running through the compound. Kwon had been there before.

"Kwon?"

"He is no more," the voice said. "He is a dream now, a memory inside of you. You have embraced this fate, Colonel, just as we knew you would. You cannot stop it. You can accept it, or you can die needlessly on your enemy's spear."

In the dark and cold, Rimes felt his body fail him, collapsing on the rough stone, the shivers becoming uncontrollable. Death throes.

Dream or delusion or fever, he was shutting down.

32

———————

9 March 2164. Several miles above the Pacific Ocean.

RIMES BOLTED UPRIGHT. He gasped in pain and looked around wildly. He was in the cybernetics lab. Kleigshoen held him straight on the workbench.

She blinked twice, then turned her head to the office door. "Brian!"

A moment later, Chin ran back into the room.

"They'll be here any sec—" Chin stopped. He stared at Rimes and cautiously snapped his fingers. "Is he really there?"

Rimes tried to reply, but his jaw was too sore, his thoughts too scattered. He got out a wordless mumble.

Wheels clattered and squealed in the hallway, and Chin stepped to the doorway, then waved and jumped to get someone's attention. A moment later, two young men stepped into the room. The smaller of the two stopped to kick at a black spot in the middle of a brass plate on the floor.

"He's alive, then?" asked the other man, a tall, bald bodybuilder.

"He just came around," Kleigshoen said.

"He's got motor problems," Chin said. "Can't speak, hasn't moved that arm where the current went in."

The smaller man began checking Rimes's vitals. "Heart rate's all over the place. You said he took a jolt from the machinery?"

Chin scratched his stomach. "Craziest thing. It should've hit me by all rights, right?"

The smaller man nodded at the larger one, and they lifted Rimes between them and carried him to the gurney.

"We'll get him down to the ER. It may be nothing—or it could be serious. That scorch mark on the floor's pretty nasty. You two got lucky."

Rimes watched the ceiling move overhead.

How close was I to dying? It's like Dana said, I can't go on like this forever. My luck will eventually run out.

~

"JACK? YOU OKAY?"

Rimes blinked rapidly and tried to focus. His eyes registered nothing but the darkness for a moment, then lights blinked. Numbers glowed softly.

He was in the cockpit of a private jet. Kleigshoen sat to his left. The instrument panel's soft glow highlighted her black jacket.

"Are you okay?"

"Yeah." Rimes rolled his head, trying to work a kink out of his neck. "Just a dream. Or a memory. Or a memory of a dream. One of those. I was just ... it's going to take a bit to get over the injury."

Kleigshoen squeezed his hand gently.

Searing pain shot up his arm. He gasped in surprise and pulled away. The sudden motion fired off a series of burning sensations. The gasp turned to an inhaled scream. Tears filled his eyes; he stiffened until the pain slowly subsided.

"I am *so* sorry," Kleigshoen said. "I forgot! I keep thinking you've healed up. They said—"

Rimes shook his head. "It's okay."

He forced himself to breathe slowly, evenly. He looked at his hand, saw the bandages covering the blisters where the electricity had entered. There was a much bigger bandage on his right heel, where it had exited.

"We don't have to meet with Jim until tomorrow afternoon," Kleigshoen said. "You'll have plenty of time to rest and let the restoratives do their work."

Rimes looked out the cockpit at the clouds floating far below them. So high up and washed in the moonlight, everything had a spectral, unearthly glow about it. They were still a few hours out from US airspace, but he already felt the pressure building inside.

His trust in the world he thought he'd known was obliterated. His trust in himself was no better.

"How does it work?" Rimes looked at Kleigshoen. He didn't even try to hide his anxiety. "Do they arrest Captain Moltke? Is it a court martial or does it go to civilian courts? What's he facing?"

Kleigshoen focused on the instrument panel rather than meet his eyes.

"I don't know. We need to present our findings to Jim. He's very interested in what I've sent him so far, but, bluntly, he's worried about the strength of the case. This is a major accusation. Involvement in something like this—murder, selling classified data, selling sensitive weapons—is huge. Everything has to be airtight.

"I guess there'll be a court martial. I can't see how he'd escape the death penalty ... for something like this."

Rimes slowly flexed his left hand, ignoring the pinprick sensation running through each fingertip. "What about plea bargaining or getting someone to testify in return for immunity?"

Kleigshoen shook her head. "You've got Moltke selling weapons to Kwon. We just need to figure out where and when that happened, and we can backtrack the rest." She looked at him, brow wrinkled and mouth pursed worriedly. "Were you ... were you able to remember the other person at the buy?"

"No." Rimes frowned. "And I don't think it's just a matter of remembering. I'm getting more and more details now. Things that were just a flash when I was connected to Kwon are ..."

"What?"

Lightning played across the cloud tops in the distance. Rimes remembered the canyons, the dark clouds, the electricity crawling spider-like across the stony surface, reaching for him.

"It's becoming real," he said. "They feel like my memories now. I think my brain is filling in gaps, separating things, sequencing them. There were things I didn't realize I saw, memories I had no idea were there, but they're coming together now."

Kleigshoen stared at him. "You remember the ... killings?"

Rimes nodded and looked away, ashamed. "He was a terrible person, Dana. What he did to his victims was inhuman." He clenched his hands into tight fists. "He saw us as animals. It wasn't just his genes. They cultivated it. LoDu encouraged it. All of it. The beliefs, the behavior, the ... killing."

Kleigshoen watched the clouds beneath them. "What about Nakata?"

"Colonel Weatherford personally knows the Special Security Council military liaison. After that, it's up to the Japanese to decide how they deal with him. But the Special Security Council won't select him for missions anymore, not once they know he's compromised."

"Can you identify the nightclub he was in yet? It'll just be your word against his. We need something stronger than that, Jack. This needs to be airtight, or we don't only look bad, we lose."

"I was hoping we could trade. Nakata's dirty. He nearly got my friend killed. He betrayed the trust of the Special Security Council. He's no different than Moltke," he said. "I give you Moltke, you give me Nakata."

"Jack—"

"I can sketch the Japanese symbols from the nightclub—kana, kanji, whatever. And the girl ... I'll never forget her face. There can't be many nightclubs with the same details—blue lights in the walls, the tables were high-grade stainless steel. Some sort of fish tank with a naked diver.

"You get the nightclub, you get Nakata at the nightclub for me. Tie him to Kwon and let him cut a deal to save his career. That's Nakata."

"Let me think about it," Kleigshoen said. "We can't risk everything over a vendetta. Keep your eye on the prize."

Rimes sighed. "Sure." He checked his earpiece's display. It was just after nine in Oklahoma. *Molly should still be up.*

"You think I might be able to call Molly?" he asked.

"Why not? You've been talking about calling her forever. I could use a minute alone."

"Thanks, Dana."

Kleigshoen exited the cockpit. Rimes listened for the toilet door shutting before synchronizing his earpiece. Several seconds passed before a noisy connection opened; another few seconds, and Molly's face came into view.

Rimes smiled. "Hi, baby."

Molly stared back coldly. "Where have you been?"

"We've been traveling." His guilt suddenly became crushing. "All over the place. It's been a real mess." He looked down as he spoke. "It's been a very ... demanding mission. I'm not cut out for this, Molly. I can't do it."

"No one said you had to, Jack." Molly looked confused. "You were meant for the military, not the ... the Bureau or whatever."

"The money is so much better, though. You'd like the way they live. Dana has such nice things—dresses, jewelry, purses. I'd like to be able to buy you things like that."

Molly pressed her lips together. "Dana who?"

Rimes stared at Molly's image for a moment. It slowly dawned on him he had never explained who he was working with. "Special Agent Kleigshoen."

"Dana Kleigshoen?"

He was on treacherous ground. "Yeah. You remember her? She was in my Ranger unit. I told you about her."

"Your old girlfriend?" Molly crossed her arms over her chest. "The really pretty one?"

"She's in the Bureau. I told you I worked with her recently."

"You didn't tell me any such thing." Molly leaned toward the console, her face seemingly millimeters from his. "What's going on, Jack?"

"You know I can't discuss the mission, Molly. Look, I'm sorry for not talking to you until now. I should be home in a couple days. I'll ask Colonel Weatherford to take me out of rotation, if possible. We'll go somewhere, visit Cleo and Alejandra, maybe visit your mother."

Molly squinted. "You disappear for a week with your old girlfriend, and you don't call me once?"

"Molly, baby—"

The connection closed abruptly. Rimes realized he'd been clenching his fists. The wound ached. He forced himself to relax and exhale deeply.

He'd felt more anxiety facing Molly than going into a live fire situation. Years of training gave him confidence he simply couldn't find in difficult situations with his own wife. He rested his head in his hands.

"You are a hard man to reach, Captain Rimes," a man's voice muttered from nearby.

Rimes spun.

A man sat in Kleigshoen's seat. He had a high forehead and dusky skin, and wore a jumpsuit, the sort that was common on orbital stations. When he spoke, his words seemed drawn out, with excessive enunciation and awkward emphasis.

"You have no reason to be alarmed. You are perfectly safe."

"Who are you?"

"You might say I am the storm, Captain." A twinkle shone in the man's odd, glistening, amber eyes. "Call me Perditori."

Rimes suddenly recognized the voice. "You were in Kwon's mind. The lightning, the presence ... that was you."

The man bowed his head slightly. "And now I am in your mind. I am very selective about which minds I use. You should be honored."

"The lightning was some sort of message? Or a seed?" Rimes guessed.

The man smiled in answer.

"You're a genie?"

"So they say. I prefer to see myself as the savior of my people, a destroyer of our enemies. Time is short. I have need of your services, Captain."

"You keep addressing me by the wrong rank. I'm a sergeant."

"Of course," Perditori said with a dismissive wave. "If you will listen for a moment, you will understand how you and I can be of assistance to each other."

"I'm listening." Rimes tried to relax.

Perditori coughed theatrically. "We share a mutual interest in T-Corp 72. While others are distracted by matters of a mundane nature, you and I both see the key to this situation as that clump of buildings nestled in that fetid swamp."

I do? But his pulse quickened.

"While I know what those buildings held, I cannot access that data.

While you have access to that data, you do not know what those buildings held. You see now the fragile balance in our relationship, and how we might pursue what is best for each of us?"

Rimes rubbed his forehead. Dealing with Perditori was taxing. "What *is* the data?"

Perditori slowly closed his eyes and gave a satisfied sigh. "It should suffice for you to know that T-Corp stole genie research from LoDu. Since LoDu and T-Corp both ended research into that line of work, we have only ADMP and EEC to carry it forward. Yet ADMP will not invest in this endeavor unless there is competition to drive them, and sadly EEC does not have access to the data or the DNA."

"You want the data taken from the compound to reach EEC?"

"Your relationship with Mr. Tymoshenko seems most fortuitous in light of this, does it not?" The smug smile returned to Perditori's face. "Nothing without a purpose ... Sergeant Rimes."

Rimes watched Perditori for several seconds. Finally, he said, "I don't have access to the data. The Bureau has it."

Perditori gave a long-suffering sigh and touched his head with his forefinger and index finger. "And now you return to the Bureau's headquarters for a debriefing. Again, fortuitous."

Rimes shifted in his seat uncomfortably. "I'm no computer expert. I could never penetrate their systems or their security."

"With my assistance, you can gain access to it easily enough." Perditori gave a melodramatic bow and rolled his hand in front of him. "The data appears to be unreadable, which it is, to a certain extent."

Rimes clenched his fists, ignoring the pain that shot up his arm. He'd let Kleigshoen talk him into thinking that it was his body that would be lacking in a fight against the genies—that the remotes would be the answer. An answer he hated.

The genie threat was more than physical.

Perditori concentrated for a moment, his face suddenly strained. "The Bureau has two of the data storage units; however, in order to decrypt the data, three data storage units must be obtained. With only two, it is incomplete, gibberish. A ruptured pattern."

"Let's assume for a moment I can get your data for you and transfer it to Tymoshenko. What's in it for me?"

"Money is not sufficient to compromise you. Would you rather have Nakata? The Bureau will not consume further resources pursuing a problem within the Special Security Council's internal operational apparatus, not unless it can be turned to their advantage."

Rimes looked up and out of the cabin, considering the offer despite himself.

Perditori pulled a handkerchief from midair and rubbed his forehead with it. "The name of the dance club you want is *Nepuchūn no fuka-sa*: Neptune's Depths. As you surmised, you have assimilated many of Kwon's memories into your own. What you touched of his is now yours. You have not yet realized the full implications of that, but once you do, you will see that we have already given you more than Nakata."

Perditori held the cloth to his mouth, breathing shallowly. His face shone with sweat. "And now I am afraid my time has run out. I will contact you again shortly before your meeting with the director. You can give me your answer then."

Perditori vanished.

Rimes blinked. The cockpit was empty except for him. Outside, the shimmering clouds rolled beneath the plane.

A moment later, Kleigshoen returned to the cabin. Her eyes were puffy. She pulled her jacket tighter around her and settled into the pilot's seat.

Saying goodbye to Metcalfe.

"How'd it go?" she asked.

Rimes rubbed at his brow. "Not well."

Kleigshoen pretended to concentrate on the control panel. "Give it some time, Jack. You knew this wasn't going to be easy."

Rimes watched Kleigshoen out of the corner of his eye. *I didn't even tell her why. What the hell does she know that she's not letting on about?*

33

10 March 2164. Washington, D.C.

EXCEPT FOR A TERMINAL that had been installed while he was gone, Rimes's office on the ninth floor of the Intelligence Bureau was just as he'd left it. He ran his hand along the terminal's smooth plastic surface for a moment, then turned to glance out the window.

He watched the people filtering out of the building, heading to the mass transit station.

How many of them even know each other? They live sealed off from each other, sealed off from anything but their own work. The important ones—like Metcalfe—work in vaults. A nobody like me gets a window. How broken is that?

Kleigshoen paced the room. She examined the walls, the chairs, then finally the window. She sighed.

She turned to glance at Rimes. "How's your hand?"

"Better." Rimes made a fist and rotated it. That was an understatement; the healing was proceeding at a staggering pace.

"And the dreams?"

He studied her for a moment. Her brow was creased. Her eyes darted. She licked her lips.

She's worried. About me? About Kwon?

He shook his head. "Nothing more, lately." There'd been no discussion of the Perditori vision, and there wouldn't be. "But I've been thinking about Kwon's memories. Dr. Michaels theorized the software sorted them chronologically. I'm not so sure."

"You said you were able to move deeper into the canyon to find older memories."

"I was," Rimes agreed. "But I also found older memories toward the canyon entry. And I found different time periods intermixed."

"So you think they were just random memories?"

"No. I think they were sorted." He worked through the thoughts as they came to him. "I think the software was weighting the memories ... I think they're what mattered most to him."

"That's pretty significant," Kleigshoen said. "You should talk to Dr. Michaels about it."

"I will. Once things ..."

A knock sounded, and Executive Assistant Director Marshall entered the room, dragging the heavy smells of cologne and alcohol with him.

Marshall smiled broadly and extended a hand. Rimes recoiled momentarily, then recovered and shook it. Marshall gave him a vigorous shake. Before it would have seemed authentic. Now it bugged Rimes.

What's wrong with me?

"Jack," Marshall said. His face assumed a sadder expression. "Dana. You have my sympathies." He took her hand, then pulled her in to give her a brief hug, then cleared his throat.

"Sorry about the wait. Good news: we wrapped the budget meeting a little earlier than expected. How about we head over to the Appalachian conference room and get this over with, so I can take you two out for a bite afterwards?"

Rimes nodded. "Works for me, sir."

"I'd like that," Kleigshoen agreed.

The Appalachian was three hallways down, across from the floor's main break room. It was everything the Fort Sill briefing rooms weren't—modern, filled with the latest gadgets, ostentatious.

Marshall helped himself to a cup of water from a side table stacked with refreshments. Kleigshoen and Rimes settled into their seats. The lights dimmed, enhancing the system displays that hovered over the table.

Marshall settled at the head of the table. "Okay, Dana, let's see what you've got."

Kleigshoen gave Marshall one of her flirtatious smiles and curled her hair back over her ears. She scrolled through the opening text. "You've seen our preliminary findings. What we've done here is to, as Brent would say—" She coughed, her voice tight. "Excuse me. We've connected the dots. This all began with the X-17 heist. We've identified five primary suspects in that operation based on means, motive, and opportunity. Captain Anthony Moltke, Sergeant First Class Edward Martinez, Sergeant Lewis Wolford, Sergeant Peter Kirk, and Corporal Jacob Stern. Each had a history of debts, mostly through gambling. A sixth potential suspect is Corporal Ladell Barlowe. He's also carrying a heavy debt load after getting his mother through rehab."

Marshall winked at Rimes and gave his most engaging smile. "I'm sure Dana's told you already we ran you through the same screening as the others. We had to be sure we could trust you."

Rimes gave a quick nod, then focused on the presentation as images of his friends—his brothers—materialized above him. He remembered his time training under Martinez, the missions with Wolford.

He'd always considered them good men, people he could trust with his life. To see them presented as corrupt, murdering mercenaries—regardless of how accurate it was—hurt.

"Of the suspects listed, only Captain Moltke, Sergeant Martinez, and Corporal Barlowe survived the mission to T-Corp 72," Kleigshoen said. "Thanks to the data we were able to recover from Kwon Myung-bak, we have enough evidence to connect Captain Moltke to Kwon."

Marshall held up a finger. "Help me out with this piece. What sort of evidence?"

"We sent messages—" Kleigshoen began.

"They were intriguing," Marshall admitted, stroking his chin. "But I can't justify a commitment based off them. You've got Moltke meeting Kwon in a bar. You can't place the bar, but you've provided several sketches and notes ... I mean, what, render an image and push it out to every police precinct and sheriff's office and hope someone can identify it? Ask them to visit every bar in their jurisdiction to see if it has a spot in it like what you saw?" Marshall looked from Kleigshoen to Rimes.

"We're working on it," Kleigshoen growled and flashed Rimes an impatient glare.

"The memories are getting easier to decipher," Rimes said. "I can recall a little more each time I think about them. Kwon's senses were engineered to be able to pick up so much detail."

"You think you could locate this bar? Eventually?" Marshall asked.

"Yes, sir," Rimes said. "I can run through missing persons files. I was planning to start that tonight."

"Missing persons?"

Rimes looked at Kleigshoen for support. She nodded.

"Kwon was a serial killer," Rimes explained. "He killed at least a dozen women. The woman he picked up at this bar was Thai, between one-hundred-fifty and one-hundred-sixty-three centimeters, forty-four to forty-seven kilograms, twenty to twenty-five years old. Dark brown hair, brown eyes, a slight scar on her chin, dental work on her incisors."

Marshall's brow wrinkled. He smiled worriedly, looking first at Rimes, then at Kleigshoen. "You could tell all that from Kwon's memories?"

"No, sir," Rimes admitted. "But Kwon could. I'm still struggling with it all."

Marshall sipped at his water while he considered Rimes's words. Finally, he set the cup down and clucked his tongue softly. "Okay, I'll tell you what we're going to do. Start your research on the missing persons data tonight. Since you're searching for a victim, not a suspect, I have authority to approve using what might otherwise be deemed profiling parameters. But I want the two of you on the first plane to Fort Sill tomorrow.

"You have one week to get me something."

Kleigshoen powered down the display, then sighed as if centering herself. "Thank you, Jim."

Marshall paused for a moment, then stood. Kleigshoen and Rimes stood as well to follow him out, but he stopped at the door and leaned against the frame. He turned. All pretense at friendliness and cordiality were gone. He drummed his fingers against the wood.

"Honestly, I was hoping for more. I think a celebration dinner would be premature at this point. Let's meet again when you've got something I can work with. You get me something actionable, I'll make it special for you."

Rimes looked down. His hands shook with anger. Marshall's attitude was misplaced, misguided. He left; Rimes looked up and caught Kleigshoen's eye. Her face was tight with emotion, but he couldn't tell for sure what it was.

One week. One week to take down my brothers and friends. One week to betray the men who are my family.

34

———

10 March 2164. Washington, D.C.

RIMES STARED at the display terminal. He rubbed his face to work away the fatigue that ate at him, slowing his reaction time and eroding his focus. He shifted in his chair, starting when his knees brushed against Kleigshoen's on the opposite side of the desk.

He'd been so caught up in his research, he'd forgotten she was even there.

She looked up from her own research, distracted. "You okay?"

Rimes stood, then stretched. His joints popped loudly, but along with the fatigue came the reassuring tingling of the accelerants and stem cell treatment at work. His foot was no longer sore, merely tender; the wound on his hand nothing but a faint scar. The nerve damage was well on its way to complete recovery.

"Yeah. I'm just tired. No surprise—jet lag, the healing accelerants ... it always takes a toll."

Kleigshoen bit her lip. "I warned you we'd need a stronger case for Jim to buy into it."

Rimes looked out the office window.

Kleigshoen sighed quietly. "I can work in the vault, if I'm bugging you?"

Rimes turned and shook his head. He was tense, anxious, ready to act, but there was no target, no clear objective. "It's not you. It's this whole situation: the way he blew us off, the search, the unknown."

Kleigshoen defocused momentarily. She shifted in her chair, a more comfortable and less worn one she'd wheeled in from a nearby conference room. "Don't let Jim's behavior bother you. He's under a lot of pressure on this. There's nothing personal in it. He can't commit resources on what we've provided so far. He's already spent so much, and all he has to show for it is ..." She stopped and touched a knuckle to her lips.

"I'm sorry, Dana. I can't imagine what it must be like losing a friend and a mentor." *Yet here I am, cooperating with you to send Martinez to his death.*

"You work alone a lot of the time," Kleigshoen said after a moment. "Brent was my partner for ... well, it felt like forever. I can't even imagine working alone now."

Rimes settled back into his seat and stared at the display.

"Any luck with the search?" she asked.

"Nearly two hundred hits so far. All dead ends."

The returns on what he'd considered narrow criteria had nauseated him. So many missing women. The implications for his own children were unsettling. And the search engine was still processing images based on his criteria, and wouldn't be complete for another forty minutes.

"I'm going to get a few things from my station in the vault," Kleigshoen said. "I—we'll need to shut things down in a little bit. Our flight leaves at ten-fifteen. I don't know about you, but I need some sleep."

Rimes grunted agreement.

She exited the office. His eyes lingered on her legs for just a moment.

With some effort, he closed his eyes and thought of Molly and the baby. She'd said from the start she'd wanted children and that she would carry them to term rather than use any of the popular proxy methods. It was a huge sacrifice. He suddenly felt selfish and petty.

An intense heat burned within him—but was it for Molly and the baby, or Kleigshoen?

Someone coughed lightly, and Rimes's eyes popped open.

"Your opportunity for coming to some kind of decision is now." Perditori sat draped over Kleigshoen's chair, wearing the same jumpsuit.

Rimes slowly massaged his brow. "You're late."

"I was otherwise engaged." Perditori waved a hand toward the hallway behind him. "Have you decided?"

Yeah. I've decided I'm insane. Or desperate. Maybe both. Or maybe I'm not even making the decision for myself. Rimes looked at Perditori's image and saw nothing to indicate Perditori was sensing the answer. "What choice do I have? I'll go forward with it for now."

Perditori pursed his lips. "Things are already in motion, and inertia can be quite a dangerous thing. Changing your mind would not be a good idea, Captain Rimes."

"Sergeant."

Perditori waved away the correction. "The data devices are in Director Marshall's office. Be quick enough, and your partner will be none the wiser."

Rimes pushed back his chair and started walking toward the door. He could feel Perditori's eyes on him the entire time. He took several tentative steps down the hallway, broke into a run, then slowed himself to a quick walk.

Perditori trailed him soundlessly.

I'm going to stop any second now and tell him the deal is off.

"What sort of security do I have to deal with?" Rimes asked.

"Nothing to speak of," Perditori replied. "The security measures were designed to keep intruders out of the building and the offices. The patrolling guard is on the floor above and will be for several minutes. You already know how to gain access to the office."

I do? How? Of course! My first meeting with Marshall.

Marshall's office door was protected by a fairly simple digital pad and card reader. Out of habit, Rimes had noted the combination when Marshall had entered it at their first meeting there. Rimes's security card information would be logged automatically, but no one should have any reason to check.

If I don't screw this up.

He swiped his card, entered the combination, and turned the knob.

The door opened. Rimes froze.

The room smelled like a lair; Marshall's musky cologne clung to everything. The office felt low, dark, and shadowed, as though a predator were waiting to jump out from behind an armchair or the desk. Digital photos hung on the wall—pictures of VIPs shaking hands with Marshall, who smiled widely, showing his teeth. Knowing what he knew of Marshall now, the pictures felt like trophies.

Bones of prey.

Rimes cautiously edged into the office.

Perditori sat on the desk with his knees crossed, then waved his hand in the air.

The bar rose off to my left. A country dance tune blared from overdriven speakers. The heat radiated from the crowd. The cologne—Marshall's cologne— drifted from the shadows to my right.

Alcohol hung heavy in the air, only overcome by the musky press of the patrons—desperate laborers and even more desperate whores—come to share company and obliterate their awareness. And through it all, the cologne—an extravagance few could afford in even moderate amounts.

Moltke shoved the napkin across the tabletop, and his partner nodded from the darkness.

"The envelope," Perditori said. "On the desk."

Rimes moved to Marshall's desk with a dreamlike awkwardness, picking up an official-looking plastic envelope. He flipped the flap up and saw two data sticks within.

Two? Barlowe said they found three sticks' worth of data.

He emptied the data sticks into his hand and set the envelope back where he'd found it.

"Now go," Perditori said.

Rimes jogged back to his office, Perditori effortlessly following.

Rimes began the data transfer process. Evidence of the transfer would be easy enough to clean up once the data was downloaded—but speeding up the transfer was out of his league.

It dragged on.

When the second data stick finally completed copying, Rimes popped it out of the terminal's base. Someone was coming down the hall: he shoved the data sticks into his pants pocket, turned off his terminal, and started to pace—then quickly sat on the desk corner and tried to look relaxed. Perditori vanished.

Kleigshoen stepped into the room. "Jack! I expected to find you still staring at the display. Did you find something?"

Rimes shook his head, hoping to explain away the anxiety he couldn't hope to hide. "I'm worried. What if I can't find her? What if my understanding of Kwon's memories is wrong?"

"It's not the end of the world. We'll find something to nail these guys with," Kleigshoen said, placing a comforting hand on his shoulder. She pulled it away after an awkward pause. "They're still sitting on a large cache of X-17. Maybe we should focus on that? How many places could they store it without raising suspicions?"

Despite all the distractions, Rimes found himself intrigued by Kleigshoen's idea. "Did the Bureau run a search of stolen or rented vehicles that could have transported the canisters? A helicopter would have a fairly limited range without refueling, and I'd imagine that's a lot easier to track than cargo trucks."

Kleigshoen seemed to center herself and shook her head. "Our best guess was that they used both—a cargo helicopter for the initial extraction and some trucks to get the load to its final destination. At one point, we were confident we'd identified the helicopter they used; unfortunately, by the time we finally located it, it had been destroyed. All that remained was trace evidence inside the cargo bay, nothing likely to withstand a good defense challenge. Even if it were allowed in trial, it would be circumstantial at best, and it doesn't get us any closer to where they would store it."

Rimes's excitement drained away. "So everything really depends on this search."

Kleigshoen settled into her chair and brought up her display. "We need to catch a break."

He stretched. "Speaking of a break, I'm going to take a quick walk, see if I can clear my mind."

Kleigshoen nodded and went back to her work. Rimes stepped out of the office. He walked several steps before turning back to see if Kleigshoen had followed. When he saw he was alone, he sneaked back to Marshall's office, replaced the data sticks, and exited, closing the door behind him.

Getting the data out of the Bureau's private Grid would be the next challenge. He regretted not having simply swapped out data sticks, but then he'd still have to get them out of the building somehow. With the data stored in his personal workspace, he would at least have access to it so long as he could access the Bureau's Grid.

He needed to somehow get the data onto the Grid. And an idea of how he might pull it off was forming.

Rimes returned to his office. Kleigshoen looked up from her work for a moment. He settled into his seat and looked at the terminal. "Damn."

"What?" she asked. "Is it done?"

"Almost. None of the hits match Kwon's memories. I don't understand. I was so sure."

Does she know about Marshall? Would she tell me if I asked her? Maybe just ask about any travel Marshall took around the time of the theft. I'd have to word the question just right, or it would tip her off.

The search finished. There were four last hits.

Rimes flipped through each image, staring, hoping, willing. The first woman looked nothing like Kwon's victim. The second had vaguely similar eyes, but nothing else. The third ... he enhanced the focus.

It was Kwon's victim. "It's her!"

Kleigshoen came around the desk and looked over Rimes's shoulder. "Duan Lek? She doesn't even look twenty, Jack."

"Reported missing in January," Rimes said. "She would have been just barely twenty. The photo's from her ID card, taken at eighteen. She was a little skinnier, a little more worn down by nirvana or some other stim, but that's her."

"The missing persons report was filed in Raleigh," Kleigshoen said. "Was she a resident there?"

Rimes flipped to Lek's travel records. "Immigrated with her parents at six. Moved from Los Angeles to Joliet, from Joliet to Baltimore, from Baltimore to Charlotte, then from Charlotte to Raleigh. Four years in the Raleigh area."

"Arrests?"

Rimes shook his head. Lek was the wrong type of person to get the attention of the overtaxed police force. She got high, turned tricks, probably committed small-scale theft. There was no room in the prison system for petty criminals anymore.

Kleigshoen walked back to her chair, but just stood for a moment before shutting down her display. "Let's pass it on to Marshall. He can have someone run it down. It still sounds like a long shot."

"Have you ever been to Raleigh?" Rimes asked as he powered down his terminal.

"Just for jump school. That was about eight years ago. I didn't really see much of it." Kleigshoen stretched, slowly arching her back. She gave Rimes a sleepy, lingering glance. "It's sort of pretty, I guess. What'd you think of it when you went through? The sort of place you'd like to go again?"

Rimes looked away. "Once was enough."

Rimes had relatives from the area; it was a dangerous place to grow up, with a lot of violence between locals and recent immigrants. Lek's experiences would have almost certainly been rough.

"What about Marshall?" Rimes asked. "Would he have any contacts in the area we could ask for help?"

Kleigshoen thought for a moment then shook her head. "I doubt it. He's from Delaware. I think what's left of his family is still there."

Rimes sighed.

"Let it go, Jack." Kleigshoen walked to the door and stopped, turning to give him a tired smile. "We can't do anything more with it until we get more evidence. We'll get what we need if we work together. We can do that, right?"

RIMES WOKE to the sound of his earpiece chiming, Molly's ring. He set the earpiece in his ear and accepted the call. The hotel room was dark except for a thin sliver of light sneaking through the drawn shades.

Molly's image took on a sickly glow. She looked weak and troubled. Rimes sat upright.

"Molly?" The display showed 0417.

"Jack? I'm sorry. I had a dream." Her voice was sleepy, her words slurred.

Rimes shook his head. "No, it's okay. I had to get up in a little bit to go for a run. This is all on the Bureau's dollar right now."

The urge to pull her close and hold her was maddening.

"I dreamed the baby was dead." Molly took a deep breath then wiped her eyes. Tears welled up then rolled down her cheeks. "You killed it."

"Whoa." Rimes threw up his hands and motioned for Molly to stop. "You know I'd never kill our baby."

Molly sobbed quietly for a moment. "Jack, I feel horrible. I feel fat and ugly and you disappeared for a week with that woman."

Rimes froze for a moment. "Molly, you're beautiful to me, you know that. I love you. Nothing's going to change that."

"Is she pretty?"

Rimes knew better than to lie. Molly had always been resentful of his old relationship with Kleigshoen. More than once, she'd worried aloud after a few drinks that he would leave her for his old flame.

There was no good answer to the question.

"She's still pretty, just like you."

"Did you sleep with her?"

"Molly, have you been drinking?" Rimes stood, fully awake now. He cursed inwardly. His blood was rushing, his parenting instincts fighting with his guilt.

"Did you sleep with her?"

Rimes began to pace. Molly had been in control of her drinking for nearly two years now. To lose control at such an important point in time …

"Molly, listen to me. If you've been drinking, you need to stop. Now. Alcohol isn't good for our baby."

"You slept with her. You bastard." Molly began crying again.

Rimes ran his hand over his head. "I'll be home in a few hours, Molly."

"J.C. said Marty's talking about leaving her."

Rimes massaged his forehead. "He'll never leave J.C. Molly, please. That's the alcohol talking. Don't let it. You're too smart for this."

"Are you leaving me, Jack? Is that it? Am I being punished for not being sexy enough?"

Rimes shook his head. "You know you're beautiful. You're everything I could ever want. I told you when I married you, it's forever. You know that."

She cut the connection.

Rimes tore the earpiece off and hurled it against the bed. It bounced off the bedspread, then settled in a tangle of sheets dangling over the edge of the bed.

She's going to leave me when I tell her. I know it. I deserve it. But I made the mistake. I've got to own up to it.

Martinez threatening to leave J.C. was nothing new, but the timing was terrible. Rimes kicked the air in frustration.

Why couldn't I control myself? Why did I have to create this situation? It's part of my training: control the variables, limit the risks. Do the right damn thing, Jack. Damn it!

There was no returning to sleep.

With a heavy sigh, he retrieved his earpiece, pulled on his sweats and shoes, and headed out for a run. When he hit the cold morning air, he broke into a quick jog. He pushed himself, fighting through the stiffness of his healing wounds and welcoming the pain, despite knowing it wouldn't save his marriage.

I'm going to save it, damn it. We're going to work through this together. We're going to have our family, and we're going to be happy.

Jogging in the darkness, alone, there was no one to tell him otherwise.

35

11 March 2164. Oklahoma City, Oklahoma.

IT WAS JUST after noon when Kleigshoen and Rimes stepped out of the Switzer International Airport terminal. He felt hollow, adrift, a failure. He shivered in a cool breeze's embrace as they loaded into an automated transport along with a handful of fellow travelers.

Rimes examined the other passengers from behind drooping eyelids. Three were businesspeople—an elderly woman with white curls, and dark, judging eyes; the other two younger, ruddy complected, dark-haired men bristling with energy.

The elderly woman spent several seconds looking down her nose at her fellow passengers, passing judgment with cold glances before finally sighing and settling back in her seat as the transport left the airport. She closed her eyes against the intrusion of these others and collapsed in on herself.

The taller businessman sat next to his heavily-modified consort, who was very publicly absorbed in mind-numbing celebrity news feeds. Rimes had seen the feeds before. They provided vicarious thrills for those who could afford the services.

The other businessman pretended to ignore his fussy assistant, a bronze-skinned Adonis in a tailored suit.

Rimes relaxed, distractedly enjoying the warmth of Kleigshoen's body pressed close against his by the cramped seats.

He stole a quick nap, waking minutes later at the car rental facility. Following a quick transfer, he and Kleigshoen were on the turnpike, heading south for Fort Sill.

Long-dead trees, weed-choked ponds, muddy earth—a dying world—drifted by. Even inside the car, the air smelled tired and depleted.

He found it hard to concentrate. Molly's accusation and relapse with alcohol; Perditori's cryptic manipulation; the T-Corp 72 data; the stolen X-17; the Commandos' involvement. Marshall's duplicity.

For just a moment, Rimes wanted a simpler life, a life without obligations to a still-forming family, a corrupted military, and a world poised on the brink of implosion.

Rimes closed his eyes and imagined himself and his team aboard a UH-121, coming in nap-of-earth, thick forest canopy skimming by a meter beneath them. There was a thrill in the imagined memory, a security and a sense of happiness. Imminent combat, life and death hanging in the balance. All the while, knowing each member of the unit had the other's back.

"You've been awfully quiet today," Kleigshoen said. "Is everything okay?"

"Molly," Rimes said, looking from the countryside to Kleigshoen. "We have some things we need to work out."

Sunlight and shadow battled across her face until a stretch of trees along the roadside draped her fully in shadow.

Rimes looked back at the road, empty except for a few automated transports and a luxury vehicle in the distance.

"She knows?"

Rimes sighed. "Knows? Intuits. Maybe. I don't know. She's very jealous of you. Always has been. She didn't take it well when I told her we were working together."

Kleigshoen stared straight ahead for several minutes, then said coldly, "I can drop you off at your apartment. We've got a case to focus on, Jack. I—we—don't need the distractions. There's no need for me to get involved."

Rimes shook his head. "We're already involved." He rubbed his knees, as if by working out the stiffness there he could drive away his anxiety. Finally, he stopped and simply grabbed his kneecaps. "Dana, I need to know if I can trust you."

Kleigshoen tensed. "Jack, what happened between us was just for fun. How you handle it with Molly is your business."

"That's not what I meant," Rimes said, stung by her dismissive response. *She hasn't changed.*

Kleigshoen glared at him. "What is it, then?"

Rimes wrestled with the idea of lying, testing Kleigshoen somehow. No easy test or lie came to him. It simply wasn't in his nature.

"How much do you trust Marshall?"

"Trust him?" Kleigshoen's brow wrinkled. "In what way?"

"This X-17 investigation, for instance. How did you and Brent end up involved with that?"

"I told you. Brent was on the fast track. This was a high-profile case. Jim was under a lot of pressure. Wrap the case, and it was a big feather in all our caps. Everyone knows Director Vaughn plans to retire after the next administration. Jim has the inside track to replace Vaughn, and then Jim would've filled his old position by appointing Brent. For leading such a sensitive investigation."

Rimes rubbed his face in frustration. "Why did you recruit me?"

She hesitated, closing her eyes and pinching the tip of her nose. "We needed someone inside your unit who wasn't compromised. Add to that your experience in Singapore and on the Sundarbans mission, and it was a perfect fit."

Rimes thought for a moment. "So how did you know it was my unit?"

Kleigshoen sighed heavily and rolled her eyes. "When Jim got the case, he called in his top analysts. The first thing they did was assess all the available intel. The second thing they did was posit potential actors. We looked at elite units worldwide—military, metacorp, mercenary, even intelligence operators. Every lead we chased down fell apart over the course of several weeks, except for one."

Rimes looked at her face, saw what he needed to see there: acknowledgment of the pain she'd inflicted and of the situation's seriousness.

It's not something petty or spiteful for her. It's real.

"So the evidence pointed to an inside job. Where could Moltke have gotten the information he needed to pull off an inside job? He's a Commando. *I'd* never heard of X-17 before word spread about the theft. None of us had."

Kleigshoen bit her lip.

"Bio and chemical weapons are illegal," Rimes said. "X-17 never should have been developed."

Kleigshoen said quickly, "It was meant to be a deterrent ... a deterrent needs to be an effective weapon, Jack. It needs to intimidate enemies. X-17 kills quickly, without leaving a trace. It breaks down quickly, so it's not generally effective over large, open areas. Wind, rain—they'd render it useless fairly quickly. That means it wouldn't be ideal for most battlefields."

"So what's it intended for? Assassination?"

"No one really knows," Kleigshoen said. Her brow wrinkled. She started to speak, then hesitated. "It's the craziest thing, if you think about it. The research was authorized nearly thirty years ago. Jim had access to the historical records, but we didn't have the need to know. Given the way it works, though, I'd say it was for assassination, extortion, close-quarters urban operations. *Maybe* limited actions. When you think about it, it's very much a weapon of modern warfare in that sense, isn't it?"

"Yes." Rimes considered the information in silence. He looked out the window, watched the devastated countryside roll by.

Marshall's involvement made less sense in light of what he now knew. Then again, the very existence of X-17 itself didn't really follow any sort of military logic.

Thirty years ago, the last vestiges of religious extremism fueled many of the world's conflicts. But now, with most of the world living in poverty, business being shipped off-planet, and the last petroleum deposits long tapped out, the extremist movements that would have made the weapon relevant had already lost most of their momentum.

Kleigshoen whispered, "Jack, why did you ask whether I trust Jim?"

Rimes watched for Kleigshoen's reaction carefully. "He was at the bar with Moltke and Kwon."

He tried not to allow vindictiveness to influence his perceptions. She'd hurt him with her revelations about his unit's involvement, and her coldness toward the damage she'd done to his marriage. He needed to be sure what he saw from her was authentic, and not what he almost wanted—expected—to see.

Kleigshoen stared at the road intently for a long, quiet stretch, her knuckles whitening on her lap.

Finally, she wiped her eyes and turned back to him.

"Brent didn't like the way Jim was handling the case. I thought—he was being overly ambitious, playing the angles, looking at how he could leapfrog Jim."

Rimes sat up straighter. "How did he think Jim was handling it wrong?"

"At first, Jim wanted us to focus only on the metacorporations. He said ADMP might be behind the theft, because they'd purchased one of the companies that had done the early research. Then the analysts showed ADMP hadn't had any resources in the area during the theft, and he had to back down. And he resisted considering military units almost to the end, giving the exact reason you did: they wouldn't have had access to the data.

"Once we locked on to your unit, Jim tried to give the case to a couple of rookies. He said their youth and inexperience would actually be an advantage in a case like this ... they'd be able to think outside of the box easier.

"Brent ... I guess you could say he sort of threatened Jim indirectly. He pulled Jim aside and told him he was putting his career at risk. If the rookies failed, there would be a lot of questioning about Jim's judgment."

Rimes kept watching her eyes. "Did you ever suspect Marshall was behind this?"

"Behind the theft?" Kleigshoen shook her head. "I thought Brent was just being greedy, trying to get us assigned to the investigation instead of the two rookies. It was our work that identified Moltke as a prime suspect. We were all set for credit. But ... it makes sense. I feel like I failed Brent by not supporting him when he questioned Jim. I ... challenged Brent's judgment."

"Does Jim know you challenged Brent?"

Kleigshoen nodded. "Jim asked me to be sure Brent was clear there were no hard feelings. They'd been friends for years. Jim mentored Brent."

They rode in silence the remainder of the way. A steady, sand-laden wind had kicked up, impairing visibility. The car pulled into the apartment complex's parking lot and stopped outside Rimes's apartment building.

"What time should I pick you up tomorrow?" she asked.

Rimes didn't answer. His eyes were locked on a barely visible highway patrol cruiser parked at the end of the row.

He could see the two patrolmen inside tracking the rental vehicle with their gaze.

Then the cruiser started to roll slowly toward them.

36

11 March 2164. Oklahoma City, Oklahoma.

His apartment building seemed miles away; the steps to his apartment seemed to stretch up forever.

"Stay here." He climbed out of the car. The dirt-laden wind knocked him off-balance. He took a step to recover.

The cruiser, an older, heavy, blocky EEC model that he hadn't seen outside Europe lately, came to a stop five meters away. He could see the two patrolmen both staring at him. He looked up the stairs again, then back at the patrolmen. The patrolmen stepped out of the vehicle, the wind nearly tearing off their brown campaign hats. Rimes's stomach flipped.

"Jack Rimes?" The driver shouted over the wind.

"Is everything okay, Officer?" Rimes couldn't stop looking up the stairs.

"We just need to talk to you, Mister Rimes. Would you mind answering a few questions?" the second patrolman asked. He was big, his voice deep, but it barely carried in the wind.

"Is my wife okay?" Rimes had to keep from charging up the stairs.

"Everything's fine, Mr. Rimes," the driver shouted. "It's about the altercation you were in at the Oklahoma City Bus Terminal recently. We just need some additional information."

Rimes relaxed. "I've been out of town for a while, so when I saw your car, I started to worry. About my wife."

"No problem, Mr. Rimes."

The taller man looked past Rimes at the rental car. "You can tell her everything's fine. This shouldn't take long."

"Right." Rimes walked back to the car, shading his face from the wind. He opened the passenger door enough to poke his head in and tossed his travel bag on the floor. "Something's up."

"What?" Kleigshoen looked past him.

"I'll explain in a minute. Just be ready."

Rimes walked back toward the cruiser, still shielding his face from the wind. He smiled at the second patrolman, who was getting into the car. "Looks like we brought this weather in from Virginia. Sorry about that."

The big man nodded cordially and waved toward the rear door, then turned toward his own door. The wind caught his hat, lifting it off his head. Instinctively, he reached up to grab it.

Rimes pivoted on his right leg and kicked the big man's exposed back with as much force as possible. That drew a gasp, then the man staggered forward into his open door, losing his hat. He recovered and turned. Rimes closed, ducked beneath a too-slow swing, and drove an elbow into the man's solar plexus before dancing back.

The big man desperately clutched at Rimes; he drove a knee into the man's groin and a quick backhand into his throat. Another strike to the jaw, and the big man dropped, gagging.

A gunshot rang out, and Rimes flinched. He dropped to the ground, grabbed the fallen man's gun, then fired off several shots beneath the car at the driver's shins. The driver screamed and fell to ground.

Rimes pistol-whipped the big man, then ran around the car to kick the driver full in the face. A second kick, and the driver was out.

"Jack!"

Rimes pulled the driver's cuffs from his belt and turned him over, cuffing his arms behind his back. The driver's gun and spare magazines were next. Rimes stuffed them into his pants. The wallet was last, tucked into a front pocket.

Rimes returned to the big patrolman, punched him again, and cuffed him as well.

Kleigshoen fought through the wind and stopped a few meters short of Rimes. "Have you gone mad?"

Rimes climbed in through the cruiser's passenger door, stretched across the driver's seat, and popped open the trunk to let the real patrolman out. He jogged back around, then pulled up short.

Empty. Where's the real patrolman?

"Do you even realize what you've done? You've just assaulted two policemen," Kleigshoen shouted.

"I told you, they're not cops," Rimes shouted back.

He checked the driver's identification. His stomach flipped. It looked legitimate at first glance. Rimes sat back on his heels and blinked dirt out of his eyes.

No. I can't be imagining this. I know I'm right.

"Let me call Jim. We can get in contact with their chief or commissioner or whatever. We can explain how this happened. You've been under a lot of stress, you felt threatened ..."

"When was the last time you saw police riding in pairs?"

Kleigshoen groaned. "Jack, did you ever think they might consider you dangerous?" She pointed at the bloodied driver for emphasis.

"They came driving toward us before I even got out of the car."

Kleigshoen rubbed her temples. "I can't believe you'd assault police on something that flimsy. They could have come by here, talked to Molly, and simply been waiting for you. We were in a rental car right outside your apartment building. How often does that happen?"

Rimes pocketed the driver's identification and walked over to the other patrolman. "How did they know you were in the car?"

"What?"

"This guy told me to tell you to drive on. He specifically said 'her.' He couldn't possibly have seen you were a female through the sand, not at that distance."

Rimes searched for the big man's identification as he talked. It looked as legitimate as the driver's. He muttered a curse.

"If they talked to Molly, don't you think she would've said I'd be with you?"

Rimes stood. He turned his head and squinted against an intense blast of wind. "Fine. But that still leaves one problem."

It was the wrong car. They don't drive EEC. They drive HuCorp single-seat cruisers.

He slammed the passenger door shut. The edge of the state patrol decal was loose.

"What?"

"There's no way the highway patrol would get involved with a case involving a bus station in town. It'd be city cops."

"Well, they're involved now," Kleigshoen said. "Either way, someone is going to call those gunshots in."

Rimes handed the identification cards to Kleigshoen and took the big patrolman's spare magazines. "I'm going to get Molly. Get ready to get out of here."

"Jack, you need to think this through. Running won't—"

Rimes thrust his jaw forward. "Check the IB database. If you can confirm those are legitimate highway patrolmen, I'll turn myself in."

Kleigshoen stomped back to the car. Rimes hefted the patrolmen into their car, locked the doors, and closed them. His heart raced as he ran up to his apartment and let himself in.

It was deathly quiet and dark inside.

"Molly?"

Molly staggered out of the bedroom. She looked ill. "Jack?"

Rimes ran to Molly and held her. "I need you to pack a bag, baby." She had vomit on her breath.

"I threw it up."

He held her tighter. "We'll talk. But now … just get dressed. I'll pack."

Jack walked to the bedroom, covering his face against the smell. He stripped the vomit-matted sheets off the bed, bundled them up, and tossed them into the washing machine. The machine kicked on, immediately monopolizing the hot water pressure. Molly squealed in shock.

A few seconds digging around in the closet, and he had Molly's travel bag. He focused on functional clothing rather than anything fancy. He wasn't sure where they'd go, but he wasn't figuring on a four star hotel.

As he detached the toiletry bag from the travel bag interior, his earpiece chimed. Rimes settled it into his ear and walked into the bathroom. Molly was leaning into the shower spray, letting the water wash over her. He quickly packed her toothbrush and toothpaste.

"Jack, you were right," Kleigshoen whispered. She was barely audible over the shower. "They're criminals."

"We'll be down in less than five minutes."

Kleigshoen went silent for a moment. "What do we do?"

"We have to assume Marshall thinks I know he's behind this. I shouldn't have let on about Kwon's memories. I just didn't know. You're committed now, whether you wanted to be or not. I'm sorry."

"We'll have to move fast. We can transfer some credit into cash cards, but only so much. They flag anything above $2,500."

Rimes heard the shower shut off. "Three more minutes." He ended the call.

"Was that her?" Molly asked. She was leaning out of the bathroom door, naked, dripping, a towel in her hand.

"Yes." He didn't know what to say to make it any better. "She's downstairs waiting on us. Please hurry, Baby. We're in danger."

Molly blinked. "I'll get dressed."

As they descended the stairs, Molly's eyes locked on the cruiser. "Jack? The cops—"

"Those aren't the cops, baby," Rimes said.

By the time they exited the parking lot, he had a plan.

37

13 March 2164. Helena, Oklahoma.

RIMES JERKED awake from a troubled nap. The heavens burned as the sun disappeared on the western horizon. Wind whistled through the watchtower's shattered glass, carrying with it the smell of approaching rain.

He shifted on the sleeping bag, listening. His earpiece chimed.

It was nearly six.

He scanned Third Street with his binoculars. They were crude and simple but functional. They were also all he could afford.

At first, the street looked empty, just another stretch of broken pavement in another abandoned town. Then he saw it: a mini-car, a rusted out HuCorp two-seater.

He focused on the car's grime-streaked window and sighed. *Better late than never.*

Rimes scanned the rest of the town; there was no movement. He opened the door to the stairwell, listened for a moment, then jogged down.

Halfway to the bottom, he pulled an ancient walkie-talkie from his pants pocket. "He'll be here in a couple minutes."

The walkie-talkie hissed as Kleigshoen answered. "Ready."

Rimes waited a moment at the bottom of the tower. "Molly?"

"I heard you. I'm going. Um, ready."

Rimes jogged in a half-crouch toward the entry gate, alternating between quick jumps and rapid jukes over patches of grass and lengths of weed-covered, cracked cement.

Aside from a few determined rodents, the James Crabtree Correctional Center had been abandoned for decades. It had been a state-run, low-security facility. Corporate-run prisons built for truly dangerous criminals rendered it obsolete. Its shutdown marked the beginning of the end for Helena.

Rimes scanned the compound interior. Long shadows draped the facility's sagging cement structures.

Nothing moved.

An iron beam wedged the rusted gate shut. Rimes hid behind a pillar until he heard the mini-car approach, then stepped out of the shadows and waited for it to brake.

Martinez stared at him from the driver's seat with J.C. next to him, anxiously twisting her hands together. They were in jeans and flannel shirts and appeared unarmed.

Martinez lowered his window and stuck his head out slowly. He scanned the gate and the prison grounds beyond. "Open it up, Jack."

Rimes kicked the beam from the gate and pulled it open. The mini-car drove through, coming to a stop next to Kleigshoen's rental car in the shadow of the old administration building's lobby.

Rimes closed the gate and jogged over to meet them.

Martinez climbed out of the vehicle, his knees making an audible pop. "You're crazy. You know that, right? Calling me up at o'dark thirty to come out to the middle of nowhere." He rubbed his knees, then straightened. "Want to clue me in?"

Rimes watched the car until J.C. got out of the passenger's side, then stood next to Martinez. What was it about her that could drive a man like Martinez—an honorable, decent soldier—to turn into a traitor? She was a wisp of a woman with a mercurial nature and a love of alcohol, but she was dead serious when it came to money.

Eighteen years of bickering and near-divorce. Eighteen years of hard partying. Eighteen years of "it's never enough."

You're the one who got him in this mess, J.C.

"You should've come alone."

Martinez shrugged. "I don't like going anywhere without J.C. anymore. Now what's up?"

"Tell me about the X-17."

Martinez looked at J.C. sheepishly. "So that's it, huh? You want in on the money, too?"

"You know me better than that. I just want to know what happened."

"What do you think happened? Moltke came to me with a proposition. We needed the money. This was worth more than any of us could make in a lifetime."

Rimes shook his head.

Martinez shrugged. "Same job, better pay, Jack."

"That's not going to wor—"

J.C.'s clenched her little fists tight at her sides. "He's taken bullets for this country. He's nearly deaf in his right ear. That knee of his is never going to be right. And what's he get for all that? Two hundred dollars a month until he turns seventy? That's bullshit, and you know it. He can't take care of me on that kind of money. He can't even take care of himself! At least he did something about it, unlike you! What kind of husband are you?"

Martinez grabbed J.C. around the waist and gently pulled her to his side, smiling at her. "She's got it right. We'll be broken men when we leave the service. If we even live to. You've got a kid on the way. How do you plan to feed three mouths on what you make?"

"We took an oath." Rimes glared at J.C. *She's twisting things, confusing him.*

"Sure we did. And now that you know about the X-17, that oath's still applicable? That stuff was cooked up by the military and intelligence communities. It was put together so we could wipe out enemies, foreign and domestic. You understand what I'm saying?"

"No, and I don't think I care." Rimes locked eyes with Martinez.

"Listen," Martinez raised his hands, palms open. "X-17 is the perfect weapon for a coup. You put the right people in the right place, and you could wipe out every single politician in the capital. No trace of anything. They authorized making this stuff after all the program cuts, and they buried it under so many layers of security, no one really knew about it until it was finally done."

"They who?" Rimes said.

"Does it matter? Generals, intelligence directors, unelected leaders. I'm no radical, Jack, but this goes against everything we were sworn to protect."

Rimes sighed. "It's too late to play the patriot."

"I'm not," Martinez said. "But you need to step off that high ground you think you're standing on and see it for what it is. This was an illegal weapons program being run by a bunch of power-hungry megalomaniacs. Making a little bit of money off it, taking away from their stockpile ... what's wrong with that?"

"What about those Americans you killed to get to it? You see anything wrong with that?" Rimes asked. "And your friends are trying to kill me. I sure as hell have a problem with that."

"No one needs to kill anyone," Martinez said, waving Rimes down. "Let me talk to Moltke. He wanted to recruit you from the start, but I told him no. He thinks you're an ace, Jack. We all do."

"It's too—"

A shadow passed overhead, and Rimes instinctively flinched. A bullet ricocheted off the cement where he'd been standing.

One of the unit's stealth-modified helicopters—a UH-121—whispered past. Rimes dove to the ground, and a second shot thudded into the dirt next to his right shoulder.

"Sniper!"

Martinez ducked and ran for cover, his hand instinctively reaching for J.C. Another shot ricocheted off a cement wall. He turned as she collapsed, blood oozing from a hole in her forehead.

Rimes rolled and scrambled across the ground, sneaking into the administration building a second ahead of Martinez.

Rimes glanced back to where J.C. had been standing. She lay on the grass.

"Is she ... ?"

Martinez's face was an emotionless mask. "You have a gun?"

Rimes knew what Martinez was going through, just like when Wolford had died. They had all learned to compartmentalize, to seal themselves off from the pain of the moment. It was the only way to survive. Rimes handed Martinez one of the guns taken off the fake patrolmen. "I'm sorry."

"Not your fault." Martinez looked skyward. "They're going to have to come in on foot now. I assume you've got some sort of plan?"

Without another word, Rimes ran for the maximum-security building, taking cover wherever he could, changing his pace, zigging and zagging. Martinez followed, quickly falling back on training and habit.

They moved through the darkness of the maximum-security building's debris-cluttered stairwell. Rimes stopped occasionally to listen to their footsteps echoing off the concrete walls. When he was confident they weren't being followed, he moved again.

They were in the compound's newest and tallest building. Not only did it have the greatest structural stability, it offered the best cover—which also made it the most likely target for a helicopter landing or fast-roping assault.

At the third floor, Rimes exited the stairwell with Martinez immediately behind him.

Rimes quickly played a penlight across the room beyond, which had an unfinished sally port and a cage door a meter beyond it. Cement, short spans of rusted rebar, and rotten tarp littered the floor. A rusty acetylene torch lay abandoned in one corner, an even rustier propane tank in the opposite corner.

"Nice place you got here," Martinez said.

Rimes smiled. It was familiar, tension-defusing banter, the sort he'd missed while working with Kleigshoen and Metcalfe. He feared it might be the last time he enjoyed it with his mentor.

"You going to be okay?"

Martinez was silent a moment. "No."

Rimes slid the sally port cage doors open, then closed each behind Martinez as they went through. Two swift kicks, and the doors were jammed with small, cement wedges. Rimes carefully stretched fishing line taut through the interior door's bars, wrapping the line around the bottom bar twice.

The room had a long, rectangular walkway around the edges but was open in the center all the way to the first floor. Another walkway bisected the rectangle, connecting the two sides. The rectangle's far end opened onto a set of interior stairs. Prison cells, stripped to the cement and littered with trash, lined the left- and right-hand walls.

Rimes pointed Martinez to the left walkway. "Far stairs."

Martinez jogged ahead, cautiously checking the cells as he passed them. "Where's Molly?"

"Someplace a little safer," Rimes said. "She can fire a gun, but I want to avoid that if I can. I've made some mistakes, and right about now, I think I'd be her first target."

Martinez stopped at the interior stairs. He checked the pistol Rimes had given him and shook his head in disbelief. "It's just us? You're expecting to hold them off with a couple of ten-mil semi-automatics? How many rounds do we have?"

"Two full magazines between us, two half-empty, plus the full mag in the gun."

Martinez looked down the stairs. They led all the way to the bottom floor, except for a piece of sheet metal covering one flight halfway up. Aside from falling back into one of the cells, they would have no cover once the building was breached.

"I hope you know this looks pretty ugly," Martinez said, searching for what Rimes saw in the position. "I'm not seeing it. Walk me through."

"Two teams. First team descends from the roof and holds in the fire escape." Rimes pointed to the sally ports at the far end of the floor where they'd entered. "Second team enters through the bottom and makes its way to the stairs, here." Rimes pointed down the internal staircase. "Second team looks for shots, can't get any."

"What, are they fucking blind?" Martinez looked at his darkened surroundings again. Nothing obscured the lines of fire but handrails.

"Just a minute. They make for the stairs in a line, three-meter stagger. Base of the stairs, they tell team one to go. Team one enters the sally port while team two ascends the stairs. Fifteen men, counting Moltke. They leave one on the roof, one at the entry below. That leaves us with thirteen. Piece of cake."

"Twelve then. Moltke would never get his hands dirty, the little coward."

Martinez glared at Rimes. "I didn't come out here to get murdered. You're my friend, Jack. I love you like a brother, but this is fucking hopeless. You're cut off from exit, you're outgunned, and you've got no defensive positions to speak of. Give it up and let me talk to Moltke. We don't all need to die over this."

"You know me better than that, Marty. I don't intend to die. I think I understand Moltke well enough to pull this off." Rimes smiled wickedly. "A limited number of exits is also a limited number of entries. It's all in how you see it. You see vulnerabilities, I see choke points."

Rimes ran his light along two narrow slits chipped out of the wall. The slits stretched a meter in length up from the floor. Rimes put the light away and said, "See? Now help me get our defensive position up."

Rimes ran back to the nearest cell. He turned when Martinez hesitated for a moment. Martinez shook his head in disbelief, then followed.

Rimes lifted a rectangle of crudely stitched and duct-taped burlap that looked a few centimeters thick. Sheet metal and packed dirt showed through the corners of the burlap.

"This and those smaller ones." Rimes strained to hold the bundle upright. "It'll stop most rounds, especially if they're loaded for close assault. We set this up where we can look down on the stairs. I've got a piece of reinforced chain link to put over the top to catch grenades. Grenade hits, give the chain link a smack to bounce it off and let the plates handle the rest."

The roof groaned as something heavy settled on it.

Martinez looked up. "Okay, I'm in."

38

---

13 March 2164. Helena, Oklahoma.

THEY DRAGGED the burlap-wrapped pieces next to the slits in the wall, then Rimes pulled a pair of leather pouches from the cell.

Rimes dug a nail gun out of one of the leather pouches. He handed the other pouch to Martinez.

"So you've been busy," Martinez said.

"You know I've always dreamed of a big renovation project."

They set to work, Martinez moving quickly and efficiently despite his grief; it took less than a minute. When they were done, they had a crude, low pillbox with narrow firing holes.

"Simple but effective," Rimes said. "I hope."

"Intimate," Martinez said.

Rimes laughed. "I'll call room service."

He opened the top, and they climbed inside.

"Okay." Martinez checked his pistol again. "So we don't die immediately. They'll still shoot through your little grenade trapper."

"I hope they think as little of me as you do."

"Loo—"

The door to the first floor burst open. Two loud pops followed. Martinez and Rimes dropped flat and knocked the grenade trapper shut. Below them, explosions rocked the bottom floor, the metallic chime of flechettes echoing everywhere. The flechettes bounced off cement and iron for a long second before going quiet. The sound of running boots rolled up the stairs.

"Here they come." Martinez licked his lips. "Last chance to surrender."

Rimes's reply was lost as the fire exit door burst open. Rimes sneaked a peek; someone in a tac-vest and open-faced helmet swept a submachine gun across the interior, its laser sight tracking over the cement wall just above their position.

It was a good forty meters and dark, and the target stood behind iron bars: it would have been a tough shot for a pistol marksman under ideal conditions.

Rimes sighted and slowly squeezed the trigger.

The bullet ricocheted off a bar. Gunfire erupted from the stairwell doorway in response, hammering the wall above them. Concrete chips and powder rained down.

"What was that?" Martinez hissed.

"Bad shot."

Martinez growled something beneath his breath and peered out his firing slit again.

"They're coming up on that sheet metal. I can take a shot."

"Do it," Rimes said.

A moment later, as the lead gunman tried to sprint up the sheet metal ramp, Martinez fired. "Got him!"

A loud crash sounded.

"Down?"

Martinez risked a glance, then pulled back as bullets thudded into the concrete and sheet metal walls. "They're pulling him back. He's not a concern."

The firing stopped.

Martinez swapped out his magazine for the other full one. "It's tough to get a good shot like this."

"Wounding is just as good as a kill in this environment," Rimes said.

"We want something more serious than a stubbed toe, I'd imagine."

"Shoot off their trigger fingers, Hawkeye."

Martinez choked back a laugh.

"I'm sorry about J.C., Marty." Rimes sighed, wondering how he would feel losing Molly. *No. I couldn't deal with it. I won't let them kill her.*

Martinez said nothing for a few seconds. "They're looking at that sheet metal. Your work?"

"Yeah."

"Is it secured? One of them's pulling at the base."

"Fire a shot at him. Don't hit him, though."

"Don't hit hi—" Martinez sighed. "And I thought Moltke's tactics sucked." Martinez took a shot at the gunman.

The gunfire came again, this time sending several rounds into the sheet metal wall protecting Martinez. Martinez rubbed at a bulge in the wall where a round had nearly penetrated.

"Kicked the fucking hornet's nest with that one," Martinez said. "I think we can safely say they're not using close-assault rounds, just in case you were still—"

Another round of gunfire drowned Martinez out. More concrete chips rained down on them.

At the far end of the building, someone knocked the wedge free and slid the sally port's outer door open. One of the gunmen squat-walked toward the second door.

Rimes fired.

Once again, the gunmen returned fire. Three gunmen were advancing into the sally port behind the lead gunman. One took up position on either side of the lead gunman, and the last ducked behind him. They were preparing for a quick assault.

"Okay, they're going to make a rush," Rimes whispered. "That means they've probably figured out the basics of this defensive position."

Martinez sighed. "We're sitting ducks. I warned you."

Rimes heard the second door's concrete wedge being kicked free. The door slid. Another quick glance confirmed the four gunmen were readying to charge, with two more waiting in the stairwell doorway.

"Shit," Martinez whispered. "They're pulling the ramp away. They're going to rush us from both directions."

"Close your eyes." Rimes swapped in a full magazine as the inner sally port door slid open the last of the way. He heard the sheet metal ramp scraping on the banister below.

Explosions rocked the building from the stairs. A wave of heat jetted over the top of their pillbox, and Martinez flinched. Then two smaller explosions sounded from the sally port.

As the explosions died down, screams took their place, and Rimes opened his eyes again.

Once again, gunfire erupted from the stairwell, this time without a hint of coordination or accuracy. Rimes pulled the walkie-talkie from his pants and activated it.

"All yours."

He switched the walkie-talkie to a different frequency and activated it again. A moment later, another explosion sounded from the stairwell.

The gunfire went silent.

Rimes switched the walkie-talkie back to its regular frequency.

Martinez looked at Rimes in stunned silence. "You had this planned all along. You knew I'd bring J.C. with me."

Rimes winced. "No ... but I had to be sure all the loose ends were accounted for. I figured you'd either show up alone and try to kill me, or they'd be following you—or following her—and they'd try to kill all of us separately. You're in with dirty people, and they don't care who they have to kill to protect themselves."

The walkie-talkie came to life. Kleigshoen's voice came in clearly. "Targets down. All clear."

"Who was that?" Martinez demanded.

"Dana Kleigshoen," Rimes said.

"That sweet thing from the *Sutton*?"

Rimes nodded. "She's also a sweet marksman. She got the pilot and the two sentries, so we just need to clean up in here. You up for that?"

"Jack, what about me?" Martinez asked, his face pained. He looked at his pistol. "They'll call it treason."

Rimes watched Martinez. "I'm sorry. I was figuring you and J.C. could disappear, start a new life somewhere, maybe down in Ecuador. You still have family there, right?"

"Yeah."

"But you need to give me the X-17, Marty. And the Sundarbans data stick you kept from the Bureau. Yeah, I know about it. And I'm guessing Marshall probably suspects."

"How'd you—"

"Later," Rimes said. He popped open the grenade cover. A quick glance at the dying flames assured him the assailants in the sally port were no longer a threat.

The improvised pillbox was battered and pockmarked. Dirt was scattered everywhere. Rimes shook his head in admiration.

Martinez squatted in front of the pillbox, rubbing his hand over several holes where dirt tumbled out. "This could've gone a lot worse."

"Let's get out of here. I want to get the data stick, and you should get on the way to your new life."

Martinez stood and walked over to the railing, leaning over it with his eyes unfocused. "Without J.C., I can't see—"

Gunfire echoed loudly from the stairs below them, nearly drowning out Martinez's quiet gasp. A round struck Rimes's right shoulder; another grazed the right side of his head. He rolled away from the pillbox.

Martinez fell.

Rimes watched for a moment, unable to understand what he was seeing. His legs gave out, and his head fell against the cement floor. Waves of pain shot through his body. He couldn't focus, he couldn't think. He was vaguely aware he'd been shot and that he wanted to get his gun, but he couldn't string together the steps necessary to do that.

Footsteps echoed. Someone was slowly climbing the stairs. One moment, they seemed close, the next far away.

It required a Herculean effort, but Rimes rolled onto his side. He blinked and managed a glance at the stairs. He saw a torso, a CAWS-5, all-too-familiar gear.

Darkness and a semblance of peace washed over him, until Moltke's face resolved out of the void, hovering above him. Moltke was saying something about Martinez. Rimes tried to concentrate on Moltke's words, but the words just couldn't connect in the thunderous roar in his head.

Where's Marty? He was here. Dana? Molly?

Moltke lifted Rimes by the front of his shirt, demanding something.

Rimes's head fell back as Moltke shook him.

A knife appeared from thin air, and Moltke pressed its tip just below Rimes's right eye. Moltke spoke again, angrier, louder. Rimes sensed there was importance to the words, that it was critical he understand what was being said.

He blinked, and his eyelashes brushed the blade. Moltke said something about knowing, about the others, about pain.

There was a pop—a gunshot—and Moltke suddenly slumped. Rimes's weight pulled them over, and Moltke fell on top of Rimes, cutting his cheek with the knife.

Moltke was mercifully silent now.

Rimes tasted something terrible in his mouth. He gagged, tried to spit. Instead, he rolled to his side and vomited, somehow managing not to breathe it back in.

Darkness.

Peace.

When Rimes opened his eyes again, an angel was kneeling beside him, babbling in the same formless language Moltke had used. She was crying.

What could make an angel cry?

Molly.

He was so tired, so very tired. He slipped into the darkness.

39

18 March 2164. Fort Sill, Oklahoma.

RIMES TRIED to swallow but simply couldn't manage it. His mouth was dry and rough as sandpaper; his throat burned. He opened his eyes and instantly regretted it; it felt like he was ripping off their outer membranes.

But with some effort, he was finally able to focus.

The all-too-familiar combination of privacy screen, monitoring systems, and wheeled serving tray greeted him.

Another hospital room.

A moment passed, and the privacy screen opened. A bushy-eyebrowed young man in hospital greens stepped in.

"Welcome back to life, Sergeant Rimes," The young man leaned in close, pulled down Rimes's bottom lids, and looked into Rimes's pupils. "Your vitals're looking awfully strong for someone who took a bullet to the head. How're you feeling?"

Rimes tried to speak, felt his throat tighten up, and thought better of it. He pointed at his throat and shook his head.

A headache exploded just behind his eyes.

"Your WBC count is up. How about opening your mouth for me?" The nurse fished a penlight out of his shirt pocket and shone it into Rimes's throat. "Just a touch of strep. We'll take care o' that. You up for a visitor? We've got a standing call for when you come around."

Rimes nodded, and the headache hit him again. He hoped it was Molly.

Waking alone in the hospital had hurt him, he realized.

She's always been there when she could be before.

"Good. I'll have the desk let Colonel Weatherford know." The nurse seemed oblivious to the disappointment flashing across his patient's face as he examined the side of Rimes's head. "Try not to move too much. Although I have to admit, I've never seen someone heal so fast before, not without aggressive stem cell treatments. And you're not showing even residual indications of brain trauma. That's pretty amazing stuff."

Rimes nodded without thinking, then grimaced.

The nurse left Rimes to his thoughts, thoughts that quickly turned dark. Not only was Molly not waiting for him, he realized, but the nurse hadn't even mentioned her. Or Kleigshoen.

Suddenly, it occurred to him that he may very well be a prisoner. He had, after all, killed several men, and there was no real evidence that Moltke was a traitor.

He searched around for the bed's controller and raised the head of the bed, then pulled the serving tray over. It was all an embarrassing struggle, his limbs shaking and uncertain, but he managed to pour himself a cup of water without spilling too much. He gulped the water down, closing his eyes against the pain.

A console suspended from the ceiling caught his eye. He found the remote and powered on the display. Flipping through the dozen or so menus was slow going, but he eventually found a news feed.

Several searches through headlines and video revealed nothing worrisome—another brushfire war in Africa, another assassination in Asia, droughts across the eastern United States. He stopped at the last set of stories: more concessions from the feckless World Trade Organization to appease the metacorporations.

Heavy, deliberate footsteps approached the privacy screen. A hand pulled the screen aside.

Colonel Weatherford's face was an unreadable mask. "I understand you have a pretty bad case of strep."

Rimes whispered weakly. "Yes, sir."

"Sorry to hear that." Weatherford's gravelly voice revealed nothing. "Can't keep these damned infections under control no matter what we do."

Weatherford patted Rimes's shoulder, sending up another explosion of pain.

"I've talked to your wife and Agent Kleigshoen. I still want to get your side of the story, of course, but by all accounts, you've eliminated a serious problem. I think the government owes you a big thank you, but I don't recommend you hold your breath waiting for it."

Rimes smiled in relief.

"The timing couldn't be much worse. This X-17 thing ... it's not going to make us look good. We need to act on this quickly and aggressively. Corporal Barlowe's under arrest and cooperating so far. CID has a team working with him to recover the X-17. He doesn't know where it was stored; that died with Moltke. The bigger problem is dealing with the canisters sold to the genies."

Rimes nodded, ignoring the pain.

"We've reached out to LoDu, played on their honor and all that bullshit. This Kwon fellow was a bit of an embarrassment to them, so they're offering a little help. At the end of the day, though, it's going to come down to us. Do you have any idea where they might have stored what they bought?"

Rimes swallowed. "No, sir," he whispered. "Kwon died before I could get much out of him."

Weatherford nodded, looking into the distance. "Well, we haven't got a lot to work with, but we'll make it count." He looked down at Rimes, then patted him painfully on the shoulder again. "Martinez was a good soldier. I hope you'll be able to remember the good about him. I think we can cover up his involvement in this."

"I appreciate it, sir."

Weatherford squeezed Rimes's shoulder. Rimes clenched his teeth against the pain. "Moltke, on the other hand, was lucky he was killed. Hard to believe Martinez got off that shot. The human body is capable of amazing things. Moltke's family will get nothing. He was a disgrace to the officer corps and to his country."

He let go of Rimes's shoulder and smiled sheepishly. "Sorry about losing my temper like that. It's just I'm very disappointed. I thought I knew Moltke better than that."

Rimes took a breath. "I understand, sir."

Weatherford moved to pat Rimes's shoulder but pulled his hand away just in time. "I also wanted to assure you your opportunity for OCS is still intact. Help us wrap up the X-17 situation, and you'll be on the next bus to Fort Benning. They say you'll be up on your feet in a week, good as new. They wanted to use you as a case study. I told them no."

"Thank you, sir," Rimes said, doing his best to hide the quiver in his voice.

Weatherford started to stand up. "Let me know if you need anything."

A thought came to Rimes: Perditori's jumpsuit. His strange accent. "Sir, there is one thing. It might be nothing ... I got the sense from Kwon that they might have the X-17 in an orbital station. I didn't get any details ... it may not mean anything."

Weatherford leaned on the edge of the bed. "Any idea which one?"

Rimes shook his head. His voice was a dry rattle. "He was all-but brain dead when I connected to him. Does the name Perditori mean anything?"

Weatherford considered the name for a moment. "I can't say I've ever heard of a Perditori, but I'll pass it along." He straightened. "For now, you get some sleep. You've got a couple of young ladies very anxious to see you."

Weatherford chuckled quietly. "I remember when I was your age." He gave Rimes's shoulder another painful pat, then disappeared through the privacy screen.

Rimes managed a smile. Apparently, Molly hadn't left him, and Kleigshoen was all right. Moltke was being scapegoated.

But the fact that Barlowe was already in custody troubled Rimes.

Barlowe was a good guy. He had unparalleled computer system skills. And Rimes needed access to those if he wanted to understand what had really happened and why.

The nurse returned with a medication cup. "That was a quick visit. You'll take two of these now, two tonight with your meals. We've had a small problem in the facility with strep lately. At least it's not something lethal." He grinned, but the effect was creepy rather than reassuring.

Rimes swallowed the pills with a mighty effort. The nurse left, and Rimes turned his attention back to the news feed—and to the possibility he'd guessed right with Perditori and the X-17.

Makes sense, after all. Kwon had connections to Perditori, and Perditori looks like he lives in an orbital station. Assuming he's even real. How can I know what's real when he can affect my thoughts?

Everything about Perditori made it seem very unlikely he lived on-planet, and it seemed unlikely a connection to Kwon could be made from outside the solar system.

Rimes instinctively reached for his earpiece to do more research, and sighed when he realized it had probably been removed when they treated his head wound.

After a moment of familiarizing himself with the remote's crude interface, he opened a workspace and pulled up a search system.

He worked through the publicly available inventory of orbitals, first filtering out those that were home to the banking cartels. These were the oldest and most established orbitals, and were home to nearly two hundred thousand people. Along with the historical distance the banks maintained from the metacorporations, the idea of one suddenly accepting what would have to be a mysterious cargo simply made no sense. Next, he filtered out anything older than twenty-five years, figuring Perditori would favor more modern facilities, from the time the metacorporations first threatened to move all operations off-planet.

Thirty-four orbital stations remained.

Rimes read through the public descriptions of each one, quickly eliminating half based on size, purpose, ownership, and history. Ranking the remaining seventeen based on what seemed most important—amenities, safety, mobility, storage capacity—gave him an idea of the most likely place for Perditori to hide out.

Rimes pulled up an image of near-space to examine the top five candidates. He rotated the view, frowning. Four of the five were within two hundred kilometers of each other, and all five were associated with major, extra-solar, gateway operations, primarily shipyards.

A quick search on other commercial activity in the area made him sit upright. He fought through the pain and dizziness and refocused on the data.

Fingers shaking anxiously, he worked his way through the first several returns: EEC, HuCorp, MDC, several SunCorps subsidiaries, Virgo, Wang—

There were hundreds of billions—trillions—of dollars tied up in the shipyards, and that just in the manufacturing, refitting, repairing, and scrapping operations. Ore processing from the intra-system mining business added even more.

It was a fortune, even by metacorporation standards.

Space—the orbitals, the colonies—was open, unregulated, the wild.

Tens of thousands of engineers, scientists, and highly trained technicians lived in orbit, willingly accepting the harsh conditions and risks for a contract and the dream of eventual ascendancy to metacorporate employment. No one knew the exact situations, but there were rumors and the occasional refugees. Everything pointed to unimaginable abuses, and the dream of future employment almost always proved a lie.

Rimes copied several links to the workspace and opened a message. He struggled for several seconds to get the data into the message, then struggled more trying to remember Colonel Weatherford's communication ID. Finally, he settled on sending it to Kleigshoen. After providing a couple of thoughts about the most likely targets, he asked her to forward the information on to Weatherford, and sent the message.

With the communication away, Rimes decided to contact Molly. He suddenly felt a wave of guilt that he'd turned to work before his own wife. He'd been doing that too much of late. He consoled himself with the knowledge that lives were at stake.

It was hard to keep the message to a handful of sentences; there was a lot they needed to discuss.

Molly, I'm awake and, except for some weakness and soreness, ready to come home. If you'll have me. Everything we've ever wanted in life seems to take me away from you, but I promise I'll do everything I can to spend more time with you once this situation is resolved. I love you.

He sent the message.

He stared at the display for several seconds, hoping she might be waiting at the apartment's terminal. It was an absurd, self-absorbed thought, and Rimes chided himself for it, but he still stared at the terminal for a full minute longer.

Finally, he closed the communications utility and returned to the newsfeed.

Minutes passed with Rimes drilling down into the latest political dramas playing out across the globe and the colony worlds. As usual, most of the world's troubles boiled down to the financial ruin wrought by the most recent depression. Energy prices drove up costs and wiped out small businesses, unemployment skyrocketed, and violence inevitably crept up. People just wanted to be able to survive—food, shelter, some semblance of security.

There was so little to be had on a global scale, yet politicians failed to deliver even the simplest, most basic needs.

An hour passed, and Rimes abandoned the newsfeed, his spirits sinking. As he brought up the communication utility, he thought of what it would be like to be an officer. His pay would be more than half again what he was making, and he would be placed in the officer's retirement system. Within a few years, he'd be making twice what he was earning as a sergeant, sufficient to get a nicer apartment with a room for their child.

The display blinked. A message was waiting for him inside the communications utility. He opened it, excited.

Molly.

It was a video from Kleigshoen. She was dressed in a tight, low-cut, blue top, and her hair was down. Rimes couldn't help noticing how bright her smile was.

"Hi, Jack. I hope you're feeling better. I'm staying at the Bradford in Oklahoma City now. Marshall authorized me to work with Army CID on the Moltke case. They really need the help."

Marshall.

Either he's got one hell of a pair, or he thinks he's untouchable now that Moltke's dead.

"I went through your analysis. You did that off a station in the hospital? You really should consider IB, Jack. You'd be a great fit. Anyway, I really like what you've done. I've forwarded it on to your colonel with a few thoughts of my own."

She leaned into the camera and Rimes found himself staring at her cleavage.

"Well, I assume you're sleeping. Here's wishing a hasty recovery!"

The image froze.

Hasty recovery? That's what you had in mind when you recorded that?

Rimes gently shook his head at the message's implied intimacy. It was just the sort of thing Molly didn't need to see, but Kleigshoen had sent it anyway.

"Sergeant Rimes?"

Rimes flinched.

A plain-faced woman in hospital greens was holding the privacy screen open, looking angry. "Your wife is here."

Rimes hastily closed the video. He twisted to see beyond the woman. He could make out the slightest sliver of Molly's face. She waved at him and smiled stonily.

The woman gave him a severe look. "Five minutes."

Once the woman was gone, Molly closed the screen and stepped up to Rimes's bed. Tears were already forming in her eyes. "I didn't even realize those old messenger things worked."

"We work with what we have available." He reached for her hand, took it, squeezed it. His throat burned with each word, but he didn't care. "Will you have me back?"

Molly wiped away her tears; anger flared in her eyes. Her nails dug into his hand. "You hurt me, Jack."

He welcomed the pain. "I know."

"And I don't know if I can ever trust you fully again." The nails bit deeper.

"I understand."

"Do you? We agreed we would have a baby naturally. We agreed I would carry that baby around for nine months. I'm taking on all this risk, all this responsibility, and you what? You hop all over the globe with her?" The nails bit deeper still.

"Molly ... I'm not proud of what I did, baby. I cheated on you. I don't deserve you."

"You're damn right you don't."

She pulled her nails free and the absence of the pain felt like abandonment. He fumbled for her hand, trying to twist his fingers among hers.

"You have every right to leave."

That's it. Now she's going to go.

Molly pulled her hand away. "I thought about it."

Rimes's heart skipped a beat.

She glared at him with renewed intensity. Along with the pain she'd shown earlier, there was hatred in the glare. "I want my own career. I'm not going to be a prisoner with no future but yours."

"I'll support your career. You know that."

"You know I don't want to be a drunk."

Rimes nodded. His heart pounded in his chest. He didn't know what to think. "You won't be. We'll get it under control."

"And I don't want to raise this child on my own," Molly said.

He felt tears fill his eyes, a welcome pain and release. "It's our child. You know that."

"When this is done, we're going to talk. The problem isn't just *her* ... you can't just do this for the money. Money can't raise a baby."

Rimes shook his head.

He watched her eyes, saw the anger softening.

Outside the curtain, the nurse cleared her throat.

Molly said, "I have to go."

"Thank you, baby," Rimes said. His throat ached, but he had to finish. "I love you."

She touched his head near his wound so gently that it didn't hurt—then she was gone.

Rimes watched the privacy screen for several long seconds, hoping she might return. When it was clear she wasn't coming back, he lay back and closed his eyes, listening to the background noise.

Finally, he brought up the messenger system again and opened Kleigshoen's video. He typed in a quick reply, then deleted the video. Kleigshoen replied almost instantly, but Rimes closed the messenger system without reading it.

40

20 March 2164. Fort Sill, Oklahoma.

THE APC INTERIOR WAS CRAMPED, and the air was thick and heavy. Rain banged loudly off the roof, and kit rattled and thumped in the dim light. The team sat in two rows on drab olive seats that squeaked with each lurch and bump. Rimes wiped his brow for the millionth time since entering the vehicle.

There isn't a personnel carrier built for comfort, but I think they went out of their way to build this one like a tomb. Feels like I'm suffocating.

Rimes looked across at Pasqual, saw him licking his lips. They exchanged a quick thumbs up: a signal going back to their Ranger days.

Bhat smiled, and Orr nodded. Kleigshoen, still deep in IB data updates, sat next to Fawcett, a freckle-faced, wide-eyed transfer who had been on Martinez's team on the Sundarbans mission.

Wolford's replacement.

I don't care what you did, buddy. No one's going to replace you.

Orr went back to fidgeting with his integrated EVA suit, checking and rechecking its readouts. It was a necessary inconvenience, a complication that worried them all. They'd never done any significant training for space combat. It wasn't really in their mandate, and they were already an expensive group to fund.

Anxious or not, we're ready to launch. We're going to do this.

The engine's growl ramped up, drowning out the rain.

"You up for this, Sarge?" Pasqual shouted. "Not too pissed off they interrupted your nice hospital vacation?"

"I'm all right. I just gargled with whiskey and glass shards." Rimes actually was feeling much better, but improved or not, he was going on the mission.

Pasqual leaned forward and punched Rimes's armor. "This one's payback," he shouted.

"Hoo-ah!" the others Commandos shouted.

They'd been spared the sordid details of the X-17 theft. As far as the official story went, Moltke had betrayed his unit and his country. Anyone else caught up in the mess was just a good soldier following orders.

However, Rimes could see in Pasqual and Chung's eyes that they had suspicions.

How are they going to deal with it when the reality sets in? The moment of realization, the new perspective on old memories, the questions of what Wolford and Martinez's betrayals meant to them. There's going to be bitterness and anger. I've been there. For now, we've got our mission, a real target, a real enemy.

The time for forgiveness will come later.

The APC came to a sudden stop, shaking Rimes from his thoughts. He looked across at Kleigshoen. She was engrossed in her earpiece's display.

Come on, Dana. Stay in this.

The rear hatch dropped, revealing the tarmac. Helicopters and VTOLs crossed the distant horizon, and dark, angular, menacing shapes loomed nearby.

Orbital shuttles.

They all jogged across the tarmac, running for their shuttle. Rimes tried to get a feel for the EVA suit. It was bulky but lighter than he'd expected. The boots were the hardest to adjust to; he felt like he was running in clown shoes. Puddles reflected their approaching forms before boots shattered the images.

As they ran up the shuttle's ramp, they were joined by another team, this one run by Lopez. Lopez was angular, even taller than Rimes, and rodent-faced. Rimes had worked with him a few times in the past.

They moved single-file through the open airlock and down the aisle splitting the ship's passenger bay. The interior matched that of the APCs—dark green, dimly lit.

The soldiers exchanged nods, whispered greetings, and bumped fists. Lopez's team took the seats on the right; Rimes's team took the seats on the left. Kleigshoen hesitated a moment before settling awkwardly into a seat in Rimes's row. She shifted as if trying to find a comfortable position before taking her CAWS-5 out of its backpack brace.

Rimes watched Kleigshoen for a moment, worried. She looked up, but seemed to avoid his eyes. Rimes looked around the passenger bay, giving each Commando a quick once-over. He stopped at Lopez.

Lopez stood in front of his seat, quietly watching his team from beneath heavy black brows.

"You ready for this?" Lopez nervously bit his lower lip.

Rimes nodded. "Let's get this going." He turned to his team. "Settle in, people."

The teams secured their weapons and buckled into their harnesses, filling the bay with rattling, clanking, and a few frustrated curses. Rimes synced his earpiece with the shuttle's systems and brought up the BAS, then overlaid the unit's data. Figures flowed in from the other shuttles as the remaining teams synced up.

An inbound communication alert caught Rimes's eye. It was Weatherford. Rimes looked at Kleigshoen to see if she might be available for the call. She was again absorbed in her display. Rimes opened the channel with Weatherford.

Weatherford's face filled the display.

"Go ahead, Colonel," Rimes said.

"Sergeant Rimes, your signal is clear," Weatherford said. He looked to his right for a moment, then looked back at Rimes. "I wanted to let you know we've moved to the operations center. You're cleared to launch in ... five minutes, twelve seconds."

"Is the mission a go, sir?"

"The launch is a go," Weatherford said with an annoyed squint.

Launch, not mission. Shit.

Weatherford's annoyance manifested as a frown. "We've got Legal and Civil Affairs *en route* to Ops. General McNabb will be joining in a few minutes."

"General McNabb, sir?"

"Things went all to hell while you were heading out to your shuttle, Sergeant. The owners have denied us access to our target."

Rimes blinked. "Come again, sir?"

"Intelligence says with ninety percent certainty the Seville Jameson Group SJG-6 orbital is our target," Weatherford said. He squinted again. "Unfortunately, that doesn't mean we can secure the owners' permission to insert your unit. They've brought in their lawyers. But we're launching."

"Sir, don't they understand that this is a matter of international sec—"

"I have my doubts they care, Sergeant," Weatherford said. He looked into the distance for a moment. "But they provided us a little data to keep us occupied. SJG-6 came online three months ago. That means all the latest safety measures and monitoring systems are in place. That's going to make our job a lot easier once we get approval."

"Occupancy?"

"Just under two thousand. When we get the names, we'll work with IB to eliminate anyone unassociated with this Perditori—apparently, he's a known element there. We've already asked SJG to prepare communication channels for us to reach the occupants we clear, pending approval."

Rimes's communication display split in half. Weatherford's face filled the right half, and the pilot's face filled the left.

"If you'll check your displays, folks, you'll see a new amber timer in the bottom right corner," the pilot said cheerfully. "We're cleared for launch in three minutes, thirty seconds. If you're not strapped in, you won't be in any shape to do anything when we arrive, so get those harnesses on tight."

Rimes waited for the other sergeants to acknowledge, then did the same. He opened a channel to the other team leaders. "System checks— suit integrity, tactical overlays, the works. No one goes into this without full functionality."

As the team leaders relayed the message to their teams, Rimes passed the same on to his.

He kicked off his suit's diagnostics, then closed the pilot's channel. Weatherford's face filled most of the display again.

"Colonel, these genies are just a big bundle of hurt. Without surprise ..."

"I've made exactly that point, Sergeant. General McNabb is ... a practical soldier," Weatherford said, looking to his left. "And on that point, I need to sign off and get some visitors here spun up on our situation. We'll be in touch once you've reached your first coordinates. Enjoy the ride."

"Rimes out, sir." The display shifted, filling with the other channels that had previously automatically shrunk. All teams showed green. Rimes nodded at Lopez, trying to project confidence. Another glance down the row, and Rimes pulled on his headgear to check suit integrity.

"Same shit, different day," Lopez muttered before Rimes's helmet sealed. It was the Army's centuries-old, unofficial motto.

Rimes opened a private channel to Kleigshoen. "Put your headgear on."

Kleigshoen cast a curious glance at him from two seats down before complying. "What is it?" she asked once she had the headgear on.

"Dana, no one else needs to hear this. For this to work, you need to act like you're in charge. I'm about to pass along status to you. When I do, you'll need to acknowledge."

Kleigshoen stared at Rimes for a moment. "Jack, this is your operation. Weatherford wants you to run it. I'm okay with that."

Rimes gave an almost-imperceptible headshake. "Operations don't work that way. This is IB's mission. You're in charge; I'm your second. I'm going to bring you in on the colonel's next call. He's not used to dealing with women in his chain, so you'll need to be a little ... forceful."

Kleigshoen hesitated. "Okay, but this is a joint operation in name only. I would've been fine with any other officer taking the mission."

"Wasn't even about to happen. They were all too close to Moltke. Look, don't panic. These guys know exactly what they're doing. Your job is to provide situational awareness and general direction."

"I know what the job is," Kleigshoen said with a frosty glare.

"Good," Rimes said with the faintest of smiles. "That means you should be okay. Don't let it eat you up. It doesn't even look like we'll receive a go."

"They'll green-light this operation," Kleigshoen said.

"You sound awfully confident." The diagnostics chimed. Rimes looked at it; his EVA was ready. "Is the Bureau working an angle?"

Kleigshoen frowned. "They have to approve it. The stakes are too high to do nothing."

"Let's hope someone realizes that." Rimes removed his headgear. A final check of his harness, another nod at Lopez, and Rimes relaxed. The counter sat at two minutes, twenty-nine seconds.

41

20 March 2164. The thermosphere over the Pacific Ocean.

Somewhere in the darkness twenty kilometers out, SJG-6 floated among a pool of lights marking a dozen loosely aligned orbitals, three hundred and seventy-five kilometers above the Pacific Ocean.

No security force protected the orbitals. The only weapons available to them were small, explosives-laden satellites designed to shatter or redirect approaching astronomical objects and debris.

Yet, thanks to the fragile state of international alliances and agreements, they'd managed to hold off thirty-six of the world's deadliest soldiers.

Rimes sighed. The mission was fast approaching impossibility, assuming they even received approval. Rimes's earpiece chimed. It was Weatherford again—or, more accurately, the operations center.

Weatherford was running the show, but General McNabb was present, ready to override anything that bothered him. Rimes synced with Kleigshoen and the other non-coms, then accepted the communication. He nodded at Kleigshoen; she nodded back.

"This is Agent Kleigshoen, Colonel. Go ahead."

"Agent Kleigshoen," Weatherford said after an awkward pause. "I wanted to provide the latest update."

"Good news, Colonel?"

"No," Weatherford said, his brow wrinkling. "Not really. Things have escalated. We have the president and SecDef syncing up. They'll be on at any moment."

Rimes and Lopez exchanged a troubled glance. Rimes had never been on an operation the president was even officially aware of; most Commando operations were structured to allow some level of plausible deniability.

"SJG continues to deny us access to their systems," Weatherford said. "However, we have a few tidbits, including the fact that SJG-6 was leased in its entirety weeks before it became officially available. The transaction is a dead end, though. No cooperation from the banks."

"Can someone bring any sort of legal pressure on the banks?" Kleigshoen asked with an exasperated sigh.

"They've got the Justice Department looking into that," Weatherford said. His expression made clear that he held out no hope from such an approach.

"What about checking travel patterns?" Kleigshoen asked.

Weatherford squinted and leaned closer to the camera. "We still don't have the residents' names, Agent Kleigshoen. SJG won't budge on the confidentiality agreement they've been standing on."

"What about tracking backwards, looking at the destinations and doing some sort of check on where the arrivals are coming from?" Kleigshoen asked.

"How do you propose we do that without their names?" Weatherford asked.

"Filter out the names you can get," Kleigshoen said. "The shipyards and mining operations have contracts with us. Force them to reveal their employee and contractor data. It's either going to come back with their residence information or not. Anyone who comes back blank can be researched as a suspect."

Weatherford nodded off-camera, then squinted at Kleigshoen. "You think IB can pull something like that off?"

A picture of a mix of uniformed and civilian people appeared in the corner of Weatherford's image.

"This is General Del Toro," one of the uniformed men said. "I'm with General Shue, Admiral Fodor, and General Wendt of the Joint Chiefs, Director Vaughn of the IB, Counselor Yost, Attorney General Hadad, Defense Secretary Jordan. We're in the situation room with President Lazaro. General McNabb, we understand there's been little progress?"

McNabb, a dark-skinned man with a thin patch of salt-and-pepper hair, adjusted a pair of black plastic glasses and stood. The operations center's camera refocused to capture a wider angle. While Weatherford sported a combat uniform, McNabb wore his dress uniform. He had a reputation for political gamesmanship and drama.

McNabb coughed. "We're still on hold pending approval, General Del Toro."

A middle-aged civilian woman with red hair leaned in to whisper into President Lazaro's ear. He nodded, then looked into the camera. "General McNabb, we've been in contact with the Special Security Council. We're hoping to receive some level of support here in the next couple hours. Can you give us the most current status?"

"We have three orbital shuttles in position twenty kilometers out from the suspected orbital station, Mister President," McNabb said. He pulled his glasses off, crossed his arms, and began tapping the frames on an elbow. "Thirty-six of Colonel Weatherford's Commandos are spread across those shuttles. It's being run by Intelligence Bureau Agent Dana Kleigshoen."

Lazaro looked across at a man. "Glenn, is this your mission?"

"It's a joint mission, Mister President," the man who must be Director Vaughn said. "Agent Kleigshoen has been working closely on this mission for quite some time now."

Lazaro extended a hand as though he were giving a campaign speech. "Colonel Weatherford, are you comfortable with Agent Kleigshoen running this operation?"

Rimes glanced at Kleigshoen, who seemed impossibly serene.

"We've seen remarkable results from our joint effort with the Intelligence Bureau, Mister President," Weatherford said.

Lazaro nodded. "I agree, Colonel. If it's any help, I've asked General Del Toro to put together a force to supplement yours."

Weatherford stiffened. "Sir?"

Del Toro's face was strained. "That's right, Colonel. We're scrambling Bravo Company of the 82nd Airborne. They've been through orbital combat simulation. They should be at your position in ninety minutes."

"All due respect, sir, but we were hoping for rapid insertion, operating on speed and agility rather than firepower."

Lazaro smiled beatifically. "It was my idea, Colonel. This is Captain Singh's group; he's an extremely experienced soldier with a great deal of potential. He also has relatives in the Special Security Council apparatus."

Secretary Jordan and General Del Toro exchanged a quick, embarrassed glance.

A serious-looking man in his mid-forties stepped into the situation room; Rimes had seen him before but couldn't place him. The serious-looking man whispered to Lazaro and the woman next to him, whispering softly. Surprise played over Lazaro's face.

Lazaro focused on the camera again. "We've just received word from the Special Security Council that they'd like a bit more input on this operation."

Weatherford frowned. "Certainly, Mister President."

Lazaro folded his hands in front of him. "I understand you have a Sergeant Rimes involved?"

"He's Agent Kleigshoen's second on the mission. Sergeant Rimes, are you receiving?"

"I'm receiving, sir," Rimes confirmed.

Lazaro blinked rapidly and offered a fatuous smile. "Apparently, Sergeant Rimes, the Special Security Council places a great deal of trust in your opinion. They'd like your input. As they've requested, we're going to add them to our channel in a moment."

Rimes took in a deep breath. "Understood, sir."

The image split to display the Special Security Council gathered in their chamber at the UN building. Rimes recognized most of them; he most often dealt with military attachés, but he'd briefed the council members a few times before.

"President Lazaro, thank you," Representative Bhatia said, bowing almost imperceptibly. "The council has reviewed your request, and we have a few questions. We appreciate you making Sergeant Rimes available.

"Sergeant Rimes, is this action related to the action taken at the T-Corp facility in the Sundarbans?"

"It is," Rimes said, amazed at the relative directness of the question; Bhatia was usually diplomatic to a fault.

"You reported LoDu agent Kwon Myung-bak killed in an addendum to your Singapore operation, yet we've been told he is somehow involved in this action. Please explain."

Rimes saw only blank stares from Lazaro and Weatherford. "We determined Kwon was working in concert with several other genies. Although he was killed in Australia as I tried to take him into custody, we were able to connect him to numerous other suspects. Those suspects led us here."

"And those suspects include this 'Perditori' mentioned in the report?" Bhatia asked.

"Yes, ma'am."

Bhatia glanced at another representative. At the other representative's nod, she continued. "Sergeant Rimes, in your opinion, do your discoveries implicate the LoDu metacorporate entity in illegal activities?"

Rimes glanced over at Kleigshoen, who bit her lip and nodded.

"Among others. But the true criminals here would seem to be the genies, ma'am."

Bhatia bowed slightly again. "President Lazaro, we hope to have the Special Security Council's official position for you within the next two hours."

Official position and unofficial political pressure. We need them if we're going to get the metacorporations to budge.

The Special Security Council connection closed. Rimes watched Vaughn, Lazaro, and the woman next to him discuss something in hushed tones.

Weatherford appeared on the screen. "Mister President, I believe we have a problem."

"Go ahead, Colonel." Lazaro smiled patiently and folded his hands in his lap. He fidgeted uncertainly for a moment before settling.

"Shortly before you joined us, Agent Kleigshoen recommended a potential backdoor research method to help identify who is in the SJG-6 orbital. The Bureau has identified seventeen residents already; we're sending those records to everyone now."

Chatter flooded the line.

Rimes opened the data packet. On the sixth record, he stopped. He'd seen the man before. A moment later, he recognized another. All told, he found four men he'd seen in Mumbai and Seoul. He flagged the records and sent them to Weatherford, Kleigshoen, and the other non-coms.

Finally, Lazaro looked up and coughed. The chatter died off.

Lazaro raised a hand again, once more ready to deliver a speech. "Colonel, Director Vaughn has just shown me something troubling. Forty-six of the people from the SJG-6 are on our Genie Watch List."

Rimes cocked his head. After decades of abuse, failure, and lawsuits, most organizations had abandoned the watch list concept.

"Mister President," Weatherford said, "we're getting employment records on these genies now. None of them hold long-term contracts with any of the orbital operations. Each and every one has held a mixture of short-term positions in the shipyards—security, engineering, construction."

"I can see that," Lazaro said irritably.

They've been inside every one of the shipyard facilities. Why? It wouldn't make sense they'd need the money. Would they hide the X-17 there somehow? Do they have weapons systems installed they could use to launch it?

The situation was surreal, absurd. They were twenty klicks out from an orbital that probably held enough nerve gas to kill fifty thousand people, yet the politicians somehow saw this as an opportunity for debate. Rimes pinched himself and rolled his head, simultaneously trying to work out the nervous tension and ensure he was awake. He wanted another stim.

Kleigshoen slipped her headgear on and signaled Rimes to do the same. Over a private channel, she said, "Jack, the Special Security Council is going to approve the operation."

"What? How do you know that?"

"Does it matter?"

"Yes." Rimes glared at her. "What's going on now?"

"I ... I contacted my father."

"Does the president know?" Rimes demanded. *What were you thinking? There's going to be hell to pay.*

Kleigshoen shook her head. "What matters is that we've got clearance from the Special Security Council. Lazaro has to give us the green light."

"Okay. So we're going in." Rimes looked around at the Commandos; everyone seemed relaxed but ready. "You going to be all right?"

"Yeah." Kleigshoen smiled lopsidedly and took a deep, cleansing breath. "It felt good proving myself. I could've done without the audience."

He nodded at her. *Of course you can do it. You were a blown-out knee away from being a Commando.*

In the situation room, Lazaro had stood and was pacing around the room's cramped confines. Rimes switched his audio back to the general conference.

"What the hell do you mean there's no one aboard?" Lazaro shouted. "Why would SJG refuse to allow us to board an empty orbital station?"

McNabb slowly spun his glasses in his hand. "President Lazaro. We're receiving a communiqué over emergency channels. The shipyards are reporting an attack of some sort. Details are sketchy, but what got out would seem to point to casualties. Quite a few casualties. They're speculating it's something in the air, or a failure of the ventilation system."

"X-17," Rimes said. *The shipyards? Their target was the shipyards? Why?*

Lazaro froze, glaring at the camera to see who had spoken. Rimes quickly muted his mike.

Weatherford said, "Mister President, I believe Sergeant Rimes is correct."

Admiral Fodor turned to Lazaro. "Mister President, we have billions tied up in those shipyards. Our largest ships are under construction. The *Powell's* still there."

Lazaro twisted, looking to his staff for guidance. No one met his glance. Finally, he turned, gripped his hands behind his back, and paced a step. He turned again and, with dramatic flair, held up both hands, looking at McNabb and Weatherford.

"We have no choice." He lowered his hands and stiffened. Faced with the potential loss of billions of dollars, he seemed to find his way. "Colonel Weatherford, you may deploy your Commandos to the shipyards immediately. Is that clear?"

Weatherford smiled grimly. His brow wrinkled, and his eyes narrowed to slits. "Loud and clear, Mister President."

42

———

20 March 2164. The thermosphere over the Pacific Ocean.

The shuttle banked hard in one direction, then in the opposite. Rimes rocked in his harness, sucking at his EVA suit's odorless, stale oxygen in an effort to fight off nausea. He twisted in an attempt to see how everyone else was doing. In the passenger bay's wan light, they were ghostly figures, phantasms. They were all caught in the same dance as him, twisting, rocking, holding on for dear life.

They've been through simulation training before. Dana hasn't.

The shuttle dipped, throwing Rimes forward against the harness. He set his jaw and breathed deep again. Genie shuttles had engaged them two minutes out from the shipyard, and they were finding their range now.

The genie pilots seemed to have a clear edge in reaction time, but they faced far-superior vehicles, and had already lost one of their four shuttles.

The Commando mission had three primary targets, two of them capital ships. If the genies managed to gain control of the ships, the situation would become elementary. The genies—and the ships—would quickly be gone.

We've got to get past these shuttles.

Rimes closed his eyes. The weight of the last few days pressed on him, and he nodded off for a moment. Shots rattled off the hull, triggering integrity alarms. Rimes jerked awake, ashamed of himself. Before he could shout a warning, the alarms cleared; the hull was fine.

The pilot suddenly initiated a radical maneuver that left Rimes disoriented. A sustained humming filled the bay: the shuttle's belly-mounted railgun array. Rimes located a blinking genie shuttle on his display just as it winked out.

Another one down!

"Sergeant Rimes, we're breaking off," the pilot said. "Orders are to proceed to the *Powell*."

"Understood."

The shuttles were a distraction, buying time.

Rimes watched the display for a few more seconds before switching his focus to their target, the USS *Powell*. The shuttle's feed was filling in details that made the mission ever more real. An idea—desperate, flawed, but still an idea—took shape.

The shipyard was a kilometer-long tube with artificial gravity capability. A dozen spokes radiated outward, with larger ships hanging off them. Shuttles from orbitals would normally arrive around the clock, depositing workers—engineers, electricians, even construction workers—and materials in the central hub to support the shipyard's insatiable needs.

Now—

The pilot's face filled a small window in Rimes's display. "Ninety seconds to target."

Rimes gripped his harness and shifted in his seat. "We're going to need two drops, Chief. I want you to drop Lopez's squad at the hangar entry. Then you'll need to drop my squad off on top of the bridge structure. I've uploaded the locations."

"Looks simple enough." The pilot grinned. "Let's hope they didn't activate those missile batteries, or this could get even more interesting."

Rimes opened a shared workspace with Lopez and Kleigshoen's earpieces and dragged the *Powell*'s floor plan into it.

"It's a pretty straightforward mission: protect the *Powell* and deny the genies control. We need to treat this just like any of our operations. We want to minimize damage, but we're authorized to destroy the reactors. We have to assume they're expecting us and are ready to repel. You can toss out any thoughts about surprise or superior training. They're faster, stronger, and smarter than us."

Lopez bit his bottom lip so hard it lost its color.

"We have a couple of advantages, though," Rimes said. "They're fighting time. And as good as they are, they can't possibly be experienced in repelling attackers in space. Nobody is."

"That's it?" Lopez said. His face twitched nervously such that his nose rose and fell.

"Our best bet would be getting in through the airlocks, but they're sure to have those covered, disabled, or mined. Maybe all three. We still have to try. Most importantly, we have to use the terminals in the airlocks in order to try to inject soft-bots into the ship systems. Software assault is probably every bit as important as our physical assault."

Kleigshoen sighed. "They're going to be ready for anything."

"We could really have used Barlowe." Rimes closed his eyes momentarily. "We have to test their defenses. Maybe it'll distract them for a moment.

"Priority one, we need to retake the bridge. We do that, we can shut down the reactors from there. Failing that, we have to disable the reactors. Four reactors go offline and they won't have enough power to make the gravitic drive work. If we can't secure the bridge or shut down the reactors, we have to render the bridge uninhabitable."

"How?" Kleigshoen asked.

"Put a hole in the hull," Rimes said, slowly balling his hands into fists, then relaxing them. "When we're dropped on top of the bridge, locate an observation porthole—one of the weakest points of the ship. We lay down explosives and set a timer. If none of us make it, the timer does the job."

Kleigshoen's brow furrowed. "We blow the bridge, what's to protect us from getting sucked out?"

"These suits have a heavyweight line off the belt," Rimes said, tapping his right hip. "There are attach points every twenty meters in the ship."

"And what if none of that works?" Lopez asked.

"Then the shuttle puts a few hundred rounds into the engines. We can't let them have this ship."

"Ten seconds," the pilot said.

Rimes checked the external cameras. "Lopez, get your squad into the airlock."

Lopez popped his harness and ordered his squad to the airlock. He stopped at the airlock hatch and pivoted, hand tight around an overhead grip. "What if the hangar isn't accessible?"

"Make your way aft," Rimes said as the airlock hatch opened. "There should be lifeboats about five meters from the hangar. You can pop the hull covers from the outside. Eject the lifeboat and override the single-purpose terminal underneath. Let the compartment decompress and you're in."

"And if that doesn't work?"

Rimes growled, "Then think of something else."

The shuttle twisted, slowed, then stopped. The airlock indicator went red. Rimes counted and watched the shuttle's aft camera view. Four seconds, and the airlock closed and began its cycle. Lopez's team was on the hull. The shuttle accelerated.

"First team is away," the pilot.

"We're on the hull," Lopez said. "Moving toward the hangar bay hatch. It's closed."

"Check if you can override," Rimes said. "Let's get into position, folks."

A new image appeared. One of the other Commando team leads was busily working at something to his right. "Sergeant Rimes, we're on approach to the *Valdez*. ETA, two minutes. What's the plan?"

Rimes forwarded the details he'd just discussed with Kleigshoen and Lopez. "Give this a look, see what you can come up with. The *Valdez* is pretty close in layout. Approach it like it's an airplane hostage rescue. I know you can do this."

"Got it. What about the others?"

"They need to secure the *Newell*," Rimes said. "Once that's done, there are two other *Newell*-class frigates they can focus on. Tell the others to pull up the plans; it's all the same basic concept, except the *Newell*'s shuttles are externally-mounted."

"Got it. Good hunting."

"Good hunting," Rimes repeated.

"Five seconds," the pilot said.

Rimes popped his strap and waved everyone toward the airlock, taking position just behind Kleigshoen. He checked the CAWS-5 attached to her back and patted her helmet. They were using the automatic 20-gauge shotgun package loaded with caseless flechette shells. The flechettes had enough power to shred most EVA suits without any real chance of penetrating an inner hull. In theory, they would be ideal for boarding actions.

Time to test that theory.

The airlock hatch cycled.

They entered and all grabbed handholds. The indicator on Rimes's display went amber as pumps began rapidly emptying the chamber. Another few seconds, and the outer hatch opened.

The team exited, gently diving toward the bridge.

Orr overshot his target, barely managing to grasp an antenna array, and saved himself from sailing over the bridge and into space.

"Orr?" Rimes called over the squad's channel.

"All good," Orr replied. His voice was tense. "Just got a little excited."

"Squad is away, Chief," Rimes told the pilot. "Take up position five klicks out. Be ready to strafe those engines if you get the call."

The shuttle accelerated away, banking hard toward the battlecruiser's aft. "Roger tha—"

A missile flew past the bridge, trailing a stream of fire.

The shuttle juked, accelerated, spat chaff, then, in the blink of an eye, disappeared in a blinding flash.

The pilot's words became a hiss.

43

---

20 March 2164. USS *Powell.*

SCATTERED pieces of debris slammed into the hull, making it vibrate.

Rimes dropped to his belly, thankful the genies had the gravitic system operational. "Lay flat. Hold on."

It may not be much, but it's enough to keep us on the surface.

Most of the debris bounced away harmlessly, but one arm-length sliver pierced Chung's left foot, pinning it to the hull.

Chung gasped. "Sarge, my suit's penetrated. I-I'm losing oxygen."

"Hold tight." Rimes gently kicked off from the hull. "Let's get the explosives planted, people."

Rimes skimmed the hull's surface on all fours as he might the muddy bottom of a shallow river, frequently gripping the surface to pull himself forward.

As he approached Chung, he grabbed what appeared to be a camera housing. Rimes's momentum spun him completely around. He grabbed another protrusion and regained his footing, then cautiously edged toward Chung. Once he was close enough, he hooked his left leg around Chung's.

Rimes pointed to the camera housing. "Hang onto this."

The debris appeared to be a sheet of heat shielding, nearly a meter long and a few millimeters thick. Rimes guessed it had barely penetrated the hull.

Where it entered Chung's boot, a fine dark mist of blood particles suspended in oxygen escaped. The blood quickly boiled away.

Rimes gripped the heat shielding cautiously, testing for sharp edges and residual heat. His gloves were lined with carbon fiber weave meant to handle such threats without trouble, but vacuum was unforgiving.

He tightened his left leg around Chung's and braced with his right, then began applying steady pressure. Seconds passed before the shielding tore free. Rimes momentarily drifted up with the force of his push.

For a fleeting moment, Rimes floated into the darkness of space. His mind filled with thoughts—fantasies or terrors—of drifting into the void, dying alone.

Chung grabbed him with his free hand and pulled him back. "Got you," Chung gasped. "That hurt like a son of a bitch."

Rimes shivered, then planted his boots back on the hull, pulled a strip of sealant from Chung's thigh pad. "Agent Kleigshoen, any update on that porthole? We need to get those explosives planted and get off this hull. Lopez, they obviously know we're here. The shuttle's gone."

"Saw that," Lopez said. "Hangar is inaccessible. We're going to blow two lifeboats to force them to cover multiple entry points."

"Good idea." Rimes pulled the sealant strip tight over the top of the boot and pressed hard against the entry and exit points, counting to five. "This isn't going to do anything for the bleeding or pain."

"I can walk," Chung said.

Rimes looked around at the rest of the team. They were pressed against the hull, their suits all but lost against the gray panels.

"Agent Kleigshoen?"

"We finally found a viewport." Kleigshoen sounded relieved. "Fawcett's planting charges now."

"Sarge," Orr said excitedly. "Take a look at this."

Rimes shrank Kleigshoen's video feed and expanded Orr's. He was looking at a small hatch near the base of the antenna array Orr had latched on to. "What've you got there?"

"I was gonna ask you that. I was thinking it looks like a maintenance hatch."

Rimes pulled up the *Powell*'s plans again and zoomed into the bridge. "No, it's noth—"

The *Powell*'s plans showed a blank area, but he could *see* the hatch. He pulled up the plans and changed his search from airlocks to hatches —bingo.

"Got it. You're right, it's a maintenance hatch. It's not pressurized, but it runs to a dedicated airlock about twenty meters inside—the manual only covered the external airlocks." Rimes opened the channel to the other Commando teams and made his way over to Orr. "I'm sending you something that may help. Find ... antenna array four on the bridge. There should be a maintenance hatch that's not on your plans, about three meters aft of that. Check your ship's plans for any reference to maintenance access."

Orr squatted next to the hatch, then brought up a virtual display to interface with the hatch terminal. He looked at Rimes, who nodded. Orr rapidly typed and swiped through the interface, and, after a few seconds, the hatch slowly rose.

Rimes tapped Orr on the shoulder and motioned for him to enter the shaft, then waved the rest of the team over. Orr entered feet first, adjusting to the sudden shift in gravity after a moment. Bhat and Pasqual, supporting Chung between them, entered next, then Kleigshoen and Fawcett.

Rimes watched the team descend. "Lopez, you still read me?"

"Copy. Go ahead."

"When I close this hatch, we'll probably lose communication until we're both inside the ship."

"Understood," Lopez said. "Good hunting."

"Good hunting."

Rimes entered the maintenance shaft and sealed the hatch. As he'd feared, Lopez's signal strength faded. Three meters down the shaft, the last of it was gone.

Rimes quickly descended the rest of the way, then dropped through another roof hatch into the airlock where the rest of the team had taken up position. They had their weapons ready. Rimes sealed the roof hatch and nodded at Orr, already plugged into the terminal.

The hatch opened onto a large maintenance bay filled with workstations, tools, and crates. Rimes signaled Fawcett to cover the entry hatch opposite the airlock.

Once Fawcett was in place, Rimes sent Bhat and Orr forward, then had Pasqual help move Chung to a workstation. Pasqual immediately went to work removing the damaged boot.

Rimes pointed to a terminal. "Agent Kleigshoen, if you can get in, dump everything we've got into anything with a chance at success."

Rimes pulled up the deck plans again. "Okay, this maintenance bay opens onto the main passageway that leads to the primary and secondary stairwells. We have to assume they have them both covered. Pasqual, you, Chung, and Agent Kleigshoen come with me. We'll take the primary stairwell. Bhat, Orr, and Fawcett take the secondary stairwell. We'll exit the primary stairwell first. Gauge our success and adjust. How's Chung doing?"

"That foot's going to need treatment when we get back," Pasqual said. "I put some local anesthetic and a coagulant on it."

"Can you still shoot?" Bhat joked.

Chung flipped Bhat off.

Rimes gave Chung a reassuring punch in the shoulder. "Dana, any luck?"

Kleigshoen shook her head. "I've tried a dozen attacks. I think two of them may have lasted long enough to matter. If they did, we should see some false signals hitting soon; we may even get lucky and have the hangar hatch open. They had the reactors locked down tight, though. But at least we had one thing go our way."

"Make it good," Rimes said.

"They haven't secured the interior hatches, just the airlocks. And I've blocked them open now."

Rimes sucked in a lungful of air and slowly exhaled. "Pasqual, seal Chung up. Assume they've detected our entry by now. Bhat, Fawcett, Orr, go."

Bhat popped the hatch and scanned the passageway, then waved the rest of his team through.

After moving to the hatch, Rimes opened a window in his display to watch Bhat's camera. The others took up their positions, Chung limping but mobile.

Rimes scanned the passageway, waved the team through, and started jogging. "Bhat, how's it going?"

"At the secondary stairwell hatch," Bhat replied.

Fawcett and Orr settled against the bulkhead on either side of the secondary stairwell hatch. Orr's fingers hovered over the open button on the access panel. Bhat stepped to Orr's side and tapped him on the shoulder.

Orr opened the hatch and fell back.

Bhat's camera showed an explosion.

Rimes froze. "Bhat, what was that?"

"And here I was hoping for a fruit basket," Bhat said. "Hatches are rigged with makeshift shrapnel devices. Um, hull looks intact."

Rimes resumed jogging. "See anything else?"

"We're waiting for the smoke to clear, but it looks open from here to the stairs."

"Bhat, lob a flashbang in there, see if it sets anything else off." Rimes came to rest against the bulkhead next to Kleigshoen. He patted her back.

A flash lit up Bhat's camera display.

"Looks clear," Bhat said.

Rimes signaled for Pasqual to open the hatch. Pasqual tapped the access panel.

Rimes tensed, ready for anything.

The hatch popped open, but nothing happened.

"No explosive here." Rimes released his breath.

Pasqual held up a flashbang. Rimes nodded, and Pasqual tossed the flashbang into the stairwell.

There was a blur of movement, then an explosion.

"One Tango," Rimes called.

Pasqual and Chung opened fire with a controlled burst of flechettes. They pinged against the walls; then the passageway was silent.

Pasqual popped around the corner again and fired a sequence of three rapid shots starting at chest height, then tracking up the stairs to the first landing. At the same time, Chung fired at ankle height and tracked up to chest height. They pulled back, and Rimes ducked out and tracked his muzzle across visible space.

Halfway up the first flight of stairs, two forms lay, moving slowly. Rimes stepped into the stairwell and fired once into each.

They stopped moving. Rimes cautiously moved up to the next hatch.

"Clear. Bhat, you get that? No fruit basket here either, just a welcoming committee."

"Got it." Bhat chuckled. "Never repeat a booby trap."

"We're three levels down from the command deck. Proceed upward." Rimes climbed the stairs slowly. His eyes jumped from the path above to edges and corners, watching for tripwires. At the landing, he spun and repeated his search.

Rimes heard a scraping noise and stopped, but it wasn't from his end of the stairwell. "Bhat, hold. We may have something. Chung, check that hatch below. I heard something over someone's earpiece."

"Checking." Chung hobbled down the stairs.

"Holding," Bhat added.

The sound of gunfire and static erupted over Rimes's earpiece. "Chung?"

If Chung replied, it was drowned out by the gunfire.

Static crackled over his earpiece. "Rimes, this is Lopez! Do you read?"

Rimes leaned against the handrail and stared up at the hatch not three meters away. "I read you, Lopez. Go ahead."

"We're just outside Reactor One," Lopez shouted. A burst of noise drowned him out for a second: "—heavy enemy resistance. One of the bastards sneaked up on Gupta. I don't know if he's gonna make it. He's bleeding pretty bad. We're stuck here until the 82nd arrives."

Rimes bowed his head and sighed. "This is going to be over before they get anywhere close."

"They're fast, Rimes. They're everywhere. They've got us pinned down."

"You need to press on and keep them engaged," Rimes said. "Keep them tied down so we can take the reactor."

"Negative. We can't move. You're on your own."

44

20 March 2164. USS *Powell*.

THE STAIRWELL above Rimes was still empty; he could see the door to the command deck.

"Okay. Hold on, Lopez. Do what you can."

"Will do."

Rimes muted the channel with Lopez. "Chung, did you check that hatch? Chung?"

"I don't see him," Pasqual said. His microphone picked up a loud gulp and the wet sounds of him licking his lips. "I can move ba—"

"Hold position," Rimes snapped.

Keep it together. Stay with what you know. Only act on what's real, not what you guess. They could be influencing our thoughts and perceptions, like Perditori.

"Dana, fall back and cover Pasqual. When he's ready to move, you toss a flashbang ahead of him and back him up. Be sure of your targets. Don't hit Chung."

Kleigshoen retreated down the stairs. "In position."

Rimes looked at the hatch above him and the command deck hatch above that, then risked a quick glance down. Kleigshoen held a flashbang at the ready.

He keyed his channel to Bhat. "Bhat, what's your situation?"

"Still holding." Bhat said.

"Something's wrong," Rimes said. "They can't possibly be everywhere at once." He came off mute with Lopez. "Lopez, do you have a strength estimate?"

"Twenty?" Lopez ground his teeth audibly. "They're firing from three positions. We can't really get a good look at them."

Kleigshoen's flashbang detonated. Rimes looked down and saw Pasqual clear the landing.

Gunfire erupted.

The hatch above opened, and Rimes turned, instinctively emptying the magazine in a broad arc of fire. Flechettes bit into the bulkhead, filled the open hatchway, and tore through the genies trying to rush through.

Rimes reloaded as he charged the hatch.

"Jack," Kleigshoen shouted over the gunfire, "We've got three of them down here. Chung's dead. Pasqual's hit."

"I'm okay," Pasqual said. His voice sounded strained. "I've got them pinned down. You move up."

Rimes stood in the hatchway and scanned up and down the passageway, then stepped back and layered Pasqual's and Kleigshoen's data feeds over the deck plans. "Lopez, consolidate your squad's BAS feeds and send them to me."

As Kleigshoen made her way back upstairs, Lopez's data filtered in, populating known enemy positions and engagement zones. The BAS merged the data and constructed a solid three-dimensional image of the entire ship; Rimes shared it with Kleigshoen.

Kleigshoen looked it over. "They're waiting for us every step of the way. Do we blow the bridge?"

Rimes shook his head. "One last thing to try."

Kleigshoen examined the BAS display again. "What? I'm not seeing anything."

"I want you to move up to the command deck hatch and wait for my signal. I'm going to see if we can give *them* a surprise for once."

Rimes poked his head through the hatchway; it was still clear. "Bhat? Hold position until I give the go. When I give the signal, make some noise. Not too much."

"Copy."

"Jack—" Kleigshoen's voice sounded angry and panicked over the earpiece; when he looked, her face was strained, her eyes were wide.

"Dana," Rimes touched Kleigshoen's EVA helmet. "I just need you to keep them occupied. Like what Pasqual is doing."

"Piece of cake, Agent Kleigshoen," Pasqual said as he sent another shot through the hatch.

Kleigshoen let out a hiss through clenched teeth and slowly ascended the stairs. Rimes watched her go for a moment then stepped into the passageway.

The passageway was still clear except for the dead genies. He stopped at a turn in the main passageway and glanced around the corner; a bulkhead several meters down blocked his view.

Rimes edged down the passageway, stopped at the bulkhead, and listened. He picked up what may have been whispering, the faint squeak of a rubber sole. The hatch was ajar. He started to peer through the opening but sensed a hint of movement.

He froze, then slid the CAWS into its brace and pulled his knife.

An unexpected sense of calm, a cool detachment, washed over Rimes. His breathing was controlled, his hands steady, his awareness clear yet wide. The usual edginess that came with combat was gone. He sneaked his head forward until he could see around the hatch edge.

A genie stood on the other side of the bulkhead, just through the hatch.

A guard.

Rimes slowly pulled back. He examined the BAS. Everyone was in position, waiting on him. He had no idea if there were other genies beyond the guard. He had no idea if there were genies at the hatch beyond, where Bhat's team waited. What he did know was that the guard had to be eliminated or nothing else would matter.

Rimes imagined the guard's exact position based off what he had seen. A lethal strike would require moving into the hatchway. That meant being visible and exposed.

It would be extremely high-risk but also extremely satisfying.

Rimes blinked. *What?*

He imagined killing the guard again.

Satisfaction. Reward. Excitement.

The sensations were alien.

It's Kwon.

Rimes exhaled silently and refocused. He still had to eliminate the guard. A quiet intake of breath, a grip of the knife in disturbingly steady hands.

He signaled Bhat, then moved into the hatchway.

The battlefield's details resolved with alarming speed and ease as he scanned first down the corridor, then at the guard. He could make out a half-dozen forms at the far end of the passageway, squatting, lying prone, pressed against the bulkheads nearest the stairwell hatch. Their eyes were glued to it.

The guard was turning, responding to a change in pressure, a sixth sense, or luck; Rimes had been silent as death.

The knife rose, not to where the guard's jaw was but to where it would be. Rimes pivoted on his right foot, rotated his hip. He threw every bit of energy he could into the thrust.

For a split second, it appeared the genie might react too quickly for the strike to connect. His eyes went wide. He swung around the submachine gun he'd been holding slack at his side. His mouth opened.

The knife struck.

It drove up through muscle and bone, severing nerves and blood vessels. It pinned the genie's mouth shut and momentarily lifted him up onto his toes.

He died without a sound.

Rimes used the momentum to pull the lifeless body through the hatchway in a single, fluid motion. The corpse twitched, its heart, not yet aware it was no longer needed, sending blood gushing through the wound.

Rimes squatted and listened, filtering out the quiet storm of his own racing heart and rushing blood. It was still quiet. The genies were focused on their ambush.

Rimes whispered, "Bhat, you've got six, probably more, just outside that hatch, waiting to catch you from behind. I want you to proceed with caution up to the command deck. Dana, on my signal, open the hatch."

"Moving up," Bhat said.

Rimes pulled his last two flashbangs and twisted back around to watch the genies through the hatchway. A second ticked by. Another.

The genie closest to the hatch panel waved the others forward. Rimes pulled the first flashbang's pin and tossed it through the hatchway into the midst of the genies. He counted to two, then ducked through the hatchway after it, sprinting toward the genies at the other end of the corridor, the second flashbang ready in his hand. At three seconds, he closed his eyes and pulled the pin on the second flashbang.

The force of the first flashbang's explosion impacted Rimes's suit. He opened his eyes, took in the genies staggering and slumping in the corridor, and hurled the second flashbang, angling it for the open bay to the right of the stairwell hatch.

Then he unslung the CAWS and slammed into the right-hand bulkhead. When the second flashbang went off, he opened fire, emptying his magazine into the stunned genies. He reloaded and spun into the open bay.

A genie lay on the ground, knocked mostly senseless by the flashbang and reaching weakly for her weapon. Rimes fired twice, center mass. Blood sprayed from flechette wounds, and the genie went limp.

Rimes's earpiece was full of thunder.

"All kinds of fun up here, Jack," Kleigshoen shouted, barely audible over her CAWS and the return fire. "There must be ten of them."

"Don't give them anything to shoot at," Rimes searched the genies for explosives, shoving three of their improvised flechette grenades into his thigh pouches. "I'm on my way. Bhat, how about you?"

"Ready to dance. Give us the word and we'll toss some flashbangs out there."

Rimes gave the bloody scene a last scan and jogged back to the main stairwell. At the hatch, he gave Bhat the go-ahead. Explosions and gunfire filled the audio as Rimes climbed the stairs, one of the improvised flechette grenades in his hand.

Rimes stopped as his head came even with Kleigshoen's boot. She had her back pressed against the bulkhead, the hatch to the command deck open just enough to allow her to glance through—and draw fire.

He ducked until the firing stopped. "Dana."

Her helmet twitched, but she kept her eyes on the hatch. "Jack."

"When I give the signal, I want you to kick that hatch open wide enough for me to throw a grenade out there."

"Got it."

Rimes examined the grenade; everything about the device was infuriatingly foreign. He had no idea how much of a fuse it had. He rotated it in his hand until he found the trigger mechanism.

"Jack?"

"One second," Rimes grumbled. "These guys may be geniuses, but they obviously don't know how to build an intuitive weapon. Okay. Go."

Kleigshoen kicked the hatch's bottom corner and pulled her leg back just as a hail of flechettes filled the stairwell. Rimes triggered the grenade and tossed it, trying to direct the blast into the chamber beyond. He ducked down the stairs and dug for another grenade.

The explosion was disappointingly modest.

Silence.

Rimes lobbed the second grenade a little harder and ducked again.

Another unimpressive explosion.

Silence. No movement. No gunfire.

Not much of bang, but the silence spoke volumes about the grenades' effectiveness. A few common-sense improvements, and they might be on to something.

"Bhat, we're clear here," Rimes said.

"Still cleaning up," Bhat replied. "One particularly stubborn ..." Gunfire drowned out Bhat's audio. "Okay, we're clear. Moving to join you."

Rimes climbed to the top of the stairs and took in the chamber and hallway with a quick sweep. Blood covered the walls. Genies lay in twisted heaps. Rimes spotted an unexploded grenade in one of the genies' hands.

Rimes opened a private channel to Kleigshoen. "It's clear. I'm going to take point. You stay tight on my six. Okay?"

Kleigshoen blinked rapidly several times, then nodded. Rimes patted her shoulder. He cautiously stepped out and scooped up the genie's grenade.

Rimes hefted the grenade as he looked down the passageway. He opened the team channel. "Pasqual, stay sharp. We're moving to the bridge."

"All covered," Pasqual said. "They've gone awfully quiet."

Rimes stopped. "Okay, change of plans. Pasqual, get up here. Take up position outside this hatch with Agent Kleigshoen. Bhat, station Fawcett outside your hatch. I think you've got some visitors coming your way. Move it."

Rimes gave Kleigshoen a thumbs' up, then jogged to the central corridor to wait for Bhat and Orr. When they arrived, he showed them the grenade he'd taken from the genie. He explained the basics of the trigger and gave the grenade to Bhat, then dug the final genie grenade out of his pocket.

"It's going to go down easy, or it's going to go down hard," Rimes said. "Easy is popping the door and lobbing these in, then doing a little close-in mop-up."

"Nothing's been easy today," Bhat said. "What's hard?"

"We blow the explosives and lose the bridge."

"Y'know, hard sounds awfully appealing right about now." Bhat pressed flat against the bulkhead opposite the hatch with the grenade ready to trigger and throw. "Ready."

"Ready." Rimes thumbed the grenade trigger and leaned against the bulkhead.

Orr opened the hatch and kicked it wide.

Rimes and Bhat tossed their improvised flechette grenades inside—but the result was more impressive this time.

A deafening explosion tore through the bridge, knocking them backwards for a moment.

Then they were almost instantly pulled forward.

The atmosphere within the bridge had begun to evacuate.

The explosive charges on the porthole must have detonated!

How wasn't particularly relevant at the moment; what mattered was sealing the bridge.

"Seal the hatch!"

Bhat was already in motion, hooking his hand on the hatch and pulling it against the force. Rimes placed a knee against the bulkhead and grabbed the hatch, adding his strength. Orr joined them.

For several seconds, they made slow progress, gaining a few centimeters only to lose one. Finally, the hatch shut and Orr slapped the control panel, closing it.

"Rimes, you there?" Lopez shouted. His signal was weak but clear.

"Go ahead."

"They stopped firing," Lopez said. "They're retreating. Just like that."

"It's over," Rimes said. He was ready to collapse. "Whoever was on the bridge somehow detonated the charges we put on the porthole."

"This engagement goes to you, Colonel."

Rimes spun, CAWS held at waist level.

One of the ruined genie corpses was staggering from the hallway toward him, blood and viscera trailing in its wake.

Its eyes were dead.

"Sergeant," Rimes said.

It waved a hand dismissively, a familiar gesture.

"Perditori," Rimes finally realized.

"Rimes," Lopez said over the earpiece. "Come again?"

Bhat had his weapon centered on the corpse's chest, hands shaking. "Colonel? A c-couple rounds to the head and he can't tell rank?"

"Rimes?" Lopez sounded worried.

"Hold on, Lopez," Rimes said.

The corpse leaned on a wall. "You denied us the resources of the *Powell* and *Valdez*, and we had hoped to do the same to you, out of courtesy. However, the time for fun and games is at an end, and we must leave this dead cradle."

Bhat leveled his CAWS at the corpse's forehead. "I could try to kill it again. Or at least get it to shut the hell up."

Approaching the corpse, Rimes held up a hand. "No." He looked into the dead eyes. "Why this ... display?"

"You have changed, Colonel. We have both changed. Even in defeat, we grow stronger. You are unreachable by my previous methods. I knew the time would come, even though I did not correctly anticipate the moment or method.

"So here we are—you, the misguided angel of death, me the creator speaking through one of your victims, an innocent bystander in an unnecessary war. I could warn you not to pursue us, but it would be futile. You will come, and we will kill you, or you will kill some of us."

The corpse smiled, dripping blood from its mouth. "In the end, it will not matter. My kind will survive and flourish, and yours will pass. You will all pass."

"Where are you going?"

"For now? Away. Eventually, beyond any place you know of. Goodbye, Colonel." The corpse bowed and gave a slow wave, then slumped to the ground.

Bhat whistled. "Shit, Rimes, what the hell was that?"

"I couldn't begin to explain." Rimes knelt to examine the corpse. After a few seconds, he stood, wiping the gore from his hands. "Let's get to the hangar bay and see if we can raise Colonel Weatherford. Something tells me this isn't over yet."

45

22 March 2164. Grandfield, Oklahoma.

Rimes stared out a filthy window at the dying lawn outside. More weeds than grass, and more barren earth than weeds, it was fenced in by cracked and rotten split rails. Beyond the fence, the ruin was worse.

So much ruin, so many failures.

A cough drew Rimes's attention back into the room.

He saw the room in a dreamy twilight where memory and reality met. He'd spent many a school night studying here, Cleo snoring noisily in the same leather chair.

In his memories, the room was larger, the furniture newer, the air fresher, Cleo stronger. Dust hung, suspended in what sunlight leaked through the windows and paper-thin curtains.

Grandfield was a ghost town, only a handful of houses still occupied. Its streets were broken pavement, its municipal buildings scabrous shells, its breath weak gusts of sand.

He sat on a battered, sagging couch next to Molly and his younger brother, Michael.

"When were you planning to tell us?" Rimes asked.

Molly squeezed his hand.

Cleo made a sound somewhere between a grunt and a cough, then took a drink from a smudged jelly jar and set it on a scarred end table. The table was as much a part of Rimes's childhood memories as the old man's penchant for cheap whiskey.

"You know now, so what's it matter?"

"How long?" Rimes asked.

"A few months," Cleo muttered. "Maybe less."

Memories lied.

The old man had never been strong, the house had never been a haven for Rimes. It had always been dirty.

Broken.

Cheap.

"I'm sorry, Cleo," Molly said, squeezing Rimes's hand again.

Cleo took another drink from the jelly jar. "For what? You didn't cause it, sweetie." He looked at Rimes. "Your brother wasn't supposed to tell you. He can't keep his damned mouth shut for nothin'."

"He told me because he knew I was considering going away for a while. He thought I'd want to see you again." Rimes breathed deep, tried to calm himself.

Cleo waved dismissively. "You're always goin' away. You ain't nothin' like your brothers. Never have been."

Rimes pinched his nose and rubbed his eyes. Dealing with his father was never easy. Saying goodbye was proving even more difficult.

The house was nearly silent—the hum of a failing console, the drip of a leaky faucet, the quiet groan of the foundation settling.

And their breathing.

Cleo looked at them with jaundiced, judging eyes, the same eyes that found them lacking as far back as Rimes could remember. Even sunken as they were, shadowed by a bony brow chiseled by the ravages of disease, they held power.

"Where now?" he said, his voice dry reeds rattling. "Another cesspool you can't even afford to take your wife to?"

"Georgia," Rimes said. He wiped away tears he hadn't realized were there before. "Fort Benning."

Michael anxiously looked from Rimes to Cleo. He rubbed his hands together. "He's going to be an officer."

"Officer?" Cleo shook his head in disgust. "What're you gonna make as an officer? Enough to move out of that little place you call an apartment? No. I could fit that place in my garage. How do you expect to have a family with a place like that?"

"They've got one on the way," Michael said.

Molly leveled a dark gaze on Michael, and he lowered his eyes.

Cleo blinked for a moment as he absorbed the news. He reached for the jelly jar with his shaking, talon-like hands and nearly knocked it over. "One on the way?" He leaned back in his chair. "Well isn't that somethin'? Wasn't sure you knew what you was doin'."

"We were going to tell you last week," Molly said. Her smile faltered. "Things went a little crazy at Jack's job. It was in the news."

"A dyin' man doesn't waste money on the news, sweetie." Cleo grimaced at Molly—it was what passed as a smile for him. "So what's this officer gig gonna pay? You gonna finally be able to afford your own car, like Steven?"

"Steven was a pimp," Rimes said.

Cleo winced, and took another drink from the jar, and turned to Michael, giving him a reproachful glance. "And I expect you'll still be tryin' to suck them dry, huh? Even when they need to provide for their own."

Rimes shook his head. Cleo was just lashing out. Rimes had to get Cleo back on track. "No car. We'll save more. When Molly finishes her degree, we'll both be making enough to get the boys a good start."

Cleo raised his eyebrows. "Boys? You got twins comin'?"

Molly smiled and kissed Rimes's cheek. "Not twins, but Jack's convinced we're going to have two boys eventually. He's already got names for them."

Cleo took another drink from the jelly jar. "I knew when I met Alejandra we'd have Steven." He stared out the window for a moment, then sighed and grimaced again. "Steven was my plan. Michael and Taylor were hers." He waved the jelly jar at Rimes. "Ain't no one planned for you."

Rimes settled his elbows on his knees and rested his chin on his hooked thumbs. He didn't want to waste time fighting with his father. Every second now seemed more precious than ever before, and he wanted to spend it with Molly.

"Cleo." Rimes struggled to find the words that had been so easy when he'd rehearsed them the previous afternoon, before he'd found out the old man was dying. "Things are changing. A lot of things are changing. I know you've never cared much for my career, but it's my calling, and there's not really much else out there folks can even call a career anymore."

Cleo snorted. "Careers ended before you were born. They were endin' before I was born, unless you consider bein' wealthy a career, or sellin' your soul. If you don't got money you can spend your life turnin' into more money, you ain't got many choices. All we got today is crime or law, mercenary or soldier. Not another option for someone not born to it. And one day, there's gonna be a reckoning. You hear me? A reckoning!"

Rimes patted Molly's hand. "Once I complete officer training, we'll be moving. Probably to Germany to start with. Other places after that."

Cleo glowered at him. "I won't be here to see your baby."

Rimes looked at his feet. His Army-issue sneakers were worn from miles of jogging. They were comfortable. Something about them felt every bit as right and natural as talking to Cleo felt awkward. "Cleo. I wanted to say goodbye and tell you that ..." Rimes took a deep breath. "Tell you I love you."

Cleo looked away, his eyes watering as he drummed his fingers irritably on the chair's arms. Finally, he wiped his eyes and said, "When I was a little younger than you, everythin' was so different. Oh, it was changin'. Things're always changin'. But if you looked at it hard enough, you could see it was changin' in a whole new way, the sort of change they probably saw back in the 1930s, maybe the 2000s.

"We'd just come off the Big One. Well, it was the Big One before this Big One. Every damn depression is the Big One. Everyone seems to want more and bigger change, so we end up with these here disasters. It was 2065, and things were boomin', relatively speaking. No more cannibalism, least not out of necessity. Jobs were there if you had the education and will to take a contract that could feed you and your family, but not much more. The land of milk and honey, just like it used to be."

Cleo stared out the dirty window, at another time. Finally, he closed his eyes and sagged slightly. "But you know what the real change was? The military. The generals said they were done firing on civilians. They were done shootin' up those who'd had enough of living like animals and wanted access to food and water the wealthy bastards had. They were done being at the beck 'n' call of corporations who offered them nothin' for the favor of eliminating some starving women who were saying no more to spreadin' their legs so they could feed their kids.

"And do you know what that resulted in?"

"The Corporate Security Laws," Rimes said, again rubbing his eyes. "They were forced to shoot anyway. I've studied history. The military's refusal to shoot only changed the uniform of who was pulling the trigger."

"Studyin' history ain't the same as livin' it," Cleo said. "They were pilin' corpses into mass graves, like you'd see in movies about the damned Nazis."

"The riots had to be dealt with, Cleo." Rimes hated discussing the military with his father, and he could see Molly was becoming upset as well. "The government felt the military was the right solution."

Cleo snorted and reached for his now-empty jelly jar. His hand shook in fury. "The right solution? Nazis had that term for killin' millions a couple centuries ago."

"So now we're Nazis?"

Michael held his hands out in a sign of peace. "Dad, no need to make it ugly."

"Ugly," Cleo said, indignant. "It is what it is. You kill millions, you kill thousands, you still killed your own people. And for what? To protect the wealthy? Revolution made this country from nothin'. Burning down those mansions, taking away what those people took from everyone else, maybe that's the only way to get us back to where we were. A reckoning! I tell you right now!" Cleo coughed and scowled. He pointed through the filthy window at the sprawl of dead grass, mud puddles, and trash that marked his yard. "You think there's a solution for what we have today? Not every problem has a solution, Son, and the military sure as hell ain't the hammer for every nail."

Rimes took a heavy breath. "It's my career, Cleo."

Cleo slapped his hands down on the chair's arms. "Billions of people go their whole lives movin' from contract to contract. And when they're asked to do something they don't agree with, they say no."

Rimes stood. "I've made my choice. You can't hold me responsible for the horrible things that the military did in your time, and you can't expect me to give up what I love out of some misplaced belief it will fix everything that's wrong with the world."

Cleo's face darkened, and he took a breath to start shouting.

Rimes interrupted him. "We've got to hit the road. The rental place said this car's sensors don't handle darkness well, and I don't want to do the driving myself. Not at night. Michael, we'll pick you up tomorrow morning."

Cleo deflated. He looked away when Rimes offered his hand. "Tell Alejandra I said hello."

Rimes stepped outside without another word.

Molly let him take a few steps onto the broken concrete before hugging him—out of sight from the window.

He held Molly close as the tears flowed.

46

22 March 2164. Grandfield, Oklahoma.

ALEJANDRA'S DUPLEX WAS IMMACULATE—BRIGHTLY painted, carefully organized, and perfectly balanced between cluttered and open, if somewhat aged and yellowed.

Rimes watched her from across a small, aluminum folding table as she set her teacup down and patted her thin lips with a faux-cloth napkin, then folded it in half and set it on her lap. It was all very proper and dignified.

Molly gazed into the steam rising from her cup. Rimes brushed a handful of crumbs from the urethane-coated tabletop and dumped them onto his plate.

As usual, Alejandra had fixed a small French pastry for them, something that grated on Molly every time they visited. It could have been the way the place smelled of something freshly baked, the way Alejandra set her modest yet perfect table with china and imported tea, or the way Alejandra claimed to have baked it herself, rather than just buying whatever was on sale and heating it up before they arrived.

Alejandra looked at him as if here were still a child. "In any organization, there are leaders and there are followers. The odds of you being a meaningful leader are much greater if you are an officer."

"Service is a noble cause regardless of the rank, don't you think?" Molly said, without meeting Alejandra's eyes.

Alejandra smiled condescendingly at Molly. Alejandra's face was still pretty, despite losing its color and accumulating wrinkles at an alarming pace, and it could project cruelty with frightening ease. "But it's rank that gets you recognized."

She looked back at Molly, waiting for eye contact. When Molly finally looked up from her tea, glaring, Alejandra continued.

"A leader doesn't just tell someone else what to do, my dear. A leader *does*. It's how respect is attained. When you begin your career—you're still hoping to have a career one day, aren't you? Well, once you begin it, you'll see what sets people of higher status apart from the others."

Molly returned Alejandra's insincere smile with a perfunctory one. When Alejandra turned her attention to Jack, Molly dropped her gaze to her tea again.

Alejandra coughed quietly into her napkin. "You know, Jack, you could always go into politics. Get a law degree, leverage your reputation and contacts. You wouldn't have to travel and risk your life all the time. You could help raise the family, too. Raising children isn't easy, and not everyone is cut out for it."

Molly gathered up the pastry dishes and noisily set them into the sink. Alejandra turned in her chair to glare; Molly opened her eyes innocently. "I'm sorry, did I do something wrong? I *am* tired. I'm not going to be much for talking tonight, I'm afraid." Molly rubbed her belly. "Travel and the baby have really been a strain."

Alejandra stood. She brought her teacup to the sink and set it carefully on the bottom without a sound. "Oh, I remember what it was like carrying Steven around. Eight months along and traveling to Texas. You know, I drove us six hours to Dallas and Cleo—he was recovering from that knee injury he suffered in his senior year—couldn't lift a thing. What a sight I must have been, my belly out to here, carrying those suitcases up the stairs to our new apartment, and me half-asleep from the drive. You go clean up and get some rest, Dear. I'll get this. I cleaned the guest room and put fresh linens in it this morning. You'll sleep better than you do at home."

Molly glared over her shoulder at Rimes as she left the kitchen. She hated the guest room. She called it Alejandra's trophy room. It was full of memorabilia dating back generations, but mostly focusing on Alejandra's younger years as a star student.

The digital awards from her career as an accomplished businesswoman could be shut off, but nothing could hide the plaques, portraits, and diplomas in the glass cases lining all four walls.

On top of that, the bed was narrow and short, and it squeaked with the slightest move, killing any opportunity for intimacy. Rimes gritted his teeth and finished his tea. He'd known when he'd suggested the trip there would be hell to pay. There was no way around such things, though, especially with reassignment guaranteed should he pursue OCS. And with Cleo's terminal diagnosis, it was their last chance to see him.

Visiting one parent meant visiting the other.

"She seems on edge," Alejandra said loudly as she inspected the dishes Molly had set in the sink. "Cleo's situation has her upset?"

"There's a lot going on right now." Rimes carried his teacup to the sink and set it down gently but not silently. "She didn't get into the PhD program again, the baby is coming … and I haven't been the best husband."

He didn't mean for it to slip out, but once out, it didn't seem too painful.

Alejandra looked up disapprovingly at the last statement. "Your father always said *that* when he tried to apologize for his infidelities, Jackson. Please tell me that isn't the case with you. You were always the special one. We all expected so much from you. I can't believe you would fall into such behavior, especially given the distance between you and Cleo."

Rimes took a towel from the sink and ran warm water over it, squeezing out the excess. "It's none of your business, Mother."

"Well." Alejandra ran water over the dishes as Rimes wiped the table. "Some things are beyond the control of even the best of parents. At least you haven't taken to drinking." She glared at the wall separating the kitchen from the guest room and raised her voice. "I hope she's not blaming her rejection on the foreign students again?"

Rimes shook the towel out and placed it on the sink edge to dry.

"Well, *were* there any American applicants accepted? If there were, then blaming foreign students is just a convenient excuse for her own inadequacies."

Rimes bowed his head and sighed.

"Don't you agree?" She sounded hurt. "It's not as if she had the highest scores. Too much partying, too little studying, just like I warned you. The schools are simply taking the best students. Wouldn't you want that? When I came to the United States, my scores were in the top three percent. I earned my place."

"Mother," Rimes snapped.

Alejandra jumped back from him, as if he'd raised a fist to strike her. After a moment, she turned her back to him. Her perfectly coiffed black hair danced as she angrily scrubbed the plates. "If you think I somehow unfairly took a US citizen's place, then the advantages I gave you were also unfair."

"I don't have time for the drama, Mother," Rimes said. "I don't have the time and I don't have the energy. I had to tell Cleo goodbye for the last time today. Losing one parent is enough."

He kissed Alejandra's cheek, then stared deep into her watery eyes. "But if you keep pushing Molly ..."

Alejandra blinked but said nothing.

"Goodnight, Mother." He walked out of the kitchen, certain her gaze was burning into his back.

The guest room was empty; he gathered his toiletry bag and went to the bathroom.

Molly was angrily brushing her teeth at the pedestal sink. She spat fiercely into the sink and watched the water rinse the foam completely away.

She sighed, then smiled at him in the mirror.

She leaned over, pushed the door shut behind him, and started the shower. They sneaked a long kiss and caress as they showered together.

They settled into the old, cramped, and uncomfortable bed, back to back but touching each other. Rimes still saw hints of coldness and pain from his breach of trust in Molly's eyes, but there was hope there, too.

"I love you," he told Molly.

She grunted.

"I'm practicing for the boys. I love you."

"I love you too, Jack."

"I love you."

"Fine, you love me. Go to sleep."

"You're going to get sick hearing me say it to all three of you, aren't you?"

She groaned and put the pillow over her head.

He pulled it back a crack. "I love you."

As Rimes drifted toward sleep, he thought of his childhood and the mistakes he'd sworn he wouldn't repeat as a parent. His children would never suffer a winter without heat or a night without dinner. They would never worry they weren't good enough.

He smiled as images of his sons laughing and playing with Molly came to him. It was the future he dreamed of. He wouldn't let anything destroy that dream.

47

———

24 March 2164. Fort Sill, Oklahoma.

STERN, powerful men of importance looked down on Rimes from the foyer of Weatherford's office. Their mouths smiled, but their eyes brimmed with knowledge: every one of them had killed, had sent other men to their deaths.

Leaders.

Rimes sat on the lone wooden chair with his hands locked in front of him.

Dark paneling, soft lighting, worn leather chairs: the office spoke to Weatherford's appreciation of the finer things. But the pictures on the walls spoke of honor, duty.

Weatherford's XO stepped out of his office and nodded at Rimes. The XO made his way to the coffee pot, tried to pour himself a cup, but found it empty. He started another pot, yawning. He was a short, sturdy, dark-eyed man, probably infantry by trade, riding a desk on his slow march up the ranks.

The coffee pot gurgled.

"He shouldn't be long. We've been swamped by all the AARs and meetings after this orbital operation. And now he's on a call with SecDef. Called out of the blue."

The XO poured the first drips of coffee into a cup and took a sip, grimaced at the taste. "You did some impressive work up there. There's already talk of building a boarding action training course off what we learned. But I doubt we'll see those genie grenades put into the arsenal. It sounds like they'll be doing a lot of inner hull repairs."

Rimes looked down at his hands. They were rough and still stained with grime.

An entire team had died in an ambush on the *Valdez*, Chung was dead, and Gupta wasn't likely to recover enough from his wounds to rejoin the unit. And they were concerned about repairing a ship.

You can repair a ship. You can build a new one. What about Chung? What about the others?

What if the genies were right? We're on our way out.

"You make a decision about OCS yet?" the XO asked.

Rimes shook his head.

"Well, I've got your approved application in the system when—"

Weatherford's door opened. The XO poured another cup of coffee, scooped in a teaspoon of sugar, and handed it to Weatherford.

"Sorry about that." Weatherford nodded at his XO, then beckoned for Rimes to enter.

Weatherford closed the door behind Rimes and made his way to his desk, settling into his chair. Desk and chair seemed to reflect the man as much as the foyer—old, well-maintained, uncluttered.

Weatherford pointed at the smaller chair across from his and watched Rimes's face from beneath gray eyebrows. "The folks in the capital are up in arms over the whole orbital nonsense, even our 'lack' of boarding action training."

"The captain was just telling me about that, sir."

Weatherford grunted. "You'd think we'd be looking at medals for saving their asses yet again. Instead we're fending off investigations. I spend more time defending us against the outrageous and absurd than I do reviewing operations and planning. My entire career, I've seen nothing but bickering and bullshit out of our leaders. Makes you wonder where that X-17 came from."

Weatherford sipped his coffee, swirled it around to mix it up, then set the cup down. "I don't want you to romanticize this career path, but at the same time, I think you're ready to take the next step. We need to replace Sergeant Martinez. We'd have to promote you out-of-cycle for that, but I've already received approval if that's what you want. Or you can pursue OCS. I've made sure you're clear of any fallout from the orbital operations. Hell, once everything's said and done, I think you may just see a medal yet."

"Thank you, Colonel," Rimes said. He was trying to keep his face blank. "I haven't decided yet."

Weatherford leaned back in his chair and stared into the distance for several seconds. Finally, he looked back at Rimes. "I know IB offered you a position. It may sound more tempting than wearing the uniform right about now, but you're a better man than that. You're a man of honor and dignity. You love the mission. You love your family. These men around you, they're your family too. You won't find that anywhere else. And at the end of the day, we'll take pretty good care of you."

Weatherford spun in his chair to look at his office. "Thirty years of service, and ... you'll have a nice pension waiting for you at seventy. Not many places offer that."

The pictures looked down at Rimes from the wall in the office, too. Rimes noticed a couple of gaps in the rows of pictures, ones that had fallen down or been removed.

"I understand, sir."

"I just wanted to make sure you were seeing things in the right light."

"I appreciate that, sir."

Impatience flashed across Weatherford's face. "You'd make an excellent poker player."

Rimes smiled. "I'm sorry, Colonel. I thought I knew my answer. Then I visited my family."

Weatherford leaned back in his chair. "What made you doubt your decision?"

"Some things my parents said," Rimes said.

The fresh, crescent-shaped scar on his right temple ached. He rubbed it and remembered Martinez's death, Moltke's strange, unintelligible words as he tried to shake some kind of truth out of Rimes. "We found out my father has terminal liver cancer."

"I'm sorry to hear that," Weatherford said.

"It's given me a different perspective. My father was a great man, once. He meant a great deal to me. Now ..." He shook his head.

"Perspective is very important," Weatherford said. "It can change over time, as we gain wisdom and knowledge."

Rimes nodded. "I need to find peace with my decision. I want to be sure I do the right thing."

Weatherford stared at the wall, looking at one of the blank spots, then over to a cabinet in the corner. He cleared his throat. "Very wise. When you're ready, contact me, and we'll get things going."

Rimes felt his eyes moisten and blinked quickly. "I should know by tomorrow, sir. I think I just need to sleep on it."

Weatherford stood. Rimes snapped to attention. Weatherford walked to the door and opened it for Rimes. It was an awkward moment, a reversal of roles.

"Thank you, sir. You'll be the first to know my decision."

Weatherford was watching Rimes's every step as he left the office, he was sure of it. He felt the stare and the weight of the judgment.

But in the foyer, the pictures on the walls seemed ... prouder. More approving.

The XO offered Rimes some coffee, but he shook his head and kept walking. Away from Weatherford's office, the halls were bare, unremarkable, worn.

There's always only so much money to go around.

Rimes stopped at the building exit to slip his beret on. He checked himself in the simple, cloudy mirror. The beret was on perfectly.

Rimes stepped through the door. The morning sun at his back, he headed for the post's confinement facilities.

It was time to talk to Barlowe. And call in some favors. A lot of favors.

48

---

25 March 2164. The outskirts of Lawton, Oklahoma.

RIMES WOKE at the sound of an approaching car and stepped from behind his tree onto the asphalt drive. He was still sweaty enough to be convincing.

The car, a restored BMW 7 Series F-25, turned onto Weatherford's private drive. Rimes knew the car well—gloss black, original engine and transmission, and authentic trim.

It was worth more than Rimes had earned his entire time in the service.

The car came to a stop; the passenger-side window lowered.

Weatherford leaned across the front seat, bracing his hand atop three shopping bags. He looked like a hiker in his blue jeans and flannel shirt. "What are you doing out here on a Sunday morning? The lake is a bit of a trip for you, isn't it?"

Rimes looked around the estate. Aside from Weatherford's house, there were eight others off the lakeshore. With only a simple wooden fence surrounding the house's broad yard, it still offered unimaginable peace and privacy.

"I went jogging this morning, Colonel. I thought I'd take you up on your offer and drop by."

Weatherford's face betrayed his annoyance, but only for a moment. "You've made a decision, then?"

Rimes nodded.

"Well, come on in. Let's talk it over."

Rimes eyed the car's leather interior. "I'm pretty grimy after the jog, Colonel. I'll follow you up."

Weatherford leaned back and gunned the engine. Rimes watched the passenger-side window close with crisp precision.

Moltke had talked more than once about following Weatherford's path: restoring an old classic, buying a nice home somewhere, planting roots in his mid-fifties.

Moltke had admired Weatherford.

Rimes jogged up behind Weatherford's car, stopping outside the carport to wait for him.

The place's rustic beauty was breathtaking. The house was fashioned after a mountain lodge, at least three thousand square feet, with a covered front porch and a stone walking path that led from the carport to the front door.

"It's something, isn't it?" Weatherford said, his voice full of pride. He closed the BMW's passenger door, then shifted the shopping bags between his hands to take it all in himself.

"It is, Colonel," Rimes agreed. He looked at the landscaped lawn. Weatherford had already begun preparing to plant flowers.

"I did the lawn myself," Weatherford said around a smile. "I could've hired someone else at about the same price when all was said and done, but there's something satisfying about getting it exactly how you see it in your head. You want things done right, you do it yourself."

"I understand completely, Colonel," Rimes said.

"This is what you could have in store for you, Jack," Weatherford said. "With your skills, discipline, and motivation, you could be a major in ten years."

"We've decided to accept the OCS opportunity, Colonel," Rimes said.

Weatherford huffed under his breath and started down the path to the front door. "Our unit's loss, but the Army's gain. You'll excel, just like you did with the Commandos. In fact, I've already put your name in for a new SpecOps unit they've started talking about forming. Your boarding assault turned a lot of heads. Let's go inside and I'll fix us a drink."

Rimes shook his head. "Thanks, Colonel, but I'll need to pass. I've got a long jog back and I need to get going soon."

Weatherford frowned. "You came all the way out here just to tell me you were going to accept?"

Something inside Rimes went frighteningly cold.

"I came out here to give you fair warning."

Rimes felt his heart pounding in his chest now that the words were spoken.

"Fair warn—" Weatherford's face reddened and his jaw worked. "Jack, what are you talking about?"

Rimes forced himself to stay under control. "I'm just trying to give you some time to plan how you're going to handle things tomorrow."

Weatherford's voice was dangerously calm. "I don't follow you, Sergeant Rimes."

"You'll need to go down to the MP Company HQ and turn yourself in."

Weatherford raised his eyebrows. He shifted his grip on the bags. "I will?" His eyes flitted across the lawn to the path and his private drive. "And why will I need to do that?"

"For your involvement in the X-17 theft," Rimes said. He took strength from the fact that his voice held.

"All right, Jack," Weatherford said with a deep sigh. "Like I said before, you'd make an excellent poker player. So, now you've shown your cards. I assume you wouldn't make your move without something to back you up."

Rimes nodded.

Weatherford chuckled. "So you want in on the action. Can't wait for the good life to come to you, you have to *bring* it to you? Patience is a virtue, but ambition is divine." Weatherford set the shopping bags down. "Let's hear it. How much do you want?"

"I don't want anything," Rimes said. "No money, at least. You've already authorized my OCS application. The captain told me yesterday."

Weatherford gave him a cold glare. "You think you have enough to make it stick? The X-17 case is closed. Marshall's putting the final touches on it. Moltke was behind the whole thing. You reopen this, it's going to be a problem for a lot of people, Jack. A lot of people who don't like problems."

"Moltke was involved. I don't see any need to try to rewrite history on that point," Rimes said. "The problem is, he couldn't have known about the X-17. Someone would've had to have told him about it, someone with access to the information. Someone like you."

Weatherford tensed. "How do you figure that? I'm just the commander of this unit. I don't have need-to-know for anything like X-17. There'd be records of me accessing it if I had."

Calm. Stay calm.

"We won't need them. When the IB went looking for red flags, they only looked for unusual spending patterns. Paying this place off early doesn't really trip any flags if you have a history of similar payments. But you dropped thirty-six thousand dollars in four payments. Twenty thousand of that thirty-six materialized from nowhere—not your accounts, not your investments."

"You're working with Kleigshoen," Weatherford said. "You have no idea what someone like her is capable of. She's leading you around by the nose, trying to get you under her—"

"The sad thing is, I assumed you were living within your own means." Rimes shook his head. "We all did. A place like this, you get in on the ground floor of a deal, get some costs shaved off because you know the right people, walk away with your dream without compromising a thing. I would never have suspected.

"But then I thought about Barlowe's arrest.

"Everyone else in on the deal has been eliminated; it's just you and Barlowe left now. Why not eliminate him?

"Martinez and Moltke were planning to sell the genie data recovered from the T-Corp facility. They were trying to cut you and Marshall out. They both had a data stick. Barlowe had copies of their data sticks and they both had a copy of his, but none of that was any good without Barlowe's decryption key.

"They didn't trust each other enough to close the deal, and everyone was getting killed, thrown right into the middle of the action. Wolford, Kirk, Stern —all gunned down during the course of duty. You used that duty against us. In the Sundarbans, you put Martinez with the trainees, hoping he would get killed. With Moltke killed, that left me as the only person with any knowledge of the whole thing, and what I had wasn't meaningful. So, end of story.

"But Barlowe knew. He came to you and told you about the data sticks. You guaranteed him no death penalty, and he would give you the decryption key."

"Ladell would never testify against me." Weatherford smiled smugly. "We have an understanding."

"I told Barlowe you were bringing me in on the deal, and that didn't sit well with him. He thought you were going to have him killed, to wrap up the last of the loose ends. I can't imagine where he'd get an idea like that—I just told him that if you hired the right person, they could crack the decryption key eventually."

Weatherford's smile faded. "It won't hold up, Jack. If Barlowe's all you've got, you made a big mistake."

"Global Threat Assessment Conference. Dallas. December, 2153. You remember that?" Rimes asked.

Weatherford said nothing.

"I did some digging. Executive Director Glenn Vaughn briefed a select group, including you and Marshall. The briefing was titled 'Transportation of Weapons Systems Using Commercial Infrastructure.'

"After the briefing, Executive Director Vaughn discussed a hypothetical scenario about transporting a theoretical nerve gas using private security and commercial infrastructure. He sought your input on security and Marshall's thoughts on counter-intelligence efforts to hide the transportation. He may have, over a few drinks, mentioned the terrible X-17 albatross around his neck."

"Vaughn won't testify," Weatherford said. "It's just wild speculation."

"We've already got Vaughn's deposition."

Weatherford flinched.

"And Marshall is cutting a deal even as we speak. Add in Barlowe's cooperation, and it seems pretty solid. It's amazing how quick folks turn on each other when they get a sympathetic ear and there's a scapegoat to be had. Colonel."

Weatherford's face flushed. "Lazaro can't handle a scandal of this magnitude, especially not in a tight election year. Acknowledging the existence of X-17 would drag his administration down. They'll silence you."

Rimes shook his head. "They won't need to."

"Twelve thousand dead in orbit, billions of dollars worth of vessels and materials stolen or damaged. Heads will roll, and if the metacorporations ever find out it was our weapon the genies used to steal their ships, that our leaders had meant to use the X-17 against them ... it'll be worse than the Corporate Security Laws. We'll belong to them, Jack."

Rimes fought to hide his surprise. *Use the X-17 against the metacorporations? I never thought of that.* "You've already sold out, Colonel. One more shouldn't matter to you."

Weatherford straightened and thrust his jaw forward. "You're over your head, Jack. There are so many things going on that you're not even aware of. They're using you. Think of the danger you're putting your family in. You've got a baby on the way. You've got to let this go. If not for yourself, do this for Molly."

"I am doing this for Molly. And the baby."

"You think you can protect your family? You're one man! They can be snuffed out at any time, and you can't do a damned thing about it!"

"Colonel—"

Weatherford advanced a step, then another. His face was red, his hands balled tight into fists. "You can't protect them. Do you understand me?"

Rimes blinked. "I think I do."

Rimes stepped away from Weatherford.

A muffled shot echoed from the woods.

Weatherford staggered, a red splatter of blood already soaking through the hole in his green flannel shirt. He looked at his chest in disbelief. He tried to lift his arms, but they were already weak and fell back to his sides. His legs wobbled beneath him, then gave out. He fell sideways, knocking over his shopping bags, his face cracking against the stone walkway.

After a few seconds, he twitched, then went still.

Rimes's knees shook from the sudden finality. He walked back to the path, leaned against the tree.

Weatherford bled out over the stones.

Footsteps approached over the dead leaves behind Rimes, walking steadily.

He didn't turn.

"They will use him as the scapegoat," Tymoshenko said. "Just like Moltke. Just like a thousand others."

Rimes looked over his shoulder. Tymoshenko carried a large, thick, empty paper sack and wore a light hunting jacket.

"Yes," Rimes said. "A rogue colonel. Vaughn will retire, just as he planned, and Marshall will decide he needs to spend more time with his family. It's always something like that, isn't it?"

"It is." Tymoshenko chuckled. "I have actually seen the script. Just fill in a few blanks, here and there. But always the same lines."

Out in the woods like this, it might take hours or days for anyone to find Weatherford. They had time. Rimes tried to tell himself that Weatherford was just another target, another enemy.

Tymoshenko coughed and stamped his feet. "I must commend your detective work, putting this all together so quickly."

"I had help. From the IB."

"Of course," Tymoshenko said. "The rifle, by the way, we took it off an IB contractor who asked too many questions in Singapore. Now he is on Mogotón, on the Honduras side of the border. Yet, how strange, his prints are still all over the weapon, so perhaps he is not where he is supposed to be? IB, they do not like to be deceived. They are known for it."

Rimes pulled a plastic pack from his pants. He held it out for Tymoshenko. "They're all in there. Data sticks and encryption key. Barlowe put it all together just before Weatherford had him arrested."

Tymoshenko took the pack. "I feel I am robbing you if I give you nothing but a dead colonel, my friend. Those are so easy to come by."

"I have my reasons," Rimes said. "Six months. Then the Special Security Council gets a copy. No sooner, no later."

Tymoshenko tucked the pack into his jacket and headed toward the woods. "I hope to see you again, Jack. We work well together," he called back over his shoulder. "A man with integrity is rare in this world."

Rimes gave Weatherford's corpse a last look.

So that's integrity.

He wended his way through the woods for a couple of kilometers before spotting Ferris Avenue, then jogged parallel to the road under cover of trees for several minutes. He finally broke into the open at Fourth Street.

He was shaking, dizzy, nauseated. No one paid him any mind.

49

---

29 March 2164. Fort Sill, Oklahoma.

THE UH-121 DESCENDED from the dark sky, its rotors shaking the treetops. Rimes dropped his line and fast-roped between two swaying sawtooth oak trees. He looked up and saw Barlowe descending next to him. Martinez and Wolford dropped to the ground across from him. They hefted their CAWS-5s and nodded toward the shadows to the north.

Rimes jogged forward, assuming his position at the point. Gunfire broke out, kicking up dirt in front of him. He tucked into a roll and came up behind a tree.

Wolford fell to gunfire. Then Martinez. Barlowe crossed in front of a tree and was dragged into darkness.

Rimes was alone, surrounded. The gunfire was intensifying, coming from all around him now. Rimes pressed flat against the tree, but the bullets came closer still.

Shadows dropped from the trees around him. He was surrounded with nowhere to go, hundreds of figures, all in masks.

They raised their masks: Kwon, Lee, Perditori, more. Genies. They fired—

But not at him.

AT 0828, he entered the Trial Defense Service office, stopping at the paralegal clerk's desk. She was an elderly civilian, silver-haired and wrinkled. She nodded at him and smiled pleasantly, then rang Captain Kibaki, his lawyer. She waved him on and returned to her work.

Kibaki's office was small, not quite two meters deep and four meters long, but it had two windows that looked down on the parade grounds. Rimes watched the parade ground flag flutter in the wind for a moment before extending a hand to Kibaki and taking a seat across from her.

Kibaki spent several seconds on her terminal looking over his file, nodding as she read the latest updates. She was big-boned, wore awkward black glasses, and fit poorly in her uniform, although the uniform itself was sharp.

Rimes was developing a strange appreciation for Kibaki's plain but friendly features. He decided it must be the feeling someone develops for a savior.

Finally, Kibaki looked up from her terminal and smiled. "Ready?"

"Yes, ma'am."

The courtroom was empty when they arrived. It had recently been remodeled, fitted with real oak paneling, gold carpeting, matching chairs, and the latest terminals and networking. They settled into their seats and waited.

The court reporter, a young, sleepy-eyed corporal in dress uniform, stepped in from a side door, followed by Major Pileggi, the investigating officer.

Pileggi had bushy, black eyebrows and scowling, pockmarked cheeks. He slammed into his chair, connected to the terminal at his table, and glared at Rimes and Kibaki.

Rimes looked to Kibaki. She frowned, then shrugged.

"We're ready to begin," Pileggi said.

The court reporter began recording the proceedings.

"Let the record show that the Article 32 hearing for Sergeant Jackson C. Rimes has begun. It is 0900, 29 March 2164. Present are Major Karl Pileggi, investigating officer appointed by Major General Owen McNabb, Post Commander, Fort Sill, Oklahoma; Captain Michelle Kibaki, counsel for the defense; and Sergeant Rimes, the defendant.

"The case being considered against Sergeant Rimes includes two charges of reckless endangerment under Article 134 and six charges of Destruction of Government Property under Article 108."

Pileggi's nostrils flared; he kept his eyes away from Rimes as he continued. "Following review of Criminal Investigative Command, Oklahoma State Police reports, and interviews with witnesses present at the event referenced in said charges, the case being considered against Sergeant Rimes is dismissed without prejudice."

Dismissed?

"Absent any input from defense counsel—" Pileggi looked at Kibaki, gripping the side of his desk and drawing his thick eyebrows together, as if daring her to say something.

Kibaki blinked rapidly. "I ... have nothing to add."

Pileggi cleared his throat with a bark. "Then this concludes the Article 32 hearing."

Pileggi looked sharply at the court reporter. She quickly shut down her station and departed. Pileggi began shutting his terminal down as well.

Kibaki stepped around her table. "Major?"

Pileggi looked up angrily from his terminal, then sighed and rubbed his head with his hand. He looked up again, more composed. "Yes?"

"Sergeant Rimes has been under the cloud of very serious charges for the last two days. Based off your presentation and questioning yesterday, it seemed as if you were prepared to proceed with what—to be gracious—felt like an extremely flimsy case. If I may ask, what has changed between yesterday afternoon and this morning?"

Pileggi shook his head. "Michelle—"

The side door opened; General McNabb entered the courtroom, nodding at Pileggi.

Rimes stood.

"General McNabb," Pileggi said. "We were just leaving."

"What is the disposition of the case, Major Pileggi?" McNabb asked.

"Dismissed without prejudice, sir."

McNabb tilted his head. "That would seem surprising given the severity of the charges under consideration."

Pileggi glanced at Kibaki for a moment. "I had a very enlightening ... interview with the director of the Intelligence Bureau last night, sir."

McNabb nodded. "I look forward to the full report."

"Of course, sir." Pileggi sighed. "If you'll excuse me, General, I'd like to get to work on that immediately."

"Thank you, Major," McNabb said.

He watched Pileggi depart the courtroom, then turned to Kibaki. "It would seem you've done an admirable job, Captain Kibaki. Sergeant Rimes and the United States Army will be forever in your debt."

Kibaki smiled at Rimes. "There wasn't much of a case against him, sir. I can't take much credit for it."

McNabb frowned and removed his glasses. He crossed his arms over his chest and began tapping the glasses on a forearm. "Three soldiers are dead, Captain, and only Sergeant Rimes knows the particulars of two of the deaths. Obviously, we want to see justice done. I'm happy for all involved that Sergeant Rimes has been cleared. Thank you. I'd like to speak to Sergeant Rimes for a moment."

Kibaki adjusted her glasses and stared at McNabb for a moment. "You're welcome. Sir." She departed the courtroom, her back as straight as a rod.

McNabb waited until the last echo of her footsteps disappeared before he spoke. "You're a fortunate man, Sergeant Rimes."

"I appreciate that, sir." Rimes felt his hands shaking. He balled them into fists and held them tight at his sides.

"Actually, I'm not sure if you're fortunate or not," McNabb said as he casually strode forward. "As the captain said, you have a cloud lingering over you that only an exceptional officer could ever hope to overcome. Captain Moltke stained the Commandos' reputation. I believe the outcome of the investigation into Colonel Weatherford's involvement and his ... murder will stain it even more. You're walking away with a commission. There will always be those who view you with great suspicion."

"Like you, sir?" Rimes asked.

McNabb shook his head. "Weatherford always spoke highly of you. He was a good judge of character."

Was he? Or was he a good judge of who he could corrupt?

"You have a good career ahead of you, Sergeant."

"Thank you, sir."

"Don't thank me." McNabb leaned against the desk Pileggi had just departed. "I'm the one who appointed Major Pileggi and pushed him to go forward with the hearing despite the lack of evidence."

Rimes struggled with the contradiction. "If you thought I was innocent, sir, why bother with an Article 32 in the first place?"

McNabb walked to the court reporter's station, examining it as if he thought it might still be recording. "To satisfy those who would only see that cloud over your head," he said finally. "People have accused me of being a political games-player, as though it were a bad thing. But it's necessary. Imagine what would have happened if no investigation and no hearing had taken place. Now look at you—cleared by CID, the Oklahoma State Police, the Intelligence Bureau, and an impartial Article 32 hearing approved by me. Playing politics won't clear that cloud away completely, but it can help defend you from worse.

"And you have a medal in the works. Colonel Weatherford's last act, you might say."

"You were close to the colonel, sir?"

McNabb turned and stared at Rimes for a moment. "Goodness, no. We came up around the same time. I was Infantry straight out of West Point, he was in Intelligence after graduating OCS. I played the game, but he got his hands dirty—dirty enough that it looks like someone eliminated him. There's a fine line, Rimes. But, warts and all, Weatherford was effective. He got things done. The Army needs officers who can get things done."

McNabb walked up to Rimes and extended a hand. "Just keep that line in mind, Sergeant Rimes. I will watch your career with interest."

Rimes shook McNabb's hand and watched in disbelief as he left. Rimes wasn't exactly sure what to make of the exchange. Had McNabb just acknowledged awareness of Weatherford's illicit activities and admitted that he'd let the situation play out until Weatherford was no longer useful?

Weatherford had always said McNabb was a crafty politician.

Molly was sitting at the kitchen table, still wearing her housecoat. Her eyes were red and puffy.

"How'd it go?"

"They dismissed the charges," Rimes said, unbuttoning his jacket. He suddenly realized he was famished. He stripped off his shirt and walked to the bedroom, returning a moment later in his jogging shorts. He took the vegetable and mealworm paste from the refrigerator and set it on the counter. "I'm starving. Do you want anything?"

Molly shook her head. "Nothing will stay down." She leaned her head in her hand and mumbled, "*She* called while you were out. Dana. She left a message."

Rimes froze, then looked at Molly's face. She looked upset, but he couldn't tell more than that. "Did you play it?"

Rather than answer, Molly walked over to the console and turned it on. She selected the message and stepped back, chewing on her thumbnail as she watched.

Kleigshoen's face materialized on the display. She seemed tired but cheerful. She wore a similar outfit to the one she'd worn the day she'd slept with him, the day Metcalfe died. Sophisticated. Elegant. Professional.

Her demeanor was serious, somber, not provocative.

"Hi, Jack. I hope you don't mind me calling, but I just got word they've dropped that court martial nonsense. Congratulations on that, and it sounds like your OCS package is moving forward, so congratulations there as well." She smiled sardonically, looking down at her hands. "While I'm congratulating, I guess I should say congratulations on figuring out how Brent saw me when I couldn't. I had a very uncomfortable moment with his family today. He left me ... something." She looked upward, blinking quickly. "It was nice, but something more than a mentor should leave for his protégé.

"I can't tell if it was just convenient for me not to see it, or if it was just a guy thing you picked up on." Kleigshoen wiped at her eyes and laughed.

"But you couldn't see me hunting you down like so much dinner. I guess that's really what I wanted to call about."

She pulled her shoulders in for a second, then lifted her chin and sat up straighter. "I owe you and Molly an apology, Jack. I've always said it was career first. I've always imagined that made me stronger, maybe even better. But I tried to take something that wasn't mine. So you tell Molly I'm sorry and that I wish I had half her strength and resolve. I thought I had a lot of strength. But some of the things I've been through lately have made me think I need ... well. I have a lot to learn. And one day, maybe you'll forgive us—me—for what I did to you.

"I guess that's it. Give me a call when you graduate. I'd like to send you both a present. Goodbye, Jack."

The image faded, and Molly turned the display off.

She looked Rimes in the eye. "If you ever fool around on me again, Jack, it will be the last time. Do you understand me?"

Rimes nodded.

Molly stepped toward him and planted a gentle kiss on his lips.

Rimes pulled her close and kissed her again. She was warm and soft in his arms; the lingering kiss seemed to suspend time until she pulled away. She smiled at him.

"We're going to get through this. You and me and the boys." She giggled quietly. "Now you've got me doing it."

"There's nothing wrong with it," Rimes said, his hands slowly rubbing up and down her back. "It's our life, it's what we make it."

He kissed her again, and this time she didn't pull away.

THE END

AUTHOR'S NOTES

Thank you for reading *Momentary Stasis*. I hope you enjoyed it. Jack Rimes's story continues in *Transition of Order* and concludes in *Awakening to Judgment*. The Rimes Trilogy is followed by the **Elite Response Force** series, which begins with *Turning Point*.

If you enjoyed *Momentary Stasis*, I hope you'll consider posting a review and letting friends know about the book. Reviews can be one of those things that really help people decide whether or not to give something a try.

For updates on new releases and news on other series, please visit my website and sign up for my mailing list at:

http://www.p-r-adams.com

ABOUT THE AUTHOR

I was born and raised in Tampa, Florida. I joined the Air Force, and my career took me from coast to coast before depositing me in the St. Louis, Missouri area for several years. After a tour in Korea and a short return to the St. Louis area, I retired and moved to the greater Denver, Colorado metropolitan area.

I write speculative fiction, mostly science fiction and fantasy. My favorite writers over the years have been Robert E. Howard, Philip K. Dick, Roger Zelazny, and Michael Crichton.

Social Media:
www.p-r-adams.com
pradams_author@comcast.net